CLINAMEN

CLINAMEN

ROBERT SLOTHUS

FOLLOW, words and music by Jerry Merrick (1943-2018).

IN THE DESERT, by Stephen Crane (1871-1900) published in 1895 as part of his collection, The Black Riders and Other Lines. "In the Desert" is the third of fifty-six short poems published in this volume.

THE WIND, ONE BRILLIANT DAY, by Antonio Machado (1875-1939).

Library of Congress Control Number: 2020906180

ISBN: 978-0-578-67182-6

Cover design by: Nicholas Stephenson

*For Deborah, who has long endeavored to
make love appear and magic happen right before my eyes*

Merit to be their only road to eminence, and the disgrace of evil, and credit of worthy acts, their one measure of difference between man and man . . .

LYCURGUS

I

Hooker's parking lot erupted with loud exhaust sounds coming from a chopper's straight pipes. Razor had been scouting the area ever since arriving in Massena. It was after midnight. A solitary corner streetlamp gave off an eerie gray light, illuminating the one chopper that was parked outside. He drove up to the entrance, got off the Harley, and smiled as he saw the Roll the Bones placard on the door. He walked into find the place dark with only a faint fluorescent light shining at the end of the second bay. As he moved toward the first lift, he heard the sound of a twelve-gauge double-action pump. He froze. The man holding the shotgun pointed at him spoke.

"That's good. Now what do you want?"

"I've been told by the man up north you were the last man to see Axel alive."

"What's it to you?"

Razor paused. "He was my brother."

"You ride with them Angels up north?"

"I did once. There's been a change in administration since I got put away. Yeah. To answer your question, I was a leader up in Quebec. Just got out. Looking to get some answers."

Workbench lights suddenly began to flicker, then came on permanently. Dan Proud Hawk walked around the back of a Dodge Dart and stood in front of Razor, keeping the barrel of the shot gun aimed at the intruder's heart.

"This garage and me. We've been known to serve a purpose . . . and even sometimes for the man up north. Who are you?"

"I am Razor."

"Don't recall ever hearing a leader by that name."

"Like I said. Been away for some time."

Proud Hawk pointed the barrel toward the Angel's knees. "All your answers got locked up out of state," he said.

"You're holding all the cards right now, you know," Razor responded, pointing at the gun pointing at him. "But think about it. Think of all you'll be losing out on when I go back and tell him that you were . . . you know . . . uncooperative?"

"You're not from around here. This is not how it works here on this reservation."

Razor remained motionless, stared at the barrel of the gun, then looked up at Proud Hawk. "Don't particularly like anyone drawin' a bead on me . . . do you think . . ."

"All right. Take it easy."

Proud Hawk lowered the weapon. "Like I said. I am connected up around those parts up north. But let's get something straight right here and now, *Razzzzor*. Big Joe and you can threaten all you want. This tribe comes first. Nobody nowhere can get me to talk."

Suddenly the overhead bay lights come on, and there, no more than twenty feet behind Razor, stood retired sheriff Henry Crow Horse, wearing an old, weathered buckskin jacket with his bowie knife strapped to the front of his waist. Moving his hand up slowly and caressing the knife's pommel, he stared at the biker.

"You may want to get a muffler for that ride of yours."

Startled, Razor put his hands up, keeping his eyes on the old Indian with the long, flowing white hair.

Henry Crow Horse walked up and stood face-to-face with Razor.

"You keep your hands up, you hear? These days it seems I can't sleep so good, so I like to ride around at night. Name's Henry. I am going to see if you got any weapons on you, so just stand still."

The old man's right hand shook slightly as he carefully patted him down.

"That's good. Put your hands down and come on over here."

Henry Crow Horse led them into an adjacent small-parts room and sat down on a swivel armchair behind an old olive-green army-surplus desk, gesturing for the biker to sit down on a crate in front of him. Proud Hawk, suspicious, stood just inside the doorway, leaning his shotgun up against the jamb.

"Hawk, what seems to be going on here tonight?"

"Well sir, this man seems to think I have some special information for him."

"What information are you looking for, friend?"

Razor looked at Proud Hawk, then turned and faced Crow Horse. "I was told he saw my brother the night he was killed. I've been away. Just got out. Wanted to know some facts."

"Strange time of the day to be walking in on a man's place of business looking for facts, don't you think? What's your name?"

"Razor."

"You and your brother, both members of the Quebec's chapter, huh?"

"Yeah."

The longtime retired sheriff pushed his chair away from the desk with his cowboy boots and leaned back as if to stretch out his entire spine, then clasped his hands together behind his neck and stared at Razor. Slowly he sat upright, stood up, unbuckled his belt with his knife in its scabbard, and placed it on the desk. Then he removed his buckskin coat, draped it on the back of the chair, and sat back down. He unbuttoned his shirt pocket, pushed his cigarettes up from the bottom in their cellophane pack, took one out without removing the pack, and buttoned the pocket again. He took a lighter from his pants pocket and lit the cigarette, then put the lighter on the desk and pulled an ashtray to him with his one steady hand.

"Well Mr. Razor Blade, there's no doubt in my mind you're a brave man . . . that's for definitely sure. And I can see you've got a lot of hard-weathered bark on ya. You know, I've lived a long time. Born here and never left for any extended time, so you see there isn't anything that happens on this reservation that gets by me. So listen up now. I am going to be straight with you because it doesn't involve anyone here. If it did, well, let's just say you would be in a heap of trouble right now, coming around here asking about our people. You understand?"

"Yeah. I understand."

"I am very glad that you do."

Henry Crow Horse took a deep drag on the cigarette and exhaled slowly.

"Three years ago the Nation of Mohawks brought together many tribal representatives from the west for a powwow right here in St. Regis. For a week we met daily and spoke about many mutual issues facing our brothers and sisters. It was at that time we agreed to have an exchange program for teen-agers who were having difficulty with reservation life. Some of our kids went to Arizona and New Mexico and some of theirs came here. Two boys didn't want to go back. They ended up doing some bad things. I am afraid they were involved in your brother's death. The FBI chased them, but they got away. Rumor has it they are still in the desert doing their best to stay away from the feds."

Razor sat motionless and silent, then turned and looked at

Proud Hawk and focused his eyes quickly on the shotgun and the knife on the desktop; then he turned his head, looked at the old man's ruddy-skinned, weather-beaten face, and stared into his black, bloodshot eyes.

"I didn't know what to expect when I drove up here. Didn't really know what answers were waiting for me here in Massena. What now?"

"If I were you, Henry Crow Horse replied, I would just say 'much obliged' and be on my way."

Razor slowly got up, his lips pinched tightly closed and his eyes focused on the old Indian's ancient-looking eyes. He grabbed his left bicep with his right hand and moved his hand slowly up and down his upper arm while measuring the distance between Dan Proud Hawk and the open door immediately to his left. He redirected his attention toward Henry Crow Horse. He stood very still.

"You've been generous, Henry, and I'll leave now, if that's all right."

"You're free to go. Oh. Just one more thing."

"What's that?"

"Give some thought to getting that new muffler."

Razor gave no reply but managed a terse smile and a nod. Proud Hawk picked up the shotgun and stepped back, allowing the Hell's Angel a path out of the room, then followed him outside and watched him leave. He returned to the parts room and sat on a big easy chair that was covered up with a few U-Haul truck blankets. He waited for the old man to say something.

Henry Crow Horse took another deep drag, exhaled, and flicked the ash into the ashtray. He leaned forward and looked down at the floor, holding the cigarette between his finger and thumb with the palm of his hand tilted oddly, resting on his cheek. He stared at the floor, then looked up and stared into space as small clouds of smoke suspended in midair surrounded his head and shoulders.

"Do you think he believed me, Hawk?"

"I don't know."

II

"Call me Patrick," I said to the men as we stood before tons of steel and the engineers who would direct us each morning. The year was 1969, and American enterprise and world commerce demanded an offering be built to the gods of mammon on the southern tip of Manhattan. The Twin Towers would begin their ascent at the intersection of Greenwich Street and the former Dey Street, where the Dutch explorer Adriaen Block's ship, the Tyger, burned to the waterline in November 1613. This worksite where I labored was many miles from my home in Moreland, New York, which was nestled in a green valley of the Catskill Mountains. The land I grew up on was greener in June than any other month of the year, and as a boy I traversed the rolling mountains in Ulster County with my brother Vincent, and we were made complete and whole by the nature that challenged us. Sometimes as I walked those mountain trails, I would look down at my feet and ask myself if I had just followed the same path the indigenous people had carved ten thousand years ago. At night, while asleep under a canopy *of oak branches, some unknown sounds could wake me suddenly and I would imagine ancient ghosts lurking about, studying me carefully and deciding if I was worthy of the wisdom they had to impart. Nowadays I am left with modern ghosts, and they appear and leave their mark more deftly on a grown man's psyche. There can be no doubt that the geography you inhabit can influence your decisions. When I decided to leave Moreland to work on high steel with the men of the Akwesasne Reservation, I wanted what they had and would never lose.*

He lived in a plain wood-framed house on top of a hill surrounded by a deep forest of tall oak, maples and conifers, not too far from the Appalachian Trail in Ulster County. Don Kaminski walked out his front door into a cold and dark morning. It was the time of day he called zero dark thirty.

Five a.m. had come and he stood in front of the hood of his old Pontiac sedan. Moving his hand around the grille, he found the release latch, opened the hood, and fiddled with two wires near the starter. The engine turned over and began to idle. Gently, he lowered the hood, making sure it was securely locked into position. He slid behind the wheel and started down what a lumberman would call a fire road, which was well over a hundred yards downhill. The slope of the road was slightly less than eight degrees with no turns and was mostly leaf covered, and many a wintry snowy night it was too slippery to drive on and passable only by foot. At the bottom of the hill the road became lightly graveled but still mostly earth laden. He stopped and got out, slowly walked around to the passenger's side, and looked down behind the car at the heavy, big-linked logging chain he had just driven over. He picked it up and struggled to attach the hooked end to an iron pole that butted up against a large wooden box sitting on a three-foot-high four-by-four post. Any deliveries would be placed in the box. Slowly walking back to the driver's side of the car, he paused and stood and listened to a gentle wind moving across the boughs of pine trees that lined the entrance to his property. Getting back into the car, he turned left on Freedom Lane, which was a properly paved state-maintained rural road.

This was the routine he'd followed for years as he left his mountain house for work at the Roam-Way Trucking Company. A cat named Huey was left behind and would not see his human until later in the evening.

From Freedom Lane he drove to Market Street, through downtown, then over the Market Street Bridge into South Moreland. North and South Moreland were separated by a wide and shallow river the Iroquois Indians named Susquehanna. A few nineteenth-century lumbermen made their fortunes cutting down hundreds of thousands of trees around this section of the county, the largest in New York State. Some parts of the North Moreland streets had mansions that the lumbermen, now called lumber barons, had kept building as they became richer off the lumber sales. County and federal courthouses were located in the city. As he drove on Route 15 through South Moreland up the big Appalachian mountain, the Pontiac's engine labored. The trucking company he worked for was at the bottom of the other side of the mountain, where Route 15 and Route 44 intersected.

He arrived at Roam-Way at five thirty. He entered the depot through an unassuming side door. Stepping into the depot from the morning darkness temporarily made his pupils close down slightly from the many high-intensity lights that hung thirty feet overhead. Bright light shone down and engulfed the men as they worked on huge engines, transmission gearboxes, hydraulic and pneumatic pumps. The place was cold and gray. He walked to the time clock, punched in, grunted and stared at the mechanic who had walked up behind him to punch out. The place smelled of diesel fuel and oil and looked grimy. Quickly he walked up a few concrete steps that joined some steel stairs leading to an incandescent-lit office with glass windows. The dispatcher handed him his paperwork. They did not exchange words and he went to his rig the way he had come. He got behind the wheel and was off. For an instant he felt as though he was an important man again but the sensation faded as fast as it came on.

The on-ramp to the interstate was unusually long and became steeper as he headed on to I-80 west. Looking into his mirror he saw the faster, oncoming trucks bearing down on him. For a moment he lost sight of them as the reflection in the mirror of the upcoming sunrise burned deep into his retinas and his eyelids shut. It was if a ball of fire had captured his sight and frozen him in time. The great Cummins diesel engine made tremendous metallic hissing and clanging noises as he quickly downshifted; the rpms shot higher as he stomped on the accelerator. The red-lined engine's sound drowned out all other sound and made the cab rattle. Cars and trucks were still bearing down on him. The cab rattled louder and shook like an overloaded Huey lifting off from a hot LZ with too much weight on board. "Come on baby, get us outta here!" he said out loud. But it was okay. It was only the sun. It wasn't a burning hooch and those were just crates of tools on board, not men clutching their own badly mangled and crippled lifeless limbs.

He drove until he reached Cleveland, dropped his load, then turned around and arrived back at the depot at 5:30 p.m. A few men came out of the entranceway and passed right by him. They were laughing and heading to South Side Tavern to have a few. Steely eyed and walking very upright and purposeful, he moved quickly to the time clock, punched out, and left the building. He stopped for a moment, glanced at a high-voltage transformer that jutted out from the back of the depot onto the parking lot, and whispered, *I warned him. Now he's dead. Shit for brains.* He remembered it was Friday.

Now what? What the hell am I going to do? Walking toward his car, feeling cold and empty inside, he thought about that transformer and the parking lot, where last month Malcolm McDonald had electrocuted himself. Memories of Vietnam, the burnt bodies near an LZ, and the smell of dried blood on a hot humid day crept into his thoughts. Electrocution can char a man beyond recognition. Plumps him up like a burnt hot dog and splits open his back, exposing the spine.

He reviewed his workday and the endless hours of driving he'd just finished over and over again in his mind on the way home. Later that evening as he lay in bed trying to fall asleep, he kept thinking and asking himself, *What's the point . . . why do I go on with this?*

In the morning he awoke when his cat jumped on to the bed. Throwing his legs over the edge of the bed, he strapped on his steel leg braces and dressed. Inside the house there was no sound, save for the little water fountain he'd made to pump fresh water into his cat's bowl. He went out the side entrance and shut the door. There was a slight dusting of snow on the ground. The sun was up and he walked a few hundred feet down a path that cut through a stand of young trees to his cinder-block two-story garage. He entered and flipped a switch to the left of the door that turned on the fluorescent ceiling lights. The room was cold. He went over and banked the coal stove. By noon the garage would be seventy degrees, a comfortable temperature to handle steel motorcycle parts. From a three-foot-square immovable steel workbench in the middle of the room he picked up two Bing carburetors and found a cardboard box next to a TIG welder to put them in. He carefully wrapped each of them with two clean dish towels and placed them side by side in the box. Starting the Pontiac in the same manner as the morning before, he got in and drove down the hill. Instead of turning left on Freedom lane he turned right and drove a mile to a dead end. Looking out the passenger-side window he saw the driveway to Grey Stone. The entrance was marked on each side by a stone pillar measuring nine feet in height and three feet wide at the base. The lane was flat and well-kept and had smallish light gray gravel, which the locals called no skid, on the surface. The crushed stones that were no more than an a half inch in size, which allowed for good tire traction in the snow. There was forest all around but the land beyond the entrance was lower in elevation then his mountain house, and he could see apple orchards and clearings beyond. He turned onto the lane, which was just over two hundred yards in length, and at its end he saw a large stone house that had been built in the eighteenth century. This was Wallace property. He stopped about halfway and veered to the right on to another lane and drove a hundred yards. At the end of this lane stood a stone cottage that overlooked a large apple orchid. The chimney was pumping out wood smoke that smelled like a campsite in summer. The sun was now at an angle that cast a sharp, crisp yellow light on the leafless apple trees.

He got out and walked to a side entrance. He knocked on the door and waited. The door quickly swung open.

"Thanks for bringing um over. Want some coffee?" asked Patrick Wallace.

"No time for that."

"Just made it. You sure?"

"All right. But I am bead blasting that Triumph's frame and gas tank. One cup. That's it. That bike's been sitting and waiting way too long for a paint job."

Both men sat down at the kitchen table. Kaminski took the box out from under his arm and placed it next to an open tech manual, tools, rags and a main drive for an old German-made motorcycle. Wallace opened the lid to the box and took out the two carburetors and put them on the bench.

"They look like new. Any issues?" asked Wallace.

"No. They meet specs. The receipt's in the box."

"I am getting kind of antsy to go for a ride. Maybe it will warm up a little and I can get her out the door."

Wallace picked up one of the carburetors and examined the brass intake valve and choke.

"Nice work, Don."

"You know, Pat, March can be a damn cold month for riding when you don't have a fairing."

"I am not a fairing kind of guy. I have a bad case of cabin fever right now. How about you?"

"I am too busy working twelve hours a day to get too far down. Driving in winter is rough going. Sometimes I see two, maybe three accidents a day on Eighty. It's some scary shit."

Patrick got up and walked to the stove. He picked up a Pyrex coffeepot and poured hot coffee into a teacup.

"Here you go."

"Thanks." Kaminski reached for the cup. "That's quite an interesting-looking cup."

"It's from my mother's set of Limoges."

"Oh . . . I see," said Kaminski.

He set the cup and saucer down, turning the cup completely around to inspect the colorful Chinese pattern.

"Pretty ornate, huh?" said Patrick.

"Don't know much about that sort of thing. What did you call it?"

"Limoges," Patrick replied.

"Sounds French. I guess all that St. James Academy book learning you got was worth something."

"Hah. Maybe so. Vin was the one that excelled at the languages and the arts, not me. I played lacrosse. It was a great school. About a month ago he brought over some of her favorite china. He's trying to be as generous as he can. They had all sorts of collections of plates and cups and such. You know being world travelers and all that. I am sure he's having a great time now, rummaging through that old wine cellar."

At the other end of the lane, Vincent, Patrick's brother, sat at his breakfast table having coffee laced with applejack. Grey Stone was built in 1789. Ninety-three years later their great-great-grandfather was the first Wallace to die in it. The floorboards squeaked as he got up from the table and walked down a hall with the bottle of applejack in hand to a darkened room, and knelt in front of a fireplace. From the age of seven he had been making fire the same way, placing kindling in the hearth Mohawk style. The dark room began to brighten from both the flames and the morning sunlight shining through a single stained glass window, giving the room an air of the exotic as it washed the wallpaper, inlaid ceiling, and the *pointier* with a kaleidoscope of colors. There were Persian rugs, a mantel clock, pewter pots, English and French paintings on all the walls, and hundreds upon hundreds of books stretched from floor to ceiling; relics of his family's past and present seemed to cover every inch of space in the library.

The house was his now. Sitting in front of the fire, he thought of his mother and how he would sit by her side in the dead of winter listening to the stories of how the Wallaces left Scotland to come to America. In his mind he could see her face now and hear her voice.

John Law, a Scottish economist, banker, and gambler who sat on the French Court, had orchestrated the contract that brought the clan to Mississippi and eventually to Louisiana. They were given some trading rights and land near New Orleans but found it worthless when they got there. Sailing upriver, they made their way to Council Bluffs, Iowa, and set up a trading camp. It was 1703 and the area was French and Indian territory. As the economy changed, they changed as well, getting involved in shipping and farming. It was during this time that James Wallace, having had two wives die on him in three years, took a Sioux woman as his wife. Together they had seven children. James Jr. was the oldest and the only one to live past the age of twenty-two. Records showed that some of his siblings drowned and others succumbed to the dangers of the frontier and illnesses; one was thrown from a horse and broke his neck and two died in fires.

Making his way east after the revolution, James Wallace's grandson Arthur Vincent settled in Mohawk territory and began carving out a trading post near the Susquehanna River. By 1900 Vincent's grandfather owned one of the three timber companies that produced close to a million board feet of lumber in all.

Vincent stared into the fireplace and poured applejack into his cup. He looked up and saw the portrait of the man who had started Wallace Lumber. He sat and drank. It was 10:00 a.m.

In the evening, Patrick walked into E. J.'s Speak Easy on Fourth Street around eleven o'clock to see a Saturday-night crowd of Moreland's yuppies, students, roustabouts, and cruisers all packed into the old 1920s bank like sardines in a can, listening to the sounds of KC and the Sunshine Band blasting through big stereo speakers. *Do a little dance, make a little love, get down tonight, get down tonight.* He stood in the dark next to a black leather couch in a rear corner of the huge hall-like room. The bar was enormous: it stuck out ten feet from the wall and ran almost half the length of the entire room. The room's ceiling was upward of forty feet high. Where the bar made a ninety-degree turn back toward the wall, there stood a highly polished steel vault some seven-teen feet high with its six-foot-diameter door left wide open. About twenty-five feet above the floor, encased in one continuous boxlike cove running along all the walls, were light fixtures that cast a

dim reddish-yellow light toward the ceiling. There was barely enough light in the room to make out a person's features.
Standing taller and broader than most, Patrick could see just
enough of what was happening around parts of the room. He
sneered at a Nycoming College professor he knew, attempting
to seduce a beautiful brunette freshmen in a section close to his
corner, while a young couple close by played Pac Man. The DJ
got up, stood on a small makeshift stage, and announced his
favorite song with an inane introduction that made no sense,
drunk or sober. Women hustled pitchers of beer through the
throngs of humanity, trying desperately to make more tips. It
was all there. The sights, sounds, and smells of a good time.
Or maybe not. He saw a man's hopes and aspirations quickly
vanish when a blonde he was working hard at impressing said
in no uncertain words, "No way, dude!"

Ian Johnson appeared at the entrance to the vault and motioned to Patrick to follow him in. Patrick saw him but didn't
outwardly acknowledge him. Both men did not speak but
walked together to the back of the sterile, dimly lit room,
where a wall of strongboxes had once been kept.

"How do you like what I've done with my office?" asked Ian.

"Looks good. Where am I going next week?"

"Well *buddy*," Ian said.

"I already have a brother, Ian, don't need another."

"Sure. Relax. Let's enjoy the night—it's just getting started."

"For you maybe."

"Have a seat. You want a beer?"

Sitting on a stainless-steel stool, Patrick watched him carefully as he walked over to what appeared to be a closet door,
which led into a small well-lit room. Patrick opened his ar-
my-fatigue field coat halfway, reached down slowly to his hip,
felt the butt end of his weapon, then brought his hand back
out. He could see pretty well what was in the room. There
was a small refrigerator, some crumpled-up shopping bags, a

couple of Chinese-food containers, and a few dime bags of pot on a glass-top table.

"Heineken okay?"

"That's fine."

Ian came out with two bottles and an opener.

"Look," Ian said as he opened both bottles and handed one to Patrick, "Pat, it's like this: things on the rez are heating up thanks to Reagan's bullshit. Lone Bear and his guy are uptight about what's been going down lately."

"So, they staying put, powwowin', or what?"

"It's time you make a trip up there. I can't move anything until I have a better sense of what's going on with them."

Patrick brought the bottle to his mouth and took a few sips. It was cold and the hops were bitter-tasting. He drank more. He set the bottle down on the floor next to his foot and leaned forward directly in front of Ian, paused for a few moments, then said, "You know, you never really understood what motivates the Mohawk."

"That's why I have you, Patrick, my old friend. Find out what's going on, will ya? Our distribution man up in the North Country tells me things need to be moving out of Quebec by the end of the month."

Patrick leaned backward, picked up the Heineken, guzzled down the remains, and handed the empty bottle to Ian . . . Okay *buddy*. I'll do the recon."

It was a little after midnight. At the other end of town, VFW Post 844 was filled with dense cigarette smoke. On a small stage stood Vincent, playing country music chords on his Telecaster, while a half dozen or more men and a few women sat at the bar. Nobody was playing pool and hardly any of the veterans seemed to be talking much. At the end of the bar, pipe in hand, sat Don Kaminski with his back to the stage, drinking bonded bourbon. The front door opened and two men, Bill Osborn and Cliff Cheetham, walked in. They were talking to each other but their voices became still as they passed him and sat down at a nearby table.

Jim, the barkeep, called everyone sir or ma'am. Betty, the sole remaining waitress, came through the swinging doors of the kitchen and sat down next to Kaminski, declaring in a loud, forceful tone that was drowned out by the band: "That's it boys, we're closed. They sound pretty good tonight, don't they!"

She stared forward and saw her face in the mirror against all the bottles that were on the shelf. She saw his face too, head down, lighting his bowl.

"That's cherry, isn't it? Smells good."

He turned his head and acknowledged her without speaking, while the two men who had just arrived moments ago got up from their table and walked over to where Kaminski was sitting. Bill Osborn said to Jim: "Give me two beers."

Both men stood close to Kaminski.

"I am not going to do this, Billy," said Kaminski.

Jim set the beers on the bar in front of Osborn and Cheetham. Cheetham grabbed hold of his bottle and took a few swigs of beer, then turned and addressed Kaminski. "We need you to stay, Don."

"I am done with all of it, Cliff. Griffiss, the Guard, both will do just fine without me. Don't worry: they'll tap someone from Hancock to take my place."

Osborn spoke up. "No one can fly as good as you."

Kaminski picked up his glass and slowly sipped his whiskey, then looked at both men. "You fellas never give up, do ya?"

Betty said, "Don't let um get—"

"Look fellas, it's like this. I know where they want to go with the Apache's electronics. Maybe I am a Luddite but it's a different feel for me. Not a good fit."

The two men quickly downed their beers and returned to their table.

The band quit playing and Vincent came over to the bar and sat down next to Kaminski.

Jim grabbed his towel and stood in front of Vincent, wiping the surface of the bar.

"May I please have a draft?" asked Vincent.

"Yes sir. Bud all right?"

"Sounds good," Vincent replied, then turned toward Kaminski. "I saw Patrick this morning."

"Oh yeah."

"Don."

"Yeah."

"I couldn't help overhearing what you were just saying. What was that all about with those two?"

"Oh, they want me to keep flying with them."

"Don I've seen you drive, fly, and take apart just about every machine around and get it back to together in no time, and it's running better when you've finished with it. Remember the time my old man broke down out on Fifteen and you and Patrick drove out there in that ancient Chevy pickup of yours? Had his old three fifty-six running in no time. He didn't miss that race at Belmont, thanks to you."

Kaminski smiled . . . "Yeah, I remember that. That was a sweet old little Porsche. I do remember that day. It was stinking hot, working on that little roadster on the side of the road. Don't think your dad ever missed a Belmont race, did he? He sure knew horses, all right. He wanted to give me some money for getting him on his way and I said no sir. He bet fifty bucks for me anyway, to place, and Patrick gave me my winnings the next day."

"So, did I hear you right? You're leaving the National Guard? New York won't be safe anymore!"

"That's affirmative. I am moving eighteen wheels down the highway from now on, Vin. No more weekend flying for me. Your brother and I want to get the old bikes up and running. Maybe take a trip out to Montana this summer, will see, he seems to be away more often nowadays. Don't get much time to work with him in the garage." Kaminski gave out a big yawn and drank the rest of his whiskey. "I am going to get some shut-eye. I am calling it a night. That guitar. You and the boys over there. You sounded really good tonight. It was good to see you, Vin. Must admit, though."

"What's that?"

"I never thought of you playing country music in a VFW hall. Can't remember the last time I saw you. What's it been, over a year since ..."

"Yeah. It's been a while. I've been staying pretty close to home when I can. A few months ago Jason Campbell called. You remember him? Used to play drums out of his garage with the Emmitt brothers. He wanted to know if I'd consider playing in this band he was putting together. I didn't want to at first. I kept putting him off."

"What made you finally say yes?"

"I don't know. Playing rock and roll always seemed to cleanse my mind. Some things needed to be washed out, I guess. Country isn't bad. People seem to really take to the songs and it's not hard to play."

"I could use some of that cleansing myself. It's always good to see you, Vin. Good night, Jim. See you next week."

"I'll be here, sir."

"Good night, Betty."

Vincent said good night to the chopper pilot and watched him as he walked out the door.

Betty looked away from the big mirror she had been staring into, picked up her glass, stood up, went over and sat down next to Wallace, and said, "Don't mean to stick my nose where it don't belong. I can tell you've known Don for a while. Have I seen you in here before?"

"No. I am not ex-military. Just a member of the band."

"A music lover, not a fighter, huh? I am Betty."

"Something like that. It's nice to meet you, Betty. I am Vincent Wallace."

"Can I call you Vince?"

The bartender cut in, the ever-present rag in hand, and commenced cleaning things off the surface of the bar. "Another beer, sir?"

"Please."

Betty leaned closer to Vincent. "How long have you two known each other? Did you know him before Vietnam?"

Vincent turned and looked at her, then turned away and faced straight ahead, staring at all the bottles in front of him. He paused and looked at her. "We go back a ways. We're neighbors, actually. Um, uh, it was nice meeting you, but I really have to pack up my amp and . . ."

"Finish your beer. No sense running off on account of me. It's just that you seemed genuinely sincere."

"Sincere about what?"

"You know, how he's doing, what's happening to him."

"I haven't seen him for a while."

"What's it been, ten, twelve years now? That war. What that bitch of a wife did. He's barely holding it together. I know. I see him here Saturday nights, always alone."

"These things just happen to people."

Betty jerked her head, then grimaced. "I don't think you're what I thought you were."

Vincent bristled. "Oh yeah, how's that?"

"Come on, get real. I don't think coming home from an overseas business trip and finding your old lady in bed with another guy, while your eleven-month-old baby daughter is sleeping in the next room is—"

"Look. I don't know you, Betty. What I do know is that it's sad, very sad and ugly, and I'd rather not discuss it with you. All right?"

The next day Patrick left Moreland a little after twelve p.m. and took secondary roads to the outskirts of the Akwesasne

Reservation, which was about two hours northwest. The Saint Lawrence River and the Canadian border were not far off. To the unaccustomed eye there wasn't much of a noticeable entrance to Indian lands. A few abandoned rusted-out cars on blocks sitting in fields of tall grass alongside broken snow-mobiles and homes that were badly in need of repair could be seen more frequently as you left the white man's neighborhood. The stark reality of poverty could not be ignored.

It was 2:30 p.m. when Patrick pulled into the Bear Den Motel, which was a short walk from the Five Tribes Center, where families would gather for meetings, to learn tribal traditions, and have potluck suppers. It looked like a quiet Sunday afternoon, which pleased him. He knew the desk clerk and requested a room at the end of the building where there was a phone booth. As with previous assignments, he was now ready to fulfill another of Ian Johnson's requests. He entered the room. It was damp and musty and the walls were covered in well-shellacked yellow knotty-pine paneling. He sat on the edge of the bed and pulled out a smallish spiral notepad from his shirt pocket. The first line read "Dash 547-2343." Other names appeared below: "Lone Bear," "James," "Joey." Some had phone numbers next to their names, while others just had neatly printed addresses. He opened his suitcase, pulled out a pouch filled with coins, and walked outside to make his calls. He opened the phone booth's accordion door, stepped in, and closed the door, and a dull light came on that lit up the glass-and-aluminum box.

He dialed.

"Hello."

"Dash?"

"Yeah."

"The man downstate wants a sit-down. Can you oblige?"

"That depends."

"On what?"

"Can you meet me out back of Ray's pharmacy? It's on Melbac Street. You know where it is?"

"I'll find it."

"See you at six tomorrow. I got to go."

Patrick made another call, went back into his room, and lay on the bed. He got up an hour later and walked across the street to the meeting center.

In a gas-station parking lot 150 yards away from the Five Tribes Center and Motel sat a Ford F-150 pickup truck. Inside, Agent Thomas Edward Price of the Drug Enforcement Administration watched Patrick enter the center, and a few minutes later he also saw Joey Skywalker enter with his wife and three children.

"PX-10, this is PX-11, you copy, over."

"This is PX-10. Yes, I copy, over."

"Just thought you would want to know that Wallace is in town at Five Tribes at this moment, over."

"That sounds about right. That's how we figured it, over."

"I'll stay with him, over."

"Roger that, PX—11. PX—10 out."

It was 5:30 p.m. and the Five Tribes Center parking lot was filled with sedans, pickup and flatbed trucks, and station wagons. Patrick walked through the front door, and made his way to one of a half dozen booths that lined a back room. Parents and children were sitting on aluminum benches attached to picnic tables. He stopped and looked at one end of the room where children were making tribal ornaments for an upcoming spring Mohawk Day celebration. A large yellow-and-red tribal flag with the Five Tribes symbol on it was hanging over the children. An open kitchen flanked buffet tables, where a Sunday supper of venison was being readied by four or five women, some dressed in traditional Indian clothing. Patrick passed older men sitting in the booths and acknowledged them with a close-lipped smile as he walked to the end booth in a corner and sat down. He stared up at the many framed pictures on the wall of Mohawk men working high steel in Manhattan. Patrick turned his head and there stood Joey in front of him. He got up from his seat and faced him. Looking over Joey's shoulder, he could see his wife and three young children by the recreation area. She was walking toward them.

"They're all doing well?" asked Patrick.

"We're making it work," replied Joey as he slid into the booth.

Joey's wife carried over a small Styrofoam cup of black coffee and a large plastic mug containing iced tea and placed them both on the table.

Patrick gave her a hug and kissed her on the cheek. "It's so good to see you, Mary. The venison smells good tonight."

"Sure does, but you know kids. They like the hot dogs and pork and beans."

"We lived on Spam and pinto beans for a year after . . ." Joey blurted out, then paused and looked downward.

"Can you stop by the house after supper?" asked Mary.

"I am going to bed early tonight. Heading north tomorrow for a couple of days, but I'll make sure to stop Wednesday on my way home."

Mary's gaze wandered to the pictures hanging on the wall. She looked back at her husband and then at a particular frame on the wall: her father-in-law standing on a long steel beam hanging in midair. The small plaque at the bottom of the frame read "Joseph Skywalker Sr., 1944–1970, Twin Tower 2." Her smile left her as she turned and walked away. Patrick watched her as she made her way back to where her children were playing. He sat down and fixed his eyes on his cup of coffee, then looked up at Joseph Skywalker's son.

"Mr. Wallace, sir . . . it's great you come up here when you can and we sit and listen to each other go on about this and that."

"You have to know, Joey, I'll always be here for you."

"Yes sir, I know."

"Something's bothering you. What's in your craw?"

"There's not enough here. What work I get is just enough. Enough, you know, for paying bills, and they get paid late most of the time. I can see why he made that long trip every Sunday afternoon into that city."

"Your father was one of the best."

"We used to miss him a lot, you know, not being with us all week. I understand it now. Didn't before. Why he did that for so long. Look at um all up there, risking their lives every day, always wanting a better way for their kids. It's been ten years. I miss him now more than ever. I got to go. Mary and the kids are waiting on me.

Just outside, an old Willys jeep with a tattered canvas top, dirty side door, and rear plastic windows veered off the main road into the Five Tribes gravel parking lot, careened around a sharp corner, and eventually came to an abrupt stop behind Agent Price's Ford pickup.

"Damn it," Price said out loud.

Henry Crow Horse got out of the jeep and tapped on the truck's driver's-side window. Agent Price took his time cranking down the window.

"Well, what do we have here? You miss your exit, J. Edgar?

"Henry."

"Shouldn't you be home with the wife and kiddies?"

"I don't think the elders would mind you sitting in here with me on a cold afternoon now, would they, Henry? Come on, get in."

"Appearances matter, you know. Ahh, what the hell. They're all in there having their supper."

The recently retired old tribal sheriff got in and cranked the window down. From his coat pocket he took out a foil pouch of Red Man and put it on the dashboard then looked down and saw a cup on the floor that contained some black coffee.

"That coffee you got there. Is it hot?" Henry Crow Horse asked.

"An hour ago it was."

Henry Crow Horse picked up the small white Styrofoam cup that was on the floor next to the shifter, threw what was left of the coffee out the window, and nestled the cup between his thighs, then opened the pouch and put a pinch of tobacco between his cheek and gum, chewed, and spat some dark juice into the cup.

"So, Price. How long you planning on keeping this up?"

"Well Henry, how long have I been trying to get you to—"

"What's your game, Price? Mine's chess. You look like a golf man. Cow-pasture pool. Damn waste of land, if you ask me."

"What . . . thought all you Mohawk men loved the great outdoors. You don't ever recreate out here on this big reservation of yours?"

"Had a horse once. Rode over every square inch of this land. Guess my dad thought it was good to have one for me on account of our surname and all that."

"That seems right," replied Price.

"*The Price Is Right*. Hah. Good game show. This Indian's a real Johnny Carson. Love Carnac."

"With all that comedic talent you got there, how come you ended up being sheriff?"

"When I was a very young man, I discovered I hated heights. My knees would begin to buckle when my dad took me with him to the high buildings. That was many moons ago. No high-steel work in Manhattan for me. Once tribal council found out about my aversion to being on high places I was done for. They trained me to be a sheriff. So, Agent Price. Why do you keep dogging Joey Skywalker like you do? You won't find anything of a nefarious nature going on in there."

"Relax, Henry. I just have to keep an eye on Wallace. That's all."

"I think secret agent man may speak with forked tongue."

"Maybe. Maybe not. You can have your opinion. I am carrying out Washington's orders and I don't plan on intentionally hurting anyone."

"There'll be collateral damage. There always is."

"How so?"

Henry spat more brown juice into the cup and wiped away some spittle from the side of his lip with the back of his hand. "You know I once heard that those Canuck agents wearing them silly red-riding-hood coats took down whole families on the other side. Your new president put them up to that? We have good people here. They be poor but good. Just 'cause you're poor doesn't mean you're stupid or dirty or mean . . ."

"Or prone to smuggle?"

"Lady Reagan says just say no. Easy for her to say, since her old man has a righteous job. She has it real good. So good she can sit around all day acting wise and passing judgment on the wicked dopers. My people been growing hemp forever."

III

Sudden, unexpected death, when it comes, delivers like a double-edge blade. With a simple single thrust there's twice the entry wound: the first being immediate acknowledgment of human loss tugging at emotion, then the second in the form of the law of unintended consequences rearing its ugly head, throwing one's world that was once orderly and purposeful into disorder and emptiness. It had been a year since our parents' plane crashed over the Serengeti. Over the years Father and his long-lost cousins from Scotland had made trips to Africa to hunt. This time was different. Age had mellowed him and his appetite for the trophy was gone. He took Mother to vacation, to sightsee, and to find and observe wildlife he thought would become extinct in the not-too-distant future. Grey Stone, with all its land and orchards, looked different now. It was family grown, but now all I was to it was a caretaker.

It was only recently that I had begun to feel somewhat disconnected to the home my ancestors built. Back in its halcyon days my brother and I knew every inch of Grey Stone's land; our father made sure of that. Before we were teenagers, we farm boys, as we were often called by others who lived nearby, were already working seven days a week, and there wasn't a chore or task too big for us to attempt. When I think about my father, I recall one day when he chose to tell me what he saw in me. He was a giant of a man and I was intimidated by him, but on that day he unmasked his Spartan persona and demonstrated a rarely seen bit of emotion. Sometime back, on the steps of the county courthouse, my father had quite unexpectedly met Mr. Walter Hutchinson, the gentleman farmer who owned the grain mill about a mile and a half from where we lived. During this encounter my father had learned of something I had done for his neighbor and old friend that made him want to see me in his study after dinner.

On those steps Hutchinson had recounted an event that to me seemed not to be a big deal. My father told me what his friend said had happened. "James," the man had said, "you should have seen him. There he was, throwing himself into that thicket, trying his best to get Lizzy out of that big bush. She got herself caught up in those thorns chasing after a pheasant and was trapped for sure. Then all of a sudden Patrick came out of that hellish patch of misery, ran into the barn, came out a moment later with a Kaiser blade in his hand, and commenced to carefully cut a hole through to my prize-winning spaniel. "He went in and picked her up and carried her out in his arms. Both of them were bloodied and I took them in and cleaned their wounds."

After he recounted the story, my father said, "Patrick, you have gumption. You'll have it all your life and it will serve you well." That's all he said to me. I said thank you and I went upstairs to bed.

As Vincent Wallace turned the ignition of the family's aging diesel Benz, puffs of blackish smoke spewed out of the tailpipe. After a minute or so the engine ran smoothly and he left Grey Stone for a one-o'clock meeting with Angus King, the Wallace-family attorney. His destination was Pierce's restaurant in Elmira, near the town hall and the county courthouse since opening its doors in 1894, where King had regularly met James Wallace for lunch or dinner. Vincent arrived promptly at 12:55 and was greeted by old Oliver, the maître d', who had an enormous handlebar mustache that had gone out of style at the turn of the century.

"Master Vincent. How nice it is to see you again" said Oliver.

"It's good to see you again, sir."

Although Vincent was thirty years of age, Oliver still called him Master Vincent, just as he had when they'd first met, some twenty years earlier. Young Vincent had accompanied his father many times for lunch at Pierce's when they made the return trip home from a weekend of visiting museums in Manhattan.

"Mr. King just arrived and is at the bar."

Both men walked through an anteroom to the bar, passing many antiques and furniture that made the Edwardian-era rooms look regal.

"Well, here he is," Angus King said. "Hello Vincent."

"Mr. King."

"If you gentlemen will follow me, I have your table ready."

Oliver walked the two of them over to a well-appointed table in a back corner of the dining room where quiet conversation could take place.

"Please enjoy your lunch, gentlemen," Oliver quickly but politely said and then retired to his post.

"I find March to be an awful month, so very gray and gloomy. Let spring get here so we can get on with things . . . damn depressing month."

"Yes sir. I see how March can be that way."

"So my boy, how you getting along in that big house you're living in now? Too many rooms, yes?"

"I think so, sir."

"Are you lonely?"

"Sometimes."

"That's to be expected."

An older waiter dressed in a crisp white shirt and dark tie and coat appeared. "Can I get you gentlemen anything from the bar this afternoon?"

King ordered a martini, while Patrick asked for a German brew.

The two men sat quietly for a short time, resting in the civility that Pierce's provided. The waiter returned with their drink order and placed the glasses on the white heavily starched tablecloth in front of them. He lit a candle and handed both men menus.

"We just received a shipment of oysters. Would they be of interest to you today?"

"Yes, that's a winner," Vin replied. "A dozen, please."

"Very good, sir," the waiter replied and left.

"I bet lamb was served yesterday. It's been on the Sunday menu for as long as I can remember. Ever have a cold lamb sandwich?" Angus King asked.

"Mother made them for us all the time," replied Vincent.

"What do you say?"

"All right."

"Good."

The oysters came and Vincent shared them with his father's old friend. In the distance they heard the sound of wood crackling in the hearth. The waiter returned and took their order and Angus King picked out a bottle of Bordeaux. Lunch arrived and both men put French mustard and horseradish on the black pumpernickel bread the rare lamb came on, ate and drank, talked about the towns of Moreland and Elmira, and enjoyed each other's company.

Having finished his lunch and being well into his second glass of wine, Angus King begun to discuss what was on his mind. "Vincent, have you given any more thought to the offer? Harold Lunnis isn't going to wait much longer for your answer."

"I don't know. I have a degree in art history. What do I know about manufacturing and marketing? It wasn't so long ago I was cutting down timber and painting at night."

"The Lunnis Company is small—maybe a hundred employees—and you have the talent. He chose Moreland to set up shop because of the work ethic the men have in that town. He's old school. I've known Harold Lunnis since the war. He has a niche with his temperature-regulated incubators and has solid backers, and needs a good man to help with getting things started."

"I appreciate you making the call for me like you did. I am not sure where my interests lie."

"You and your brother, you both had so many interests you acted on. How long did Patrick work on high steel in the city? He worked on the World Trade Center, didn't he?"

"He most definitely did, him and his Mohawk crew. They put a good percentage of that superstructure up. I believe he worked over a year on Tower One."

"How's he doing now?"

"We both seem to be moving forward. But it's slow moving, I must admit."

"It's been over a year since your parents' plane went down," replied Angus King.

"Yes, I know. Doesn't seem like that long ago though, to me. Patrick has not confided in me at all as to his status. We always kept our personal affairs to ourselves. I don't pry."

"His status? I know you love your brother, Vin."

"Love, love is for poets. Look, I need to know what I can provide. Can I give him more money?"

"The money you receive from the trust is yours to do with—"

"Yes, yes, I know that. But . . ."

"We've been over this before."

"Where's that waiter? I need something to drink," Vincent exclaimed.

"The trust is irrevocable."

"All I know is I am up in the main house and he's in that

tiny cottage. It's wrong. What were they thinking—he was going to live off the profits from his apple farm?"

"Well, that may be the case. I don't know what your father was thinking. Wills can be strange things."

"You were his oldest and most trusted friend. You both went to Princeton. Crewed together. You're telling me he didn't discuss his reasoning, ever?"

"No. He did not."

"Pardon me, but I think that's rubbish. I don't believe that."

The waiter appeared.

"I'll have a Drambuie," said Vincent.

"Very good, sir. And for you, sir?"

"Coffee, please."

It rained and cleared and rained some more. The drive back to Moreland seemed to take forever. Too many unanswered questions and a career decision kept Vincent's mind unsettled. The back roads he always enjoyed driving on now seemed to twist and turn out of proportion as he pushed through a downpour. The grayness of the day, the *tat-tat* sound of rain falling on the roof, just as it had on his parents' coffins when he and Patrick and Don Kaminski carried them from the hearses to their graves, caused him to shiver.

At about the time Vincent arrived back at Moreland, Patrick was leaving the New York side of the reservation on his way to Montreal. Driving north on Route 37, he noticed a sign that read "Bridge to Canada." Turning off at the next exit, he soon came upon a 1940s-era customs bridge spanning the Saint Lawrence River. Cars and trucks were lining up in different lanes and customs officials were inspecting and questioning impatient drivers. Further in the distance he could see a smaller sign that read "Thank you for visiting Massena New York, IT WORKS, for business, for family, for you." The river stretched for miles in both directions, frozen and still, with trees on either side. He crossed the bridge into Canada without incident and drove nonstop until he reached the borough of Ville-Marie in Montreal, where he entered a small parking lot at the corner of Melbec and Spruce Streets. Patrick positioned his car in the rear of the lot facing the one and only entrance and sat low in his seat and watched, eyes gazing in a continuous sweeping action. Dusk had arrived but he could see well enough. He was surrounded by three walls, one of which was the rear entrance to an old, dilapidated four-story warehouse, another the rear of a Chinese laundromat, and the third the back of Ray's Pharmacy. There were two cars in the lot with space for another half dozen. It wasn't very long before a young man walked out of the pharmacy. He was well groomed and looked pale and thin. Under an open raincoat, Patrick could see he was wearing a tie and what appeared to be a smock that a barber would wear. He stood still and stared for a moment, and when he saw Patrick behind the wheel, he walked directly to the passenger door and got in.

"I am glad this day is over. Let's get out of here."

Patrick started the car and drove away. They left the city limits and drove west until they reached a dirt road that led them to a house trailer nestled beside a stand of pine trees. Patrick stopped the car and turned off the engine, then rolled down his window, listened, and heard the sounds of a nearby brook. The night was pitch black.

"You live here?" Patrick asked.

"This is my uncle's place. He comes here when he goes fishing. You said you wanted privacy."

"Go in there and turn on some lights."

Dash did as Patrick ordered. He found the key above the door frame and let himself in. He lit two kerosene lanterns, then started an electric generator. Soon the place had light and heat. Patrick entered and sat down on one end of a couch. Dash sat on a chair facing him and Patrick began questioning him on what he encountered over the few weeks.

"Stay cool, Dash. Now just take your time and think. Think hard and carefully. Tell me everything you can remember. Okay?"

"Yeah. Sure, Patrick. About a month ago some guys paid us a visit. They were from Boston. The guy that did the talking . .. he called himself Mr. Brown."

"How many?"

"Three. Brown and two others."

"And?"

"They shook us down. Said we were to pay, um, twenty percent. They said that some very powerful men were watching us and he would protect us from them coming in and taking over our whole operation."

"What did you say?"

"Nothing, I listened. I almost shit my pants. This guy Brown, he said he knew I was young and so were my boys, and they were in the business to help guys like us. He knew about our Indian friends too."

"Then what happened?"

"He got up real close to me and said he'd give me two weeks to get the money to him and every month thereafter."

Patrick stared out a bay window into the darkness for a while, then looked back at Dash.

"You did all right. That was a tough spot for you. For anybody, no matter how old they are."

"What are we going to do?"

"If it were up to me I'd pay them. I don't see us having much of a choice. They know where you work. Probably where you live, too."

"But it's not up to you, is it?"

"You know the answer to that question. Stay cool. You hungry?"

"Starving," answered Dash.

"Let's see what your uncle has in his pantry."

Both men walked toward the end of the trailer.

"Here we go," Patrick said as he opened a closet door that was next to a small refrigerator.

Bingo.

"Look here. Cans of Campbell's soups and sardines. And OTCs. Bet your uncle was a seafaring man.

"How's that?"

"Hardtack."

"Huh?" replied Dash.

"Old Trenton Crackers, son. The whole Union army ate them, and most sailors too, in the nineteenth century. They will keep forever in a can like this."

Patrick opened the can and pulled out what looked like a small ball of baked dough about the size of a walnut and banged it on the countertop.

"These are great, Dash. They have very little moisture in them, but crack um and put them in soup or coffee and your stomach will fill full again in no time. Hunger goes away pretty quickly."

Patrick heated up a can of tomato soup on the stove and Dash found a half-empty bottle of Yukon Jack in a cupboard above the sink. They ate the sardines and soup and drank the liquor, and Patrick told stories of his experiences with Mohawk tribesmen and how fearless they were, both at sports and in working on skyscrapers high above the city of Manhattan.

Patrick sighed. "I am bushed. Time to hit the sack."

Patrick walked a short distance from the dinette table down a narrow hall and found the bedroom. He flipped on the light switch and saw two sets of gray steel military-style bunk beds. At the end of each bed was a neatly folded dark green heavy wool army blanket with a rough, old-looking gray-striped feather pillow placed on top.

"Good. We both can sleep in the bottom bunks. Turn off that generator, will ya?"

Dash lit a kerosene lantern and went outside to shut off the generator. When he got back inside and went to the bedroom, Patrick was in his bunk.

"That's much better now. That damn thing is noisy as hell."

Dash got into his bunk and turned off the lantern. Both men lay quietly for a good while.

"Hear that?" Patrick asked.

"No. What?"

"The tongue of the brook. What a peaceful sound it makes."

"I can't hear anything."

"Lie still. Quiet. Hear it?"

"Yeah. I think so. Oh yeah, I hear it now. Man, that's all right. All the years I've been coming up here . . . guess I never really paid much attention to what's around. Those stories you were telling. You know. About our Akwesasn friends."

"Yeah, what about them?"

"You know a lot about them?"

"I know enough."

"Like what?"

"Well, they knew about Wanasi."

"Wanasi? What do you mean?"

"The eagle before it was the eagle was Wanasi, the talker. Wanasi really liked talking. He talked a lot. He talked so much he could only hear himself. He couldn't hear the water flowing in the brook or the wind, not even the fox. Then one day a crow came and said to him, 'Wanasi, the fox is hungry. If you quit talking you'll hear him and you'll hear the wind, too.' And the crow said, 'When you hear the wind, you'll soar.' From that moment on Wanasi decided to stop talking and Wanasi became its true nature: the eagle. And Wanasi soared and flew so very high that he could see all the lands and everything, and its flight said all it needed to say. Get some sleep. Try not to worry too much about Brownie and his Boston friends. I know some badass Mohawks just down the road that can solve all your problems."

Patrick was up first the next morning. The inside of the trailer was cold and dark, but that didn't matter to him because he was used to sleeping outside when the occasion was called upon. Getting up at the break of dawn would get him back to Montreal in time to drop Dash off for work at the pharmacy. He knew some people in the city and would try to learn what he could about the men from Boston that put so much fear into the minds of Ian Johnson's pot-smuggling crew.

Patrick poked his head into the bedroom. "Dash. Time to get up. Get a move on. I have a lot to do today."

Patrick lit a lantern, stood in the kitchen area of the trailer, and looked into all the cupboards for coffee, but there was none.

Dash appeared a few minutes later and was dressed.

They stepped down out of the trailer into a cold morning, just when the sun was starting to rise above the timberline. Dash got into the car but Patrick went behind the trailer toward the edge of the forest and stood still. A short distance from where he stood, he saw the brook he'd heard during the night and watched the water flowing over the rocks, twisting and turning its way until it was out of sight. He walked over to the brook, lay down next to the water, and drank, and when he stood up, he heard a screech that seemed to have come from the treetops. He went back to where the truck was parked, got in, and together they drove off.

"What did 'Mr. Brown' look like?" he asked Dash.

"Huh," Dash replied.

"Try hard to give me a good description, okay?"

"I could remember better if I had some breakfast."

"There will be a place down the road. Soon we can stop for some."

"I could even go for some of that . . . what'd ya call it? Hartic?"

"Hardtack."

"Yeah . . . right. Give me a second to think, will ya? Well,

I remember he had sort of a chin full of hair—dark but not too dark. Kind of a half beard, I guess. He wore a black wool watch cap."

"What about his eyes?"

"They looked dark . . . black, I think. He was a lot smaller than you. Maybe a little shy of six feet. Medium build. I know . . . ever see *The Deer Hunter*? He looked like that guy De Niro. Yeah. Robert De Niro, you know, the actor."

"I remember the movie. That's good. I have an image now."

They drove for a short while, stopped at a diner, and had breakfast, then continued on to a suburb of Montreal and pulled up to Dash's apartment.

"You live alone?" asked Patrick.

"Yeah."

"I see. What time do you have to be at work?"

"Ten."

"You're going to make it. I'll be in touch."

"Before two weeks are up?"

"You can count on it."

"That's good, 'cause I like breathing, ya know."

"Stay cool, Dash," Patrick told him as he pulled away in the direction of downtown Montreal. As he drove into the west side of the city, he made an action plan in his head of what he wanted to investigate. He turned on to Center Street, then made his way over to what the locals called down-and-out row. He saw a caramel-colored hooker walking down the steps of an old hotel, counting her bills. As he drove farther, he saw a bearded man with long gray hair wearing an army-green coat that was tattered and filthy sitting on a flattened cardboard box at the entrance to an alley. He watched him as he held a small brown paper bag containing a bottle up to his lips while stretching his other hand out to a guy who was passing by wearing gray checkered pants and a white tunic. As Patrick drove past them, he could see the cook in the rearview mirror, handing the man a big loaf of French bread. Patrick turned right at the next light, stopped in front of a large six-story apartment house that was in need of some repair, got out, walked up some steps, and entered. He climbed five flights of stairs before entering a dingy and smelly hall and knocked on a door that had a piece of masking tape with the name Jim Cantonese printed on it in ink stuck above a peephole. Jimmy, as he liked to be called, was a drug mule who had worked in a peripheral way with Patrick a few times in the past two years. He knocked, knocked again, and once more. A voice shouted out, "I am comin' I am comin'. Who is it?"

"You see me."

Three locks were unbolted and the door opened. "Come in."

"That was not much of a greeting."

"I was kinda asleep. Please, come on in. Cop a squat while I make myself a little more presentable."

Patrick entered a small living room, sat in the middle of the long end of an L-shaped sectional sofa, and looked down at a large oak-and-glass coffee table. An open three-ring binder and maps were lying out on the glass top. On one particular map Patrick could see a line drawn in red that started at Nova Scotia and ended at Long Island. Jimmy walked back into the room wearing an old ankle-length patch-quilt bathrobe and sat down next to Patrick.

"You didn't say what time you would be dropping by when you called. Too early for a Molson?"

"Sure, why not?"

Jimmy looked down at his paperwork lying on the coffee table.

"Guess you can tell what I've been attending to. Let me get those beers."

"Jimmy."

"Yeah?"

"No. Go ahead. Get those beers."

He went into the kitchen, returned with two open bottles and handed one to Patrick, then sat down.

"So. How goes it?"

"It's going," Patrick said as he sat back. "However, there's been a kind of momentary snag for us in how things are flowing south."

"Oh yeah? How's that?"

"You know. You've been in this business longer than I have, and well, we've always been good with passing info back and forth."

"Yeah. I've been cool with that. Yeah, sure. We've helped each other out when things got hot."

"I could use your help identifying someone."

"All right. Lay it on me."

"A few weeks back a guy by the name of Brown—that's what the dirtbag called himself—he and two of his boys paid a visit to one of my guys. Ever hear that name being talked about around town? Said he was from Boston."

Jimmy sat back in the couch. "Can't say that I have. What did he look like?"

"About five foot eleven. Medium build. Dark hair with a kind of half beard. Dark eyes."

"What did he do? I mean. What did he say to your guy?"

"Wants a piece of our action. Twenty percent."

"You think he's Mafia?"

"Don't know. Could be."

Jimmy took a sip of beer. "Hah. Maybe he thinks he's working for Escobar."

"Can you help me?"

"I don't have a clue, but I may know someone who might be of some assistance. This guy . . . draft dodger. Been here since sixty-nine. Tends bar and cleans up at the Shamrock over on Champlain. We both get high together from time to time. He's cool. Couple of times when I met him there, I saw some big-ass black cars parked outside. He may be tight with some of those guys who eat there. Worth a shot. Yeah?"

"Yes. That's good. What's his name?"

"Maurice. He likes to think he's French. Hah. I'll call and see if he's there. I'll make us some lunch first and we can head over there."

"Okay."

Maurice was working that afternoon. The three of them spent a better part of an hour talking at the bar. It was agreed that Maurice would help Patrick get an audience with Joseph Lanszetti. Big Joe, as he was called, was friendly with Maurice because he liked the way Maurice made his perfect Manhattans and liked even more the exceptional women he procured for him. Patrick and Jimmy went back to Jimmy's apartment. Patrick returned to the restaurant at 9:00 p.m. and sat at the bar. Lanszetti sat alone in a booth sipping Grappa from a tiny gold-rimmed stemmed crystal glass. He lit a La Gloria Cubana, Maurice walked Patrick over to the booth, and Patrick sat down. Being huge men, they appeared to consume the entire booth.

"Maurice tells me you're from Moreland," said Big Joe Lanszetti.

"Yes, that's right."

"Been there once. I like the country. Would you care for something to drink?"

"Yes."

Lanszetti motioned Maurice over.

"Two more Grappas."

"Yes sir," replied Maurice.

"What brings you to Montreal?"

"I am looking for someone."

"Yes. Maurice explained to me you needed some help in that way."

"May I inquire as to what else Maurice told you?"

"Just that I may be able to identify someone for you. You know. Because of the line of business I am in. I have from time to time opportunities to acquire many shipments of cigarettes and redirect those shipments back into the States. You may be in a position to help me with some of *my* logistical problems."

"Yes, I can see how I could assist in that problem." Patrick then explained his need to find the man that Dash called Brown.

"I have come to know very recently of this character of whom you speak. He's a new arrival to our fair city. A wolf. A lone wolf. But a wolf nonetheless. You see I . . . I travel in the pack and the pack I run with gets results. Ask around."

"I do not doubt you."

"That's good."

Both men sat like NFL centers facing each other at the line of scrimmage.

"If I can deliver this wolf to you, do we have a deal?"

"Mr. Lanszetti, I can assure you that if my employer instructs me to agree with your request, we can do business."

"Ahhhhh . . . you are a man who knows how things must be done."

"Like you, I run with a pack. The ancient clan and a tribe run through my veins. We both know how things must be done."

Patrick got up and walked to the bar, said good night to Maurice, and thanked him before walking out into a city that he was not familiar with. Lately he'd felt more at home in the woods, so he drove far out of the city in the direction of the reservation and found a roadside motel to stay the night. Lying in bed, he thought of his Latin teacher, Mr. Harper. Always remember, Mr. Wallace . . . *manus manum lavat.*

"Good morning. FBI Albany office, Miss Eldridge speaking. How may I direct your call?"

"Agent Purcell, please. Randall Svensen calling."

"One moment, please."

"Mr. Purcell, I have Randall Svensen on line one.

"Thank you, Cherie."

"Randall, how are you?"

"Good morning, Gary."

"How's the DEA doing on the reservation?"

"We may be moving on something. Gary, I see in my notes that you wanted to meet today."

"Yeah. We want to coordinate as best we can with you."

"Is the RCMP on board?"

"That's affirmative. We can go over everything when we meet.

"Very good."

"Let's meet at that same place. Make it noon."

"Roger that. We will be there."

"That was a quick exchange. What did he say?" asked Agent Price, who was sitting across the desk from Randall Svensen."

"We're on for today. The Triangle at noon."

"I'll call and reserve that back room," replied Agent Price.

"All right, we better go over our notes one more time," said Agent Svensen.

Svensen and Price walked out of Svensen's office into a meeting room to carefully review the facts they had gathered over their six-month investigation of reservation activities.

Patrick slept in. At 8:00 a.m. he got up, shaved, showered, dressed, and left the motel after 9:00 a.m., and was back in his car on Route 37, heading west toward the reservation. As he drove closer to St. Regis, he became uneasy about not having made telephone contact with Lone Bear the night before. He knew that coming unannounced would add more anxiety to an already tense situation, so he decided to stop for lunch and place another call to Ian Johnson's main man on the scene. About a half mile from the reservation he turned into the parking lot of the Triangle Restaurant and Trading Post. Since the 1940s the Double T, as it was called by locals, had been a roadside stopover for tourists looking for bargains on moccasins on their way to Niagara Falls. Patrick walked in and was quickly seated at a booth. The place was starting to fill up as it was now close to the lunch hour. A waitress named Tushanna came over to Patrick's booth, handed him a menu, and took his order. While he waited for his food to arrive, a quiet voice reached his ears as if from nowhere.

"May I join you?" asked Henry Crow Horse.

"Of course. Please sit down," replied Patrick.

Out of the corner of her eye Tushanna saw the retired sheriff and came back over to the booth with a coffeepot and two cups.

"Tushanna, you're looking well. How's Tom? How are your boys and that daughter of yours?"

"Oh, you know, they can't wait till schools out. My Jessie will be starting Little League this year."

"That's great. Tom coaching again?"

"Yeah . . ."

"Tell him I said hello."

"I sure will. Can I get you something?"

"How about a hamburger and some fries?"

"Coming right up," said Tushanna as she walked back toward the kitchen.

"You ever want to go back up on the high steel in Manhattan?" asked Henry Crow Horse.

"Don't know if I have the stomach for it anymore."

"I read about the plane crash. I am sorry."

"Thank you, Henry."

"Joey Skywalker . . . I know you keep in touch with him. That's good of you. He's struggling."

"I know."

"Well, I'll be damn . . ."

"What's that?"

"Just look at me and keep on talking. The feds just walked in."

Patrick's back was turned to them, but Henry Crow Horse had a keen view and could make them out clearly. Henry was just about to bolt when he saw them being ushered to the other side of the restaurant.

"Patrick. I think it would be wise if we continued our talk another time."

"Yeah. I'll get the check," said Patrick.

"Looks like they went in the back room to talk. Let's go," said Henry.

"I'll hang back until you're outside," Patrick replied.

Patrick drove out of the parking lot onto the main highway and entered the reservation. He could feel the steering wheel getting moist and slick from his palms. Up ahead he saw a gas station, found a phone booth, and called Lone Bear. Like the night before, there was no answer. He drove to Lone Bear's trailer and knocked on the door several times to no avail. Looking first to his left, then right, he gently turned the door handle. The door opened and he slowly walked in and shut the door behind him. The inside was undisturbed and well appointed. Patrick looked in all the rooms and saw nothing out of the ordinary or out of place. He found a notepad on the kitchen counter and wrote Lone Bear, asking him to meet him at the Bear Den Hotel after 2:00 p.m. He fixed the note to the front of the refrigerator with a Washington Redskins magnet and started for the door. As he opened the door he walked straight into Joey Skywalker. Both men looked into each other's eyes and Patrick seemed to sigh and fold into himself as his head dropped.

"Ah, Joey. Jeeeez. I was afraid something like this might happen someday. Did you walk here?"

"Yeah."

"Come on. Let's get out of this man's home."

Both men got into Patrick's pickup and drove off. Neither

man spoke until they reached Rose Valley Lake, which was located at the northwest corner of the reservation. Patrick parked the truck and they sat for a while staring at the water.

"Patrick."

"Yeah?"

"You're not going to ask me why?"

"I figured you'd tell me what I already know."

"We used to come here when I was a kid."

"I know, Joey. Your dad told me all about the fishing the two of you did here."

"It's like this. You know. Like I was saying to you the other night, I am without money most of the time. Mary and the kids, they need things."

"They need you most of all."

"Yeah. I know the risks."

"How long have you been hooked up with Lone Bear?"

"Jerry?"

"Is that what he's calling himself now?"

"Yeah. That's the name he likes to go by. We started talking a couple weeks back. Told me he could use some help."

"Did he tell you why?"

"Just what's been going down around here. He can get the stuff, get it through, and get away."

"Anything else?"

"Just that he had a visit from somebody a couple of weeks back. He didn't talk about it much. You know. Nothing specific or anything. He said he could use a guy like me. Called me a warrior and said I had much power and I could be of great service to him. Talked up the warrior-nation movement. You know, that kind of stuff."

"You've known him for quite some time, haven't you?"

"He was a couple of years ahead of me in school. We never hang out. He's a single man, you know."

Patrick nodded, then looked at his watch.

"I have to get back to the motel before two. Will talk later. All right?"

Patrick drove Joey home and then went on to the Bear Den to check in and wait.

The Double T's lunch crowd had emptied out. The noontime gathering of FBI and DEA agents had just finished their lunch. DEA Agent Tom Price got up from his table, walked out of the small private dining room, and found Tushanna behind the counter.

"We will be needing the room for a while. Is that okay?"

"You have it until suppertime," she replied.

Price asked Tushanna for the check, told her they were not to be interrupted, returned to the room, and locked the door behind him. Price began the meeting . . .

"Gentlemen. Shall we get started? Gary, the DEA wants to thank you and the FBI for lunch," said Price as he handed the receipt to Agent Gary Purcell.

"We'll buy next time," quipped DEA Agent Randall Svensen.

"All right, fair enough," replied Purcell. "So. Randall. You said this morning that you may be moving on something? Can you bring the FBI up to speed?"

"The main problem, Gary, as we it, is that these people are extremely distrustful of outsiders, non-Indians. Relations have not been amicable. Putting that aside for a moment, we've seen something recently that's new to the reservation," replied Svensen.

"What do you have?" asked Purcell.

"A syndicate connection."

"Manhattan?"

"No. Scranton."

Purcell sat back in his chair and said, "Interesting . . . Buffalino is more into coke distribution these days. They're smoking the stuff in Miami."

"Yeah. I read that last report. They're making it into a solid and cracking it up. A small piece is going for twenty-five," replied Price.

"What do you have so far?"

"DEA intel purports that Scranton wants in on the action here and has contracted with a guy by the name of Lanszetti in Montreal to squeeze Ian Johnson's crew," reported Agent Svensen.

"Maybe they're thinking the Manhattan crew will be so knee-deep in this new crack distribution op that pot transport will fit just right in their business plan," said Purcell.

"Our Johnstown office has made good inroads into our yuppie's traffic business down in Moreland. He's been a busy-bee distributor downstate and in central PA, too," said Price.

"Boy, he's something, isn't he? Ian Johnson. Born on first base, thought he hit a triple. Jesus. Poor bastard is totally clueless to the crap that's coming his way," said Purcell.

"He's been lucky so far, not having Manhattan to contend with," remarked Price.

"Well, he has Wallace up here and in Montreal, asking a lot of questions. Some Scranton boys paid Johnson's crew a visit two weeks ago. Got um uptight and hunkered down. At the moment they aren't moving anything for him," explained Price.

"Agent Purcell sat back in his chair and looked at Agent Price. Patrick Wallace. I remember you talking about him a while back . . . interesting sort of guy. He can't save Johnson's bacon from getting burned."

"He's real tight with the Mohawk," Price said.

"Without them our young yuppie would be relegated to selling little baggies to college kids out of the trunk of his car. So what have we in real time?" asked Agent Purcell.

Patrick pulled into the Bear Den Motel's parking lot a little af-ter two o'clock. His tiny room was warm and stuffy. He walked over to the only window and cranked hard on a half-broken rusty handle until it opened louvers made of milk glass, lay on his motel bed, and waited. Fresh cool air slipped through the louvers and he nodded off into a light sleep while waiting for his contact, Lone Bear, to arrive. It was after 4:00 p.m. when a knock at the door awakened him. Patrick opened the door a few inches, then slowly swung it completely open when he saw Lone Bear, who raised his right hand upward, palm facing Patrick. Patrick did the same.

"Please, will you come in, Lone Bear?"

Lone Bear did not make eye contact with Patrick or say anything. But he lowered his hand, looked past Patrick into the room, and slowly came forward as Patrick backed into the room in a relaxed manner, being careful to keep a distance. This distance was not out of fear but respect.

"You know the ways of the Mohawk, Patrick. Many do not understand our customs."

"It's not easy Lone Bear," said Patrick, offering a cigarette. "I work at understanding what is important to me. Sometimes I get through faster than at other times. And sometimes . . . I guess I never get through."

"It is the work, not the time that is important, maybe? Thanks for the smoke. Good brand."

"Let's sit for a while," Patrick said as he walked over to a small table in the corner of the room and sat down on a rickety rattan chair. "I was getting concerned when I couldn't reach you."

Lone Bear lit his Marlboro. "Sorry, Patrick. No answering machine. Been up-state since Saturday, moving my sister into an apartment. She got a job in Albany."

"Your younger sister?"

"Yeah . . . she just turned eighteen. She wasn't keen on leaving here, but the job was right for her and the pay is good. My mother and father, they're going to miss her."

"She'll be back every weekend, Lone Bear."

"I am heading back to Moreland tomorrow. Before I go I am stopping by the Skywalkers'. Promised Mary I would drop by before heading home."

Lone Bear's expression changed.

"Mary's a good cook, I hear. Good woman. There's something I have to . . ."

"I know. When I was at your trailer this afternoon, I ran into him."

"I want to explain, Patrick. Please." Lone Bear's voice grew solemn and remorseful.

"Of course you do, and thanks for being straight with me," replied Patrick. "You know where my intentions lie when it comes to Joey and his family. I know the difficulties that are here. You don't need to get into weeds about reservation life. He's a grown man, Lone Bear, and can make up his own mind."

"I should have put him off right away. He's got kids," replied Lone Bear.

"Lone Bear, you can be certain I'll talk to him. I believe I know what to say to him," said Patrick. "Right now I need to hear from you about what's been happening around here lately. I've spent some time making inquiries. Dash told me the same guys who visited him paid you a visit. I don't have any concrete answers right now, but I am working hard on understanding what I have uncovered so far. Let's talk about these guys . . . okay?"

Lone Bear sat back in his chair and in a more relaxed voice said, "Very good then. Here's what went down."

Patrick listened as Lone Bear told him what had happened the day he met the three men from Scranton. When the sit-down was over, it was clear to Patrick that Brown posed a serious threat to Ian Johnson's pot-smuggling enterprise. Having heard the specifics delivered with much concern in Lone Bear's voice, Patrick tried to calm Lone Bear. Once he felt he had done that, he ended the meeting.

Lone Bear got into his pickup and drove off. Patrick stood

in the doorway and watched him leave, then walked to the phone booth in front of his room and called Mary Skywalker as promised. As the phone began to ring, he thought about whether he should stay the night or drive back to Moreland. The phone kept ringing, and the more it rang, the more he thought of Joey and what he'd say to him.

Joey sipped at a beer while the phone rang repeatedly. The kids ran in and out of the living room, where Joey sat on a recliner in front of a television set.

"Mary . . . Mary . . . you there? You expecting a call?"

"I'll get it," she said, half out of breath, having just walked in from the garage with bags of groceries.

"Hello."

"Mary, it's Patrick. I am not interrupting your dinner, am I?"

"Patrick. Oh no . . . haven't started that yet. You coming by?"

"I don't want to intrude."

"We all want to see you. There's enough food."

"All right. I'll settle up here and be over there shortly."

Mary hung up the phone on the wall and began to make a meal of spaghetti with meatballs and hot sausage. Joey entered the kitchen.

"Hi," he said. He hugged her and helped her put away some canned goods in a cupboard.

"That was Patrick."

"Oh yeah?"

"Yeah. He's goin' to join us for supper. Remember when we saw him Sunday, he said he would come by today?"

"Yeah, I sort of remember you saying something about that."

Joey's mood changed. He walked over to the kitchen table and sat down facing the sink where Mary was starting to cook. "I'll set the table," he said.

Before he could get up from his seat, their three kids ran in and surrounded him. His daughter put her arms around his shoulders and tugged him toward her while her younger brothers milled around and pawed at him.

"Daddy, can we go outside?" shouted the two boys.

"It's almost suppertime," Mary replied.

Patrick paid his bill and drove out of the motel parking lot toward the Skywalkers' house. He stopped at a convenience store and bought some food items for their larder and ice cream for the kids. He pulled up to the house and parked his Chevy half-ton pickup. He gathered his packages. While he was closing his door, a large German shepherd suddenly appeared, barked twice, sniffed his feet, then walked away. Patrick made his way through the yard to the front door of the log longhouse. Before he could knock on it, the door swung open and Joey and Mary's children were on him, wrapping their arms around his legs and tugging at him as he passed over the threshold and into a warm, inviting home.

"Whoaaaa, guys! Patrick exclaimed as he made his way into the living room, then the kitchen.

"Let's give Uncle Patrick a chance to settle in before—"

"That's okay, Mary."

Joey got up from the table, walked over to the sink, and tried to peel his kids off the man who was once his father's best friend.

"They're always like this when you visit," said Joey.

"I'll tell you what," said Patrick to the youngsters. "How about after dinner, if it's still light outside and it's okay with your mom and dad, we explore the backyard."

"Yayyyyyy," they all shouted together.

"Can we go now? Please. Please."

Patrick smiled and shook his head a couple of times, then shook Joey's hand. Mary put a colander filled with pasta down into the sink and gave Patrick a big hug.

"You kids sit down now," said Mary. The three reluctantly followed their mother's order and made their way over to the kitchen table.

Patrick placed the bags he was carrying on the countertop and whispered into Mary's ear. "Hope it's okay, I got them some ice cream."

"They'll like that," Mary quietly replied.

"All right, let's all sit down," Joey said.

Mary placed a large bowl of spaghetti in the middle of little kitchen table and Joey carefully spooned out equal portions to his kids, making sure each one got a meatball and a slice of bread. Mary came over with a pitcher of grape juice and poured some into the children's plastic cups, then sat down. She poured some into two tall glasses, then handed one to Patrick and the other her to her husband.

"It's like wine. Drink up," she said.

Patrick sat and enjoyed his meal and talked and laughed with the children and Mary. She was excited about all the prep work she was doing for the upcoming Mohawk Celebration Day. Joey sat in silence. Patrick watched him as he sat in his chair, hunched over his plate, picking at his food and looking smaller than his true stature. He was a shy, quiet man of over six feet, four inches tall who tipped the scales at 235 pounds and had long, black shiny hair that he tied in the back.

When dinner was over, Patrick led the kids out into the backyard, and they had the ice cream he had brought them. He and the children walked farther out into a large field past a cistern, then stepped into a spring house, where they stood and looked for crawfish in the water trough. It was getting dark and difficult to see the little scary creatures, but Patrick did his best by holding his Zippo lighter above where he thought they may be. It was getting close to eight o'clock and already dark.

Mary stood on the back stoop and called out, "Time to come in."

"Look, there's one," the youngest boy said.

"Grab it," said his sister.

Crawfish scurried about and the two boys reached for the one they had cornered and pinned up close against the side of the stone wall, as water splashed everywhere, getting Patrick and the girl wet.

"Got it," said the older boy.

"It's time to go in, gang," Patrick said as he began to walk out of the spring house, still holding the lit cigarette lighter in the air.

Mary stepped down from the porch and walked towards the cistern. She smiled as she watched her children follow Patrick as he led the way with the faint yellow glow of a tiny flickering flame. It was dark now and they marched proudly and happily toward the back of the cabin trailing the big man in a single file with the oldest boy first in line, holding the tiny catch of the day at arm's length for all the night to see.

"Mom. Mom, look what we caught!"

"That's good hunting. Go and show your dad now, then it's time to wash up and get ready for bed," she said.

The children rushed into the living room. Patrick stood in the doorway of the kitchen and saw Joey sitting in his chair in front of the television. The kids told him of their great adventure and the hunt and he listened and carefully inspected the crawfish they presented to him.

"Patrick, can you stay the night?" Mary asked. "We just have the couch for you."

"I am expected back in Moreland tonight."

"It may take me a while to get them washed and to bed, so I'll say good-bye now."

"Dinner was good."

She hugged him and kissed him on the cheek.

"He'll be okay."

She looked at him with eyes of concern. "Talk to him."

"I will."

Then she walked down the hallway into the bathroom and called for her children. They jumped onto Patrick and grabbed him around the waist and legs and said good night to him, then they ran into the bathroom. Patrick walked into the living room, picked up a chair, and moved it next to where Joey was sitting so he could talk quietly. He could also see down the hall to the bathroom, where Mary was running water into the bathtub.

"On second thought, maybe this isn't the best place to have this . . ."

"Let's go outside," replied Joey.

"All right."

They walked out the front door and got into Patrick's pickup. Joey sat quietly and stared out at his longhouse, saw the window to the bathroom and his children's room, and saw shadows of his family on the walls.

"Why do you think Lone Bear wants your help all of a sudden?"

Silence engulfed the cab of the truck.

"Joey, listen. There's going to be trouble and he needs muscle. Hell, I am surprised he didn't call on the whole Mohawk Nation to help him."

"Do you think it might come to that?" asked Joey.

"I am not getting into any details. The less you know the better." Patrick looked at the cabin and pointed to the windows. "That's your concern," he said firmly.

Joey turned his head away from looking out the passenger's window and looked straight at Patrick. "You went to college. Tell me, isn't there a better way for us?"

"All I know," said Patrick, "is that you can't change the past. The future isn't here yet, whatever it's going to be. So all there is . . . is this . . . the present space we occupy."

"This reservation we live on. This is our homeland. Our space. If we can get the pot across our land, that's our right. Who's it hurting? It's money in our pockets—not for shit things we may want but real things we need."

Patrick sat quietly and listened.

"I am not leaving the rez. My kids are going to know our

ways. My father had that opportunity. I don't. We don't. There's no climbing the high steel for us for good pay anymore."

Patrick drove off the reservation and headed south. There was little if any moonlight coming through the thick, dark clouds above, which left only an ever-present consuming blackness and gray eerie shadows appearing on the road in front of him. Only the headlights of an occasional oncoming car would jolt him out of a trance he was going in and out of as he headed back to Moreland. He drove fast through the mountain passes and around sharp, winding curves that had no guardrails. The more he thought about what Joey had said, the more thoughts he had of the accident in 1970 that had killed his friend. For more than a hundred years the Mohawk had been building the tallest bridges and skyscrapers, and there were accidents and men died. That was a fact of life, and Patrick was always good at rationalizing irrefutable facts and moving on with life, never looking back. He drove faster. The total blackness of the night surrounded him and entered him and he could not shake the realization that he was culpable in the death of another human being. As he drove toward home, thoughts began to flow into his mind about Manhattan and the towers and Joey's father. The winding roads, the afternoon with Lone Bear, and the talk he had just had with Joey kept his thoughts going to just one place. It was all there now in front of him as if it were yesterday. The day, the blackness of night, the late hour, and fast driving all swirled together, and uncontrolled memories flowed uninhibited.

"I forget. What floor is this?"

"It's the ninety-third," replied Joseph Skywalker.

"The fog is pretty bad today," said Patrick.

"No wind though."

Visibility was good enough to see the kangaroo crane operator give the thumbs-up sign and Patrick and Skywalker moved to another section to accept the belly band that was slowly being dropped into their position.

"Let's weld some metal!" Skywalker shouted.

Both men worked competently and quickly. Heating the metal was a precise and sophisticated process. The steel had to be maintained at a constant weldable temperature for a flawless weld. Patrick held a propane torch and directed it constantly toward the metal area that Skywalker was welding. After Skywalker's pass Patrick scrubbed the weld with a wire brush and broke off some slag with his chipping hammer, then brushed the surface once again before Skywalker made his second pass.

The air had been heavy and damp when they started work. The morning fog finally broke around ten o'clock and warm sunlight quickly fell on their necks, shoulders, and backs. The other ironworkers on the floor were moving and positioning and connecting fabricated materials into their final destinations. When completed, the two buildings would contain 100,000 tons of steel.

Skywalker finished his last pass and put down his gear and glanced at his watch.

"It's noon. Let's eat."

He took his welding helmet off and put his hard hat on and walked over to where he had stored his lunch pail.

Patrick surveyed what they'd accomplished since 7:00 a.m., and feeling good about their efforts, joined Skywalker.

"How many you think work here?" asked Skywalker.

"You taking a census?"

"Maybe."

"I heard five hundred or maybe a little more," replied Patrick.

"Seventeen more floors to go, then we hit the next one," Skywalker said.

"What else you have in there?" Patrick asked as he peered into Skywalker's lunch box.

"Ahhh, you lookin' for one of these?" replied Skywalker as he reached into his coat pocket, pulled out two Twinkies, and threw one to Patrick.

Patrick smiled. "You know me too well now. You going to miss living in Brooklyn?"

"You going to miss the Village, with all those beatniks and them zippy hippies?"

"Joseph, don't be making fun of my poets now. You liked that book I got you last month."

"I did," replied Skywalker. "Mr. Whitman used to live not far from where I am staying. I think he understood our nature. Good book. Good man. I won't miss the drive every Friday, that's for sure. It's best not to get me thinking about leaving Brooklyn or what's coming next: we have another one of these to build, you know."

"Why did you ask me about the number of men working here?"

"Just curious. Guess I wanted to know how many it takes to get this kind of project built. It took a couple dozen back home a weekend to put up a home."

"That's how the Amish do it," replied Patrick.

"Got a letter from my wife. Joey, my oldest—he just turned thirteen—she said he's going to help build my brother's house next weekend. Want to come?"

As Patrick drove on, he remembered the weekend he spent with Skywalker and his tribal brothers who came together one Saturday at dawn to build that home. Many ironworkers and their fathers and uncles were there to lend a hand. Late Saturday afternoon families began to arrive and create firepits to roast elk and venison. When supper had ended, many of the older men who had been riveters and welders back in the twenties sat on the ground in a large circle, and one by one they told stories about what they had built and what they had seen while living in New York City. It seemed many a story would eventually come around to Skywalker's father, whose strength and wisdom was unmatched. More than one told of how Standing Arrow could hammer a rivet into place with one blow. Patrick later learned that a one-strike rivet was a very rare occurrence. As the evening was coming to an end, the men had broken away from the women and brought out their pipes, and they smoked and shared quiet words with one another, then parted and went home.

Skywalker and Patrick had had to leave Sunday afternoon so they could be back at their worksite at 7:00 a.m. Monday morning. On the ride back they'd talked a lot about their weekend together and how well-organized the men were. At some point on the trip back Patrick had noticed Skywalker's tobacco pouch lying on the dashboard, and it had reminded him of the men and their pipes. He had asked Skywalker what they were saying to one another as they smoked. Skywalker had told him that tobacco burning means that you're communicating with the creator and giving thanks to the creator, and as you burn the tobacco it rises up and the creator knows that you're speaking to him truthfully and honestly and you're being thankful.

"That's why we always carry tobacco—it's just a little bit of medicine to help you. We always have it close by . . . they were just communicating those thoughts to one another before going to sleep," he said.

Patrick was less than thirty miles from Moreland and noticed that fatigue was setting in. Arriving a little after midnight, he went into his cottage, turned on a light in the smallish den, and walked directly over to a dry sink. He opened the bottom cabinet and took out a bottle of brandy and poured two fingers into a large snifter. He sank down into a big, old cushioned chair that once belonged to his grandmother and slowly sipped the brandy, and when he was finished he went into his bedroom, undressed, and got into bed. He was sound asleep soon after his head hit the pillow.

He did not wake up until twelve hours later. Slightly drowsy but awake and still lying in bed, he went over each detail in his mind of the report he would deliver to Ian Johnson later in the evening. His thoughts were interrupted by the sound of an engine. He got out of bed and stood next to a window and saw old Bill Mack coming up the lane, driving his ancient two-toned Dodge pickup with his son Willie by his side. Old Bill had been tending to the apple orchards throughout growing and pruning seasons long before Patrick was born. Patrick watched as they made their way down the lane toward a Quonset hut where the farm's machinery was kept. Patrick stood at the window for a while and watched them both open the heavy prefab hut's big sliding door. They both went in and started to poke around and after what looked to be a prolonged cantankerous discussion Willie reluctantly started to do the maintenance on the tractor while his father looked on. Patrick stood there with a slight grin on his face and remembered the time his father told the story of when Bill came to run the apple farm.

It had been the day after Pearl Harbor was bombed. Bill lived in the Newberry section of Moreland, which was the east side, the poorest part of the town. Bill and a half dozen other Negro men were on the sidewalk heading toward the town's municipal building, while at the same time Mr. Wallace was stepping over the threshold of his office's front door and onto the sidewalk. The two men crossed paths. Bill tipped his hat to Patrick's father.

"Bill Mack!" Mr. Wallace said in a declarative voice.

"Mr. Wallace, good afternoon to you, sir." His companions momentarily stopped. "Go ahead, I'll catch up with you," he said to them.

"How's the winter treating you so far, Bill?"

"I am doin' a little of this and that. I miss the mill, sir."

"Yes, I miss the ol' days too. Where you headed?"

"Goin' to enlist in the army."

"Now, that's very admirable. What do you know about apple orchards?"

"Sir?"

"You ever take care of them?"

"I know deer can clean them out pretty quick but other than that, no sir."

"Army, huh? If I recall correctly you have a young family."

"That's right, sir."

"Well, it just so happens I have a need to fill a position. If you're so inclined to discuss it with me, I will be home before dark. Stop by then if you're interested."

"Why thank you, Mr. Wallace. I just may do that. I'll need to think it over a spell."

"I understand," Mr. Wallace replied, and the two men parted company.

Patrick looked on and saw father and son going over the old tractor with a fine-tooth comb. Since the spring of forty-two, Bill had faithfully attended to the family trees and the equipment needed to keep a working farm in good order and profitable.

Patrick turned away from the window, got dressed, went to his kitchen, and made himself some eggs. When he had finished eating, he telephoned Ian Johnson to find out what time he wanted to meet with him that evening at E. J.'s.

It was 9:50 p.m. when Patrick walked into E. J.'s. He walked directly to the entrance to the vault, then turned around, walked a few steps and stood and waited at the end of the bar. He could see anyone who entered or exited the vault. It was Friday and the place was packed.

Johnson had bought the old bank and the entire block a couple years back with money from his inheritance. Johnson had inherited a lot of money from an uncle in the pharmaceutical business, money he spent on the disco club to prop up his ego and open some access to the party crowd. He had been Patrick's roommate for all four years of college, in part because of the aid that Patrick could provide the slightly built Johnson when push came to shove. The robust, steely-eyed Patrick towered over the bespectacled Johnson, and even spoke for him at times.

Patrick didn't have to wait long. Johnson appeared and both men walked into the vault and sat down on a black leather couch. The thumping bass sounds from the disco could still be heard, so Johnson got up and shut the inside door to his office to quiet the room.

"You sounded down when you called. It can't be that bad," Johnson said.

"It's not good, Ian."

"Come on, we've been in—"

"No. Not this time. This isn't something we're ready for."

"What do you mean?"

"This situation. It has too many unknowns. I can't say we can trust what I learned."

"Okay, let's hear it."

"You don't need this aggravation, Ian. You could stop your operations anytime. You don't need the money."

"Yeah. That's right."

"Then why?"

"Why are you in it, Pat?"

Patrick sighed. "That's a little complicated."

"So come on. What went down?"

"Two weeks ago three guys—one named Brown—they confront Dash and Lone Bear with an ultimatum."

"And what was that?"

"Either pay twenty percent or else."

"Or else what?"

"Come on, Ian, you're not—"

"Okay, okay, twenty percent. I get that, but how would they ever know what that would amount to?"

"Well, for starters they must have some idea of the cost of

a kilo and what we are moving."

"That makes sense. The going price is pretty standard these days, but how the hell do they know how much we import? How would they know? You know exactly?"

"I don't know, Ian. It's hard to say how they know for sure. Maybe they've been watching things real close, but I think we need to come to the conclusion that they know and they will be expecting a right amount on a regular basis."

"Shit. Who the hell are these guys?"

"That's what's bothering me. I am just not sure. This, my friend, is the oldest game to have ever been played. Could be Mafia out of Boston."

"Come on, Pat. A shakedown? Jesus! My operation is small potatoes. What did you find out about this Brown guy?"

"Nothing I can trust. The whole thing smells to high heavens. I was able to meet this guy by the name of Lanszetti. He gave me the impression he's tight with a crew but I haven't verified that yet."

"A crew?"

"Yes. That's Mafia talk, Ian. A crew."

"Shit."

Patrick stood up and walked over to the door that led to the small room with the refrigerator. He opened the door and went to the refrigerator and took two cans of beer, walked back to where Johnson was sitting and handed him one of the cans.

"Here. Let's keep it together, okay? We have to do our best to break down what I've learned."

Johnson pulled the tab on the can and took a sip. "So. Lanszetti. What's his game?"

"He says he can deliver Brown to me."

"For what? To make a deal with us? But you're not a hundred percent sure what that deal is."

"That's right. Not completely, but he told me that if we can help him get his products across the reservation and over the border into New York, he'll alert us to who this Brown guy is."

"Man oh man, Pat. This looks pretty gray."

"Tell me about it. We're dealing with people who will turn on a dime in a second. I could go up there next week and have a shit storm rain down on me."

"Hector has ten keys just sitting in his garage up there in Nova Scotia and the ice. That will be gone in a month," said Johnson.

"Lone Bear has other routes he can use," replied Patrick.

"I know, but his snowmobile is the safest bet.

Patrick opened his can and drank while staring for a long time at an old wood-framed picture of some Indians standing next to Lewis and Clark that was hanging on the wall directly in front of him, then turned toward Johnson. "I like *my crew* and I don't much appreciate them being messed with."

"That's noble, Pat, but—"

"But nothing. I have my reasons to think the way I am thinking now."

A phone rang. Johnson picked it up. "Hello. Oh hi, baby. No, it's not too late but I am in the middle of . . . uh-huh . . . uh-huh . . . yeah. You're where? . . . Put Jackson on the phone."

Johnson grabbed his beer and gulped down what was left in the can. "Pat, I have to take this. It's Sarah. She's outside at the bar. She's yammering."

"I thought coke calmed her down."

"If you lace it with enough Valium," replied Johnson.

"Sorry, boss," Jackson Louge said. "She just took the phone off the wall and . . ."

"It's okay, Jackson. So. She's at the bar now."

"Yes. She's standing right here in front of me."

"All right. Get her to sit down if you can and keep her there. Can you manage this?"

"Yes sir."

"Good. I'll be out as soon as I can . . ."

Johnson hung up the phone, walked over to the refrigerator, and got himself another beer and one for Patrick.

"I can tell it's going to be a long night. Here . . ." Johnson said as he handed Patrick the can.

"We can shut all of this down right here and now. I know you. It sounds to me you want to head north and make this problem go away."

Ian Johnson's bartender, Jackson Louge, put the phone back on the wall and walked around the bar to where Sarah Taylor was standing. "He's with someone right now, talking business. But he said to me I am to entertain you. So. What can I get you, Sarah?"

"Mon ami. Tonight? More of everything."

"Well. Don't think we have that on the menu at this moment. You set your lovely self down right here on this stool and I'll fix you something. What would you like?"

Oh, Jackie boy. Romance is on my menu tonight," she replied.

Patrick got up from the couch and started for the vault's main door, then turned around and walked over and stood quietly for a moment beside his friend.

"What?" Johnson said.

"Nothing comes from nothing," Patrick whispered.

"You're going then," replied Johnson.

"I am. There's a devil to pay."

"Tomorrow we can sit down and map out the details the best we can. All right?" asked Johnson.

"I'll see you tomorrow, Ian, and don't leave your best work in the sheets."

Johnson got up from the couch and put his arm around Patrick's shoulders and walked him out. Both men stood for a moment outside the vault's threshold and gazed out on the disco scene. Ian looked over at the bar and saw her. Patrick also looked at her sitting on the bar stool, then he looked at

Ian, shook his head a couple of times, and revealed a slight grin. "Better you than me."

"I'll never learn, will I?"

"Good night, Ian," Patrick said and he left.

Johnson walked over to where Sarah was sitting. She was drinking white wine. She gave him a big smile as soon as she saw him, and he stood next to her.

"You look good," he said.

"Thank you, darling," she replied. "Guess I interrupted something really important, didn't I?"

"What do you mean?"

"For a moment I thought Jackie was going to put a bear hug on me or something, if I tried one more time to see you."

Johnson looked at his bartender, who was washing and drying a few glasses a few feet away, and gave him a wink of approval.

"I thought you said you were staying until Sunday," Johnson said to her.

"I couldn't take her anymore. She's high most of the time now, and I don't much care for her friends."

"Jackson, how about a Heineken? Where were you now?"

"Mon darling Ian . . . don't you remember? She's in Ville-Marie. Been there since summer. I couldn't wait to get back. Two weeks was enough. That place is such a downer. No night life, just a bunch of old farts and all that cold . . . no wonder she's lit up most of the day."

"So, Sarah, your mother really likes good pot, huh?" said Johnson.

"Her new boyfriend seems to keep her well supplied with good stuff, that's for sure. I think he's . . ."

"He's what?" Johnson asked.

"Nothing. He's just bad news, that's all I can say about him. It's funny though."

"What's funny?"

"He's got this accent. He kinda sounds Italian but his name is Brown. How can that be, she said?"

She picked up her drink, finished what was left in the glass, and set it back down on the bar. "Take me upstairs, will ya? I missed you."

Patrick stepped out onto the sidewalk and walked north one block, then crossed Fourth Street and entered a nightclub called Franco's. He sat at the bar and drank a beer, then returned to his car and drove home. Not feeling tired or hungry but feeling restless, he walked into the kitchen and stood in front of a window and looked out onto the backyard. It was 10:30 p.m. and it seemed to him every creature out there was asleep. He thought he probably should be doing the same thing. He turned around and made his way to his study and sat down at a desk. It was an old turn-of-the-century oak rolltop desk that had belonged to his father and sat in the office of the family lumber mill forever. He grabbed the edge of the last slats of wood, raised the top up, and slid it back, exposing a pile of newspapers and *Time* and *Newsweek* magazines, bills, and unopened correspondence. He rooted around in the clutter and found his .38 revolver. The wheel gun was a Rossi five-shot snub nose. He then opened a bottom drawer, took out a box of cartridges, opened the box, and counted the bullets, then took both the box and gun with him outside for a walk. The night was moon bright, and it was cold and raw, and like most March nights in the valley there was much dampness in the air. He walked down the gravel lane he had driven on a few moments ago and began to create what he thought to be a good plan to take care of the Brown issue. *Failure is not an option*, he kept saying to himself. In the morning he and Johnson would finalize the plan, if there was to even be one, and he told himself the ultimate decision lay with Johnson. But that thought didn't sit well with him. He kept walking and thinking about all of what he'd seen and experienced over the past week. He started to turn around and walk back, but then saw out of the corner of his eye headlights then red taillights heading toward the main house—his brother's house. He walked a little farther on the gravel driveway, then turned and started down an orchard row that led him to the back of the main house, where the faint red lights had finally gone dark. By the time he arrived, his brother's car was in the garage. He stood outside the rear of the big stone manor house for a moment, looking up and into the mudroom through a blurry plate-glass window, and observed Vincent's shadow silhouette appearing on a wall. He moved forward and climbed steps that led to the mudroom door, quietly knocked twice, and opened the door an inch or two.

"Saw your lights going up the lane," Patrick said quietly.

Vincent was setting his guitar case up against a wall and had his back to the door when he heard Patrick's voice. Startled at first, but when he turned toward the door and saw it was his brother, a concerned expression turned to a small smile.

"Patrick."

"Vincent."

"What brings you out this time of the night?" Vincent asked.

"Didn't feel much like sleeping."

"Come on. Get in here. There's nothing like a walk in the orchards on a moonlit night, is there?"

"I don't know about that. Always seems to me at night old Ichabod Crane could be riding down the rows and I am in his way and, bam, I am dead meat. So you're playing in a band?"

Just finished practicing. "Just started up again with Jason and the Emmitt boys. Tomorrow we're at the Legion Hall in Lock Haven."

"Jeeeeez . . . the Emmitts . . . they're still rocking?"

"Close that door and get in here," Vincent said as he started to walk toward the kitchen. He stopped to let Patrick go in front of him and they made their way through the kitchen and into the dining room. They sat down next to each other at the large oak table where they used to have all their evening meals together as a family.

"I am playing country now."

"Music is music, I guess," replied Patrick. I like that Johnny Cash song. What was that song, oh yeah, I remember now, *How many times have you heard someone say, if I had his money I could do things my way* . . . something something . . . *a satisfied mind.*"

"That's a good one, all right. I heard him sing that a cappella on a very old record."

Patrick looked up at where the chandelier was fastened to the ceiling and stared for a few moments at an indentation in the plaster, then turned to Vincent and said, "I am still surprised we didn't get a whipping for breaking off those low-hanging pieces."

"I can't recall. Did you shake that champagne bottle a little bit or did it blow like that on its own?" Vincent asked.

"You're joking, aren't you?" replied Patrick. "I remember pretty well how it went. They were finishing their cocktails in the library and I thought I would be like Jeeves and ready the bottle. What were we then . . . nine? I guess I wasn't very gentle with how I handled that bottle before I dropped it into the bucket."

"Boy, did the cork explode into that crystal like a forty-five. You took the agrafe off, didn't you, before putting it in the bucket? Who would have ever thought it would have hit a weak link like that and, well, that glass sure flew and ricocheted all over," replied Vincent.

"Good thing the soup course hadn't been served yet," Patrick said with a slight sardonic chuckle in his voice.

"We played the VFW hall last Saturday. Don was there. He said something about you two heading out west this summer on your motorcycles."

"Been wanting to see Montana for a long time. Maybe on the

way we'll pass through Council Bluffs and try to find the old homestead Grandmother always spoke about," replied Patrick.

"Had lunch with Angus last week."

"Oh yeah? How's that old codger doing?" replied Patrick.

"He turned me on to a job. Management."

"You going to take it?"

"Don't know for sure yet. But I am thinking of settling down."

Patrick sat quietly for a moment, then got up and walked over and stood next to the breakfront. "You keeping the family standards in full supply?"

"I'll get some glasses," replied Vincent.

Vincent left, returned a few moments later with two small snifters, and placed one on the table in front of where Patrick had been sitting, then sat down and placed the other glass on the table directly in front of him.

Patrick opened a little door at the base of the breakfront and knelt down and peered inside. On the bottom shelf, way in the back, he found a dusty old black bottle with the number 1952 hand painted on it in burnt orange. He slowly and carefully took the bottle out, walked gently to where Vincent was sitting, and placed the bottle on the table in front of him.

"Here, little brother, I'll let you do the honors.

"You always did like the port."

Vincent slowly lifted the bottle and decanted the wine ever so slowly into the glasses, being careful not to disturb the sediments. Both men lifted their glasses to inspect the port.

"Good pour, Vin. It's been a long time since we had this."

"That's for sure. The old man didn't bring this out very often. This may be the last of it. So, what do you want to drink to?"

Patrick put his glass down and sat still and once again became quiet. Vincent could tell he was giving the question a lot of thought.

"Vin. I am heading north tomorrow."

"To the reservation?"

"Yeah."

"You look like you have something on your mind. What do you want to tell me?"

"I just wanted to stop by before I left. That's all."

"You in some kind of trouble? You've never gotten over that accident, have you?"

"I am responsible for someone. Let's just leave it at that."

"It's the boy, isn't it?"

"He's grown up. Big as Paul Bunyan now, except he has a ponytail."

It was only then that Vincent saw the butt end of Patrick's pistol protruding out from his army fatigue coat's side pocket.

"Why don't we see our buddy Don tomorrow before you go?" Vincent asked Patrick.

"I have an early meeting downtown."

"You need anything? Is there something . . ."

"No, Vin. Just know that . . ." For a few seconds Patrick remained still and stared into his glass, then turned to his brother. "Knowing that our lives are not always under our command can sure be unsettling. But I wouldn't have it any other way. Never wanted to be a slave to my thoughts."

"You know, I think that everything outside of us is more familiar and better understood than anything inside of us that's always been there," replied Vincent.

"Damn right."

And with that, Patrick raised his glass and Vincent did the same.

"To everything outside of us," Patrick exclaimed.

She looked asleep. Johnson got out of the waterbed and stood for a moment looking at her, bobbing up and down with the waves he had just made, then turned and went into the bathroom. He stood in front of the toilet naked and half asleep, staring at the wall in front of him, then looked out a small window and thought the time to be close to 7:00 a.m. He relieved himself, then went over to the sink and rummaged through the medicine cabinet, looking for aspirin and found none. Seeing his bathrobe hanging on a hook on the back of the door, he put it on and made his way down the hall to the kitchen, where he made coffee. He sat down on a small padded chrome chair that was part of a Formica dinette set in the center of the room, which looked like it belonged in an Air Stream trailer from the fifties. He waited and watched for the coffeepot to begin to percolate and thought about Sarah, comfortably asleep in his bed. The phone rang.

"Hello."

"You ready, Ian?" asked Patrick.

"Yeah."

"All right. I'll be there in about a half hour. I want to be done with you and up at the reservation by midday."

"You're not going to believe this."

"What?"

"Seems Sarah's stepmom has been doing a guy up there in Ville-Marie who calls himself . . . get this . . ."

"Yeah. Okay what?"

"He's known up there as Mr. Brown."

"Well, I'll be damned."

It was a two-hour drive to St. Regis and the middle of the afternoon when he got there. Patrick drove once again to the Bear Den Motel and went into the office. Charley Lightning was sitting watching the Knicks game on a little black-and-white TV set. He got up and went around the desk.

"Would you like your old room?"

"That works for me."

"Weekly rate's the same. Twenty-eight dollars and one eighty for the governor. Almost forgot. Phone call came in for you about an hour ago. You are to call a Mr. Johnson."

"Very good, Charley. Thank you."

Patrick got the key, walked to his room, went in, shut the door, and placed his bag under the bed. He closed the curtains and stood for a moment to one side of the window, then pulled on the outer edge of one curtain just enough to look out the window at the main road that cut through the reservation. He watched the traffic come and go, then went outside to the pay phone and called Johnson.

"Hello."

"It's Patrick."

"You on a secure line?" asked Ian Johnson.

"Yeah. Of course."

"Okay, good. About a half hour after you left, Hector called. He seems to think some Mounties have been interested lately in his comings and goings. We better execute Plan B."

"I understand."

"You all right with it?"

"I am good. We've planned for something like this."

"Patrick."

"Yeah."

"Nothing."

"Don't worry, Ian."

"I am cool," replied Johnson.

"I'll call you when we have the goods secure."

Patrick pressed down on the phone cradle with his free hand and listened for the dial tone, put a quarter into the slot and called Lone Bear, then Dash, and told them to meet him at his motel at 8:00 a.m. and to be prompt. He got into his pickup and drove to the Double T. It was early and the restaurant was empty, save for him. He ordered the Sunday special, which was a T-bone steak, and he had a glass of red wine and he ate slowly and thought about Plan B.

Randall Svensen turned off Route 37 and drove down a partially ice encrusted road that eventually ended at a stand of woods. There was so much snow and ice that the trees sagged from the extra weight.

"All right, let's check it out," Svensen said to Tom Edward Price.

Both men got out of the white Ford Bronco with DEA plates and traipsed over land that eventually led them to a clearing overlooking a frozen Saint Lawrence River.

"It's going to be dark soon, Randall."

"I just want to take another look."

"Look at this, Tom," Svensen said as he pointed across the vast frozen stretch of whiteness to the woods on the other side. "We've got Canada over there and the reservation here and over there."

"It makes things difficult," Price replied.

"A sovereign nation and borders and ice bridges. Come on, let's go," Svensen said, and they turned around and started back toward the Bronco. ""I heard from Purcell this morning. He has two more agents on board and some local and state cops out of New York, ready for containment, and four Mounties stationed on the north shore."

"Now we go see Henry again. Right?" Agent Price asked as they approached the vehicle.

"Some of the tribal police around here hate these smugglers," Agent Svensen said as he opened the driver's-side door and got in.

"What about Henry?"

"He's next."

Svensen turned the Bronco around and they headed back the way they came. When they reached the pavement, it was dry and clear of ice and snow. Svensen accelerated and some trapped ice wedged in the tire treads caused them to slide and the Bronco ended up on the berm.

"So much for four-wheel drive," Svensen muttered. "These tires are too damn wide."

"When it comes to this icy crap, less is more," Price replied.

"Let's just sit here for a minute and think about how we want to deal with Crow Horse and the others."

After finishing his meal, Patrick sat for a while, and from his booth he could see, through a large plate-glass window, some kids across the street playing hockey. The young boys had brooms with the straw cut off at the bases and were chasing a Coke can, sliding on their shoes on rough and uneven ice. The waitress brought the check and he paid the woman who was sitting behind the register, then he went outside and walked across the street and stood for a while and watched the boys. It was getting dark and they soon quit, and Patrick watched them walk together in the direction of a group of trailers that were nestled together at the base of a hill not too far away. Patrick turned around, and standing right in front of him was Henry Crow Horse.

"Patrick."

"Good evening, Henry. You're quieter than a mouse," Patrick replied.

"Two Sundays in a row. You must like the food at the Double T. What did you order?"

"I had the steak special."

"Haven't had my supper yet."

"It was good."

"Did you play hockey growing up?"

"Yeah, as a kid. But I mostly played lacrosse when I got bigger."

"Will you walk with me?"

They walked around to the other side of the ice field, then down a snow-covered trail that meandered through a stand of thick hemlock and young oak trees. Side by side, both men walked silently. After about five minutes they reached a clearing and their destination, which was an old lean-to made of narrow hand-hewed logs. Darkness began to fall and the old Indian stepped into the hut and found a lantern that was hanging on a hook from one of logs over his head, and he took it down and lifted the glass and lit the wick. Slowly, a faint golden light began to emerge from the glass, and he put the lantern back on the hook and adjusted the flame so that the light was not too bright. They sat down on small wooden stools made of cobbled tree branches and seats made of half logs.

"Most of what I know about you comes from what my brothers say."

"And what do they tell you?" replied Patrick.

"What's that song—I ain't old, I just been around a long time? I am sixty-nine years young. Was once sheriff of this land. That was many, many moons ago. Silver Heels liked to say that on the radio to his ranger."

Patrick let out a small chuckle.

"You know, the only weapon I carried during that time was a big knife strapped to my front like my grandpa used to. The hilt was made of persimmon and had two wolves baying at a full moon carved into it. The federals made me give it up. They said it made me look too menacing with it hanging down in front like that."

"My father told me once that anything old is good . . ." Patrick said quietly.

"Wise man. Last Sunday, just down the road apiece, I was invited to sit in a DEA agent's F-150. The agent didn't say much but revealed much. He really didn't say anything but said a lot."

"Beg your pardon?"

"I hear tell the Sioux course through your veins."

"That's correct."

"Intuition. We have that going for us, don't we?"

"Is your intuition telling you something now that I need to hear, Henry?"

"It's taken me some time to put the final pieces together, Patrick."

Patrick got up slowly and walked a few steps out from under

the shelter and stood and looked out on a field with the remains of chopped-off frozen cornstalks and the forest beyond.

"I just can't pack up now and head back to Moreland."

He stood still for a moment, then turned around and looked
at the retired sheriff and reached into his coat's breast pocket
and pulled out a unopened pack of Marlboros. He walked back
into the lean-to and presented the old man with the tobacco.

"Lone Bear. My brothers, they were right. Please. Sit with
me."

Henry partially unzipped his coat and put the pack of cigarettes inside his shirt pocket, then reached into his coat and
took out a beaded pipe bag. He opened the bag and pulled out
a long wooden stem and a brownish wooden bowl and joined
the two together, then took a pinch of tobacco from the bag
and threw it to the Four Directions. He filled the bowl with
herbs and tobacco, then offered the pipe to Patrick. "Let's
smoke the sacred pipe symbol of truth so that there will be
no lies between us."

They sat and smoked and talked of many things, old and
new, and when finished Patrick had the information he needed
and the two of them walked back to the restaurant parking lot,
where Patrick got into his truck and drove back to the motel.
Henry Crow Horse went inside the Double T. He ordered
the steak special.

Patrick woke in a neon haze—an unnatural light created by
the motel sign just outside his room. He rolled his wrist over
and confirmed 00:24:40 on his barely readable, stainless GMT
wristwatch. He looked at the ceiling and peripherally at the
room around him. There was something familiar about the
light—or the feeling that the light created:—like a full moon
over a lake, or some other kind of light that contorts normal
everyday objects into distorted shadows not immediately
recognizable. There was something supernatural and alien in

the light to which he had grown accustomed. Sleep had not come easily. He had learned just hours ago that Chief Dan Tails, duly elected head elder of the St. Regis Mohawk Nation, was making secret deals with Brown through Lanszetti and some Hell's Angels from Quebec. He closed his eyes. A few moments later he sat straight up, his heart thumping hard against his rib cage. Quickly he found the lamp next to the bed and turned it on, then threw his legs over the side of the bed, hitting his duffel bag with his heel. He reached down and pulled the bag out from under the bed and opened it. He stared into the bag and saw his snub nose, then saw the 1911 in its shinny brown leather holster. *Bikers*, he thought. "I hate Harleys," he said out loud, then reached down and pulled the 1911 out of its holster and shoved it under a pillow. He turned the light off and fell sound asleep.

The next morning Lone Bear and Dash appeared at his motel door and the three of them got into his pickup and drove north.

"What I am about to say. Jeez I'll just say it: Chief Dan Tails is behind Brown's action."

Lone Bear and Dash became quiet, then Lone Bear quipped, "He started that big mansion of his up on the north shore at Rose Valley and couldn't finish it. Ran out of money, I heard. Guess now he can."

"Well, his action is running smack-dab into ours and that's not all," replied Patrick. "Brown has those knuckleheads from Quebec with him."

"You mean the Angels that came down here last August and made off with that shipment of Canadian Club and Marlboros?"

"Yes, that would be them," replied Patrick.

Dash sat quietly in the middle of the bench seat with a look of concern that he could not conceal.

"Come on, little man . . . lighten up. We've made the run

how many times? Eight, nine times? Tell him, Patrick."

"It's not Dan Tails or bikers. It's the DEA that I am concerned about. We've stayed clear of them. We fly under the
radar and this place has made it happen for us. You know, for
all the right reasons. You *know* what I am saying. But with
all these others wanting a piece and now Hector calling Ian
getting nervous on account of some Mounties snooping around
his neighborhood, my little voice . . ."

"What's it saying to you?"

"Dash, don't interrupt."

"It's saying that maybe the juice just ain't worth the squeeze
tonight. What's Hector's ETA?"

"He'll be at the safe house before nine," answered Dash.

"We've gone over this before, so there is nothing more
to say. When the time comes I know you'll be cool and stay
with the plan."

Patrick drove across the reservation, keeping to the speed
limit with his crew by his side, and he eagerly listened to
them as they bantered back and forth, with Lone Bear doing
his best to keep Dash's imagination from getting the best of
him. As he listened to them talk about how fast Lone Bear
was at racing dirt bikes in competitions all across the state, he
joined in and kept up with the conversation but he couldn't
shake his uneasiness.

"You boys hungry?" asked Patrick.

"I could eat," Dash fired back quickly.

"You're always hungry. You sure you don't have a tapeworm
or something?" asked Lone Bear.

Up ahead Patrick could see a drive-in. "This will do," he said,
and he turned into Stella's motor court drive-in restaurant,
home of the Stella burger. They ordered hamburgers and fries
and mugs of root beer. A pretty girl wearing a buckskin coat
with long, braided black hair brought the food out on a tray
and Patrick lowered the window so she could set the tray on

the glass edge.

"You guys are lucky."

"How's that?" Patrick asked.

"We opened for the season . . . just today. I have a parka inside 'cause I know it's gonna get cold again. That'll be eleven eighty-five, please. Hiiiiiii, Lone Bear," she said as she stretched her neck to get a good look at who was inside.

"That will be fine. Here." Patrick handed her a twenty. "Keep the change."

"Thanks, mister. Come back real soon. Bye, Lone Bearrrrrrr."

Dash stared at Lone Bear while handing him his food. "Who was that?"

"Let's eat," Patrick said with authority.

They finished their food and he started the truck. He drove it out of the northeast corner of the St. Regis Mohawk Indian Reservation and on to Route 37 through St. Lawrence County. They were now in Upstate New York. The road became more and more cracked and bumpy the closer they got to the river. He turned onto an unmarked road that ended at the tip of the northwestern part of the reservation, with Canada just in sight.

"Feels good to be on our own sovereign nation," exclaimed Lone Bear.

Patrick put the truck in four-wheel drive and Lone Bear got out and locked both of the front wheel hubs, then got back into the cab, and he drove in second gear down a snow-encrusted road that was barely passable. He drove slowly for about a mile. He stopped the truck and they got out and walked a trail until they reached a small hunting cabin that belonged to Lone Bear's father. It was midday and the sun shone down on them through the treetops in random columns as they walked single file through melting snow. They approached slowly and saw no evidence of intruders, and Patrick entered through the only door, the front door. Lone Bear and Dash walked around back to a detached outbuilding where their two snowmobiles had been stored. They immediately went to work getting the machines ready.

Joey Skywalker finished his lunch, got up from the kitchen table, and walked over to the sink with his plate. He washed it and a stack of breakfast dishes, and when finished he dried his hands and stood motionless at the sink, looking out a window directly in front of him.

He saw, covered with snow, the top of the swing set and monkey bars he'd gotten his kids a few summers ago, and beyond his backyard he could see acres of snow-covered fields, and he remembered when he was a very young boy, how those fields were farmed and they had sweet corn in August. He looked out about a hundred yards to his left and saw his neighbor's backyard. The top of an old motorized washtub was sticking out above the snow. There was snow and more snow in every direction. There was so much snow he could only see the upper half of a 1960 Rambler station wagon and remembered watching his father and their neighbor put it up on cinder blocks after the transmission seized. The sun shone brightly, and the brightness helped him to steel himself for what he had to do later in the night. He turned away from the sink and started to walk toward the back door to meet Dan Proud Hawk at Hooker's garage but stopped when Mary came into the room with a laundry basket.

"I didn't know you were still here."

"Proud Hawk got me some work, driving tonight. Maybe even tomorrow. Don't know for sure yet. I have to get over there."

"You never had to drive at night."

"Well, I don't have much of a choice now, do I? He's the man. Not sure when I'll be back."

"Joey."

"Yeah."

"Please be careful."

"I will."

"I know."

"I got to go."

"Don't go just yet. Wait a few minutes. Please. I know things aren't going our way right now. You'll see, Joey. This reservation. All of us working together. We'll figure something out."

"You sound pretty sure about that. Wish I had your strength."

"You've got enough for the both of us."

He bent over and hugged her and kissed her on the cheek. She put her hands on his massive neck and shoulders, then reached around his upper back and gently caressed his ponytail with one hand.

Joey pulled into the back of Hooker's parking lot and shut the motor off and sat for a while, thinking about Mary. He got out and locked his truck, then walked slowly up to the back door and stood still with his hand on the doorknob, turned his head, and looked back at the truck, then turned and faced straight ahead, staring at a sign on the door that read Roll the Bones. Beneath that was a skull and crossbones. He opened the door to find two members of the Hell's Angels standing next to a couple of pickup trucks.

"You Axel?" Joey asked.

"Yeah. You're driving. Get in. Harry, you keep up with us, you hear?" Axel shouted to the driver of the other truck. They drove off Hooker's parking lot and headed north.

Randall Svensen pointed his Bronco due north. From his vantage point on a high bluff he could see pretty well through the evening night most of the snow-covered terrain. "PX-10, this is PX-11, you copy? Over."

"This is PX-10, read you five by five, over."

"I am in position, over."

"Roger that, PX-10. PX-11 out."

It was becoming dark. Tom Edward Price sat in his Dodge Power Wagon about five miles west of Svensen's lookout. The land was completely covered with snow and ice, and from his location with the gibbous moon overhead, he could just about make out an ice bridge and a few islands off to the east.

"Mountie 3, this is PX-11, you copy? Over."

"This is Mountie 3. I copy. All quiet here, over."

"Roger that, Mountie 3. PX-11 out."

A trooper rolled up in his Wagoneer with a trailer and a snowmobile in tow and got out and walked over to the Power Wagon's driver's-side window. Agent Price lowered the window.

"Fifteen miles of this and look at those damn islands. Those Canucks get wind of anything?"

"All's pretty peaceful. Price said quietly.

"I am going to push off my ride."

"You got enough gas for that Ski-Doo?" quipped Price.

"Yeah, but if they get me in that maze . . . Look at that clump of islands over there. You know what I mean? We sure could use a few more machines."

"A fifteen-mile border and tonight we're looking at just a third of that land," said Trooper James Mattoon Scot.

He's right, Price mused. *A true cat-and-mouse game for sure.*

"You hear that?" shouted Scot.

"Get that thing started. Sounds like two of them. Mountie 3, this is PX-11, you copy? Over."

"PX-11 Mountie -3 here, I copy."

"We're hearing some snowmobile sounds about two clicks from my northwest position. See or hear anything? Over."

"Negative, PX-11. Over."

"Damn . . ." Price said out loud as he threw the communication device down on the floor of the four-by-four. He slammed the Power Wagon into gear and sped off to the northwest while the trooper raced northward toward where he thought the snowmobile sounds to be the loudest.

Dash stayed on Lone Bear's tracks, never farther than twenty yards from the toboggan directly in front of him. He looked down at his speedometer—fifty-eight, sixty, sixty-five miles per hour. They were flying fast over smooth ice that had very few undulations. Lone Bear careened through one turn after another, and the toboggan loaded with 250 pounds of Canadian weed slid perfectly in tandem with every move his Arctic Cat would make. Dash turned his head and saw his sled doing the same. Their homemade sleds were working perfectly as designed. Across one ice bridge, past two small islands, their engines screaming without their governors. Dash smiled and the cold he was feeling suddenly went away.

About a half mile out to the west Price saw two light trucks traveling south at a fast speed. He reached for the two-way.

"Shit. Where did that thing go?"

He bent over, contorting himself, searching for the phone handle.

"Gotcha."

"PX-10, this is PX-11, you copy?"

"Roger that PX-11, what's going down?"

"In immediate pursuit of two vehicles going southwest of my last position heading for Rural Road 36 . . . Trooper running down two Cats with his machine. Can you assist? Over."

"Negative, PX-11. You're the very end of it . . . could be a diversion. Over."

"Roger that, PX-10. Looks like two sets of trouble coming my way. Over."

"You see that over there?" Axel grunted.

"Where?" Joey replied.

"Look to your left."

Skywalker turned his head and saw Price's headlights coming straight for them. He could make out it was a Power Wagon and it was closing fast.

"Get this thing movin' Tonto," said the burly biker.

The cab suddenly began to shake violently as Joey accelerated and raced for the drop-off site. The road was hard pan
with patches of ice and snow, crushed rocks, and pea stone.
He struggled to maneuver around blunt rocks jutting up from
the surface and potholes that looked big enough to swallow
a Volkswagen Beetle.

Axel bent over and pulled a TEC-9 out from under the
passenger's seat. He looked to his right, and in the side mirror
he could see the other truck trying to keep up.

"Harry can't drive that thing for shit."

Axel looked to his left and saw the Power Wagon's lights
getting closer.

"I smell bacon. Lose this fucker."

"Hang on," shouted Skywalker.

Patrick had parked his truck on top of a snow-encrusted
embankment that ran parallel to the edge of the Saint Lawrence River and the northernmost boundary of the reservation,
where RR 36 could be easily accessed. From his present position he could barely make out the ice bridge his crew would be
crossing. Dark clouds had suddenly moved in across the night
sky, consuming what little moonlight had been in existence
only moments earlier. His breathing quickened slightly as
he got out of the truck and began to walk toward the trailer
where Lone Bear and Dash were expected to arrive at any
moment. As he reached for the door of the trailer, he heard
their engines off in the distance, and a few moments later
he saw both snowmobiles heading straight for him. Patrick
smiled and gave out a quiet sigh, then turned and walked a
few paces away from the trailer and stood and watched his
crew pull into the yard.

"Both of you. You're a sight for sore eyes. Come on. Let's
get these unloaded ASAP."

"You did good, Dash, said Lone Bear as he dismounted
his machine."

Patrick quickly walked over to Dash's toboggan and they all began to grab the canvas bags, carrying them quickly over to Patrick's truck. From out of nowhere the two pickup trucks being driven by Harry and Joey appeared at the entrance to the property, traveling at a fast speed. The lead truck, with Harry at the wheel, slid off the thick ice-encrusted driveway and came to a stop a few feet from the trailer. Joey, in the second truck, careened around the corner, stomped on his brake pedal, slid sideways, and crashed into Harry's truck just a few yards away from both snowmobiles.

"What the hell!" Lone Bear shouted as he jumped out of the way of the second oncoming truck.

Coming from the north, the trooper raced over the ice bridge on his Ski-Doo and stopped just on the other side of the embankment.

Price turned the wheel sharply and the Power Wagon skidded and ended up in a snowbank, facing the second truck. Price got out with his pump twelve gauge.

"DEA! DEA!"

"Drop it!"

"Get out, get out!"

"Drop the gun!"

"Don't do it!

"Drop the gun, drop it!"

"Don't do it."

"Scotty!"

"Police! Everybody down!"

"You motherfucker!" Harry yelled as he fired.

"Look out!"

Patrick turned to Dash. "Get down."

"Don't fucking move!" The trooper yelled.

Axel jumped out, fired, and hit Price in the right shoulder.

Joey bailed out onto the snow and began to crawl toward the trailer. The trooper drew down and fired on one of the two bikers with his .357 magnum. Patrick jumped down next to Dash. "Crawl. Stay low. Move to that side of the trailer . . . go."

He reached behind his back and from under his army field coat pulled out his .45 and fired at both Hell's Angels, allowing Dash to retreat, then rushed toward the DEA agent who was lying next to his vehicle. Price turned and struggled to pump a shell into the chamber of his shotgun and swung around to point the weapon in Patrick's direction.

"Don't shoot," Patrick yelled as he extended the .45 outward, pointing it straight up in the air.

Agent Price recognized him from his picture from their briefing. "Wallace . . ." Price said out loud.

"These guys are going kill us if we don't make a stand . . . *now!*" Patrick responded in a commanding voice.

Price put his free hand on his upper arm and when he removed it, he saw plenty of blood.

Damn it.

"Can you fire that thing?" asked Wallace.

Price tried to raise and shoulder the heavy Remington pump. The bullet had entered his upper arm high up on the outside and the exit wound was in a rotation at the rear such that turning his shoulder, he could see both wounds clearly. He dropped the weapon.

"No."

The shooting stopped. Axel and Harry reloaded and moved toward the trailer. The trooper tumbled down the embankment, ending up face to face with Wallace.

"Those were your boys on the Cats."

"Yeah . . . and they're unarmed," replied Patrick.

"I am useless here," said Price.

"Bullshit," replied Scot. "You'll be surprised at what you can do."

Price sat up and looked at him. "I'll call for backup." He grabbed for the door handle and opened the truck's passenger-side door. A few rounds went through the Power Wagon's driver's-side and passenger's-side windows. Glass rained down on him.

Harry yelled out, "Hey shitheads, I've got your boy here."

Patrick crouched down behind the hood of the truck and looked toward the front of the trailer. Through the darkness he could see Dash being pushed around by the biker.

Joey stood up and ran and took cover alongside a metal shed, and he could see Dash at the front door being held by Harry, who had his weapon pointed at his head. A small snowball suddenly landed in front of his feet.

"Joey. Over here." It was Lone Bear.

Skywalker looked to his right and behind a stack of cut firewood he recognized Lone Bear, who was down on one knee gesturing to him to join him. He quickly crawled over snow and ice toward Lone Bear's position. He leaped forward and slid behind a tall stack of logs that were piled up alongside Lone Bear.

"I've been watching," said Lone Bear. "You know, for a big guy you can really move. Some jackpot we got ourselves into . . . yeah?" Lone Bear looked to his left and pointed in the direction of the snow-covered embankment. "Patrick's over there behind the Power Wagon with the law."

"He ain't going to be happy to see me here. What are we going to do?" asked Joey.

"They got my buddy Dash . . . see . . . look at the porch over there . . . at the front door."

"That's Harry," replied Joey. "He's crazy. He'll kill him for sure if . . ."

"We're goin' to free him. You with me?"

"Yeah," replied Joey.

Lone Bear looked around. "I don't see the other one."

"That guy's name's Axel. Tough monkey, he is."

"You have a gun?" asked Lone Bear.

"No."

"Don't suppose these guys would listen to you and just head on out if you could talk to them."

"All I am to them is a driver that knows our land pretty good . . . an expendable Mohawk."

"Just thought I'd ask. This Indian hates unnecessary killing," replied Lone Bear.

The trooper moved over next to Patrick, while Price sat in the snow, holding his bleeding arm with his left hand. Price turned his head and looked toward them while he propped himself up against the rear wheel. Both men looked at Price, then at each other, then at the biker with his machine pistol pointed at the kid's head.

"Don't move," shouted Axel.

Price saw him first, standing there on top of the embankment. Scot and Wallace froze.

"That's good. I got a thirty-round clip in this thing . . . it'll fuck you all up quick. Drop your weapons and show me empty hands."

"I know this trailer. It's my uncle's," Lone Bear said quietly.

"What's the plan?" whispered Joey.

"We can get in through the back. There's a window that can be loosened up and in we go. Come on."

"You two. Turn around. Slowly now."

Scot and Wallace did as Axel said.

"You and that twelve gauge just stay still."

Axel moved down off the embankment and stood next to Price and kicked the shotgun out of his reach.

"Get up. Now let's all start walking toward that trailer. Nice and slow. Move. Harry, we're coming in," Axel shouted.

Harry whispered into Dash's ear, "It's your lucky day, boy, you get to live."

Axel pushed the muzzle of the short-barrel TEC-9 hard into Price's back and led the three of them up onto the porch.

"Where's Tonto?" Axel asked as he walked up to Harry.

"Well, what do we have here? That's some sorry-ass-looking deputies you got there, boss."

"Did you see him or not?"

"That Indian. Sheeeeeit. He's probably halfway to Quebec by now. He run off when the fun got started."

"Let's get um inside. Try opening that door."

Harry did as Axel ordered and grabbed the knob. To his surprise the door was unlocked. He started to push Dash across the threshold.

"Wait a minute," Axel said.

"It's okay, boss. This place is empty. Fuck, it's cold in here," replied Harry.

"All right, let's go. Follow your boy in there and keep your hands where I can see um."

The dark clouds that had suddenly crossed the sky obscuring the moon only moments ago moved on toward the east, leaving a faint grayish light that crept into the trailer's living room through a big bay window. Axel was the first to be hit from behind and his feet flew out from under him as he was brought down hard. Muzzle flashes lit up the trailer. Patrick was spun around and when he righted himself he saw Joey twist Axel's neck, killing him instantly. A spray of bullets hit the trooper and he fell on top of Price, who was already on the floor. Patrick leaped toward Harry but Lone Bear already had hold of him, and before he could stop him, Lone Bear broke his neck. Dash was unhurt, standing motionless up against a wall. Patrick stood up, walked over, put his arm around him, and led him over to the kitchen galley. Dash was trembling.

It's going to be okay. You're not hurt. You're all right. Maybe you can try to find some candles or something, so we can have a little more light in here, he said to him, then he turned and walked back into the living room.

He stood still, looking at Joey and Lone Bear, who were

standing off to the side of the room. A rich tang of gunpowder hung in the air. He looked down at the dead bikers, then looked up at Skywalker and Lone Bear, made his way over to where the two of them were standing close together, and looked them both in the eye.

I want you to take Dash and get on those machines and go home. I'll hook up with you later on when I think the time is right, he told them, and he turned around and went over to see what condition Price and the trooper were in.

IV

New York and Central Pennsylvania -
Monday, September 15, 1984, a year and a half later

*T*wo of us were led out of the Massena County lockup on to a
half-sized school bus that was painted battleship gray. On
the side of the bus, boldly printed in black, were the words *Federal
Bureau of Prisons.* We left the Empire State, and five hours later
we got off the bus in the old stone back courtyard of the penitentiary. Inside the walls the prison looked like an ancient medieval
castle or fortress . . . maybe a monastery for Trappists or some
obscure sixteenth-century order of Ascetics. Stone corbels accented
the outside and the interior was French Gothic architecture. The
arched doors were made of oak that appeared to be three—maybe
four—inches thick. They were hung on huge oversized steel gray
ornamental hinges that shut quite solidly. Opened in 1932, this
maximum-security prison known as the Big House had held men
such as *Alphonse Capone* and *John Gotti,* together with political
prisoners like *Jimmy Hoffa* and *Alger Hiss.*

We were lined up and the guards did their sardonic best to read
off our names. The first group of prisoners was ordered to the in-

firmary, while the rest of us went to the hole. From what I could make out by the dim hallway light that came thru a small barred window in the door, roaches and maggots scurried and slithered around and competed for available space in the sinks and toilets. The hole was a dungeon like two-man cell. The floor was sticky, and the five-by-nine-foot cell had a foul petroleum smell that almost made me gag. As I tried to walk around the small space, the soles of my shoes stuck to the floor. The intensity of the stench was inescapable. I had the top bunk, which had a very thin plastic sleep pad on it, and some of the bedsprings had worked their way through to the surface and could pinch my skin if I slept flat on my back. All the heat, humidity, and stagnant, foul-smelling air seemed to be hovering over my head, and for a while I had some difficulty breathing.

When I finally fell asleep, I was awakened by screaming. I quickly jumped down from my bunk and looked at my cellmate and asked, "You all right? What's the matter?" "Get um off me!" he said. "I don't see anything," I replied. "Rats," he shouted. "They were all over me!" I looked around the cell. There was not enough light to see much of anything. I couldn't see where there were any holes big enough for rats to crawl through. I thought maybe mice or a couple of large roaches had crawled across his bare chest or past his face and ears. He was really shaken and it took a while to calm him down. I remembered, as I lay back in my bunk, staring upward at concrete, that this was going to be my life from now on, and I fell asleep and did not dream.

The next day two guards appeared at Wallace's cell and they took him out of the hole. He was given some clothes and bedding, and they walked him up the steel steps of South Block Level 2 and onto a catwalk passing mostly empty cells. As they neared the end of the row of cells, Patrick noticed a pair of hands protruding out from the bars. He was placed into his one-man cell and a guard told him that it was exercise period and most men were outside. He was left alone to set his cell in order, and he made his bed and stepped out onto the catwalk and stood at the railing looking down into the cavernous dark holding areas below, then turned to his left and walked to the end of the row to the last cell and saw it to be inhabited but temporarily unoccupied. He looked in and saw a small writing table and a poster of Jimi Hendrix hanging on a wall and a poster of Richie Havens on another wall. He also noticed wooden planks sticking out from one end of the bed frame, giving the bed an additional one foot of length.

"That's Zeb's home."

Patrick turned to his left and the pair of hands he'd seen a few minutes ago, sticking out from the bars, had vanished. Now he could see that those hands were attached to Francis Bunnyard, who was standing a few inches away.

"Zeb?"

"It's short for Mr. Zebadiah."

"And who might you be?"

"I am Bunnyard. Francis P. But you can call me Bunny."

"I am Wallace. First name's Patrick."

"Well, how'd ya do."

All of a sudden, coming from the lower bowels of the jail were sounds of banging metal, and men's loud voices flooded upward and seemed to clash hard with the bars and the old concrete walls of the cells, bouncing around and becoming louder and louder. As the prisoners walked up the steel steps of South Block Level 2 and onto the catwalk Bunny's cellmate, Big Harold, said loudly,

"Motherfukin' Carlos has a lot of fuckin' nerve. Fuck him and the horse he rode in on,".

"Here they come," said Bunny as he turned and saw the tall, lanky, afro-headed Zeb coming down the catwalk back toward his cell followed by "Big Harold" Dubois.

"Whoa. You're bigger than Big Harold," Bunny said as he

stared at Patrick, who was standing in the entrance to the cell.

Bunny was so white his skin glistened. Patrick had never seen skin so white before in his life. He was short. He stood five feet, four inches tall with his boots on. His greased-up black hair was combed straight back and when it hit the back of his neck it flipped up about an inch or more. On the inside of his left forearm he had a tattoo of Bugs Bunny, who was standing up cross-legged holding a half-eaten carrot. Patrick backed away from the cell and Zebadiah Campbell lowered his head considerably and walked in and sat down on his bunk. A moment later he got up and went over to his tiny desk and looked down at a guttered candle stub then looked upward at the poster of Hendrix.

"You know what today is, Bunny?"

"Today? Sure I do, . . . It's cabbage day."

"That may be on tonight's menu, but that's not exactly what I am referring to. It's the anniversary of his death. My main man died in London on this day, this very day fourteen years ago."

"Oh . . . that day," Bunny replied.

Zeb lifted the candle stub up and began to pick at it with his fingers, then placed it back down close to a piece of cardboard that had a small sheet of white, lined paper glued to it. The cardboard was leaning up against some books. Patrick could see that it had some writing on it. He stood quietly by and waited.

Zeb turned around and looked at Wallace, then spoke up. "So you're the new man come to join our iron commune?"

"Wallace. Patrick Wallace. Good to meet you."

"Zebadiah Campbell. I take it you met Bunny."

"Yeah."

Zeb looked away from Patrick and looked at his posters and pointed at Hendrix and said,

"Nineteen sixty-nine. I was there at the farm with all of

them. Summer of love. Can you dig it, Patrick Wallace?"

"Too bad it lasted only a summer," Patrick replied.

Zeb smiled, then picked up the cardboard square and handed it to Patrick.

"Some of us are still cool."

Patrick read the few handwritten words: "When the power of love overcomes the love of power the world will know peace."

"I can dig that," Patrick quietly replied.

Zeb looked Patrick over. "Bunny's goin' to have to get you some decent clothes. Don't want you lookin' like some new fish. Hear that, Bunny?"

"Uh-huh, I understand. I'll be getting to it directly."

The three of them walked out of Zeb's cell and stood on the catwalk next to the railing. They looked out across empty space to the rows of cells above and below and directly opposite them. A phalanx of men—muscles, pungent sweat smell, tattoos, noise—all of them jockeying for position, with the oppressive summer heat making them more on edge than usual.

"Over there ..." Zeb pointed his finger down toward the west block. "Them are Colombians under the stairwell over there. Mexicans without any compadres ... see um ... they be over in that corner." Then he pointed to the north and east blocks. "And right across from us, those be the Aryans and bikers."

The captain of the guards yelled out, "Count! Count! Recount! Recount!"

"Idiots!" Angry shouts from all over, bouncing off concrete and iron. "Learn to count, asshole!" "Morons."

"Recount. Recount. Let's go, people."

"Tonight's cabbage, lettuce, bread, and potato night," Bunny said with excitement.

"Waltz ... Billy! Waltz ... Billy? Waltz? Waltz?"

Silence.

"Man missing! No Movement! Recount!"

Zeb whispered into Patrick's ear: "The Cubans. See um over there? They be the loudest. It all started back with them Mariel boat people. A dozen whites equal a half dozen Mexicans, which equals a couple of brothers that equals just one Cuban. Noisy bunch, they are. Call themselves refugees."

"Pay attention and shut up, Too Tall. You three get moving," shouted Captain Bruno Sheetz. They're shipping Waltz out for a while. Check your clipboard, Plough."

They marched to the end of catwalk with Plough, black baton in hand, directing them forward to the top of the stairs. As they began to descend to the ground floor, a voice shouted out at the new inmate from across the abyss that separated the upper and lower rows of cells.

"Don't be hanging with them niggers."

"Say what?" Big Harold shouted back.

It was an Aryan or maybe a biker. Although a hundred feet of space separated the two groups of inmates, the warning rang out and met its intended target. Wallace paid no attention and continued to follow the men in front of him. They were heading toward the large hall that was detached from the main cellblocks, and as he walked through the double-wide arched entryway, the smell of boiled cabbage suddenly hit him and he jerked his head slightly backward.

Vincent Wallace pulled out of the entrance to Grey Stone, turned on to Freedom Lane, drove to Don Kaminski's mountain house, and parked his car at the bottom of the hill. He turned the engine off and sat and waited. A few minutes passed. Kaminski appeared out of the forest and walked over and unhooked the logging chain that was barricading the entrance, then got into the car, and together they drove up the leaf-covered fire road.

As they approached the house at the top of the hill, Kaminski said, "Let's go in the shop."

Vincent turned the car sharply onto a narrow path that led to the garage. He parked the car by the front door and both men got out. Kaminski unlocked a steel door and Vincent followed him to his office, which was at the back of the shop, all the while watching his step as he negotiated his way through a narrow opening past old motorcycles, tool and die machines, lathes, and various types of welding equipment. Vincent saw his brother's old bike and paused for a moment and stood staring at it. Kaminski stopped and turned and watched Vincent.

"Come over here. I want to show you something," said Kaminski.

Over in the corner of the room there appeared to be bikes with white sheets draped over them. Kaminski went up to them and pulled off the sheets, exposing two new BMW K-series bikes.

"I've had um for a while. What do you think?"

Vincent stood quietly for a moment, then walked around the bikes, carefully observing the details.

"That engine design. Looks pretty radical."

"Yeah. You're right, it is. Some call it the flying brick," said Kaminski.

"I can see why it might be called that. Four cylinders in a row in a perfect rectangular box," Vincent replied.

Kaminski stood next to the bike painted metallic red and put his hand on the throttle, then looked over at the other bike. "That one's Patrick's."

Vincent's eyes slowly closed, then he lowered his head, looking down at the floor. He looked up at Kaminski, then reached into his back pants pocket and pulled out an opened envelope that was folded in half.

"Look at this, Don," Vincent said as he handed the envelope

to Kaminski, who took the envelope, pausing to first look at the return address on the back, then pulling out the letter. He began to read.

> brother of Patrick,
> Please excuse my poor writing. I had a stroke and have lost some dexterity. Many of us wish to help Patrick. If there is a need, we shall be there.
>
> —Henry Crow Horse

Kaminski placed the letter back in the envelope and handed it to Vincent. "Will never really know how things went down that day, will we?" said Kaminski.

"Those Mohawks know. You can bet on that."

"Come on. Let's go where it's a little more comfortable to talk."

They walked into the office and sat down on what was once a rear seat from a 1957 Chevy.

"You know they transported him out of the state yesterday," said Vincent.

"No. I didn't know that. I am ashamed to admit it, Vin, but I've lost track of many things lately. You ever spoken with this Crow Horse fella before? Patrick ever mention him?"

"Never heard of him. He pretty much kept me in the dark when it came to his Indian friends. Just before it went bad for him I was getting a little suspicious about his comings and goings, but we . . . we never talked about what he did up there."

"Says he had a stroke. Must be kind of old, don't you think?" asked Kaminski.

"I don't know. Old, young—what's the difference? They pretty much have their own isolated, protected nation up there, don't they? We found that out at the trial, didn't we? What's the use in what an old stroked-out Indian has to say anyway? Our government put Patrick away and now ... now what do we have? I am driving to Pennsylvania to see him next week."

"I'd like to go with you."

"They only allow one visitor a month."

"All right. Then I'll go along for the ride."

"That would be good. I would appreciate the company."

"You going to write the Indian back?"

"I don't know. Maybe."

Now sitting on the edge of the two-toned leather-and-vinyl seat, Vincent cupped his head in his hands, leaned forward, and looked down at the floor.

"For now I just have to get it together for next week and ..."

"Come on, man. I know it's dark ... real dark for you now. I miss him too."

"I know you do. Seeing that old bike of his and then the new one really ..."

"Did you have supper?" asked Kaminski.

"No."

"All right. Come on. I'll make up something for us to eat."

Patrick sat at the end of the bench alongside Bunny and across from Zeb and together with two other inmates, Skeeter and Calvin. They ate soup and shared loaves of bread. The chow hall, as it was called, was set up with ten-man metal tables with benches bolted to the floors. The noise the men made now didn't sound the same as what was heard in the cellblocks only moments ago. Supper was for eating and some low talking, and for some who had the ability, a temporary state of mind that would stretch the time away from the block and the night's solitude that was awaiting them. Some civility was indeed mandated by rules and regulations, but there was a certain self-imposed propriety and fellowship that didn't go unnoticed by Patrick. At first no one acknowledged him. He sat quietly and ate. Zeb and Calvin carried on a conversation about the impact a recent increase in the price of cigarettes would have on Zeb's dealings and then questioned one another as to whether men preferred hard or soft packs and if anyone ever gave any serious attention to the surgeon general's warning label.

"Billy's in the hospital having a lung removed right now," quipped Skeeter.

"You saying it were his Pall Malls that gave him the cancer?" said Zeb.

"Who said it was cancer?" replied Big Harold.

"Billy Waltz got whacked with Dioxin while he was fightin' in Nam," Zeb replied.

"What's *deoxane*?" asked Bunny.

"It's Dioxin. Agent Orange, Billy called it. They used tons of the shit to kill all the trees in the jungles."

Zeb was the first to speak directly to the man who was the latest addition to the South Block Level 2 eating table. "Were you over there?"

"No. I didn't have to go. A buddy of mine went over there in sixty-five. He made it back a couple of years later."

"Too many brothers got sent over there. My people are from Tupelo, Mississippi. Way back when Elvis lived there and was just a pup ... the brothers knew no better. I left for Philly in sixty. They never got me."

Big Harold listened to the table talkers, then looked over to see Wallace just as he was finishing up his soup and noticed he was looking around as if he wanted to know if he could get more food.

"Here," Big Harold said to Wallace. He handed him some bread that was nearest to his side of the table. "I know what it's like. You'll get use to the feelin'. Ain't never enough for me neither."

A loud buzzer rang out throughout the hall and Patrick jerked his head quickly to the left, then right, to see what was happening. Plough appeared along with other guards and they stood at the head of each of the tables. The buzzing noise stopped, and from that point on not much was said. They got up from their benches and deposited their empty trays and were herded back into their cells. Patrick sat on the edge of his bed and looked at the walls and listened to his stomach making sounds. He was still hungry. Hours later, at ten o'clock, another high-pitched buzzer went off and the bars slammed shut. The cellblocks grew quieter and Patrick felt a strange kind of stillness that seemed to flow from the catwalk into and through his cell and through him. The quiet and stillness reminded him of fall, when he would get up at dawn to pick apples, and while he stood at one end of a pond, a foggy mist, traveling ever so slowly across the pond's surface, would pass over and around him and he would feel the dampness attacking his bones. He had that same feeling now. He lay down on his bed facing the bars. One hour. Two hours went by. Lights went out. He lay there and could look out at the cells that were across the chasm that separated second floor north from South Block. There was just enough ambient light coming down from the atrium for him to see if men were standing or if they were lying in their beds. Suddenly a dark silhouette appeared and stood in front of the bars and Patrick closed and rubbed his eyes to make sure he wasn't dreaming. When he opened them, the figure was gone. He tossed and turned throughout the night, and just before dawn he dreamed of his apple orchids and some of Moreland's black men who would join him in the harvest. He saw himself with the fall sun slowly setting on his back while he crouched down to open up a cask of last year's Jack. It was the end of a good and productive day. The men stood around the Quonset hut and were tired and they ached from all the reaching and bending. When they saw him take a mallet and pound a wooden spigot into the barrel, they immediately went and retrieved their mason jars from their pickups and jalopies and commenced lining up single file behind Patrick. The head of the line suddenly recoiled a few feet to allow old Bill Mack the honor of the first draw. His son Willie smiled as he looked on from the back of the line.

The lead corrections officer, Lieutenant Miller, took hold of the big circuit-disconnector leaver and pushed it upward, and as he slammed it into the upright position, all four of the big electrical boxes were engaged and the loud banging sounds that were created by the power surge could be heard throughout all the cellblocks. Instantly lights came on and Patrick opened his eyes, got up, and stood in front of his cell door, grasping the bars. He could see a new set of guards milling around at the end of the cellblock. Suddenly the high-pitched buzzer sounded and the cell door uncoupled, steadily moving from right to left, making him quickly pull his hands off the bars.

Bunny was the first to appear, then Big Harold and finally Zeb.

Bunny stepped out, turned to his left, and saw Patrick, and with a big smile on his face announced, "It's Wednesday . . . pancake day," then turned around and walked straight back into his cell.

Zeb walked farther out and put his hands on the catwalk railing and stood and looked at the Aryans at the end of North Block, then saw a biker move toward the Aryan leader. Patrick stepped up to the railing and looked in the same direction that had Zeb's undivided attention.

"I got a feelin' they be talkin' about you. That cracker there . . . that's Highway. He's in command of the Angels. That's the one that yelled out at you."

"Who's he talking to?"

"That'd be the Terminator," answered Zeb.

"The Aryan leader, no doubt?"

"He's not the man they'd be all bowin' down to lately. Ever hear of the Order?"

"No. Can't say that I have," replied Wallace.

"This guy come in from Colorado. He got one hundred ninety years. Name's Erik Edwin Payne . . . he brought the *Or*der into our house."

"That's some major time. Do you know what they nailed him for?"

"Antigovernment shit. Murder of some big-shot radio guy who was a Jew. White power and hatin' on the brothers and the Jews. That kinda shit. He and a couple of other Natzzeee wanabees started it out west."

The horn buzzer blasted out two quick bursts. A shout followed: "Morning chow . . . move it."

Big Harold led the procession down the stairs with the new rookie guard, Peter R. Kowalski, making sure everyone stayed in line. They entered the chow hall, got their pancakes, and sat down. The room was different now: full of loud chatter, not like the night before. Patrick scanned the room, getting a sense of who sat where. He spotted a tough looking inmate they called Highway, talking to a long-bearded, bald-headed, bulbous-nosed character whose tattoos completely enveloped his neck and appeared to engulf and flow down his arms, eventually reaching both wrists.

"Skip the preamble, Z. What exactly did he say?" asked Highway.

"Well, that's just it. Payne gave me nothing except to say to tell the Highway man to chill out."

"That motherfucker. He knows that new fish has some worth."

There was a sudden damping down of talk and action around the tables. Patrick looked away from the bikers and turned his attention to the hall's entrance. A short, stocky man with a crew cut, wearing black-framed glasses and a suit and tie entered and began to walk down the rows, moving quickly from row to row. It was a surprise appearance of Warden Rudolph Conrad Klump. He was flanked by Captain Sheetz, three lieutenants, and two guards. Around the room's perimeter there was a half dozen correctional guards brandishing twelve-gauge pump shotguns. Sheetz had a clipboard in his hands and wrote down what the warden was saying. As Klump passed South Block Level 2 eating table, he stopped and stared, then pointed his finger at Wallace.

"Have this man in my office by eleven hundred."

"Yes sir," replied Sheetz. "Anything else Warden?"

"No."

The Warden continued making his way past more tables and was almost out of Patrick's line of sight when suddenly he stopped for a brief moment to speak to an inmate, then left the same way he came in.

Patrick turned to Zeb. "Who was that the warden was talking to?"

"That's him. That's Payne."

One brief horn blast announced the end of breakfast and Kowalski appeared, stood at the end of the table, and ordered everyone to get up. Returning to their cells, most of the men began their day just like any other with no variation, feeling like time was stretching out longer and longer and moving inordinately more slowly than its true nature. Some who were lucky enough to have outside work details or permanent assignments to laundry and shop rooms were escorted out of the block to begin an eight-hour shift. These men welcomed the minutes and hours they were given and look forward to any and all work that awaits them. Around midmorning Kowalski returned and stood in front of Patrick's cell and did his very best to bark out an order.

"Wallace. In one hour I am taking you to see the warden.

Have yourself presentable. You understand?"

"Yes," Patrick replied.

"Yes what?"

"Yes I understand. One hour."

The young rookie, dressed in his starched gray uniform and wearing black high-top high-glossed, tipped boots, bristled and quickly pivoted to his left and walked away.

Patrick heard a faint sigh and then a laugh coming from Zeb's cell.

"Jesus, Mary, and Joseph . . . he didn't get a yes sir from ya. That boy been trying real hard to show us something since he got here but he be knowin' one thing for sure . . . we don't give a rat's ass about what that cracker has to say. Respect is somethin' you got to earn in here."

"Any guards worth respecting?" Patrick asked.

"Hell no. The hacks are all prick bastards. Except . . . well maybe . . . Plough."

Young Kowalski deposited the new inmate outside the warden's office. "Sit down."

Patrick sat on a wooden bench and waited. A few minutes passed, then suddenly a door opened, revealing Klump sitting at an oversized mahogany desk with his captain standing behind him. The room was oak paneled and well lit from the late morning sunlight shining in from huge plate-glass windows that allowed Klump a panoramic view of the yard. A trusty named Arthur Rishel stood just inside the entrance to the doorway and motioned with his hand to enter. They walked in and Kowalski pointed to where he wanted Patrick to stand, then he and Rishel left the room.

I am Warden Klump. This is Captain Sheetz. Your number is 12873-057. It's best you remember it. We've just finished going over your file, Wallace. When I ask you a question and if the answer requires an affirmative or nonaffirmative response, you will follow your reply with *sir*. Do you understand?"

"Yes . . . sir." Patrick eyed the distance between them.

"As an educated man you would like to be put to work on a detail that requires some thought. Am I right?"

"Yes . . . sir."

"Here." Klump handed him a smallish spiral-bound notebook containing rules and regulations for inmates and a leather-bound Bible. "Those twenty-three pages in that pamphlet outlines very carefully what you cannot do in my prison. Pay attention to that rule book and you won't have any trouble from me. You live in a pressure cooker now. Anything and everything can set a man off. I'd grow eyes in the back of your head real quick. You cause any trouble in my prison, and it will be time in the hole for you with nothing more than bread and water and your own thoughts to keep you company. With time and with good behavior you may be assigned to a cellblock where you may find a population more suited to your own kind. You go ahead and read that Old Testament now, and when you're finished, we will talk again. Captain. See that this man returns to his cell. That will be all."

Kowalski returned Wallace to his cell. He sat on the edge of his bunk and opened the Bible to the inside cover to see, written in India ink, the words *Brüder schweigen.*

It had been three days since he got off the federal corrections bus. It was Thursday and the heat wave that had made the cellblock temperature rise to over ninety degrees had ended. He finished reading the Pentateuch and was on to Joshua when lights-out was called and moments later the block became dark. Around midnight cooler air streaming down from the atrium made for a better night of sleep. Things seemed to settle into a routine. Men were locked in from 10:00 p.m. to 6:00 a.m. and head count occurred four times a day. At 4:00 p.m. inmates were in lockdown and made to stand inside their cells facing the bars, answering to their name when ordered. There were boring times in the cell. For hours and hours he listened to the aimless chatter of *motherfuckin'* this and *motherfuckin'* that and various other laments coming from all over. After breakfast men congregated in pod rooms, and he kept an eye on everything that moved, and he began to see a rhythm to the actions and the talk, and this relieved some of his boredom. After the noon meal it was his time to enter the yard and exercise. He picked up a handball game, and when that ended, he sat alone on the stone bleachers that ran the length of the yard. Zeb, Bunny, and Big Harold quit shooting hoops and walked past him and sat down not too far from where he was sitting. From the top row at the farthest end of the bleachers, a huge figure walked away from where a small group of men had gathered and then down the bleachers. Big Harold saw him first and jabbed Zeb with an elbow, who responded by putting his index finger to his lips, making the sign for silence. The Terminator came down to the concrete yard and walked toward Patrick, then and stopped and stood directly in front of him. They were equal in size.

"All right if I sit?"

"Go ahead."

"Name's Britton. I work for the man up there. He wants to talk to you. You all right with that?"

"He's the talking man, huh," replied Patrick as he turned his head and stared at the far corner of the bleachers where Payne was sitting.

"People listen to what he has to say."

"Well then, if that's true I can't pass up that opportunity, now, can I? Always been a good listener."

Britton nodded, acknowledging approval in the reply. "You may find what he has to say interests you. I believe you know where we live. You'll be hearing from me when the time is right."

The Terminator now looked directly at Zeb, stood up, and walked away in the direction of the upper end of the bleachers.

Patrick watched him as he went back up to the top row and talked to Payne, who seemed pleased, then Patrick turned and looked at Zeb, who lowered his head slightly. Zeb and the others got up and returned to the basketball court to continue playing, as Bunny liked to say, round ball.

V

Razor slowed his chopper down as he turned and glided into the Bear Den Motel's parking lot. It was half past one o'clock, cold, pitch black except for the red light coming from the No Vacancy neon sign he saw in front of him. The Harley's big 1200 cc engine he was straddling gave off some heat but not enough to warm his body.

Now inside his room he flopped down on the bed and lay on his back, staring at the ceiling. One month had passed since his release. Each week he had reported to his parole officer. For the next eleven months it would be once a month. Lying still and trying to get to sleep, he thought about the eight years he had been locked up for second-degree manslaughter. All he saw when he shut his eyes was the old Indian sheriff he'd seen at the garage, and he tried hard to remember what his brother Axel looked like.

The next day he rose early, got on his chopper, and began his return trip to Quebec. Traveling on two-lane roadways, he saw quite a few ponds, grasslands, and wheat fields that had begun to turn yellow and brown, and he noticed a flock of Canada geese and wondered why they weren't farther south by now. By late afternoon he was approaching Montreal, where he planned to meet up with some Angels who lived on top of a bar and strip club.

When he pulled up in front of the bar, night had already fallen and the parking lot was almost filled with choppers, old vans, and cars. He went in. There was a man tending bar who looked familiar to him. Eight years is a long time to be away and he was uneasy about all the lost time. He knew Nomads and Rock Machine infiltrators were around and that this would make Montreal's newest leader, Mom "the Butcher" Denton, anxious and more than ready to draw blood at any provocation. The North American Hell's Angels had their reputation to uphold. He sat down on a stool and the barkeep looked at him.

"I remember you. When'd you get out?"

"About a month ago," replied Razor.

"What can I get you?"

"Beam with some ice, and put some Yukon Jack in it."

"Coming right up."

At the other side of the room a dancer wearing very little appeared and stepped onto a small platform, grabbed a pole, and began to dance to some loud music.

"Here you go. This one's on the house. I was here in seventy four, seventy five. Do you remember me from back then?"

Razor thanked him for the drink, looked at the dancer, then looked back at him. "You look familiar. There weren't any Viet girls dancing here back then."

"*The times they are a-changing*," the bar tender replied in a half-singing half-talking cadence.

"Dylan fan, huh?"

The bartender started to speak but suddenly stopped when

he saw a half dozen Hell's Angels pass through the front door. He lowered his head and started wiping the bar top with a dishrag. Five of the men were surrounding a lone figure as they moved past the bar, when suddenly one man peeled off and stood alongside Razor, while the others continued toward a set of stairs that led to the second floor.

"Manny, two bottles of Johnnie Walker.

"I got to get um out back, I'll bring um up to yah," replied the barkeep as he started walking away toward the rear of the bar.

The biker turned his head and looked at the figure in the middle of the nest of bodyguards; Mom "the Butcher" Denton threw an appreciative nod at him as they approached the stairs. The biker stepped away from the bar, moved toward Manny and shouted, "And don't forget the glasses and the ice. Make sure you announce yourself or you'll get your head blown off . . . you hear me?"

The biker made an about-face and started to walk past Razor, then stopped and stared at his old tattered and faded blue-jeans vest and noticed 1976 under the blood-red Hell's Angels embroidered banner.

"Razor, that you?"

He recognized the voice, then looked behind him. "How's it goin, Jake?"

"Damn. You're out?"

"Yeah."

"Jesus. How long's it been?"

Razor stood up. The two men clasped hands as if they were going to start to arm wrestle, raising their hands together, pulling each other close.

"It's been a while."

"A while? Shit, man. It's been too fucking long."

"Jake the snake. Looks like time's been good to you."

"I am doin' all right. For me."

"Look. I really want to hear what's going on with you but

I gotta get upstairs. We're under new management."

"So that's him. Mom."

"Yeah. You've heard of him?"

"Just what I read in the papers."

"You want to meet him?"

"What. Tonight?"

"Having a poker game up there. He has to know about you and Ax ..." Jake abruptly paused. "I'll talk to him. Hang here for a while, okay? Man, it's good to see you."

He started to walk toward the stairs.

"Jake."

"Yeah?"

"Thanks."

The biker stopped and looked back and smiled, then walked toward the steps.

Sounds of machine pistols erupted, with bullets flying past Razor's head. Razor saw Jake get hit in the back and go down. There were two Nomads spraying the bodyguards with 9 mm rounds. Grabbing a bar stool, Razor raised it above his head, then brought it down on one of the Nomad's outstretched arms closest to him. The Uzi fell to the floor. Manny quickly took a scatter gun out from under the bar and fired a tight pattern that hit the head of the remaining shooter, blowing skull and brains everywhere. Razor dropped down and quickly silenced the other killer. The Viet girl wouldn't stop screaming. The men guarding their leader only seconds ago were now piled in a heap at the banister. Some moaned; some lay dead. There was movement from under the pile. Mom pushed a body off of him, then slowly got to his feet, looked around, and saw Razor and Manny standing over the assassins. Manny unhooked a set of keys from his belt and threw them to Razor.

"Here. My Mustang's out back. Get him to the safe house."

Razor caught the keys, bent over, and picked up the Uzi, then walked over to where Mom was standing.

"Who are you?"

"My name's Razor. You hit?"

"No."

Razor offered his hand. "Come on. I got to get you out of here."

Mom moved his right hand around his back reaching for his .45, which was lodged in his belt, but suddenly stopped when he saw the faded colors on the back of Razor's vest. He stared into his eyes.

"Old school, huh?"

He grabbed the outstretched hand and Razor pulled him over the bodies, then they both began to make their way past the shooters toward the back door.

"Hold it" said Mom. He stopped. Staring down at one of the killers, he drew a buck knife from his belt, knelt down beside the dead man, cut off an index finger, and shoved it into his coat pocket, then turned to the next man and did the same.

"All right. Let's go."

Out back Razor saw Manny's blue Mustang. He opened the door and shoved the Uzi under the driver's seat and climbed in and pushed the seat back as far as it could go. He put the key in the ignition. Mom opened the passenger's-side door and got in. When they got to the main highway, they drive west toward Ville-Marie.

"Jake got it in the back, didn't he?"

"Yeah. He did," Razor replied.

"That piece you got there under the seat. It's a full auto. Mounties will come down hard on you if they find you with that. You know how to get to Ville-Marie?

"Yeah. I was born right next door, in Lafayette."

"When you pass the union hall, turn onto Champlain Street. Got that?"

"Yeah. I got it."

"You know who I am?"

"Yeah. Jake told me. Mom 'the Butcher' Denton."

Mom looked out the passenger's window as they proceeded to the safe house. A half hour passed.

"Streets are always deserted this time of night. Thursday night. Can you believe it? They roll up the sidewalks in this town after ten. Jake. He was good at doing what was asked of him. Slow down. This is it. We're here. Right here. Pull in."

Razor turned into the driveway and stopped ten feet from a garage door. Mom got out and lifted up the door and Razor drove into the bottom of a split-level ranch-style home. He turned the engine off and pulled the Uzi out from under the seat. Mom closed the garage door and turned on a light, then started for the inside door that led into the house but stopped when he saw the weapon in Razor's hands. He got back into the car and shut the door.

"That's a TEC-9."

"How's that?"

"It's a MAC Ingram . . . an Uzi copy. We have some extra magazines for that inside.

Razor turned the piece in his hand. It had a dark green Parkerized finish to it. He found the safety and made sure it was clicked on to the fire position.

"We were followed when we started our last run. We'll be safe here. Machine pistols. They did a lot of damage tonight on us. You need a job?"

With a loud bang lights came on. Fifteen minutes later a horn buzzed twice and cell doors opened. The South Block Level 2 inmates began to emerge. Bunny was again the first to step out on to the catwalk. He grasped the heavy, thick metal guardrail with both his hands and stood motionless, then leaned up against the railing and stared across the dark, lifeless divide at the upper and lower rows of cells that were a hundred feet away. From somewhere high above the prison's atrium, the early morning light of dawn broke through and dissected some parts of the dark abyss that separated north and south cellblocks. The sound of coughing and hacking up phlegm began. Toilets flushed. Big Harold came out, then Zebadiah, and finally Wallace. Each of them also stood at the railing in front of their own cells and they watched and listened to what was happening across the divide. On the other side, men did the same thing. They stared.

"French toast day! Bunny proclaimed, then walked over and stood beside Big Harold. The two of them go into Big Harold's cell.

"How long we've known each other, Bunny?"

"Let me see." Bunny began to count on his fingers. "Fourteen years. That's how long it's been."

"I can't figure it," replied Big Harold.

"Figure? Figure what, Hal?"

"How'd you always get what we'd be havin' for breakfast all the time?"

"We goin' to play round ball today, Hal?"

"No. That was yesterday. You're going to work today."

"I have a good job, don't I, Hal?"

"Yeah. Yeah. You better get a move on. Get yourself cleaned up—we be heading to the chow hall now. Hurry it up."

"All right, Hal, I am goin'. It's French toast day."

Big Harold shook his head and managed a slight smile. "That's right, Bunny. Got to get them French toasts, don't we?"

Although the lighting was not so good, Zeb could see ZZ and Highway staring at Patrick. "They're going to be scoping you out for a while. Until . . ."

"Yeah. I know. Payne just can't wait to talk to me. Do those two work for him?"

"They have some kind of agreement with him. They're bikers through and through. The Angels carry a lot of weight in this place. But to answer your question, they respect what Payne says. That's all I can make out. They don't want me anywhere near their redneck country club, that's for sure, so I don't know shit. This brother stays clear of um. I am fixin' to get me some pod time this morning. How about you?"

"I didn't request any time, replied Patrick.

"Don't worry about that. My man Rishel, he's got the clipboard this week. We be cool. He who controls the clipboard has the pod power," replied Zeb.

Out of the corner of his eye Zeb saw the kid hack Kowalski with his black baton in hand.

"Shit. Here comes needle nuts," said Zeb.

Kowalski stood at the end of the catwalk.

"Let's go. Chow in ten, he barked out loudly as he slowly walked down the catwalk smacking his baton on the railing.

Zeb went back into his cell and Patrick stood alone at the railing going over in his mind what he had seen so far after just a week. Released from their cells at 6:00 a.m., men were free to roam the compound relatively unrestricted until 10:00 p.m., when they were locked up for the night. There were always two guards stationed at the end of the two-tiered upper and lower cellblock stairwell. Work details began at 8:00 a.m., exercise in the yard happened from 2:00 p.m. until 4:00 p.m., and pod-room privileges were assigned throughout the day. There were four pod rooms, one for each cellblock, each containing two coin-operated telephones. Adjacent to one pod was a visitors' room, where rows of prisoners sat behind glass windows on one side of a concrete wall and their visitors sat on the other side. As this would be his first time in the pod, Patrick wondered who he might want to call or, if a visitor appeared, would he want to see anyone?

It was midmorning. South Block Level 2 pod erupted with a buzz. Patrick walked in and sat down next to Zeb. All around, the buzz got louder as the pod began to fill up.

"Look at um. There all working it. Working and rappin'

all the time. Nonstop. We've got Bloods and Crips, Mexican-American *chulos*, Cubanos. Them the crazies and the loners over there. The Aryan Brotherhood are down that hall in Pod 1. We be here, we're the gentle group. Every shade of pot smuggler is here. Boat captains, pilots. You name it. Seven pot guys with a total of three hundred years in sentences all in a row. The feds. The new law. They're out of control, ain't they? These people can sure do some outrageous things to us."

"I know something about what the law can do," replied Patrick.

"I thought you did. New clothes fit okay?"

"Yeah."

"That will be five packs of Luckys, Mr. Patrick."

"Don't have any money just now, but I guess you knew that already, Mr. Zebadiah."

I am the 'getting man,' and being a new celli like you are living next door to me and all that, well, I know the score. You're good for it. Right? I can read people pretty well. I am not in it for the money anyway, but I have my name and my good standing around here to hold on to.

"Does Payne get stuff from the 'getting man'?"

"Never been approached. Won't get guns, won't get the hardest of drugs. That's what the bikers want. Men been known to kill an enemy or themselves around here with weapons and heroine. Don't want no part of that. No sir. Now if you want some reading material, booze, a little reefer, and such, I'll be glad to provide. For a price of course."

Patrick offered up a slight grin. "Of course," he whispered.

Patrick's grin was replaced with a more pensive expression as he gazed far down the hall in the direction of Pod 1.

"You fixin' on seeing Payne soon?"

"How's that?" Patrick replied.

"Saw Payne's man approach you yesterday. Hell, we all saw his big skinhead goon come down from the mountaintop where them Aryans always be hangin' and plottin' all the time when they're outside. You got a first-class priority-one invitation extended to you."

"So Mr. Zebadiah. Payne wants to powwow."

Zeb looked in the direction of where Patrick had been staring. "Well, Geronimo, that'd be that Terminator heading this way."

"I noticed. Guess he don't like to be kept waiting too long," replied Patrick.

The Terminator stared at Zeb. "Take a hike, tall boy."

Zeb remained still.

"Now *BOY* . . ."

Zeb got up slowly and left.

Jim "the Terminator" Britton sat on a bolted-down steel stool and locked eyes with Patrick, who was sitting alone, directly across the table from him. He wore a sleeveless olive-green muscle shirt. A collection of tattoos adorned his arms, neck, and chest. Daggers dripping in blood, naked women, skulls, and battle axes, each one done in a bluish-green ink. These were not street-parlor tattoos. These were convict freehand tattoos that men using sewing needles and melted-down toothbrushes either carved into themselves or had other inmates do it for them. The ink was used in filling out prison forms and was easily obtained in all institutions. Even though they were drawn and inked at different times and in different jails and prisons, they all had the same color, and each was considered a badge of honor. Britton was hairless. Patrick could see on his upper chest a tattoo of a clover leaf and the numbers 6 6 6.

The noise in the pod lessened and inmates temporarily stopped what they were doing to turn and look at the two men.

"Don't think I properly introduced myself yesterday. My name's Britton. Jim Britton."

Patrick looked at him with his cold, clear, calm eyes. "I suppose today is as good as any. All right. Let's go meet with your talking man."

They got up and walked out of the pod with Britton leading the way up the steps to the second tier, onto the catwalk of South Block, past ten—then twenty—cells, some occupied, some empty, until they reached the next-to-the-last cell.

"Wait here."

Britton walked to the end of the row and entered Payne's cell. A few minutes later he stepped out and motioned to Patrick to come over.

The leader of the Order sat at a small writing table reading a book. When Patrick entered the cell, all he immediately could see was Payne's back, but on further observation he noticed he had very short cropped black hair and bleached white skin, and was of slight build. On the back of his neck, tattooed in large, thick letters, was the word *Mephistopheles*.

The Terminator stood in the entrance to the cell at parade rest with his hands clasped behind his back, staring straight ahead out into the cellblock, his enormous size filling almost the entire entryway.

Payne, without moving or turning his head, said in a soft yet firm voice, "Please. Have a seat. I'll be with you in a moment."

Patrick sat on a steel-armed chair that had a leather padded seat, the kind that can be found in any American military base office around the world. He sat in the middle of the cell facing Payne's back. Above the writing table was a bookshelf with a dozen or more books and right above the bookshelf affixed to the wall was an eleven-by-fourteen-inch pencil sketch of some kind of heraldic-looking emblem or crest with writing in German. At the center of the drawing was a German iron cross and immediately above the cross Patrick focused on the same words written inside the front cover of the Bible the warden had given him: *Brüder Schweigen*. He then looked at some of Payne's reading material on the bookshelf. *The Turner Diaries*, *The Diary of Malcolm X*, and Goethe's *Faust*.

English Translation from the Deutsch:

Thou art my battle axe and weapons of war: for with thee will I break in pieces the nations, and with thee will I destroy kingdoms

    —Jeremiah 51:20

With book in hand Payne stood up and turned his chair around then sat back down. The men were now six feet apart, facing each other.

"Irony. It never ceases to amaze me."

"How's that?" replied Patrick.

"Just started studying this chapter on anthropology, and lo and behold, I find out the origin of word *Aryan*."

"You sound disappointed."

"He had to know they were indigenous to India and dark skinned."

"If true, then it's indeed ironic that your Führer picked that word," Patrick continued. "But I wouldn't be too disappointed. Sometimes ancient languages and historical facts can paint an incomplete picture. Happens more often than you think."

"Klump told me you were educated."

"I've studied history. What else did *der* warden tell you?"

"All in good time, Mr. Wallace. I hear patience is a virtue. I am Erik Payne. But you probably already knew that. Speaking of the present administration. The warden and Sheetz like to put new men in South Block for a while, but I've seen new fish go directly where the she males and Sodom mites live. Do you like living in South Block?"

"It's been a week. Can't say one way or another."

"Let me ask you something, Mr. Wallace. On the road of life do we make our luck or does it find us?"

"I imagine it's probably a little of both."

"When I was sent here a year and a half ago, I got lucky. I was given an opportunity that to this day continues to . . . well, just baffle the hell out of me."

"How's that?"

"Well. You see. The warden, he's always had an appreciation for what some call the Teutonic ideal. Ever hear of the German American Bund?"

"Came about in the thirties, if I recall."

"Yes. Very good, Mr. Wallace. Started in 1933 actually. The Bund was to consist only of American citizens of German descent. Its main goal was to promote a favorable view of Nazi Germany. The Bund was established formally in thirty-six, but a few years earlier Rudolf Hess got American Germans in New York and Chicago to form the Free Society of Teutonia."

"Wasn't that the name of a Marx brothers movie?"

"A student of the cinema as well a historian. Bravo, Mr. Wallace. But no. Members of these movements were very earnest in their attempt to legitimize national socialism and take down capitalism and communism. I digress. Let me get to the point of my good luck. You see, Warden Klump's father was active in the movement and at a big rally in thirty-nine he was killed by police when violence broke out. It seems someone took offense when FDR was referred to as Frank D. Rosenfeld. Probably a guy planted by the FBI to get upset and start a riot. Anyway. Ever since good ol' dad got whacked, his only son has, shall we say, harbored some ill will toward certain elements in our country, and when he opened the dossier the FBI gave him on me, well . . . let's just put it this way . . . he likes my views."

"I guess everyone's entitled to their own view of things. That's America for you."

Payne stood up and walked over and stood in front of a pile of magazines that were stacked up high in a corner of the cell, next to his tiny desk. He started to rummage through them and about halfway down he found what he was looking for: he pulled out a copy of the March issue of Time dated 1976 and handed it to Patrick, then sat back down.

Even the pious peanut farmer running for president got it right but then had to apologize to save his political ass.

Patrick opened the magazine to the page that had a piece of tape sticking out from it and read a paragraph Payne had underlined:

> *I have nothing against a community that is made up of people who are Polish, or who are Czechoslovakians, or who are French Canadians or who are blacks trying to maintain the ethnic purity of their neighborhoods. This is a natural inclination . . .. Government should not break up a neighborhood on a numerical basis. As soon as the government does, the white folks flee.*

Patrick looked up and handed the magazine back to Payne. "I believe the French Canadians like to speak French and want to keep it that way. Sounds reasonable."

"But there's more," replied Payne.

Payne stood up and walked past Patrick, then stooped down, looked under his bunk, and grabbed a stack of papers. "Look at this. Just last month."

Payne handed Patrick a copy of the Washington Post. Patrick read a section that was circled.

> *Rev. Jesse Jackson refers to Jews as "Hymies" and to New York City as "Hymietown" and coming to Jackson's defense The Nation of Islam's leader Louis Farrakhan threatens, "If you harm our brother Jackson, it will be the last one you harm."*

"It appears there are people who are upset about some things, Mr. Payne. What does all this have to do with me?"

"I could say you are a useless new fish who understands nothing about anything. But I know as sure as God made little green apples that with time your intelligence will make you a valued commodity, and I want you to know you have options."

Payne got up and grabbed *The Turner Diaries* off the bookshelf and handed it to Patrick. "Here. Take a look. Someday soon I hope to meet again to discuss some theories."

Patrick stood up, looked past Payne, and stared at the etching on the wall above the bookshelf.

"Can you tell me what *Brüder Schweigen* means?"

"Of course. It means 'Brothers keep silent.'"

"Thank you."

"Jim."

The Terminator did an about-face. "Yes sir."

"Mr. Wallace can leave now."

Patrick began to leave, but before he passed through the entryway he stopped. He turned his head and looking directly back at Payne, he nodded and smiled, then walked past Britton onto the catwalk. He returned to the South block pod room, where he sat on a metal stool affixed to the floor, directly adjacent to one of a half dozen round tables that were spread around the large space. A few minutes passed, and Zeb got up from where he was sitting and walked over and sat down next to him. Two other inmates, Skeeter and Calvin, were sitting at the table.

"There's new law and old law. Shit, man. Half these motherfuckers would never be here for some of the shit they did if they did it five years ago," Skeeter said loudly.

Patrick sat quietly listening while looking down, thumbing through the pages of the book Payne had given him.

"DEA and shit. Jail, prison, the penitentiary, the whole fuckin' federal correctional bullshit system. Lockup. Lockdown. And look at Attica. All the brothers shot dead by them state troopers. Those hostages. They were all gunned down. Shot by the man. No brother killed a hack with any fuckin' knife. I know that shit 'cause my cousin survived that shit and told me. Told me with tears streaming down his cheeks. I never had no motherfuckin' father, Calvin. Just me. Me and my brothers and sisters and my mama. You know what I am saying, man? And how about you homeys? You just got here. Tell me I am wrong."

Patrick lifted his head and looked at Zeb and then looked at Skeeter. "Mercantile ethics."

"Say what?" replied Skeeter.

"My grandfather told me about some neighbors of ours who lived in the hills a few miles up the road from us. They were moonshiners. He said they made white lightning during the twenties since the government made drinking illegal. Granddad said if it hadn't been for selling that stuff the family would have starved. There was no work back then. No jobs anywhere. It was the Great Depression. Then there were these government-bought deputies, the *revenuers*, who were hired to chase down men who were making the stuff. Chased them all over the county with bloodhounds and caught them and put them in jail for quite some time to set an example.

"Ain't no justice nowhere," bellowed Calvin.

"Justice. What the fuck's that?" replied Skeeter.

Zeb sat with his hands clasped on the table. He looked at Skeeter. "I don't know about any justice Skeet but booze, grass . . . ain't no difference in my book. Depression recession. Hell. In Mississippi there was always a depression goin' on. Poor is poor. If there ain't no work, there's plenty of pain to go around. Man has a right to dial back the pain."

Patrick turned his attention away from the table when he noticed a figure wearing a uniform standing alongside the entrance to the visiting area. All he could see was the correctional guard's back.

Skeeter looked at Patrick. "So homey. What's your story?"

Patrick refocused. "Yeah. Right. Dial down the pain. I like that. Guess the government had an issue with *my* methods of dialing back that pain. In their eyes I am guilty. Case closed."

The guard disappeared. Coming around the corner, carrying his clipboard with one hand and pushing a metal cart with the other was old trusty Arthur Rishel. He shuffled along, slowly dragging his deformed leg behind him, handing out mail to inmates. He stopped and stood behind Zeb and Patrick.

"New man. You got a visitor's request for one week from today."

"Do you know who it is?"

"It says a V. Wallace."

"Didn't think I could see anyone that soon."

"It's not that soon. Warden's decent when it comes to some things . . . especially family."

"You got anybody on that clippie board of yours for me to see?" asked Zeb.

"Not to worry, tall man. You'll hear it first from me when it comes hot off the Western Union. I am here to please."

Rishel leaned in closer to Zeb's ear. "Speaking of pleasing . . . my daughter's having that baby any day now. That fifth of brandy come in yet?"

"Should be here Friday."

Skeeter grinned and looked at Calvin, then at Rishel. "So Rish . . . you're goin' to be a grandpappy, huh? Far out. That's righteous."

Calvin tapped Skeeter's upper arm with the back of his hand, then looked in the direction of the hallway. Highway and ZZ were standing at the entrance to the pod.

"There's the *mail man*," shouted Highway.

"Fuckin ABs. Why they got to mess with us today?"

"Politics, Calvin. Politics," Skeeter replied.

The two members of the Aryan Brotherhood entered the pod and walked up behind Skeeter and Calvin. ZZ stood behind Skeeter, while Highway moved around to the other side of the table and stood alongside the trusty with his back toward Patrick.

"You got my *Popular Mechanics?*

The old man looked away from Highway. He coughed.

"You're a bit deaf, aren't you?"

He cupped his hand over his mouth and coughed again. "I heard you."

"Then just go over there and get my magazine."

The old con stumbled, got his footing, then moved away from the table toward his pushcart.

Highway looked at Patrick. "Man oh man . . . ever seen such a relic walking on two feet?"

Above the pod room, near the entrance to East Block, shouting started.

"Get the fuck away from the door, you big black queen. Don't be looking at me like that. You must be fuckin' insane."

"Fuck you, you big white bitch. Don't be talkin' that way to me no more or I'll slap you into next year."

"Oh yeah?"

"Oh yeah, motherfucker. I am right here anytime you think I won't, honey."

"Fuck you."

"I'd love that, sweetie. But first I need someone with a dick."

Highway looked up in the direction of Level 2 East Block, turned and looked at Patrick, then shifted his body directly in front of him, lifting his arm up at a ninety-degree angle, exposing his bicep, which was inked with a large tattoo of a swastika. "You hear that shit up there? We'll handle that later. What do you think?"

The noise level decreased as inmates stopped and stared at the two men.

"I try not to," replied Patrick.

"Where you from?"

Patrick stood up. "And what business is it of yours where I'm from?"

Highway looked at Patrick's eyes for the first time. Blackish gray. At once shiny and totally opaque. Like wet granite orbs. "Just ask these boys. Go ahead. They'll tell ya. I am *all* business."

"There's a time to have transactions and a time to recreate."

"Yeah. You get the general idea. All transactions are made right down that hall. You'll see. Z . . . get my magazine. Seems to me this man likes being an Oreo."

Mom reached into his coat pocket, pulled out the two fingers he cut off the assassins' hands, and threw them down in the middle of the dining-room table. Gang members sat around the table and stared at the fingers, then looked up at Mom. In the kitchen a blonde woman with honey-colored, tan skin and legs that seemed to go on forever wearing a white cotton tank top and faded cut-off jeans was making dinner. The house smelled of fried onions, garlic, sausage, and peppers.

Mom "the Butcher" Denton of Quebec began to address his inner circle. "There's not much more to say about the shit storm that's just come down on us. Want you all to meet Razor.

He'll be in charge of security now."

After Mom finished the introductions, Razor stood behind him.

"Right now, we've got to find out what we can before any of our distribution lines are disrupted. So. What are you hearing? What do you know? Billy, you first."

Billy Grimes took a swig of beer. "Got a Rock Machine mule tied up in my fuckin' basement. Been squeezing him hard all day. Before I left to come here, the guy was finally coming around, said he knew about a lot of that new crack shit coming in from Miami. Said some Machine asshole boosted a lot of the shit in Nova Scotia and Boston Harbor, and now it's here in town."

"Gerald. What say you?"

"Right now, Mom, ain't hearing squat about any action against us. We've been digging around looking for anything that smells."

The doorbell rang. Mom turned around in his chair and looked up at Razor.

"Get that, will you?"

Razor left and a few minutes later came back into the room and whispered into Mom's ear.

"It's all right. Let 'em in."

Razor went out of the room and came back, followed by Lanszetti and his associate Brown.

"It's good you could make it on such short notice."

The two men joined the leader of Quebec's Hell's Angels at the table.

Mom opened two cans of peanuts and doled some out on the table in front of him, then passed one can to Billy and the other to Gerald. They passed them around. The blonde woman entered holding two pitchers of beer and placed them on the table, then picked up empty pitchers and walked back into the kitchen.

"Here's how I see it. We've got all seven gangs in Canada. That makes us the largest chapter in the world. We're a cartel now. We've got the numbers. I don't need to tell you. Let's use them."

Joe Lanszetti pulled out a fat Arturo Fuente from his inside vest pocket and lit it up. Large clouds of smoke began to billow around his shoulders, then move upward and hover at the top of his head as he started to speak.

"You pretty much either decapitated or brought in the Machine and the Nomads last year. My sources in Scranton say—well, they say Bufallino recruited a few of those who got on their bikes and headed for the hills of Pennsylvania. Crack is where it's at now. It's in demand all over. He wants access through the reservation. By taking you out he may get what he wants."

Mom stood up, walked over to a sideboard, picked up two glasses, and placed them in front of Lanszetti and Brown, then reached for a pitcher of beer and poured beer into both glasses. He stood behind Lanszetti.

"Beer and nuts is all we got, Joe. Enjoy the hors d'oeuvres."

Gerald passed a can of nuts in the direction of Brown. Lanszetti reached for his glass. Mom pulled a carbon-steel bowie knife out from behind his back and slit his neck to the bone. Both carotid arteries burst and a jet of blood shot across the table, hitting Billy in the face. The dead man's head, barely tethered to its upper torso flopped, then fell forward onto the table. Blood and peanuts congealed on the tabletop. Mom returned to his seat and looked at Brown.

"So Eddy. Come here and sit by me."

Gerald got up from his seat, allowing Eddy Brown to sit at the right hand of Mom.

"This man just earned his center patch."

The bikers stood and raised their glasses. Mom got up and put his hand on Brown's shoulder. "For more than a year, Eddy, you've done a job that has given us everything we wanted."

The men cheered.

"All right, all right . . . the rat may be gone but we got to be just as skillful now as ever. We know Buffy's reputation. Don't forget he took out Hoffa."

Mom walked over to a swinging door that led into the kitchen. He pushed it partway open.

"Martha. Where's that dinner?"

Razor, Billy, and Gerald stood over Lanszetti. Billy grabbed him under his armpits and lifted.

"Jesus, Gerry, this guy's one heavy motherfucker. I'll get a sheet."

"Hold it. I'll be right back."

Razor left and came back with the shower curtain and towels from the bathroom upstairs. "This cuts down on spillage."

Gerald glanced at Razor, then looked at Billy.

"See? Mom sure knows talent when he sees it. Razor here, he's got some experience with this kind of shit."

They dragged him into the garage, threw him into the trunk of Manny's Mustang, returned to the dining room, and wiped down the tabletop.

Mom looked at them and smiled. "A very competent disposal. Let's eat. MARTHA!"

The kitchen door swung open and food was placed on the table.

"So . . . where are we? We've got some renegades backed by a family who think they can gain access to St. Regis. Well, fuck that. Tomorrow we roll south." Mom laughed. "I hear Pennsylvania is a pretty colorful place this time of the year, with all those fucking autumn leaves. Eat well and toughen up your assholes 'cause we're going to be riding long and hard until we get what we're after."

It was midnight when Billy got behind the wheel of the Mustang and backed it out onto the street, then took off, followed by Gerald in his pickup. The house was empty except for Mom and Razor. Martha was cleaning up.

"Hey. Head of security. Come with me."

The two men walked through the kitchen and out a back door onto a wooden deck.

"Cigarette?"

"I could use one."

Mom lit his cigarette, then handed the lit lighter to Razor. "You know in the short time I've known you, I've seen you go into action and take charge. You certainly have shown me you can handle yourself when things gets hairy. Your experiences have certainly paid off."

Razor lit his cigarette. He exhaled and smoke poured out of his nostrils. He looked at Mom. "Experience is a great teacher and a fool will learn from nothing else."

Mom looked up at the night sky, then at Razor. "I read somewhere that someone said that experience is the name everyone gives their mistakes."

Razor took a drag on his cigarette. "That guy could be right but I can't say for sure."

"Yeah. Being too sure about anything can sometimes getcha into trouble. I know one thing for sure, Mr. Head of Security."

"For sure, huh? What might that be?"

"Well, Razor. That crime scene we left last night. All those fucking bodies lying around everywhere. The Mounties have impounded our rides by now . . . that's for sure. But I got a remedy for that. Come on. Follow me."

They walked into a garage behind the house. Mom flipped a light switch on, walked over to where two motorcycles were parked, sat on one, and put both hands on the handlebars, throttle, and brake grips as if he were going to drive away into the night.

"I've been working on these for a few months now. This one here. Picked it up a few years ago. You should have seen the rust. I retooled the motor and tranny, put these ape hangers on, and got rid of the saddlebags. A Heritage any one percenter would be proud of."

"One percenter?"

"That's what the Mounties call us now. They say outlaw gangs are one percent of the bikers who ride Harley iron. What were you riding the other night?"

"A Touring Classic that belonged to my brother."

"What's he ride now?"

"He doesn't ride anymore."

"How come?"

"He's dead."

"Dead."

"Yeah. It happened a few months before I got released from Causapscal. All I know is, he was killed on Indian lands."

"St. Regis?"

"Yeah. I think that's right. And I got a feeling."

"About what?"

"Well. You know that guy you whacked tonight . . . I think he was somehow involved.

"What's your brother's name?"

"Axel."

Mom looked away from Razor, then pointed to the other Harley. "You take that one."

"I can't do that."

"You need wheels. When the time is right, we'll talk with Eddy Brown about your brother."

At dawn they drove off to rendezvous with carefully select-ed center-patched members south of Montreal. The posse, as Mom called them, was already assembled in the parking lot of Sonny's Roadhouse when the two of them rolled in. Morning sun beat down on rows of chrome and steel. After a preliminary meeting in an RV, the "Pennsylvania Run" was underway. Twenty-five bikes were traveling now, like a black swarm, so close together that mirrors were clipped, knees were grazed and lungs filled with exhaust.

It was dark when the posse arrived in Scranton. Mom raised his hand up past his shoulder and his men immediately geared down. A low rumble of engine sounds echoed in the streets as they made their way toward the Gennetti Hotel where Buffalino was known to be having dinner. The bikers turned into the alley directly behind the Hotel. They got off their bikes and huddled in front of Mom. He quickly gave final instructions to his men then they all entered the hotel from different entrances. A few minutes later a half dozen gun shots rang out from within the five story building.

Razor was the first to come out of the front door and down the steps of the hotel, followed by Billy and Gerald. Sporadic chatter of automatic pistol fire and the loud explosive thunder-clap sounds of shotgun blasts flooded the street, echoing along building walls. A Cadillac and a Lincoln Town Car's tires were flattened. The drivers, desperately trying to maneuver the cars away from the attack, ended up driving the vehicles onto the curb and sidewalk. A wounded driver got behind one car and opened up on the hotel entrance. Razor dropped down behind a car that was parked in the portico and slapped another clip into his machine gun. Rounds shattered glass and careened off exterior concrete walls, splintering benches and wooden doorjambs and moldings. It was a dark, moonless night and all you could see were muzzle flashes. Everywhere the smell of gunpowder permeated the atmosphere like the smell of fire-works. A misty, milky layering of expended gunpowder smoke trapped in damp autumn air seemed to hover horizontally above the asphalt and concrete. There was a break in the firing and Razor turned, crouched down, and maneuvered quickly alongside parked cars toward the hotel's rear entrance. Inside the hotel Bufallino lay dead. As Razor turned the corner he saw Mom and Brown exiting the rear of the hotel and getting on their Harleys. Mom saw him and gave him a thumbs-up. Angels got on their bikes and scattered, leaving town in all directions. Sirens sounded in the distance. Billy and Gerald caught up with Razor, and the three of them raced down an alley and got on their motorcycles.

Together with Mom and Brown they rode north through state forest lands. They crossed from Wyoming County into Susquehanna County. They crossed into New York State at Corbettsville and they rode up through hills covered with tall, thick hemlock where asphalt turned to dusty dirt roads, staying far away from Binghamton, then headed west. The night was pitch-black. Hundreds of miles to the northeast was the Saint Lawrence and Canada. Suddenly it was dawn and on both sides of the road acres of goldenrod came into view. Cold nights caused the weeds to wilt and attract road dust causing them to droop downward onto the berm of the road. They rode up through a pasture along Castle Creek in Broome County and into the low hills. The creek was shallow but clear and green, with fallen petrified trees slumped over the embankments and bluffs. Stopping to drink, they scarcely spoke with one another. At midmorning they passed through the ruins of an old logging camp on a stony escarpment where there were dilapidated cabins and rusted machinery that had not been used since the 1930s. An ancient mill. The wreckage of an old wooden sluice among new tree growth.

They rode on. Coming out of the forest, they drove onto dry, cracked pavement and over potholes, and in the afternoon they descended through low rolling hills and into St. Regis and the Akwesasn Reservation. They drove up 37 and turned onto Elk Road and rode up Paw Paw Road past the Five Tribes Center and the Bear Den Motel past the Double T Restaurant and headed north toward Rose Valley Lake. As they reached the crest of a hill, Chief Dan Tails's sentries could be seen standing in the middle of the road. One man held an

M-14; the other a short-barrel coach gun. Mom raised his hand and they stopped. After a few words were exchanged, they were permitted to pass. They drove down a hill, then onto a narrow dirt road that hugged the lake, making their way toward a large A-frame house made of logs with a green metal roof. The house was completely encircled by a wooden deck that was stained a brownish red. The loud sounds of their exhausts shattered the stillness of the tranquil lakeside property. The chief stood on the threshold and watched the men pull in and dismount their Harleys. Mom walked alone up to the front of the house, then climbed some steps to the deck, stood in front of the Mohawk elder, and raised his hand. The chief's right hand went up.

"Daniel."

"Malcolm."

"Sorry about the noise, Chief."

"No worries. What's the Harley motto . . . Straight pipes save lives."

Both men gently grabbed each other's right shoulder and held on and laughed.

"It's always good to see you, Malcolm."

"Me and my men . . . we're worn out."

The chief looked at Mom and then at the Angels, who were standing next to their motorcycles. Both men and machines were covered with dust, grime, and road mud. "There's plenty of room. Come on in."

Mom turned and motioned to the men to join him. They climbed the steps to the deck and followed him and the chief into the house. Once inside they entered a great room and walked past oversized leather couches, BarcaLoungers and a pool table, then walked up to a massive stone walk-in fireplace that consumed the entire width of the room. On every wall there were mounted heads of elk and deer. A woman standing in a kitchen doorway walked in.

"This is Tushanna. She will see to your needs," said the Chief.

The men showered and after eating a meal found two rooms containing bunk beds and went to sleep.

Mom awakened before dawn and walked into the great room. As he looked through a window he could see the sun starting to come up and saw a shadowy silhouette of a figure, a man, sitting on a rocking chair outside on the deck. It was the chief. Mom made his way through the room and stood in the doorway and looked out on the lake. The leaves were almost completely off the trees and the lake had a covering of a milky mist floating on top of the water moving ever so slowly from right to left.

"Come join me."

"All right."

"Before I moved into this place, I lived on this land in a shack. Most mornings I would start my day with a walk down that path over there. There's a clearing on the other side. You can't see it from here. Every year I would grow corn on that piece of land. A strange thing happened this year as I walked."

"What was that?"

"Must have lived here twenty years, more or less. In all that time crows would fly over me going here and there. This year they started to walk with me."

"I am a city man. Don't know about the wilds but that does strike me as peculiar."

"They're very social and supportive in their ways. Saw them stay by a dead body for three days straight. One of their own. Dead by natural causes, I think."

"Natural or unnatural. Does it make a difference?"

"I suppose not. All living things have an arc. A natural flow."

"You're probably wondering why I made this unscheduled visit. These past few days . . . I've had to change that flow. Had to alter the business plan, Daniel. There'll be a change in personnel."

"Were your suspicions correct?"

"Yes they were. Big Joe got greedy. His arc. Well. It's been permanently flattened. Ed Brown will be providing you with everything for the foreseeable future."

"Ahhhh ... Malcolm. I thought I detected bloodlust in your eyes when I saw you yesterday. Sometimes you have to cut off a finger to save a hand."

Mom smiled. "Can't argue with that, Chief."

"People in this tribe have benefited from our working relationship. Don't see how this change you made will produce any downside to my goals." The chief stood up. "Did you see that pool table in there? They just delivered it last week. What da ya say? How about a game of billiards before breakfast?"

Ten miles away, at the other end of the reservation, Henry Crow Horse sat in his jeep,

patiently waiting for Tushanna to come down the stairs of her apartment, which was atop the Double T Restaurant. She wasn't working the breakfast shift at the restaurant but instead was traveling once again across the reservation to Chief Dan Tails's lake house to cook and clean and see to his overnight guests. He saw her come down the steps and got out and walked over to her car. He stood by the driver's-side door and faced her.

"I am late," said Tushanna.

"This will only take a moment."

"Do you have any idea what he will—"

"Please. It's important. We can park way back over there. No one will see us."

"All right. But if I am late he'll ..." She fumbled through her purse, looking for keys. "Damn it. Just get in."

She drove the two of them around to the back of the restaurant and parked next to a Dumpster.

"Dan Tails had some visitors come in late yesterday afternoon. Were you there?"

"Yeah. They were those bikers from Quebec."

"Any names thrown around?"

"Mom. They called one guy Mom. He must have been the leader. The chief and him were alone together most of time."

"Tushanna. Anything you hear ..."

"I know. I'll let you know."

"Be careful."

Chief Dan Tails put his arm on Mom's shoulder and together they walked out of the great room and entered a darkened room that smelled of smoke and ash from the burnt logs that were smoldering in the fireplace. The Chief pulled a chain attached to a shiny brass light fixture suspended over the pool table. Three green shaded incandescent lamps came on to light up the tabletop.

"So you're a billiards player?"

"You mean pool, Chief? I've been known to shoot a game of eight ball from time to time."

The chief picked up a smallish hardcover book. "I've been reading the rules. Ever hear of ball in hand?"

"No. But I got a feeling you're going to teach me a few things."

They stood on either side of the table, which was made of oak with bear and fish carved into the thick oversized legs. The chief took a plastic cover off the table and rolled it up and set it down on the back of a BarcaLounger. The table's felt was maroon colored with no sign of dust or lint.

Tushanna drove to the lake and was waved through the checkpoint. She continued up a dirt road to the rear entrance of the Chief's house and entered a back door that led directly to the kitchen, where she began her breakfast preparations. The kitchen was dark when she entered and as she moved through the room to switch on the overhead stove light she noticed a bright light coming under the bottom of the door that led to the great room. She could hear the chief and Mom talking.

The chief stood in front of a rack of cue sticks and ran his hand over them while inspecting the labeling at the bottom of each one. Mom picked up the rule book and saw that page two was dog-eared. Underlined in pencil was item three: "Ball in hand." He quickly read the passage and put the book down.

"Here it is. This one's mine. Come over here and pick a good one, Malcolm."

He racked the balls and handed the cue ball to Mom "the Butcher" of Quebec.

"You break, Chief."

He broke the balls and they played eight ball and the Chief beat him easily, walking around the table and chalking his cue with a deft, quick circular motion and announcing the shots with quiet authority. He played slowly and studied every potential move and the overall lay of the table, and as he studied and played, he spoke of the Mohawk tribes that inhabited North America and the history of St. Regis.

Mom bent and sighted and hit the seven ball down the entire length of the table into a corner pocket. He studied the table. He bent and shot and stood and chalked his cue.

"I have to ask a question, Daniel. I know you won't . . . no . . . . check that . . . can't get into the weeds too much on this, but I have a guy with me sleeping in that room down the hall there whose brother got killed in that fuck-up on that ice patch a couple of years ago. He just got out of Causapscal and wants to know how his brother ended up here dead. Ordinarily I wouldn't give a rat's ass about this kind of shit, but this guy saved my ass a while back and, well, I guess, no . . . there ain't no guessing about it. I do owe him something; some answers if I can get um."

"What is your question?" replied the Chief.

"The accounts of what happened he'll get from the newspapers, but I have a feeling that's not enough. He's on the trail of something more. He ain't going to stop until he hits pay.

dirt, and when that happens, I know that will get him killed, and that's going to put a strain on our relationship."

"Go on, Malcolm," the chief said as he studied the table. He chalked, he moved.

Mom bent and banked the ten ball into a side pocket then stood and surveyed the table. "Eddy Brown gave me what little history he could on how it went down that day in that trailer on the ice. Those Hell's Angels both getting their necks broken like that."

"And what else did your Mr. Brown tell you?" said the chief.

"Look. I don't want to push the issue but I got to tell this guy something. Eddy said what really happened was two Indians from out west did the killing and they never been seen since."

Chief Dan Tails looked at Mom and smiled and looked at the table. "The feds sent a man to prison in Pennsylvania not too long ago. Maybe you could have this man go down that rabbit hole. Find what he's looking for in there."

"That may work," replied Mom.

"All kinds of things have been known to happen in prison, Malcolm. That's the best I can do for you."

"I'll give that idea some thought, Chief."

"This man . . . you've got to persuade him that all his answers can be found in a prison, not here."

Mom looked at the chief, then he looked at the table. "I read you loud and clear, Chief. The Mohawk Nation can't ever be seen to have been involved."

Mom bent to shoot and missed his shot and stepped back from the table.

The chief ran the remaining balls off the table, then stood quietly looking out the window toward where he'd once planted corn. "Let's get some breakfast, and later, if you like, I'll introduce you to those walking crows."

"Well, Daniel. You're a damn fine *billiards* player."

Tushanna walked away from the door. The sun was up and

the men emerged from their bunks. Tushanna served them breakfast, and as they ate, the chief regaled them with stories of how the men of his tribe built the skyscrapers and bridges of New York City.

Mom saw that Eddy Brown had cleaned his plate. "Eddy. It's time you sewed on your patch. It's in my saddlebag. Come on. Let's get this going."

The two men got up from the table and walked outside. Mom opened a saddlebag and took out the patch. "Before we go back in we need to talk."

"Sure. What's up?"

"It's Razor. He's asked me if I can help get him get some info on Axel. They're brothers—were, that is."

"Oh. That's, uh ... um ... that could open up a whole hornet's nest that would be bad for business."

"Yeah. We sure can't go there."

"You have something in mind?"

"You remember ZZ?"

"Sure. He disposed of that Rock Machine asshole. Benny "the Fool" Johnson. Damn shame he got nailed for that one. He's never getting out."

"What's the name of the guy that got busted for all that shit that happened on that ice patch?"

"Hmmm ... yeah, that guy. He was from Moreland, New York. Let me think ... Wallace. Yeah, that's it. His name was Wallace. A drug runner from downstate."

"Wallace. That's his name? Very good. Look, Eddy. I want you to go see ZZ. Get him dealing for us again. He and his boys can always use more income. Right?"

"From what I hear, guys doing serious time like this new crack. I can make that work, Mom."

"I've got to get Razor to believe this Wallace guy whacked his brother. ZZ could spin it that way. You know ... ZZ could get Razor to see there's no question in anyone's mind that this

Wallace guy did it and our Angel brothers in there all know he killed him."

"So ZZ is to only know what we want him to know. Is that it?"

"That's right. As far as ZZ is concerned Wallace killed Axel all by his lonesome. Only you and I will know what went down."

"All right. I'll go see him. We got a budget for this job? I'll need to whet his appetite."

"Feel him out. Have him throw some numbers out at you. When we meet with Razor, let me do the talking. You just agree with everything I say."

"Okay, Mom."

"Let's get back inside and get that patch on your back."

VI

*M*y brother Vincent arrives today to see me. Haven't seen him since my sentencing came down. Haven't seen anyone, for that matter. Don't much blame them.

At St. James Academy our Latin teacher once spoke about St. Thomas Aquinas and his use of the word grace and how it encompasses the idea and ideals of duty and love. All those cases and declensions written on the blackboard flow into my consciousness as I sit on my bunk waiting for a guard to take me to see him. In my head I see only the word disgrace. Our history and rhetoric teacher liked to play up the importance of the Spartan way of living. "What did the Greeks know?" he asked us over and over again. I over-romunticized the Stoics and their steadfast resolve. I was hooked by what I thought was their insightful ways. I would have been better off with Aeschylus. Yes. Poetry. It's impossible to get the news from poems yet we die miserably each and every day for lack of what is found there.

I sit. I wait. I am not sure it's a good idea to have a family *member come visit. Images are now being conjured up from my unconscious of past and better times. This can't be healthy for me. Prison is prison. To think by having a few moments of interaction with someone that cares for me will do me any good is foolish. To the contrary. It can only make things worse. In prison one must be a Stoic or one cannot survive. Better to set my sights and resolve on to the true facts of life here in the Big House then to fall prey to some dreamy notion of the possibility of some kind of a better life inside these walls. But it seems I cannot stop this flow of unconscious remembering, if indeed that's what it is, how on Friday afternoons at St. James the old Presbyterian minister lectured us from the New Testament with great love in his heart on how life could truly be made better if only one believed and had faith. The old man delivered his weekly speeches as if our lives depended on what he said and fervently believed to be true. Monday through Thursday we received knowledge of the Titans and Olympians. But on Friday, souls needed to be saved. The revealed religion was thrust upon us with great enthusiasm and hubris.*

The beginning gray light of morning appeared in Don Kaminski's bedroom. The clock on his nightstand read 4:00 a.m. It was the first Monday after Daylight Saving Time ended, and Huey's stomach told him it was time for breakfast. Cats know exactly when it's time to eat. The meowing started promptly at five like previous days. However, today would be different. There would be no tractor trailer driving to Ohio. Today he would drive with Vincent Wallace to Pennsylvania to see his old friend who was locked up in one of the oldest federal penitentiaries in the country. Like every other day he sat on the edge of his bed and strapped on steel leg braces, and when they were firmly affixed to his tibias and fibulas, Huey began weaving back and forth in a figure-eight motion through his legs, purring and leaning into steel, skin, and bone.

After feeding the cat, he made coffee and sat at his desk and looked out his window toward the east and saw a light blue sky dotted with white clouds accented with orange and pink hues. He turned and looked at a framed picture of himself together with his flight-and-gun crew. The photograph had been taken in Da Nang in 1967. He had just turned twenty-three years old. He remembered the very early morning sky in Vietnam to be just as colorful and beautiful as this sunrise. Huey sat on the floor staring at his human, then jumped on his lap. The sun's yellow light now broke through the windowpane and the two of them sat together and soaked in the warmth of the sun, in a mountain refuge so quiet and still they could hear each other's breathing. For a brief moment they were, two sentient beings depending on each other for the same thing.

A short while later he left the house and drove to Grey Stone. Vincent was already standing at the front door when he arrived and the two of them got into Vincent's car and left Moreland for Lewisburg, Pennsylvania.

Four hours later they were at the prison's main entrance. A guard stepped out of a tiny one-man gatehouse and peered into the car as Vincent lowered the window.

"Can I help you?"

"I believe I am on the list to see Patrick Wallace."

"Your name?"

"Vincent Wallace."

The man checked his clipboard. "Yes. Today is your day. May I see some identification?"

Vincent took his driver's license out of his wallet and handed it to the guard.

The guard looked at the license and handed it back, then looked at Don Kaminski. "What about him?"

"He's going to wait for me."

"All right. He'll need a badge if he plans on walking around out here. You can ask for one when you get to the visitors' check-in. Go on through."

"Thank you."

The guard raised an old wooden crossing guard barrier to the upright position, and the old Mercedes pulled forward, spewing black diesel exhaust out the tailpipe.

"Jesus, Vin. Look at this place. It's as if we just stepped out of a time machine. Look at those ramparts. Medieval for sure."

They parked and found the office of visitation.

"What are you going to do while I am with him?"

"Like the man said, I am free to walk the perimeter as much as I want. Saw a picnic table over there by the woods. I'll wait there."

"All right."

Big Harold walked out of his cell. He saw Patrick sitting on his bunk staring at the wall in front of him.

"My man *Patrrrrrick*. What'cha sitting all by yourself like that for?"

Patrick got up from his bunk and walked out onto the catwalk. "Waiting on a visitor."

"Hell, man. They better be hurryin' it up. It's getting close to chow."

Harold saw a guard walking toward them. "Plough's comin'. It's cool. He'll be taken ya."

"You ready?"

"I guess I am as ready as I'll ever be."

"It's tough for some . . . the first time," replied Les Plough.

Patrick looked at Plough. His face was pale, prematurely wrinkled, and there were dark bags around his eyes, yet the eyes were clear and enthusiastic-looking. When Plough opened his mouth, Patrick saw two teeth missing, the result of breaking up a fight a few weeks back. Well over six feet in height, with straggly blondish-brown hair, he was large-boned and sinewy but not robust. To Patrick he seemed out of place.

"You know, ever since I got here I've had this feeling . . . you've been watching me, haven't you?"

"You might say that. Come on. Let's get going. The warden puts a time limit on these things."

They entered the visitors' room and Patrick saw his brother sitting at one of six partitioned cubicles with a brown paper bag on his lap. Plough directed him to sit on a wooden chair directly opposite Vincent, then left the room. Thick glass separated them. Simultaneously they picked up telephones. Vincent was the first to speak.

"Willie Mack picked these for you."

"Season's just about over, isn't it, brother?"

"Yeah. That's about the last of them."

"How'd the jack turn out?"

"Willie did his usual thing. It's got a good kick to it, that's for sure."

"What else do you have there, Vin?"

Vincent held up a small, ancient-looking book bound in a tattered, faded red cloth.

"Is that . . . damn, no, *Le Morte d' Arthur*! The Malory edition?"

"I looked all around the library and thought this one would do."

"That's going way back, Vin. What were we? Eleven, twelve, when we read that one?"

"Yeah, I think so."

"Remember when Father told us how, as far as legends went, King Arthur and his knights were right up there with . . . remember? What were their names?"

"King David was one," answered Vincent.

"Yeah, that's right, and Alexander the Great and Charlemagne."

"Yeah, but those three . . . they were real guys. The Arthur legend . . ."

"I know, Vin. But as a kid . . ." Patrick paused. "Well, anyway. Thanks for bringing it with you. And the apples."

"Don came with me."

"He still driving the eighteen wheelers?"

"Yeah. He is. But, uh . . . I have something here I'd like you to look at." Vincent took out a small piece of paper from his shirt pocket, unfolded it, and pressed it up against the glass. "Received this from upstate."

Patrick read the note from Henry Crow Horse. "That was good of him. That beat-up crippled old sheriff. Not even a stroke can keep him down and out of the game."

"Before I go, I am going to speak with the guy in charge and try to see what I can and cannot bring you. Don wants to see you."

"I'd like to see him. Tell him that, will you?"

"This one-visitor-at-a-time rule makes things difficult. He'll come next month."

"How's that new job of yours going?"

"Good. Real good, actually. Angus hooked me up with the right guy, all right. It's a small fabrication plant right now, but there's growth potential. I am putting in ten, twelve hours a day. Manufacturing. Never knew much about it, but it's something I seem to take to pretty well. I understand the concepts."

"Remember what Grandpa would say to us, Vin? He'd say, 'It's always good to make things, boys.'"

"Yeah. I remember. He and old Bill Mack were always out in that barn or at the mill putting things together for this and that. The constant needs and repairs to that lumber mill never seemed to stop."

"And then one day the logs just stopped coming in. There were hardly any more trees left."

"Conservation was never their strong suit, Patrick."

"Yeah."

"Tell me. How you making out in here?"

"Remember growing up and hearing all those stories about the Sioux? You know, how if you threw um in jail they would after a while just up and die. Sometimes I can see how that could be. But then I think . . . there's the Wallace in me."

"That's right, brother. Don't forget why Hadrian's Wall was built. The clans joining together; that was strength alright. The Romans knew they had to keep us Highlanders up in the North Country and out of England.

"I never paid very much attention to politics. But in here, there's a lot of politics going on. Power and all that. Who has it, who wants it, and how to keep it is the reality of this place. Do it to the other guy before he does it to you is the rule around here."

"There's much strength in you, Pat."

"Strength and power . . . they're both fleeting. There is one thing that I am having some trouble with."

"What's that?"

"I can't see the night sky in here. Remember all the times at night we'd lay down on the grass near the orchards and look up at the moon? I miss the moon's phases—seeing it shed its shadow."

"Those harvest moons . . . they're the ones I liked the most. Big and yellow filling up the horizon."

"We were lucky growing up, being country boys, weren't we?"

A guard came in and put his hand on Vincent's shoulder. Vincent looked up at the man.

"Time's up," the guard said quietly.

"Already? Seems like I just got here. Look, uh, I . . . I brought these for my brother."

"I'll have to check everything that's in the bag, but there shouldn't be a problem with him getting these kinds of things."

"Can I have just a few more minutes?"

"We're on a tight schedule. You'll have to say your good-byes. I can give you a minute or two."

"Thanks."

"See if you can get here by nine thirty the next time you come. You'll have more time that way."

"Well, Vin, this is it."

"I don't know what to say. I just can't find the . . ."

"Yeah. Me too. There are no words for any of this. Just know that coming here like you did today—that was a tough thing to do. Good-bye, Vin."

Plough came into the room and escorted Patrick out into the hall and had him sit on a bench while he went into the visitors' office. Moments later he was back, standing next to Patrick.

"Here. They check out okay. No saws. Come on, let's go. Time to get you back for chow."

The other guard opened the door to the visitors' room and Vincent exited and walked down the hallway past administration offices, all the while quickening his pace. Then he saw an old oak door that looked like it opened into a tiny custodial closet, but on further inspection he could see a small metal sign screwed above a door marked Lavatory. He stopped and turned the corroded brass doorknob; it opened. He walked in, locked the door, stood at a tiny sink, and splashed cold water on his face, then sat on the toilet, propping his head up with both hands. His eyes welled up with tears. After a while he got up and walked out of the building, never looking back. He felt light-headed and his breathing seemed to be racing out of control. He kept looking around, then suddenly his feet began to move and he found the picnic table where Kaminski said he would be waiting. But he was nowhere in sight. He scanned the area. He could see steep hills to the north. Suddenly Kaminski appeared, moving down from one of the hills through the trees toward him.

"What were you doing up there?

"You know . . . you can see into the center of that place pretty well from up there."

"What did you see, Don?"

"It's probably what they've called it forever: you know . . . the yard. Just like in those old-time movies. And it's a *big yard*, there's no doubt about that. How is he?"

"I'll tell you on the way back. Right now I've got to get out of here."

At the parking lot Vincent stretched out his hand to Kaminski. "You feel like driving?"

Kaminski grabbed the keys and got behind the wheel. Vincent sat alongside him in the passenger seat. Kaminski found what he believed to be the right key, then looked for the ignition on the column.

"You forget, Don. This is a sixty-three Benz."

Kaminski smiled at Vincent, then looked down and to the left of the wheel below the dashboard. "Germans. Why they always have to be so different?"

He put the key into the ignition and turned it a quarter turn. The glow plug light came on, then went off, and he turned the key as far as it would go. After a few cranking sounds the starter engaged the diesel engine and it turned over, blowing out dark smoke from the tailpipe. As soon as the engine began to idle smoothly, he drove out of the lot back toward the gatehouse. Right before they reached the exit area, Kaminski saw a sign telling him to stop and be checked out by the guard. Seconds later, upon hearing deafening motorcycle exhaust sounds, he slowed down to see two Harley riders at the gatehouse entrance. The bikers quickly pulled away, heading in their direction. Suddenly the second biker abruptly slowed his chopper to almost a standstill and locked eyes with Kaminski, then proceeded on down the road toward the prison. Kaminski and Wallace turned in their name badges to the guard, then drove onto Route 15 and headed north to Moreland.

"Did you know that guy?" asked Vincent.

"Haven't been stared at like that in a long time. No. Never seen him before," replied Kaminski.

Eddy Brown and Billy Grimes parked their choppers close to the picnic table and dismounted. Billy reached into his saddlebag and pulled out hoagies and two bottles of beer, and they sat and ate and waited until it was time for Eddy to meet with ZZ.

Plough walked Patrick back to the South Block entrance, then up the steps and onto the catwalk, past men standing in their cells waiting to go to noon chow. Patrick stepped into his cell, then turned around and faced the guard.

"About your question. Yes. I've been watching you."

"Any particular reason?"

"I am finishing up a psychology degree at Penn State. Warden Klump, he's allowing me some access to inmate files."

"Am I to be one of your case studies? Is that it?"

"The file indicated you had a superior IQ."

Double horn blasts screamed out from atop the atrium.

Plough shouted, "All right, people. Let's move."

Men stepped out of their cells and walked single file toward the stairs. Patrick followed Bunny, who was following Big Harold, with Zeb at the end of the line. Plough walked away from Patrick's cell and stood next to the railing, making sure order was maintained. Down the steel steps they all went past cellblock pod rooms and through a long, dark cavernous hallway. Arriving at the entrance to the dining hall, each man received a tray and eating utensils from a supervised attendant, then stood in line to wait for the noon meal to be served. Once they had their food they moved directly to their assigned table, where Skeeter and Calvin were sitting. Skeeter dove into a pile of pasta and twirled the thin, white slippery noodles around his fork, then placed it in his mouth, chewed, swallowed, and turned and looked at Francis Bunnyard.

"Pass the ketchup, will ya, Bunny?"

"Here you go. Pasta is good today, isn't it?"

"Yeah, yeah just yummalicious . . . but it needs some help."

"It would be nice if just once they could serve up a meatball and some spaghetti sauce with it," said Zeb.

"Meatballs! How you going to make a goddamn meatball out of green baloney . . . you know that's all the meat we ever get around here," muttered Calvin.

Big Harold let out a loud baritone laugh. Zeb noticed Patrick staring at the tin metal tray in front of him, slowly moving his food around with his fork, not wanting to eat. "You up for some round ball this afternoon, Mr. Patrick? We got hard-driving-to-the-hoop Harold here, and there's his main man Bunny, whose been known to be super fly under pressure, and then over here we've got the speedy Gonzaleses of the half court, Skeets and Calvineo. They've all been just chomping at the bit, waiting to show this ol' man how fresh their legs are and how I am *way* past my prime. How about you and me take um on, huh, Mr. Patrick? What do ya say?"

"I'd like that."

"Good," replied Zeb.

Harold smiled a big Cheshire Cat smile, exposing two of his upper front teeth that were made of fourteen-karat gold.

"Now Bunny," Harold said. "Listen up now . . . ya hear? As soon as you get outside, you get to working on them layups of yours. Youz got to remember you're the great *White Hope* of South Block. Ain't that right, y'all."

"Now you just hold on one minute there," replied Zeb. "Bunny's got some competition now. My man here, he's a force to be reckoned with. Aren't I right, Hoss?"

Patrick managed a slight smile and began eating his pasta, then paused. "Hoss. Huh . . . could that name be possibly used for identifying oversized white guys that can't dribble? Hand me that ketchup, will you?"

Big Harold let out another laugh.

"When I was a kid in Mississippi that's what we called good ol' white boys that were dependable."

"Well, all right then; Hoss it is," replied Patrick.

"*Right on*, my man Patrick."

The old Mercedes-Benz engine labored as the sedan climbed yet another series of mountain summits. Kaminski downshifted as faster cars passed them. "We're about three hours from home. How about we stop for lunch?"

"All right," replied Vincent.

Up ahead they saw a sign for the Mountain View Café, and Kaminski pulled in and parked. Vincent eased himself into a booth, while Kaminski went to wash up. He lifted the menu from the wooden rack where it stood along with the ketchup and mustard. Don returned and scooted into the booth opposite Vincent.

So . . . what do you think's better to have on this stretch: that four-door tank of mine or your Freightliner?" asked Vincent.

"It be nice if yours had a few more gears." Don took a menu. "What are you havin'?"

"I see they have hot beef sandwiches," replied Vincent.

"Think I'll have a cheeseburger and a chocolate shake."

The waitress came and they ordered. Vincent got the beef sandwich with mashed potatoes and gravy.

The ex-chopper pilot took an unopened hard pack of Marlboros out of his shirt pocket, smacked the end of the cellophane pack on the tabletop a few times, tore off the cellophane and opened the lid, then pulled out a cigarette and put it in his mouth. He lit it with an old Zippo lighter. Vincent saw that the chrome skin of the lighter was worn so thin he could see brass. He also saw what looked to him to be some sort of military emblem on the side of the lighter but it too was so worn, beaten up, and scratched that he could not make out what it clearly was.

"I can see you've had that for a very long time; what's the emblem say?" Vincent asked.

"Seventh Cavalry."

"Like in Custer's outfit?"

"Yeah. The army traded horses for Hueys."

Don sat smoking, holding the cigarette pencil wise in his fingers, flicking ash into a small black plastic ashtray, while keeping his eyes fixed steadily on the lighter—rubbing and opening and closing it. Then with the fleshy part of his thumb he began to slowly and deliberately rub the raised army insignia. "Are you all right?"

"I am all right."

"You haven't said a whole hell of a lot, Vin. Don't you think it may be good to talk about it?"

The waitress came, carrying a large round tray with the food and drinks, and stood still for a moment, staring at Kaminski. He moved the ashtray and she set the plates and glasses on the table, asked if she could bring them anything else, then left. They sat quietly and ate. Vincent mopped up the beef gravy with a Parker House roll. "I was hungry. Truth be told, I am far from being okay. But what the hell can I do about any of this wretched situation he's in?"

Kaminski sucked the last bit of chocolate shake out of his glass with his straw, then took out the pack of cigarettes from his shirt pocket and held the pack and the lighter in the same hand. He set them on the table and looked straight into Vincent's eyes.

"Been thinking about it. I can get him out."

"You know Don, as crazy as that sounds I think you could."

"Two things are critical. One, timing, and two, deflection. Calculating distances won't be difficult for time coordination, so the first one is just plain mathematics, and I think I have the answer to the second issue."

"Deflection. You mind telling me what you mean by that?"

"Bullets, Vin. If a round hits a hydraulic or fuel line, well, then all bets are off. But I think I can give us more time before they start shooting."

"You're crazy."

"I know I am, have been for long time, my friend; but hear me out."

Wallace looked around to see if anyone could hear them.

"What the hell, a good fantasy like this one is a good distraction from the reality of this fucking nightmare I've been dealing with. Go ahead . . . lay it on me—tell me about your deflection."

"Well, you see, we need something plausible that will make the guards hesitate. You know, keep um from firing once they see me touch down. We need a kind of Trojan horse thing, and here it is. I can liberate a medivac from Moreland Regional. They got this pretty, new white Huey with red crosses all over it. I met the pilot a while back. No sweat with getting my hands on that little honey. You'll see. Those guards, they'll think there's been some kind of accident or emergency and that, Vin, will be just the thing to give us the time we need to get him out and increase our odds of not getting shot all to hell. I saw them up there with their M-14s. Those aren't 5.56-caliber rounds. No sir. Those boys on the towers are old timers, they mean business using those 7.62 mm rounds; they'll tear a hole clear through the fuselage and do some major damage for sure. I know. Been there, done that, too many times. Been on the other side of an AK and don't it like much."

It was three forty-five, and four loud, rapid-firing horn blasts erupted from atop the atrium. All inmates were now expected to be in their cells before four o'clock. Just like every other day, men went into their five-by-nine-foot cells and stood facing the bars, waiting to be counted. To not adhere to this mandate would be a major violation of one of just many of Warden Klump's standing orders, and any violators would be swiftly sentenced to the hole for a week or sometimes longer. Les Plough's shift ended and the rookie Kowalski came on and marched up and down South Block's Level 2 catwalk, wearing his Waffen-SS-looking uniform and clenching a black baton and tapping on anything made of steel. Many months, if not years, of weight lifting had made his upper torso look abnormally large compared to his head and legs. He strutted from one end of the walk to the other in his short-sleeve shirt, which couldn't seem to contain his unnatural-looking, pumped-up chest and oversized biceps. Finally he stopped his parading when he came to the end of the catwalk and stood at his post next to the top of the stairs; one single deafening horn blast rang out and all cell doors opened simultaneously. Patrick moved out of his cell, then leaned over the railing, looking down at East Block Level 1. He saw ZZ talking with Highway.

When ZZ finished speaking, Highway lowered his head, turned, and faced his cell, and grabbed two bars with his hands. Head still lowered, he slumped slightly, standing motionless for a long time, then let go of the bars, stood up straight, slowly turned around, and stared at ZZ. He looked up at South Block Level 2 and saw Patrick.

"That son of a bitch," said Highway.

"You knew him, didn't you? You knew this Axel guy," replied ZZ.

"Yeah. I knew him all right. We rode together. We rode together for a hell of a long time, and that motherfucker up there killed him."

Patrick walked away from the railing and stood and faced Zeb's cell. "Told you I wasn't much of a dribbler."

"We did just fine, Hoss," replied Zeb. "There was a time though, I had the fastest moves and got to the boards pretty damn quick. I hate to admit it—I am feeling my age."

Zeb took his shirt off and stood at a sink no bigger than a shoebox and began to wash up. "I got to try to get this stink off me. You can come in if you want."

Patrick took a step forward, then paused and stepped back when he heard something he'd never heard before. He looked over to his left and saw Harold playing the harmonica in front of Bunny's cell. Patrick stood at the entrance to Zebadiah's cell, watching the big man with his enormous hands gracefully caressing the tiny chrome instrument and sliding it back and forth against his lips, doing his best to make the blues come alive. Kowalski walked by them and made an ignorant comment. Harold ignored him and played on. Patrick walked back into the cell.

"Hand me that towel over there, will ya?" said Zebadiah.

"Those two."

"Who?"

"Harold and Bunny."

"Yeah, what about um?"

"Playing basketball with them like we did today and just now seeing Harold making music . . . they're kind of an odd pair, but there's something . . ."

Zeb dried himself off and put on a clean T- shirt. "That something goes way back, Hoss."

Patrick stood quietly looking at a large poster on the wall next to Zeb's bunk of a tall, bearded black man in a long, flowing robe, strumming vigorously a worn, scratched-up guitar.

"You familiar with him?"

"No. Can't say that I am."

"That's my man Mr. Richie Havens. Saw the brother at Woodstock. I can lie here at night and look up at him and remember that day like it was just yesterday."

"Sounds like he made an impression on you, that day up there on Yasgur's farm.

"Were you there, Hoss?"

"No, I wasn't, but my home was in the same county: Ulster County. I lived about twenty miles away, in Moreland. That summer I was in Manhattan, working construction."

"That's too bad, Hoss. It was a *real blast*. Mr. Havens started the whole thing off. He was the first act onstage . . . can you believe that? There's this song he does . . . when you listen to it, it's . . . it's like he takes you to the place he's singing about.

You feel you're there. You know what I mean?"

"I think so."

"I liked it so much I learned some of the words."

"You're the getting man and a folk singer?"

"That's right . . . multitalented and handsome too, don't you think? Wait a minute. Be cool . . . I'll be right back."

A few moments later Zeb returned, then Harold appeared and stood at the entrance to the cell; Bunny was there, right by his side. There was not enough room in the cell for the four men to stand without pressing up against one another like smelts in a tiny tin container.

"All right. Whenever you're ready," said Zeb.

Harold put his blues harp to his mouth and started to play a hymn-like song. Zebadiah waited for the intro to end, then began to sing soulfully, melodically:

> *The rising smell of fresh-cut grass*
> *Smothered cities choke and yell with fuming gas*
> *I hold some grapes up to the sun*
> *And their flavor breaks upon my tongue.*
> *With eager tongues we taste our strife*
> *And fill our lungs with seas of life.*
> *Come taste and smell the waters of our time.*
>
> *And close your lips, child, so softly I might kiss you,*
> *Let your flower perfume out and let the winds caress you.*
> *As I walk through the garden, I am hoping I don't miss you*
> *If all the things you taste ain't what they seem,*
> *Then don't mind me 'cos I ain't nothin' but a dream.*

Harold's final notes ended gently.

"I've still got some more to learn," said Big Harold.

"You were right. For a while there . . . I was in another place far away," said Patrick.

"I think he's right about that, Hal. I can go places when I

hear you play your songs."

"Right on, right on, Bun man. Good-sounding words can do that," replied Harold. "Come on, let's go. It's almost suppertime."

"Chicken à la king tonight," Hal.

Harold shook his head and smiled and looked at Zeb and Patrick. "I don't know how he does it."

"It's a gift," said Zeb.

"Hell, ain't no gift at all; he's just got a nose on um like an old coon hound," replied Zeb.

"Thanks for the songfest," Patrick said as Harold and Bunny leave to go back to their cells.

"My pleasure. It's mighty fine to have another music lover on Level Two," replied Harold.

Patrick looked at Zeb. "You mind if I ask that question again?"

"I don't mind. I guess by now you can tell Bunny just ain't completely right."

"Yeah."

"Wasn't always like that though."

"What do you mean?"

"Francis Bunnyard was a twenty-year-old kid when he got here. Was from some backwater South Carolina place no one's ever heard of. His folks were sharecroppers. From what I could gather, they were as poor as they come. The two of them never were close back then, but Harold's from down that way, and from what I could tell, their families were kind of the same. Always being abused by the man. You know, always keeping um down keeping um in the place they was in."

"I heard that part of the South never really changed much."

"That's true for sure. Me getting to Philly when I did was a blessing—well, in some ways it was. For a long while Bunny had a hard time getting used to all this."

"At twenty . . . who wouldn't?"

"Don't need to get in too many details, but Bunny had some guys around him that wanted to get friendly—if you know what I mean. He did his best to protect himself, but this place can be really bad for some of the new young ones."

"You mean they raped him?"

"Yeah. Not just once, either. Sometimes you could see the blood that dripped down his backside through his pants."

"Jesus."

"One day Harold was near the stalls and walked in on them when it was happening. He turned into a raging bull and took all five of them on, but as he was kicking the shit out of those queens, Bunny fell and hit the side of his head on the edge of a sink. I know a good ol' boy in the infirmary who told me that when they carried him in, he saw some of Bunny's brain had leaked out the side of his head. Never been right since. So you see, Harold's been looking out for him. Guess he feels kind of responsible in some way. That's the *something* I was talking about when you asked."

"I know how that feeling works: guilt can be a motivator," replied Patrick.

"You had a visitor this morning."

"How did you know?"

"Harold told me. I asked him what was up when I saw Plough take you away."

"Yeah, my brother came down from Moreland."

"I bet you two were always pretty tight. No man knows your life better than a brother near your age. He can know who and what you are best than most anyone on the earth. A brother's a brother. Visitation, on the other hand—that cuts both ways. I've been here so long I can't remember the last time I had a visitor. But I can remember the first. In the beginning my sister came up from Mississippi to see me. It was nice to see her, but then later on it was not good. They have their world and we have ours. I found it best not to mix them two up with past memories and all that kind of thing. Too much for the old head to handle."

"Is that why you asked me to play basketball with you guys today? To get me to think about something else?"

"Hell no, Hoss; *shitttt*, I just wanted to see if you New-York white boys can jump, pass, and dribble with both hands."

"Hah ... I'd be glad if I could do that with one hand," replied Patrick. He started to leave, then paused. "That was decent of you Zebadiah. Thanks."

After supper Patrick was lying on his bed reading the book his brother had brought him when he sensed a close presence; he looked up from his father's first edition of *Le Morte d' Arthur* to see James Britton staring at him from the entrance to his cell.

"What can I do for you?" said Patrick.

"There's some news Mr. Payne has just received that concerns you. He thinks it would be useful for you to know this information and suggests that you come with me," replied the Terminator.

"That sounds kind of ominous."

"Huh? Ommina ... how's that?"

"Never mind. An evening out, you say? Damn. Now how can I pass this up? All right, by all means ... lead the way."

They went down the steps, across the divide to North Block Level 1, and continued walking past mostly occupied cells until they reached the next-to-the-last cell.

"Wait here," said Britton.

Britton walked to the end of the row and entered Payne's cell. A moment later he stepped out and motioned to Patrick to come over. Patrick walked in and saw Payne sitting at his table reading with his back to him. The Terminator moved in, turned around, and stood in the entrance to the cell at parade rest with his hands clasped behind his back, looking out across the divide toward South Block. Patrick waited, then coughed;

Payne turned around and looked up.

"Please, have a seat."

Patrick looked down at the little three-legged stool. The seat cover was padded and had an embroidered swastika.

"All right. Sure."

"I've become aware of some facts," said Payne.

"And I am to assume this involves me?"

"Usually it takes months or years to acquire enemies in prison. You, uh, well, may have set a new standard."

"Sounds like a standard I can do without," replied Patrick.

"I am the Aryan Brotherhood in here, Mr. Wallace. My *Order* keeps order, so to speak. The white race will never be undermined. Never. But that is not for discussion here at this time. I was hoping to bring you into our way of thinking, but unfortunately something has come to my attention today that, well, let's just say . . . time is of an essence, and I felt I needed to act now so that you might have a future—maybe even a future with us."

"Well, that's very kind of you."

"Kindness has nothing to do with it. This is about business and how *the Order* maintains command and control in this prison. The Aryan Brotherhood deals with many gang members from all over the country: LA, Chicago, Houston . . . our reach is extensive and permeates all prisons. There's a Hell's Angel in East block that goes by the name of Highway that got some news today from his second in command that has, well, how should I say this? It appears to me and my associates that he's about to do some damage. Normally, I wouldn't try to alter the intricate movements of the universe, but you see Highway is a savage. His tenure with the Hell's Angels is legendary. He exudes viciousness like no other I've seen. Over the years Warden Klump has had him in the hole for months at a time."

"I get the picture; the ultimate badass."

"Highway's real name is Thorval Saxon. I know him pretty well. We've done business together but he's a rogue element, so to speak. He's been known to be a subcontractor for other gangs and, well, the Brotherhood has tolerated him, more or less, because he gets results for us."

"I am still not clear on why you're telling me this now, but you certainly have my attention."

"Look. The warden has shared with me things about you and I believe you are someone that we can profit from."

"So what's the beef Saxon has with me?"

"His second, ZZ, was told today that you killed an Angel by the name of Axel up in some ice patch in Canada a couple years back. Seems Highway and this Axel grew up in the same foster home and did all kinds of nefarious things together, including running street gangs and becoming Hell's Angels. He's in for four consecutive life terms. Jimmy here . . . has been the only one to face him in a fight, and that ended in a draw."

The Terminator slowly turned his head, looked at Payne and uttered a grunt, then looked back across the huge chasm that separated the two cellblocks.

"He's kind of sensitive," said Payne. "Pride, Mr. Wallace— one of the seven vices we must all try keep in check. Now I don't know whether you killed this guy Axel or not, but that doesn't matter."

"Yes, I can see that. The die has been cast."

The single loud buzz sound from atop the atrium alerted both inmates and guards. It was nine forty-five, and men had fifteen minutes to return to their cells for head count and lockup.

"There's no such thing as life without fear or terror and the spilling of blood, Mr. Wallace. I never thought people could live in harmony with one another. On the outside I used to see people who would think that and I 'd look at them and say they've given up their souls and they were no more than slaves to an ideal that to me looks like weakness. The Order in here creates a species that devours and survives."

"I'll remember that," replied Patrick.

After finishing their lunch, Kaminski continued driving north toward the New York border. By early evening they had reached the summit of Bald Eagle Mountain and were now making the long descent down Route 15 toward the Susquehanna River and Moreland. Home was ten minutes away. They crossed over the Veterans Memorial Bridge and drove through town, continuing north a few more miles, then turned onto Freedom Lane and entered the Wallace estate. Driving down the graveled two-lane access road toward the main house, they noticed a Willys jeep in the semicircular car park adjacent to the main entrance to the house. As they came closer to the old, rusted-out World War II jeep, they could now see more clearly a man with long white hair that flowed down just past his shoulders slumped over the steering wheel.

"I think you're about to meet that Indian of yours, Vin," said Kaminski.

"Hope he's not dead."

They both got out of the car and when they slammed their doors shut, Henry Crow Horse sat up and looked out the driver's-side window. Vincent slowly walked over to the jeep and motioned for him to crank down the window, and the Indian complied with the nonverbal request.

"You all right in there?" asked Vincent.

"I am looking for a man named Wallace. You him?"

"Yes. I am Vincent Wallace."

"I knew your brother; my name's Henry. Henry Crow Horse."

"You're the man that sent me the note a while back."

"That's right."

Vincent looked over at the chopper pilot. "This is Don

Kaminski. Why don't you come inside and we can talk for a while?"

"That would be good. Never was much fond of night dampness. I am much obliged."

The retired sheriff slowly got out of the jeep and as he stood alongside the vehicle, Vincent could see that the right side of his body was somewhat contorted. When he looked at his face, he saw darkened, leathery skin with deep, furrowed lines in his cheeks and forehead, and when he looked into his eyes, they appeared bloodshot and ancient but also shiny and keenly aware and alert to all of his surroundings. The old man offered up his hand in friendship to Vincent, and Vincent shook his hand, then shut the door to the jeep. Kaminski and Wallace walked alongside the visitor and into the house. The floorboards creaked as they stepped into the foyer. Vincent pushed a button on a tarnished brass plate and faint lights in wall sconces came on and illuminated the ancestral hall. He closed the door, and he and Vincent removed their coats and placed them over the back of a hunt chair, concealing two pheasant etchings that were carved into its back. Henry Crow Horse kept his buckskin coat on, and together they slowly went down a cold hallway, past dimly lit oil portraits of forebears, and into the kitchen.

Vincent fixed coffee, then rummaged through the refrigerator and found a ring of German baloney. He put cups, plates, forks, and knives on the table. He opened the door to his larder and took out jars of pickles and mustard and placed them on the table, took the meat and put it on a cutting board that was in the middle of the table, then turned on the oven to warm the kitchen. When the pot stopped percolating, Vincent walked over to the table and poured the coffee into the cups and then sat down, joining the other two men, who had been quietly sitting at the table watching him maneuvering through the old-style, antiquated kitchen.

"Please help yourselves," said Vincent.

The Indian drank the coffee, then spoke. "Your brother, how is he?"

"Well, it's . . . look . . . um, may we call you Henry?"

"I see now how like your brother you are; both know so much about the honor of the past. The respect Patrick has amongst my people . . . he has many friends up north. Yes, I am Henry to you, and to you, Mr. Kaminski."

"Well, Henry; it's pretty coincidental that you ask . . . We just now saw him late this morning. Been to Pennsylvania. That's where he's been sent."

"When I awoke this morning, I had a strange feeling of urgency come over me that I could not shake from my head. Not sure if it's me getting on in years or the nature I've encountered over those years that moves deep within me, but that's why I am here. I have important news to share."

"Kaminski looked at Vincent, then back at the old man. "What is this news?" said Kaminski.

"A woman I know and trust reported to me that these men who visited our reservation . . . these Hell's Angels, they were, from Quebec, she overheard them saying they wanted to set Patrick up for a killing he did not do and that very soon a couple of bikers would be heading to that prison in Pennsylvania to communicate with a Hell's Angel inside to make sure Patrick was known to have been the killer."

"For what purpose? Why would anyone want to do such a thing?"

"Vin . . . remember those two at the gatehouse when we were pulling out of there?"

Vincent sat and stared for a moment at Henry Crow Horse, then turned and looked at his friend and back at the sheriff. His face became flushed and he hit the table with the bottom of his closed fist, then stood up.

"God damn it! My brother didn't kill anyone. He got put away for drug smuggling . . ."

"Easy."

"I got to get some air. This is just too damn . . ." He went out and shut the door. It was dark outside and cold, and a thin gray blanket of dampness seemed to roll over the land. He walked out onto the grass and stood slumped over with his head down like some supplicant to the bleakness of the night and to the sadness of the day that had just ended. When he raised his head he could see out toward Patrick's orchards and he stood there for a long time looking in the direction of his brother's cottage. What he loved in Indians was what he also loved in men like his brother and Don: the vital spirit and the ferment of the vital spirit that ran them. All his reverence and his admiration and all the leanings of his life were always for the straight shooter and fair minded and they would always be so and never be otherwise. Anger returned, and the taste for revenge swelled up strongly in him, and he felt his chest expand and contract as he breathed in and out, trying to regain his composure. He looked up into the night sky and saw a few planets and stars beginning to appear. He focused his eyes on a flickering Jupiter, taking deeper and deeper breaths, and slowly he became steady and clear minded. He turned around and went back into the house. He walked through the little mudroom and stepped into the kitchen.

"Who wants some more coffee?" asked Vincent.

"Are you all right?"

"I'm all right, Don. Now tell me, Henry, who the hell are these people?"

"I don't know, Mr. Wallace. I used to think they were the same ones we've always had to deal with coming and going through our reservation. They're not like the ones my pappy had to deal with back then in the twenties when they were running molasses for whiskey makin'. In the fifties it was cigarettes and liquor and I could manage them. Now they're runnin' dope, and these bikers from hell shoot first and ask no questions. I ain't sure we've seen people like these before;

they'll stop at nothing," said the old man.

"We're running blind here, but we've got to assume some-one in that prison has or will have been told that Patrick was involved in the death of one of these guys. It doesn't matter why or who right now, but we've got to get word to him ASAP. Is that how you see it?" said Kaminski.

"Yeah, you're right. I'll go back tomorrow and get word to him somehow." Said Vincent. Henry . . . why don't you stay here tonight?"

"That would be much appreciated, Mr. Wallace."

"Please, call me Vincent. You're more than welcome to drive down with me. The rules dictate we cannot see Patrick; inmates are allowed one visit a month."

It was after midnight. Patrick sat on the edge of his bed staring at the blank wall in front of him, trying hard not to think about Payne's message. Listening to the multitude of tonal sounds of snoring that were reverberating in all direc-tions helped redirect his thoughts, but thoughts of Highway kept pouring in. Out of the corner of his eye he saw a dark silhouette walking past his cell. It was Plough. The guard stopped, then turned around and stood in front of Patrick's cell. Patrick turned his head toward him but in the darkness he could not make out who it was.

"Can't you sleep tonight?" Plough asked quietly.

Patrick got up and walked to the bars. "It's you . . . the psychologist."

"Not yet," Plough replied.

"Pulling double shifts. That can't be good for class atten-dance."

"Kowalski called in sick."

"Sick? Huh."

"Actually I am glad you're up. Been wanting to ask you something ever since we got back up here from your visit."

"Well, as you can see, I am not going anywhere . . . ask away."

"That little book over there on your table; the one your brother brought you. Why did he bring that one to you? The Arthurian legends?"

"I think it started early on; maybe we were eleven or twelve years old. Both our parents were, well, kind of different, to say the least. We'd joke about it—called them parental units. They had some unusual ways of parenting."

"How so?"

"This part of your study?"

"Maybe."

"Well, they made sure that the teachings of the Episcopalian church came first, but then along came ancient Greece and mythology. Seemed Vincent and I couldn't get enough of the myths. I think our parents found them to be a way to communicate with us that made them feel more comfortable around us, or maybe that's how they were brought up. There were never any televisions in the house. Storytelling was what we had."

"I studied the legends in my freshman year."

"What school did you go to?"

"Bob Jones; the Seminary school."

"You're a man of the cloth?"

"Used to be. Not anymore."

"Speaking of stories; if you don't mind me saying . . . that's got to be a pretty big story to be carrying around. You feel like filling in the particulars?" said Patrick.

"Hey. I thought I was the headshrinker around here."

"Didn't mean to overstep any boundaries. It's just that I can't sleep and a story just might do me some good. Got some things on my mind."

"Want to talk about it?" said Plough.

"I'll tell you what, you go first."

"All right. Why not? You're looking at someone who walked away from something my ancestors did for five generations;

the patriarchs were all preachers. My life was planned from the time I was born."

"What made you quit?"

"I had this nice little congregation in Uniontown; it's about a two-hour drive from here. It's a small steel town on the Monongahela River near the West Virginia border. Simple, poor mountain people in need of some spiritual reassurance. I was their man, all right. Had a wife and three kids."

"Had?"

"I am divorced now. But getting back to your question. In November of sixty-five I buried a nineteen-year-old boy by the name of Edward Grover Castle Jr. He was killed at the Battle of Ia Drang, in Vietnam. After his body was put in the ground and the earth shoveled over him, his father took me aside and with tears in his eyes looked at me and asked me why. What did he die for? I could not answer him; I had no answers. The next day I read in the paper about a Quaker man from Erie who sat down in front of the Pentagon, doused himself with kerosene, and set himself on fire to protest the war. I sat at my kitchen table and saw pictures on the refrigerator of my wife and children, and at that moment I decided I needed to . . . well, I needed to think long and hard about all of what was coming down around me. Something just gave way in me."

"What was that?"

"Faith. I had none. And when it left me, Mr. Wallace, I knew it was time to find another vocation. But first I needed a job and this one came along. Then after some time I realized that being a humanist with an education in theology, psychology just might be a better fit for me. So here I am talking to you in the middle of the night, going to night school, paying alimony and child support, trying my best to make sense of all I've seen and felt."

"Do you think you might have an answer for the dead boy's father now?"

"When I saw that book your brother gave you I had a flashback to when it was discussed and analyzed at Bob Jones. At first read, the knights seemed so determined."

"You mean their belief in God and the true meaning of the Grail quest?"

"Yeah. That's right," said Plough.

"Do you believe in God? You know, an all-knowing, all-seeing power in heaven? A God of love? A God that sees all?"

"I don't like to use the term *God*. I do want to believe there's holiness in everyone . . . human holiness. Everything else is just power plays, masks, expressions, and hocus-pocus. I don't think you can ever really understand what human holiness is, but it's something to cling to . . . something obtainable, lasting until your time is up. What happens to us then when we become worm food, we don't know, do we? Poets, preachers, musicians, and saints . . . they're the ones that get a glimpse into what we cannot discern . . . the inconceivable. They see and understand it sometimes but not always—bits and pieces maybe. For me, it's a comfort to think about human holiness. The warden . . . when you first got here, he gave you the Old Testament to read, didn't he?"

"Yeah, I started to read it the other night," replied Patrick.

"There's a good reason why he didn't want you to read Matthew, Mark, Luke, and John. There's no attainable love here. Agape maybe, if you're lucky. But what Jesus preached can only be found outside of this prison. What did Dostoevsky say . . . 'What's hell? The condition of not being able to love.' That's what this prison is all about."

"Whenever the word *love* came up in conversation Vincent would say, 'Love is for poets.'"

"Did your brother ever tell you what he meant by that?"

"We grew up with books. All kinds. The Grail quest, I think, was something our father wanted for us to see as something noble. A code to live by. Love was perceived as a weakness. We were taught to be Spartans. As I got older, I began to look at how Indians see nature and how they rely on their instincts; I still believe in that. I think he meant that love started with the Renaissance, at least the way we think of love—you know, courtly love with chivalry and all that."

"Yeah, that's how I pretty much see it too, but in that same time period it was realized that rationality could solve our problems," replied Plough.

"You're talking about control, aren't you?"

"Well, it's my understanding, after taking all these psych courses, that the ability to reason is only half of it."

"What's the other half?"

"The unconscious has always guided us, and I think those Indians of yours have always understood it and have lived and died using what they know—the nature around them—and to trust their instincts. The medicine man or shaman could tap into it, and when he did, he could be a helper ... a guide."

"Like a psychologist, huh."

"And then you have the legend of Parzifal and the myth of the Fisher King," replied the guard.

"Ah ... the wounded king and Parzifal, who comes into his kingdom and helps to save him from himself. Vincent and I read it more than once."

"It's been a long time since I read it, but I remember the story pretty well; it's about a young prince who goes out into the forest to prove his courage so he could become king. If my memory is right, the forest is a metaphor for showing the connection with the unconscious and this connection gave him his naturalness and innocence with all the spontaneity and natural warmth and openness that goes with a young boy growing up. During the day he walks out of the woods and goes fishing and catches a salmon, then comes back and makes a fire. Now, while he is spending the night alone in the forest, he's visited by a sacred vision and out of the fire appears the Holy Grail, the symbol of God's divine grace. Suddenly a voice says to him, 'You shall be keeper of the Grail so that it may heal the hearts of men.' But for a split second he's blinded by greater visions of a life filled with power, glory, and beauty. In his heightened state of radical astonishment he feels for a brief moment not like a kid, but he feels invincible, like a god, so he starts to grab for the Grail and the Grail suddenly disappears, and when he comes too close to the fire, he is wounded. His wounding, when it came by fire . . . now, that symbolizes the spirit. Then a little later he tastes a piece of fish . . . and that symbolizes wisdom and knowledge. The fire, the spirit, is encountered within the forest, and like Adam and Eve in the garden, the knowledge the prince experienced in the unconscious caused his fall from innocence. How am I doing, so far, Mr. Wallace?"

"Yeah, more or less, that's how we came around to thinking about it," replied Patrick.

"The wound of the young prince drives him away from the fire and wisdom of the divine in fear, repelling him from the one object which might heal him, the Grail, which of course symbolizes the love of God, which has poured out for him. His inability to approach the Grail keeps him separated from God and constantly cold, or without feelings. His inability to accept his unconsciousness-based feeling function separates him from his own divine origin and source."

"Whoa, now hold on there . . . his unconsciousness-based feeling function! That's some kind of new territory for me. I learned a long time ago that when you stay too long in your own head, you're behind enemy lines."

"Yeah, I like that, 'behind enemy lines,' that's true, but that's the psych stuff I am learning. You've heard the saying he 'stood too close to the fire.'"

"That's what happened to the young lad—got his groin burned," replied Patrick.

"In this myth that burning symbolizes the loss of his ability to create. I learned that the left side of the brain is where we analyze and do mathematics; that's our rational world. Few if any of us have personal encounters with the divine in our left-brained, rational, material world. The divine is encountered through occurrences of the irrational, the unexplainable, the unconscious. That's what the medicine men and shamans of ancient tribes understood; they connected with the right sides of their brains. The force and power of such encounters are most often totally overwhelming. In the old days, such experiences were referred to as 'standing too close to the fire,' and these occasions have led to fear and insanity, as it did for Neitzche, so modern man fears control by his own unconscious, which he experiences as a manifestation of divinity."

"Ahhh . . . and that's where our errant knight Parzifal comes in. He and his brothers, they've gone into the business of knighthood; defending the faith with their swords and lances . . . fighting for what's right and good and against wrong and evil," said Patrick.

"Yes . . . and as the boy grew older and became king, his wound grew deeper, and one day, life for him lost its reason. He had no faith in any man, not even himself. He couldn't love or feel loved. He was drunk with freedom and sick with experience. The only pastime that could relieve his pain was fishing in the lakes and ponds near his castle; his fishing of course symbolizes him seeking the unconscious for understanding and help."

"Of course," said Patrick.

"But no help comes. Time stands still, and the king and everyone around him loses their substance as they become less material, as life slowly fades away for them. They are near death for much of their existence, yet cannot die. So the people of the Grail castle await a savior. Then one day a young, innocent squire training to be a knight, our young Parzifal, comes on the scene and finds the Fisher King fishing. The king tells him how to get to his castle, and in the evening Parzifal witnesses a parade and the healing of the sick. But unaware of how things are and lacking confidence in himself, he does not ask anyone why the king does not receive healing nor what the Grail is or how it can heal. In the morning he realizes it's too late and saw his mistake and goes off and spends the next twenty-five years fighting in battles. Then he realizes that all his life fighting for king and faith has been a waste of his life and he now clearly sees the suffering he has inflicted on others. By the time he's reached middle age he realizes that the way he's lived his life has all been a mistake. And then, Mr. Wallace, fate brings him back to the Fisher King. And once again he is invited into the castle, but this time he asks the question, who does the Grail serve? Parzifal wants to know, he needs to know how his own misery can be stopped and how the king's wound can be healed and how he can find meaning to his life. And the answer comes: serve the Grail King! Serve something greater than yourself."

"And in order to heal ourselves of our own wound, we have to serve something greater than ourselves and to do it freely and openly—not because of some kind of guilt," said Patrick.

"You sound like a man who knows something about guilt and being wounded," replied Plough.

"I can't go behind enemy lines, at least not just yet; how about finishing your story?" replied Patrick.

"All right, here's how I see it. For men, today, their most pernicious wound is the wound of the Fisher King . . . its cost is the loss of feeling of value. No material things . . . money, success, women, cars, homes can heal the wound. It is a wounding of the very capacity for feeling. But a man's wound and his pain can also be his teacher, for it gets him ready for an awakening to his mistaken way of living. None of us can escape the pain so long as we are overly rational, power hungry, exploitative, unfeeling, and selfish. When we've had enough of the pain, we'll be like Parzifal. We'll ask ourselves, who does the Grail serve? What will it take to stop all of this pain? What am I doing; why can't I make my life work? And then, Mr. Wallace, just like Parzifal, we'll see that the Grail serves the Grail King. In order to heal ourselves of our own wound, we must serve something greater than ourselves. Each of us is the Grail, the Fisher King, and Parzifal. We are the healers who must heal ourselves. We are the seekers of knowledge and wisdom who must face our own fear of who and what we are and grant ourselves love and unconditional acceptance, and we must go stumbling through life, learning by trial and error, mistake after mistake, until we recognize that the way we see ordinary life is an illusion filled with pain. We have the power to heal ourselves; we only have to ask the question, who does the Grail serve? And when we do that, we're ready to ask ourselves the most important question any of us can ask, how is life to be lived? What is it that gives life meaning and purpose and beauty?"

They stood quietly. After a while Patrick said. "Years ago my parents died in a plane crash. You lost your faith when you buried that soldier; I completely lost my way when they didn't come back from their trip to Africa."

"That's a lot to be carrying around. You want to . . . like you said, 'fill in the particulars'?" replied Plough.

"Go behind enemy lines?"

"We have time."

"Well, all right. You did go first and I do try always to do what I say I am going to do. All right, here goes. It actually started long before their plane went down. Back in seventy-one, when I worked in Manhattan. I was part of a crew that put together the World Trade Center and that crew consisted of Mohawk men from the St. Regis Reservation; those guys walked on beams and superstructure like no others could or would. Fearless, they were. These Indians from up around the Saint Lawrence built the tallest bridges and buildings in the world, and I was accepted into their crew; I was accepted into the brotherhood of Skywalkers. In sixty-eight I learned about the Twin Towers and I knew how to weld. You see, those towers had two hundred thousand tons of steel in them, and I wanted to put together something grand and lasting, and wanted to stand a quarter of a mile up in the sky and be part of something bigger than anything ever built before. The Koch Erecting Company had developed a way to erect those buildings using these massive-looking things called kangaroo cranes that were placed on top of the completed infrastructure. There were four cranes on each building and they lifted the panels and belly bands of steel up and into rough position, then gangs of plumbing-up men—ironworkers—set them in place. Each one of those cranes could lift thirty-five tons a day, and they needed hundreds of welders to secure all that metal to metal.

"That's certainly a 'heavy load,'" said Plough.

"Did you ever do anything you were ashamed of to the point where you would never tell anyone?"

The guard thought about the question. "Yeah, I'd have to admit . . . yeah; I've been there, he said."

"This is hard."

"Take your time."

"We were on the ninety-ninth floor of Tower Two, which was eleven floors directly below a kangaroo on the side of the building where we could look over and see Tower One. You could count the remaining floors just by looking across the divide. Eleven more and the center would be finished. We'd been on the ninety ninth for a couple of weeks. Lunch break was over and clouds were just starting to come in from the west, but visibility was still good. I noticed some winds were picking up but no horns sounded to stop work. There were a dozen of us on the floor, but I was far away and out of sight of the others when I started to begin preliminary work on accepting a treetop from the kangaroo . . . this thing that looked like a giant tuning fork. I was with a man I'd spent the last two years of my life with—every day we worked side by side together, welding and fabricating, and we shared a tiny apartment in the Village with four other men from his tribe. We were a tight-knit crew."

Patrick raised his hands upward, grabbing the bars to his cell, then lowered his head. "I . . . no. No, I don't think I can do this."

"You don't need to if . . ."

"His name was Joseph. Joseph Skywalker. The first ever in his tribe to be given that surname. The operator patiently sat at his controls, waiting for my signal, and when he started his final move to lower the tree, the thing just started to sway and twist out of control and . . ."

"It's all right, Mr. Wallace—Patrick—just let it come."

"I flew backwards into him and . . ."

Plough placed his hands on Patrick's clenched fists and he released his tight grip he had around the bars but kept them there. The guard did not let go. Patrick raised his head and looked straight into the guard's eyes.

Plough could see tears, and listened as Patrick's voice weakened.

"He had ahold of my ankle and then . . . the next thing I know he just, he just went down and the net caught him, but the way he fell into it . . . well, it didn't save him."

Patrick backed away from the cell door and sat on his bunk and leaned forward and cupped his head in his hands.

"It was a terrible accident . . . you couldn't've . . ."

He raised his head and looked in the direction of the guard. "That's not it. No." He got up and stood in front of the cell door and looked at Plough. "I've never . . ."

"It's all right, it's okay," replied Plough.

"I pulled myself up and quickly turned and lay flat on my stomach and looked down at him and I stretched my arms down over the edge, pretending to reach for him, then they all came running from the other side of the floor and surrounded me, and they looked and saw him there, all curled up motionless in the net. I lay there and didn't move. I couldn't move. They thought, they really thought I tried to hold on to him but I didn't. I didn't try to do that . . . it never even entered my mind to try."

"You wanted to live."

"Yeah, sure, I wanted to do just that, but that's not how I played it. They all thought something else. They were convinced I had tried and I didn't do a thing to make them think any differently."

"You did what you had to do to survive."

"I don't see it that way, no sir . . . not one bit. I am a liar. I am nothing but a God damn liar. And you know what happens to guys like me? You're looking at it. And I won't be looking for the Grail anytime soon. Liars have to pay what they owe."

"Do you think maybe you've paid enough for that? I mean . . . look around at all this."

"This? This is nothing. This is all lawful. You know what the biggest curse is? To be a coward and to see that and be reminded of it each morning when you look in the mirror. You've been kind to me tonight and I appreciate all you've said, but you have your work to do now and I am . . . I am going to try to get some sleep. I got this feeling tomorrow will be a hard day—could even be a day of atonement."

"What do you mean?"

"Ahhh, it's just that my past never wants to let me just . . . be. I'll have to leave it at that. Maybe someday I'll see the Grail, huh? Look, I want to thank you. You know, Doc . . . I think you're going to be one hell of a headshrinker someday. I am grateful you took an interest in me. Good night, Doc."

"Good night," said Plough and he turned away from Patrick's cell and walked along the catwalk, down the steel stairs to continue his duties on Level 1 of South Block.

Lieutenant Miller made his way to the main panel and slammed the disconnecter lever upward into place, and all the electrical boxes engaged loudly; lights come on and Patrick opened his eyes. A horn sounded and his cell door uncoupled and slid to one side. Bunny was first to come out. Across the divide in East Block Level 1, ZZ stepped out and walked past a half dozen inmates and into Highway's cell.

Thirty minutes passed.

A buzzer sounded; the morning meal procession was underway.

"You got it down? You ready?" asked Highway.

"Sure, I am ready," replied ZZ.

"Good. No fuck-ups, you hear? Let's go," said Highway.

ZZ returned to his cell, got in line, and they began to move forward.

On the opposite side, in South Block Level 2, Bunny turned toward Harold, who was standing in his cell entrance.

"We're going to have our eggs today, Hal," Bunny announced.

Zeb, standing at the railing, looked at Harold. Harold shook his head a few times and smiled.

"At least they're not powdered," said Zeb.

"Line up . . . move," barked Kowalski.

Skeeter and Calvin began to march. Bunny followed Calvin, Patrick fell in behind Harold, and Zeb followed, with Kowalski prodding Bunny with his baton as they walked down the catwalk toward the stairs.

"No talking, egg boy," said the guard.

Patrick entered the hall, got his tray, and moved down the line. The server scooped up some scrambled eggs from a big stainless-steel container and plopped them down on his tray, then ladled some grits alongside the eggs. Because it was Sunday, hot biscuits and gravy came at the end of the line. He got his coffee and moved to his table and stood for a moment, peering over at Payne and the other North Block inmates, who were all seated a few rows away. Payne looked up from his tray and stared back at him, then slowly turned and glanced at Highway and ZZ and went back to eating his breakfast. Patrick finally sat down and took a sip of coffee.

"You seem like you're kind of preoccupied with something this morning," said Zeb.

"Who, me?" replied Patrick.

Kowalski walked by the table, then made his way toward the Aryan Brotherhood section of the chow hall. He stood against the wall directly behind Payne.

"Look at that puffed-up pecker head. Did you see how that cracker poked our man?" said Harold.

"I know what I'd like to do with that baton of his," said Zeb.

"His ass is too tight for that thing . . . you could never pry it into that natzzzzzzee prick bastard," replied Harold.

"Look at him standing there, next to those ABs . . . he's on their payroll for sure," said Skeeter.

"They keep g'tting' their dough from selling that new crack shit," replied Calvin.

"And our brothers are buying it . . . that's starting to piss me off," said Skeeter.

Bunny turned to Patrick. "After breakfast I've got cart detail."

"Oh yeah," replied Patrick.

"Mr. Rishel got put into the infirmary Friday . . . he's pretty old, you know. You know what he did?"

"No, what did he do?"

He put in a good word for me with the warden. I get to go to the library after breakfast and get Mr. Rishel's cart and give out the books and magazines. I'll be just like the mailman. There's really two carts, you know."

"I didn't know that."

"Yep. One for each top level. I have to put the stuff in this thing they call a dumbwaiter, and then it gets lifted up to the top floors, and then I unload all of it onto the cart. Don't have to do that on the first level. There's just one cart down there."

"I see. Sounds like a good way to manage all that."

"Sure hope Mr. Rishel gets better soon."

"Me too, Bunny. He's a good man."

"Patrick."

"Yeah?"

"Why does that guard act that way—always being mean to us?"

Harold and Zeb looked at Patrick. "I don't know, Bunny. Some guys just plain enjoy making trouble for others."

"You mean he can't help himself?"

"Yeah. That's right. He's defective," replied Patrick.

"There's good defective and bad defective," replied Bunny.

"How's that? What do you mean?" asked Harold.

"I know I am not right inside—I'm a good defective . . . I don't do bad things to people."

"You ain't no defect," declared Harold.

Patrick put his hand on Bunny's shoulder. "You got to listen to Harold; he's right."

"It's all right, you guys. Don't think I don't know how it is . . . how I am. But what's his excuse?"

A half hour later a horn sounded, indicating breakfast was over, and Kowalski marched them back to their cells. Lieutenant Miller stood in between North and South Blocks on a spotless, shiny concrete floor and looked down at his clipboard, then he yelled, "COUNT."

At each level a guard shouted out an inmate's name, got a reply, then put a check next to the name on his clipboard.

Roll call ended, and the Lieutenant walked over to his control station, pressed a button. A buzzer sounded. An hour passed. Patrick completed his morning routine, then stepped out of his cell and stood next to the railing and looked down across the divide to see nothing out of the ordinary except for Kowalski leaving the vicinity of ZZ's cell. Many of the prisoners were staying put, but some went to shower, while others who had pod time headed to one of the four pod rooms adjacent to each cellblock. He saw Harold and Zeb in their cells, lying on their bunks, and Bunny standing in the entrance to his cell, eagerly waiting for someone to take him to the library. Out of the corner of his right eye he noticed Kowalski walking down the catwalk, coming toward him, then saw him suddenly stop at Bunny's cell.

"All right . . . let's go, mail boy," said Kowalski.

He watched them as they walked toward the stairs, when suddenly something inside of him seemed to forcibly grab his thoughts, urging him to follow them. He headed down the catwalk—past Skeeter and Calvin, then down the steps—and peered around the corner of East Block and watched them pass pod rooms and the chow hall. He kept following, never losing sight of them and being careful to stay out of range of Kowalski's peripheral vision. They entered a series of dark, narrow connecting hallways, then suddenly the guard stopped, looked around, turned into another black, cavernous hall, and disappeared, leaving Bunny standing alone in a dimly lit alcove behind the prison trades shop. He heard the sound of a latch and could see a steel door slowly opening; before he could utter a word, Bunny was out of sight. His heart pounding and his mouth dry, he raced through the doorway and there he was, face to face with Highway, who had Bunny in a half nelson. Before Patrick Wallace could make any kind of move from behind the door, ZZ laid into him with a pipe that missed his head but caught him squarely on the lower portion of his neck and shoulders. He was bent over, and ZZ leaped into the air and slammed both knees against the back of his spine. The two of them went to the floor. Highway dropped his captive down hard on the floor, rendering him unconscious.

Like a wounded grizzly bear, Patrick rose up and sent ZZ flying across the tool room, where he ended up face-first with his nose split apart by the butt end of a table vice. Highway stepped over Bunny, then grabbed a hammer and swung it at Patrick's head. Patrick saw it all unfold slowly in front of him: the hammer coming directly at his eyes. He rolled backward, ending up against the table. Highway lunged once again but missed, plunging the hammer into the table. He grabbed his wrist and pounded it several times on the table's surface; the weapon dropped to the floor. With his free left hand the Hell's Angel gouged Patrick's eye and hit him hard with his right fist on the jaw. Patrick stepped back and was up against the wall.

Highway seemed surprised. Patrick ran his tongue into the corner of his mouth and tasted blood. He knew his eye had been bludgeoned and felt wetness coming down his cheek. Highway stepped back and pulled a knife from his belt, and before he could react, Patrick was cut across the outside of his forearm and upper chest. Highway moved the knife with incredible speed. The knife came across Patrick Patrick's chest again, then hacked deep into his abdomen. The room swirled. He slowly dropped to his knees, then slumped forward into the arms of an enemy he never knew.

Highway whispered into his ear. "That's for Axel."

Bunny regained consciousness. Awake but dazed, he could make out Highway standing over Patrick, who lay still with his eyes closed. He got to his knees, crouching. He fell and got up again. Kneeling, he pushed against the ground to rise, then began to run. Running through the maze of darkened corridors and hallways, he entered the kitchen of the chow hall, made his way past the East Block, then up the South Block stairs past Skeeter and Calvin, and stopped when he got into Big Harold's cell. Harold was sitting on his bed.

"Come. Come quick." Bunny wheezed, gasping for breath, then fell to one knee.

Harold got up, bent down, and looked at Bunny. "What.

What happened?"

Skeeter and Calvin ran down the catwalk and into the Big Harold's cell. Calvin yelled out, "Zeb . . . get in here."

Zeb ran into the cell.

Harold helped Bunny to his feet. "Tell me. What happened?"

"Patrick. He's hurt. He's down."

"Where is he?"

"I am not sure. But we got to go . . . we got to get him."

"Tell me where he is."

Bunny bent over and put his hands on his knees, gasping for air.

"Think. Try to remember . . . where's Patrick?" Harold asked once more.

"Tools. Saws. Workbenches."

"Sounds like the shop. Let's go," said Zeb.

VII

*D*ays turned into weeks. I could hear but not understand the vague sounds from around my hospital bed. I was alive but for some strange reason could not rejoin the living. There was no day or night but just an acknowledgment of my respiration, and if I tried hard I could make out the distinct sound of my heart beating quietly, rhythmically, in concert with my breaths. No thoughts could be conjured up. A feeling of complete and utter inadequacy floated in and over me. Suddenly I was plucked out of a vast blue sky and placed on a great and beautiful Midwestern prairie of wild grasses that flowed like ocean waves, weaving back and forth and around me, gently caressing me with whirling breezes that blew from all directions. Then all at once the winds stopped and a Buffalo gently nudged my back with her forehead and nose.

"Where do you want to go?" she asked.

"I don't know," I replied.

"That can be a good start."

She turned sideways and looked at me, then, straining her neck,

looked up at the sky, and I followed her lead, and together our eyes
saw a solitary crow, slowly circling overhead.

He woke in a dimly lit white room. He raised his hand and
touched the top of his hip bone and felt pain across his belly.
Slowly he put his hand down. He wondered if he might be
approaching death, and in a moment of urgency and grief, he
felt a deep surge of sadness fall upon him like a waif starting
to cry. It drew pain into him so he began to slowly and me-
thodically breathe, counting each breath, over and over until
a calmness came to him and the pain subsided. He turned his
head to the right. He tried to adjust his eyes to what seemed
like twilight to him. There was someone there. He could sense
him and he focused until he saw a silhouette.

Henry?

Henry Crow Horse put an index finger to his lips and
whispered, "Welcome back."

Holding two coffee cups, Vincent walked past the nurses'
station toward where a guard sat just outside the entrance to
an intensive care room. He passed the guard and went into
the room and saw Henry bending over his brother's bedside,
then saw his brother's eyes were open. Excitement and joy
flooded his senses. He stood still and restrained himself, then
walked quickly to the other side of the bed and leaned over
and looked into his brother's eyes.

"You were always a fast healer, brother Patrick."

"Vincent . . . that you?"

"Shhhhh . . . yeah . . . it's me, buddy. There's a rent-a-cop
just outside and . . ."

"But Vin."

"You've got to lie still and be quiet . . . hold on."

Vincent handed the cups to Henry Crow Horse, then turned
and cocked his head toward the entryway and motioned with
his eyes. Henry took the coffee and sauntered up next to the

guard and handed him a cup.

"Thanks, Chief.

"You think the Eagles can beat Washington tomorrow?" Henry asked.

"EAGLES! Every time I watch them they lose. They stink. Pittsburgh . . . now that's a first-rate class-act team."

"I see you have a paper there. What do they say about tomorrow? I thought Bradshaw was on the injured list."

The guard turned and picked up the paper off the floor and started to rifle through the pages, looking for the sports section. With his free hand Henry reached behind his back and slid a glass partition closed, while Vincent rolled down the blinds.

There. Now we're set. We don't have a lot of time. "Man. it's good to see you awake. How do you feel?"

"Stomach's tender—some pain, but it's okay."

"Look, as soon as that nurse comes in here and sees you're out of that coma. you'll be sent to the prison infirmary."

"So?"

"I brought you another book. See? It's on the nightstand there. You must take it with you."

"All right, but what's so important about that one?"

"Inside the back cover . . . you're going to have to carefully peal the fabric off . . . are some plans."

"Plans? For what?"

"Your escape."

"Escape!"

"Yeah."

"You got to be kidding."

"Nope. I am dead serious, brother. Don and I and your Indians have it all down. It's a plan that will not fail."

"One minute I am in a Nebraska field with a lady Buffalo, and now I am here with you, talking about getting out of the Big House. I must be still dreaming.

"This isn't a dream. Don's going to fly you out."

"From here?"

"No. No. You got to heal first. When you're fully patched up, Don will pick you up in the yard. The toughest part of this is where to put you once you're out, but Henry's on top of that."

"Well, that's certainly good to know."

"This Highway guy."

"Yeah."

"Well, he's not going to stop until . . ."

"Yeah. I know. How do you know about him?"

"It was Henry at first; came to us with the facts, but it's this fella Les Plough who's been talking to me about Highway."

"Plough?"

"Yeah. He's been here checking on you just about every day."

"Well, I'll be damn."

"You just lie there and rest and let me fill you in on how it's going to go down."

The phone rang in the kitchen at the Hell's Angel's safe house. Martha turned down the flame under a cast-iron skillet that was overflowing with half-cooked bacon, then picked up the receiver.

"Hello. Who's this?" she said.

She listened.

"It's Eddy Brown," shouted Martha.

"All right, I am coming," replied Mom.

The leader of the Quebec Hell's Angels left Razor standing on the steps to the rear entrance of the kitchen.

She handed him the phone.

"Uh-huh. Really. He's here now."

He hung up the phone, shook his head, then sat down at the kitchen table and said to Razor, "Come on in."

Razor sat down opposite him. Martha finished frying the bacon, then whisked some eggs around in a glass bowel and dropped them into the heavy black pan.

"You're getting scrambled," she said.

Razor quickly looked up at Mom, then he looked over at

the blonde's small, tight acorn-shaped ass and back at Mom.

Mom looked at Martha, shook his head and smiled, then looked back at Razor.

"With those legs . . . she can have all that attitude she can muster up. After breakfast how about we go for a ride?"

"You got any particular place in mind?"

"Let's just head out and see what comes our way . . . maybe we'll go out toward St. Regis," said Mom.

They ate and drank the last of the coffee.

Mom wiped his mouth with a paper towel, pushed back his chair, then rose. "Come on . . . let's go," he said.

After an hour on the road, shadows of clouds were beginning to give way to more sunlight. As the bright sun broke through the veil of overhead grayness, the cool air and early-morning dampness quickly disappeared. The big Harleys flew down single lanes with straight pipes blasting out monstrous sounds that cracked like thunder, then echoed outward against houses that were close to the road. When the exhaust sounds hit the house walls it made another crackling sound loud enough to wake the dead. Coming out of Ville-Marie, past Trois Rivieres, they rolled on to Route 37 and rode south, parallel to the Saint Lawrence River. It was early June and the light-brown muddy-colored river was still flowing fast, a final reminder of the long Canadian winters that had to be endured year after year. They rode on through valleys of hemlock growing higher up on the hills, past a gorge, on to a barren wind gap, and parked among the rocks. They looked out over the country to the south, where the Mohawks of the Akwesasne occupied Cornwall, Ontario, to Rooseveltown, New York, and down to the town of Massena.

"I don't know what it is about that reservation down there," Mom said.

"Maybe it's the name . . . St. Regis . . . don't sound Indian to me."

"When I was a boy I knew all about them. Started with them

cultivating maize around 1000 AD . . . the first ones were all around the Great Lakes. Cartier and Champlain wrote about them. They shared a culture with other Iroquoian groups but they had a language of their own, called Laurentian. Then a stronger Mohawk group came up from the South and waged war against the Saint Lawrence Iroquoians to get control of the fur trade and hunting along the river valley. By 1600 some mixed Iroquois like the Mohawk, Oneida, Onondaga, and Seneca had migrated from New York, and there was a Catholic mission set up in that village right there. Many converted. That's how it ended up with the name. Come on, let's sit over here for a while."

They walked back from the rock ledge and sat on a downed ash log.

"There's something I want to talk to you about. That guy you found out about . . . the one that killed your brother—did you know he was attacked last month?"

"Yeah. Eddy told me what happened to him and who he was. Actually . . . I think I may have met him once."

"Who? The guy who cut up your brother's killer?"

"Yeah."

"Huh. Small world, isn't it?"

"When Axel and I got sent away to different foster homes I'd sometimes go visit him. This guy Highway and him were tight. Really tight, you know. Thorval is his real name. Guess I owe him a debt of gratitude. Don't really matter how the bastard got it . . . payback—it's a motherfucker, ain't it? Wish I could have done it myself . . . you know . . . for Axel."

"That phone call I got back at the house . . . that was Eddy. He just heard from an inmate friend of his down there in Pennsylvania . . . the guy survived."

Razor got up and walked back to the rock ledge and stood there looking out on Indian territory. Mom sat watching him and waited. When Razor didn't move for a while, he got up and slowly sidled up next to him.

"What do you see down there?" asked Mom.

"I don't think I see what you see," replied Razor.

"I suppose you're right. You see a place where your brother was taken away from you by an evildoer. All I see . . . all I care about is holding on to the power I got, and that chief who lives way over there by that lake—it's his greed I am counting on to keep me on top. We're untouchable down there . . . thanks to him."

"I think I'd like to talk with this friend of Eddy's," said Razor.

"I'll arrange that. But think about this: all the time you put into getting something back . . . trying to make a wrong thing right . . . well, remember, there's only so much time to go around. In our line of business . . . time's a luxury you can't afford to waste."

"Look. You made me head of your security, but what do you see here in front of you right now? I'll tell you . . . a lot of long, gray hair and a expanding belly . . . how do they say it? 'He's gettin' to be a little long in the tooth.' Maybe that's how it's goin' to be. But I'll tell you this: for whatever time I have left, what I don't want to be is a fake human being. The way Axel got it down there on that reservation . . . some things just have to be made right. It's a matter of personal honor, pure and simple."

"I never had a brother, so I can't relate to how it is with you."

"I am not done with this just yet."

"That seems fair enough. Come on, let's head back. Crazy Martha just might have something special cooked up for supper."

Kaminski stopped at the sentry checkpoint. An army sergeant approached the vehicle. Bending over slightly, the soldier looked at him, then raised his hand to his forehead just above his eyebrow and held his salute.

"Lieutenant Kaminski . . . how are you, sir? It's been a long time, sir."

Kaminski saluted the guard.

The soldier lowered his hand.

"Dalrymple. Pulling guard on the weekend, huh?"

"Yes sir. My turn in the barrel. I see the colonel has you down for eleven hundred. You coming back regular?"

"Have to see what he's offering."

"Very good, sir. Have a good one."

Standing tall, the MP saluted and smartly waved him and his ancient Pontiac sedan through the checkpoint. As he drove across what was once a World War I training camp, he immediately began seeing dark olive green everywhere. He passed the PX, a motor pool, and a munitions depot, and a row of World War II-era white wooden clapboard barracks that were set back behind the parade field. He could see the choppers in the distance, all lined up neatly in a row. He pulled up in front of the main hangar and parked. It was a short walk to the operations and personnel office, where his meeting was to take place. He got out of his car, stood at the fence, looked out on the tarmac, and saw a white Huey with a red cross painted on the aft fuselage and across its nose. He heard a car door slam shut behind him. A tall man in uniform walked up alongside him.

"Thought you might be out here."

Kaminski turned and faced the colonel, then offered up a salute.

"Colonel."

He returned Kaminski's address.

"Good to see you in that flight suit, Don."

"Good to see you too, sir." He turned and looked at the choppers. "What's with Moby Dick over there?"

"Civilians. Always wanting to get in on our action."

"Action, sir?"

"Disaster weekend coming up. Going to have joint exercises with the two hospitals and civil air patrol."

"Sounds like a prudent thing to do. Always good to be prepared. I see the Chinooks are still in good shape. We certainly saved those Westinghouse engineers' asses with them, didn't we?"

"You know Don, seeing you flying over DC, carrying that thing of theirs, then lowering it like you did, smack-dab in the middle of the Pentagon, was sure a beautiful sight. The top brass was pretty happy that day. Made um see how we can get things done in a hurry. Congress loves to see how their appropriations money can be used in such an innovative manner."

"Roger that. But who would have thought they'd build something so big and so heavy they couldn't get the damn thing through the doors and inside?"

"You're one hell of a pilot. You ever fly those in country?"

"No sir. Just the slicks. Although once I went out on a patrol with the Rat Pack . . . flew a Cobra with those 2.75-inch rockets on board. Boy, those things could light up a VC command post pretty quick. Chinooks . . . they were a big-ass target. I was always grateful I didn't get tapped to fly them around in the Nam."

"Damn fine beautiful day for flying, isn't it? No sense going inside. What did you want to talk to me about?"

"Do you mind if we walk and talk? I'd like to see inside that new bird."

They walked on to the flight line and stood next to the medivac. Kaminski opened the door and stepped up and into the pilot's seat. "Hell . . . she only has a hundred hours on her."

He sat and stared down at the Plexiglas chin bubble at his feet and moved the tail rotor anti-torque pedals. The colonel climbed aboard and into the commander's seat.

"I still remember my first strip alert at Dau Tieng," said Kaminski.

"That was on that old rubber plantation outside of Saigon, wasn't it?" said the colonel.

"Yes sir. War zone C. I can smell it right now."

Kaminski kept looking down at the clear bubble at his feet, remembering the extra protection he was issued—the chicken plate, they'd called it. A twenty-two-pound piece of chest-shaped armor worn inside his flight jacket and another piece of armor he attached to the side of the armored seat that would give him side and head protection. Once they were in place it was impossible for him to shut the door; his gunner would have to do that for him. He turned and looked astern and saw only medical gear, then looked back down at the Plexiglas bubble. He thought back to 1965, when he was taking six US infantrymen or ten Vietnamese into combat assault missions. They had no armor under them. They sat on their helmets. His thoughts turned to the present and the eighteen wheelers he drove to Ohio five times a week, then suddenly Patrick's face flashed in front of him.

"Remember your mission," Kaminski said to himself.

"Did you say something, Don?"

"Um. Uh. Yes sir. That's what I wanted to talk to you about. I want to be a weekend warrior again."

"How are your legs?"

Kaminski rolled up a pant leg past his calf muscle, exposing a brace, then knocked with the knuckles of his hand on one of the steel bars that ran from his ankle up to his knee. "Well sir, the biggest trucking company in the country says they're just fine. I have to think Uncle Sam would tend to agree. Don't you think so, sir?"

"You know we want you back, Don. If the flight surgeon says okay and headquarters gives the green light, then it's a go. Good timing, too."

"How's that, sir?"

"After this weekend's disaster drill, we spend the next week with county and state officials, then do it all over again next month."

"Yes sir. Next month would be just fine, Colonel. Yes indeed. Just fine."

With the afternoon head count concluded, Zeb and Big Harold stepped out of their cells and stood at the rail, looking down at North Block. They saw Payne with the Terminator at the entrance to Payne's cell, then noticed ZZ as he walked out of his cell wearing a shiny metal cone in the middle of his face. He made his way to the very opposite end of East Block, where he waited in front of Highway's cell.

"A lot of chatter going on down there. You got a cigarette?"

Zeb pulled out a cellophane pack and flicked his wrist upward, and the tip of a Camel popped out from the pack. Harold pulled it out and put it to his lips, then lit it with a match.

"Thanks. I hear he don't have hardly any nose left."

"That cracker wasn't ever easy to look at to begin with. But without a nose—*shittttttttt* . . his own mother won't recognize him now."

"Wonder what they're all jabbering about."

Zeb turned his head to see Rishel pushing his cart down the catwalk. The old man, walking ever so slowly, dragging his leg along the way, stopped in front of Bunny's cell.

"There he is, *my man*," said Zeb.

"How you doing, Rish?" asked Harold.

"Doc says I am as good as new."

Bunny stepped out, wearing a big smile on his face.

"Want to thank you, Francis, for making all my deliveries for me like you did," said Rishel.

"Glad I could do it. How you feeling?"

"Doing just fine, son . . . just fine. Did you hear the news? Wallace is in the infirmary. Just arrived a few hours ago, as they were booting me out."

Harold looked at Zeb.

"That's what they were talking about. Jesus . . . news sure flies fast around here, don't it?" said Harold.

Rishel and Bunny walked together down the catwalk, handing out magazines and paperback novels.

"What are you thinking about, Hal?"

"Thinking about how much trouble there's goin' to be when he gets back. Revenge killing. Can't stop that shit once it's begun."

Zeb leaned over the railing and looked at Highway, who was now out of his cell, standing next to ZZ.

"Wallace seem like a killer to you?"

"Can't say one way or another. Rishel might know a thing or two. He was in the infirmary with Tin Nose down there."

"Look at um," said Highway. I am getting fuckin' tired of them two always lookin' down at us like that. That shit's got to stop."

Mouth open, making faint wheezing sounds, ZZ stared at Highway, then looked over Highway's shoulder to see Payne's number one walking toward them.

"I gutted that bastard good. If you'd hit him harder we . . . what's with you?"

"Nothin' . . ."

The Terminator walked up behind Highway. ZZ's eyes darted in the direction of the big man, then stared directly up at him. Highway turned around.

"Jimmeeeeee . . . long time no see," said Highway.

"Thor*vallllllll.*"

"What brings you down to our end of paradise alley?"

A half dozen East Block Hell's Angels noticed the Aryan and began to gather behind Highway. ZZ moved to his boss's side. The Terminator looked at ZZ's face, squinted one eye, grimaced, then looked at Highway, ignoring the Hell's Angels in the foreground. "Mr. Payne wants to meet with you two."

The Angels were now directly behind Highway. He turned around. "It's okay. It's about time we discuss some things."

Highway and ZZ stepped in front of the Terminator and walked out of East Block. As they approached Payne's cell, the Terminator moved in front of them and put his body in the entranceway to Payne's cell.

Payne was standing in his cell. "Thank you, Jim. Let um in."

The terminator stepped aside and they entered. He stood at parade rest, hands clasped behind his back, facing the catwalk.

"The day has finally arrived, hasn't it?"

"Yeah, we heard. The warden's investigation seems to have run aground. Did you have something to do with that?" asked Highway.

"Let's just say Warden Klump and I have similar interests, and when those interests are jeopardized, certain actions will and have been taken."

"What did you want to see us for?" asked Highway.

Payne moved to the back of his cell and laid a hand on top of a book, then looked up at the Aryan banner above his bookshelf. He stared at it.

"It was during the Dark Ages the Aesir made themselves known to our race. We're a hardheaded race but take great pleasure in our friendships, drinking and eating, lovemaking and outwitting strangers and avenging wrongs and . . . of course . . . fighting bravely. But before Odin and Thor, Greek antiquity shed light on the great Zeus and how he created us mortals.

Highway turned, looked at ZZ, closed his eyes, and slowly moved his head from left to right, then back again. He refocused on Payne and the Aryan banner. "Did he have a special purpose for us . . . this . . . Zeus?"

"Not so much a purpose but a spark."

"Spark? What spark?"

"All of us are the descendants of Zeus. He breathed into us a spark . . . a divine flame that allows us to reason things out to logical conclusions, and he gave us the will to act. Once you have that eternal flame, nothing—not even Zeus—can extinguish it from your body."

"Act on what?" asked Highway.

"To attain the good and to avoid all that is evil. Remember, Thorval . . . you can't waste your life agonizing over the things that are not dependent upon your will, and you shouldn't spend one minute of your time on this earth trying to avoid things that aren't dependent upon your will. We cannot allow ourselves to spend our feelings on things beyond our power. Remember, if a man is unlucky, that is his misfortune . . . his own fault."

"What else did Zeus have to say?"

"The Order wants its people to understand Zeus's gift of the faculty of reasoning. We detest those who tremble and moan and seek to avoid misfortune. Zeus has endowed us with great resources, and we relish the chance to be tested and challenged—and those who succeed in those challenges bring honor to themselves and to the Order."

"So what's your *reasoning* for all this Zeus talk? I am not an educated man. I move when I have to move."

"Ahhh . . . Thorval . . . that reminds me of a poem I just finished reading. You swerve."

"Poems now!" bellowed Highway. He looked at ZZ, then back at Payne. "What poem? What do you mean I swerve?"

"It was written by a man named Lucretius who lived in ancient times . . . he was a Roman thinker. The poem he wrote was called *On the Nature of Things*. The swerve—or *Clinamen*, as it's called in the Latin language—means the unexpected, unpredictable movement of matter. You fulfill the laws of nature when you *move* as you say. We are all moving atoms and nothing more. But here is where Zeus's gift comes in. You can reason things out. The crack that your people bring into this and other prisons is making the Order stronger. Don't you see, Thorval? We keep the black man where we want him with that white powder. If you keep trying to kill people in here, there's going to be a full-blown all-out federal investigation, and that could compromise our enterprise and possibly weaken the Order. Is my *reasoning* becoming clearer to you now? Do you *see* what is at stake?"

The Terminator turned and stood directly behind Highway. ZZ motioned with his eyes for Highway to look behind him.

"I see things, all right. You know, when Klump stuck me in that hole for a month, I stared at a wall that had some writing carved into it. Some guy back in thirty-two named Crane chiseled it into the concrete. I memorized it, saying it over and over day after day . . . here's a poem for ya, Erik . . . . Highway looked at the Terminator, then stared at Payne:

"In the desert
I saw a creature, naked, bestial,
Who, squatting upon the ground,
Held his heart in his hands,
And ate of it.
I said, is it good, friend?
It is bitter—bitter, he answered;
But I like it
Because it is bitter,
And because it is my heart."

Six white enameled steel beds lined up side by side. I am lying here alone in one of them in this windowless infirmary. It's been a week since I was delivered here. A trusty just left. About an hour ago he stood by this bed and we talked about what's been happening in South Block, then he walked with me down the corridor and into the rehabilitation room. They have me ride a stationary bike, then I do some push-ups. My strength is slowly coming back. The doctor has been in and I've been told I'll be here for a while. When I try to get a definitive answer from him, he smiles and says, "A tincture of time is what you need, and besides, the food is better here, so there's no need to speed up the healing process now, is there?" I keep staring at the book Vincent brought me that's lying on top of a steel cabinet just a foot away from my head. The escape plan seems sound. One short visit from him and the wheels begin to turn and lives change forever. It is said, Greater love hath no man than this that a man lay down his life for his friends. How is it they are willing to do this for me. How can this be? I've been told he is coming tomorrow. In another month I could be far away from this place in some distant land. But to put them all in such jeopardy; can I be that selfish? And then there is this maniac somewhere right now in East Block plotting to kill me as soon as I am released from this room. I walked in on him once and I don't want to confront him anytime soon. It's not because I am afraid. I don't think that's the case at all. I am willing to fight and will accept a fair fight, but the odds are against me in the game that's at hand. I sure don't much like the idea of always having to look behind me all my waking moments. Would I be taking the easy way out to go along with the plan? I can now relate better to Hamlet and his questioning maybe to go to sleep for good. By confronting the madman and losing the fight, I'll end the heartache and the thousand natural shocks that flesh is heir to. I'll be permanently asleep, that's for sure. That is the ultimate question, isn't it? To be or not to be in this place for the next twenty-five years. If I want to . . . be . . . I either kill him or get on that chopper.

Plough stood at his duty station at the end of North Block and observed Highway and ZZ leaving Payne's cell. He waited ten minutes and began walking slowly past the row of cells, and when he reached the Aryan leader's cell, he stopped for a brief moment and looked at Payne, then walked away. He entered the block's pod room, then walked around a corner into another room that had a pay phone heavily bolted and chained to a wall. Four inmates sat at a pod table playing cards. A few minutes passed, then Payne suddenly entered the pod with the Terminator. Payne walked around the corner and stood by the phone, while the Terminator stood by the card players, putting himself in between them and the entryway to the phone room.

"Any luck?" Plough asked.

"I don't know. You have to approach him in a certain way."

"And what way might that be?"

"Appeal to his sense of biker supremacy. Being direct won't work. You can't make any deals with him when he's like the way he is now."

"I see."

"Even if I were to lean hard on ZZ for more information about Wallace's accuser on the outside, it wouldn't matter. He's convinced Wallace did it. It won't make any difference now . . . I am sorry to say Wallace is a DMW."

"How's that?" asked Plough.

"Dead man walking. Although I don't think I'd be too quick to bet against him. He seems to be able to survive major damage. Look . . . I did what I could. It's decent of you to get involved but you know how it is."

"Yeah, I am afraid I do."

"Highway should be locked up in some damn insane asylum far away from here. What are you going to do now?"

"I don't know."

Late in the night Patrick woke from a troubling dream and made his way down the dark infirmary hallway and asked to use the telephone. He dialed the number in Moreland and leaned on the counter and listened to it ring. It rang a long time. Finally Vincent answered.

"It's Patrick. I know it's late."

"*Pat . . . what time . . . hold on . . . you okay?*"

"They told me you were coming tomorrow."

"*Yes, that's right . . . I'll be there in the afternoon. Don will be up in Massena, meeting with the Indians one last time. Why . . .*"

what's the matter?"

"I don't want you to come."

It was midmorning when Henry Crow Horse drove up to the back entrance of Hooker's garage. He got out of his jeep and stood in front of a badly weather-beaten wooden door that was attached to an unpainted clapboard wood-framed vestibule that jutted out from the concrete-block building. He opened the door, walked into a dungeonlike room that served as a reception area and office, made his way down a dimly lit hall to a bay, and stood next to a white Chevrolet van that had been made to resemble an EMS transport. Under the van's dashboard, directly below the steering wheel was Dan Proud Hawk, who was completing the last bit of wiring to an ambulance siren and rooftop lights. Proud Hawk stopped working and looked up at the old man standing in front of him holding a small brown paper bag. "You got um."

Crow Horse pulled three license plates out of the bag. Proud Hawk carefully inspected the New York, Pennsylvania, and Arizona plates.

"That's real good; the tags haven't expired. We're gettin' there. Just got to get these lights and horns up and running," said Proud Hawk.

"We're legal now," said Henry. He reached into one of his lower coat pockets and pulled out three wristwatches.

"Kaminski gave me these last night so we can all be coordinated. He'll be here soon."

"Did he give you the chopper's radio frequency? I need to double-check it with our CB."

Henry opened his coat, reached into his shirt pocket, pulled out a small slip of white paper, and handed it to Proud Hawk.

"Okay, I'll tune into this but we need to test it. Did he tell you when he can get back on that army base?"

"He'll be there a week from today."

"All right then. Once we've made radio contact, we can go anytime."

A few minutes passed. Lone Bear and Joey Skywalker arrived. Together they stood at a workbench, reviewing Kaminski's notes and going over small maps of Central Pennsylvania, Arizona, and a larger map of the United States that was pinned to the wall. Behind them they heard the sound of someone clearing their throat.

"Good morning, gentlemen," said Don Kaminski.

Henry turned around. "Good morning, Captain."

The five of them stood next to one another in front of the workbench, looking down at maps.

"Let's go over it one more time, shall we?" Kaminski took out a plastic protractor, placed it on a map directly over the prison's location, and rotated the protractor so that it was aligned with various reference lines on the map. He marked the map along the edge of the protractor at the desired headings then extended bearing lines toward three exact points using a straightedge. He marked a location with a red grease pencil.

"At one hundred knots we've got a two-hundred-mile radius . . . that's two hours air time; this first area here in the Allegany Reserve, just west of Elmira, will be our first LZ. From where we are here in Massena to this point is a hundred ninety-one miles. Hand refueling will take me thirty to forty-five minutes; it's another hundred seventy-three miles to the extraction point, then twenty-nine miles to our second LZ. Vin will have the pickup camper here at the Bald Eagle State Park at the west end of this lake when we land, then it's Route 66 to the canyon and that Havasupai reservation. Lone Bear . . . how are you getting along with those barrels?"

Proud Hawk and Lone Bear walked over to the back of the van and opened the doors, exposing two fifty-gallon barrels filled with JP-4 fuel.

"I've got it now that all they have to do is slide them down this ramp I've put together," said Proud Hawk.

"All right. Well done."

Proud Hawk and Lone Bear returned to the workbench.

Kaminski looked down at his notes and the drawings he'd made of the prison. "Joey . . . once you've dropped off the fuel, you'll get back into your car and follow Lone Bear in the ambulance to the extraction point."

"When we get to the entrance, should I follow behind him?"

"I'd peel off to the side of the road as you get close to the checkpoint and wait. Give Lone Bear a minute or two to get through, then drive up to the guard. Lone Bear . . . once you're inside the perimeter, turn those big blue rooftop lights off and proceed to this point here and park. You have the white coat?"

"Yes."

"And you will get a haircut, right?"

"Yes."

"Once you're in, Joey . . . you'll park here, near the van but not too close."

"Yeah. I understand. I know, I know . . . get rid of the ponytail, right?"

"Roger that."

"Lone Bear . . . as soon as I am on my final approach, I'll signal you. With that delayed relay installed, you'll have thirty seconds before the siren begins to blast and the lights go on. Joey will have the trunk open for you. Joey . . . just stay put until you hear the sound of my engine, then head back to the guardhouse. All eyes will be on me and the van. What are you going to say if that guard asks why you're back so soon?"

"We were told there's a medical emergency and all visitations are canceled until further notice," said Skywalker.

"Good man. Then it's back home for you two."

It was noon. Patrick was sitting on the edge of his bed, staring at the floor. A tall figure walked out of the patient ward past the trusty Rishel, then out the infirmary entrance. The trusty was pushing his cart, making a meal delivery to the sole patient in the infirmary. Patrick heard the squeaky wheels of the cart and looked up as the old man entered the room.

"Mr. Patrick . . . how are you feelin' this fine Sunday afternoon . . . did you have a visitor?"

"Oh . . . hello, Rish. Yes, my brother came today."

"He be that tall fella that just left, huh?"

"That's him . . . that's Vincent."

"You look sad . . . how come you look so down, my friend?"

"I think I may have upset him."

"Oh. I see. Well, how about something to eat? Here . . . there's enough here for the two of us. I'll have lunch with ya."

"Why that would be just fine with me, Rish. I could use the company."

Patrick sat down on a steel stool that was next to an examination table at the very back end of the ward, and Rishel grabbed an antique wooden chair and placed it close to Patrick so they could talk quietly.

"Looks like meatloaf you got there."

"Yeah. That's yours. I got this cheese sandwich here for me. Let's eat."

They sat and ate. After a while an orderly walked in and looked at them, then walked out.

"We got plenty of time—he won't be back for a while," said Rishel.

"Can I ask you a personal question, Rish?"

"Sure."

"How did you get that injury . . . your leg?"

"It's my hip. Back in sixty-three I was in the shop . . . in fact the same place you and Francis had that run-in with the bikers. We'd just finished packing up these crates of furniture and while loading a big one onto the back of a truck, the crate fell on me. I was pinned down for a long time before they got help. That happened nigh on twenty-some years ago. I remember I had just turned fifty. Half a century and all that."

"Does it hurt now when you walk?"

"No. Just hard to do some steps and things like that. I hear you're getting out of here tomorrow."

"Yeah. That's right."

"I can see now maybe why you aren't so . . . I mean . . . how that could be a problem. Tell me about your brother."

"Vincent. He's a stand-up kind of guy. A Renaissance man, actually."

"Can you tell me why you said he was upset? Seemed he was in a big hurry to leave."

"He hates indecisiveness in men."

"Oh."

"It's kind of complicated, Rish. I'd just be opening up a whole can of worms, trying to explain."

"That's all right. There's a lot of things that go on between brothers."

"You see things clearly, Rish . . . all the years you've been in this place . . . you've taken in much."

"I guess time has a way with that sort of thing."

"This Highway guy. He's going to try kill me again, isn't he?"

"Yeah. That's right. Francis will be the bait again. You know I am mighty fond of him. We have some things in common."

"I think I understand about you and Bunny. I've seen you two together enough to realize that."

"I've spent all of my adult life in here, and one thing I've learned is that all of us in some way try very hard to find some sort of connection with one another that keeps us going."

"What do you mean?"

Well, I remember one day, many years ago, I had family-visitation detail and witnessed something this visiting Quaker man brought to my attention. It kind of put things right for me. You know we always had preachers come in . . . you know, trying hard to get us to have a relationship with God and that sort of thing. But this man. He had a way of making things seem so . . ."

"Clear?"

"Yeah. That's it. Kind of like shining light in the sky after a thunderstorm. A lot of these preachers were all talk, but not this fella. I learned a long time ago anything worth knowing must enter you through another place. Talk just ain't going to do it for me. We sat there for a while just being quiet and then he asked me if I believed in a personal God. I said no. I was expecting him to move on, but he sat still, then looked around and saw a mother and baby who were visiting a young man on the other side of the holding area. I'll never forget what he said to me. He said . . . I know there is a God and I can prove it."

"He had proof?"

"Yeah . . . he did, all right. At least for me he did."

"Really. Just like that. What did he say?"

"Well, first he said, 'Through love God gives rise to all things.' Then he said, 'Look over there . . . that young mother holding her baby . . . when I see the beauty of unconditional love, that to me is the distinguishing proof of eternal life—that is a sign of the existence of God.'"

"I see what you mean. That has a kind of burning-bush element to it, all right."

"Then he said—this is what was the frosting on the cake for me . . . he said he lost his faith once and then one day he was listening to someone being interviewed on the radio who said that if there is a God we must see him, and if there is a soul we must perceive it; otherwise it's best not to believe. Better to be an outspoken atheist then a hypocrite."

"Hmmm. That makes sense. But can you honestly tell me you've seen something that even comes close to unconditional love in this prison?"

"Sure, Mr. Patrick. Like what you did for Francis in that shop. No one said you had to try to save his life like you did."

"You're positive Highway is going to . . . how did you say it . . . use him as bait to lure me in?"

"Francis is more vulnerable now than ever. Zeb and Harold will try to protect him, but the bikers will win this one."

"No doubts?"

"No, Mr. Patrick. No doubts at all."

Les Plough appeared and stood in the doorway to the patient ward. "Rishel! There you are," said Plough.

"Okay boss. I am a-leaving."

"Klump was asking where you were. Better get up to his office right away."

"We're all lookin' forward to seeing you back up on South Block."

"Thanks, Rish. That means a lot. You've helped me shore up some things that have been rattling around in my head. I know what I have to do now."

Rishel left. Plough walked in and stood next to Patrick.

"And what is it you're going to do?" said Plough.

"Go on living."

"I've talked with the guards. The ones that I know well and trust. We'll do what we can to help you."

"Thanks."

The night engulfed Don Kaminski's bedroom and spread its darkness like an opened black umbrella above his mountain house and the surrounding lands. The forest was still, its inhabitants resting quietly. He struggled to sleep. He tossed and turned. In a few hours he would leave his longtime sanctuary, never to return. Huey slept near his feet, unaware of the adventure that awaited them.

He dreamed of being in Southeast Asia, taking off from an army base and landing near a rice paddy in close proximity to a jungle clearing. Bullets whizzed by his windscreen. His door gunner returned fire. Suddenly the landscape shifted and he now saw a forty-foot wall in front of him and worried if his tail rotor or boom will clip the top of the wall as he attempted to land inside that medieval fortress of a prison.

It was still dark as he was coming out of his dream—half asleep, half awake—when the phone rang. He looked at the old radium-dial Accutron wristwatch on the nightstand and picked up the phone. "Yes," he said.

"I am leaving now. Will see you at the lake," said Vincent.

He listened to his friend for a minute. Then he said, "By tonight we'll be on the other side of the Ohio; Arizona will be just a few days away."

"All right. It's time."

"Vin."

"Yes."

"All I can give him is ten seconds once my skids hit the yard."

"He knows. He'll be at home plate at four."

"Roger that, Vin. See you at Bald Eagle."

"Good luck, Don."

He got out of bed, strapped his leg braces on, went into the kitchen and made coffee and fed Huey, then took his cup into the dining room and stood over his dining-room table and inspected the aeronautical chart that was spread out on top of the table. The route to Lewisburg was laid out perfectly, plotted with exactness, and for a pilot with his experience there was really no way he could possibly get lost. He had seen the prison and pictured in his mind the exact hole he was to drop the chopper into. Like an athlete before a big game, he was all pumped up, ready to go. *Man, it will be a breeze, piece of cake*, he thought. He sipped some coffee and thought some more. *Sure . . . if the tower guards don't shoot and if Patrick is there on time and the LZ doesn't have loose crap lying around that will fly up into the blades or intake manifold.*

He showered and shaved, put on his flight suit, then filled up a small plastic bottle with water and put it and a small blanket into the little camouflaged carry-on case he'd made for Huey. He searched for his utility cap and found it behind his helmet and flight bags. He put his shaving kit and toothbrush into a ditty bag and put that into his duffel, gathered up his charts, put Huey in the cat carrier, and left the house. At first Huey meowed loudly as they drove down the bumpy mountain road, but he finally settled in and was quiet after they were on the state road for a few miles.

Saturday morning started with a loud bang, followed immediately with low-intensity lights coming on at the ends of the catwalks. Cold and grayness permeated the air. Fifteen minutes later a horn buzzed twice; cell doors opened. South Block Level 2 inmates began to stir. The sounds of coughing and the hacking up of phlegm emanated from above and below. Toilets flushed. Bunny was first to come out of his cell. He stood at the railing, looking across the chasm that separated South and North Blocks. Big Harold came out, then Zebadiah, and finally Wallace. Each of them stood at the railing in front of their cells and observed what was happening across the divide.

"Porridge day!" Bunny announced, then walked over and stood beside Big Harold. The two of them went into Harold's cell. At first Patrick stood up against the railing but then leaned over, looking down at the lower row of cells. A cloud of dusty early-morning light crept through and past the dark abyss and into Payne's cell, then Highway's cell. Patrick stared at the first rays of the morning. Zebadiah walked over and stood next to him. Patrick didn't move. He kept looking down at the ends of the light beams.

"Zeb."

"Yeah."

"I, uh . . . just want you to know that you've been, uh . . ."

"Something on your mind, Hoss?"

"No. Well, yeah, I just wanted to say . . . these last few days . . . since I got back you've . . ."

"You know we don't have much here except what we wear and what we say and do to one another."

"Yeah, we're rightly connected, Zeb. I never thought I'd make it in here. But then you and Harold just . . . since day one . . . you let me in. No judgments, no third degree. No matter what happens, I just want you to know I'll never forget."

Zeb looked away from Patrick. He scanned the area below. He saw what Patrick was focusing on, then realized he was staring at Highway's cell.

"You thinking he be comin' at you today?"

"Today, tomorrow, I don't know. But very soon it will be finished."

Zeb reached into his shirt pocket and pulled out a pack of cigarettes and flicked his wrist upward, and the tip of a Lucky Strike popped up and extended out from the pack. He pulled it out and put it to his lips and lit it with a match, drew smoke deep into his lungs, then exhaled. "Cigarettes in here are like money. I'll tell you what," he said.

"Tell me."

"We're gonna keep doin' what we been doin'. Harold stays near Bunny."

Zeb lifted a knife out of his boot, palmed it, and slid it into the pocket of Patrick's trousers. Patrick pulled it out of his pocket. It looked better than what he'd expected. A switch-blade with a slightly damaged handle, made in Italy, some brass showing through the plating on the bolster. He pushed a button, it clicked open, and he closed it and slid it into his boot. They stood together, the tall black man's face pondering. Serious. As if he'd thought of every sort of consequence that could happen.

"Thanks. I don't know if I'll be needing it."

"Well, Hoss, you never know . . . but just in case . . . yeah."

"You're right. It could come in handy."

"Remember me telling you about us starting up with soft-ball again?"

"Yeah. I remember. You had me down for shortstop."

"Game starts at three."

"When I was in the infirmary Rish showed me a list that had my name on it and the schedule of all the games to be played."

"When you're fully healed, we sure can use you. You can coach third base for now . . . okay?"

"You know, my friend . . . that may work out just fine for me this afternoon."

Kowalski walked past ZZ, passed another half dozen cells occupied with Hell's Angels, and stood in front of Highway's cell. Highway was sitting on his bed.

"It's time to go."

The guard took Highway out of East Block. The two men did not exchange words as they walked down corridors past numerous checkpoints, passing through sliding steel-reinforced doors manned by security guards. Kowalski led him into the visitation room. He sat in front of the glass and picked up a phone attached to the partition separating him from the empty cubical on his right. He motioned to the man on the other side of the glass to pick up the phone bolted on a ledge in front of the glass. He lifts the phone to his ear.

"Who the hell are you?" he said.

"Name's Razor."

"I don't know you. What do you want?"

"When we were kids, I met you a couple of times."

"What? What are you talking about?"

"I am Axel's brother. My name's Phillip."

"That was a long time ago."

"And you're Thorval."

"All right. Yeah. You got that right, ace. But it's Highway now."

"All right."

Highway sat up in his chair then leaned forward, staring at Razor. He sat back. Bowed his head slightly. His head jerked up. "Shit! I remember now. You're that little shit Philly!"

"I am called Razor now."

Highway laughed loudly. "All right. All right. With a name like Razor you must be pretty sharp, huh?"

"Sharp enough."

"Axel used to talk my ear off about you. How you two would boost cars and roll old guys while they took a piss in public shitters."

"Bus and train stations were the best for that. You know it's impossible to turn around and fight for your wallet when you're taking a piss in front of a urinal," replied Razor.

Highway looked Razor up and down, his eyes finally drawn to his blue-jeans vest.

"Stand up and turn around, will ya?" said Highway.

"What?"

"I want to see your colors."

Razor complied with the request.

"So you're a member up in Montreal. I've heard about your new leader—this Mom guy. He consolidated all the membership up there, didn't he?

"Yeah, that's true. I am in charge of his security."

"He must be one smart son of a bitch." Highway glanced over to where Kowalski was standing, then looked back at his visitor.

"Don't worry. I know the routine," said Razor.

"So why do I have the pleasure of your company this morning? You drove all the way down here for something . . . isn't that right?"

"A few months back a guy by the name of Eddy delivered some info to your man ZZ."

"That's right. He gave me that bit of info and I acted on it."

"I just needed to see you and . . . uh . . ."

"Well, you're lookin' at me now. What gives? What do you want from me?"

"Just tell me: you plan on finishing what you started?"

Patrick didn't go to eat at noon. He sat eyeing the yard and tried to picture in his mind what was going to happen. He thought men walking past him were looking at him. Then he thought they were trying not to. He said quietly to himself that soon, all that was about to happen could get men killed. His friends killed.

Today, like the previous day, was sunny. He checked the time on the clock on the administration office wall. He looked at the width of the shadow of the wall in front of him. When the yard was half in the shade it would be four o'clock, just like the day before. It was the east wall he was examining, the wall Don Kaminski would be flying over in just a few hours.

After a while he got up and walked down to where Skeeter and Calvin were preparing the field for the game. He helped them set up the bags for the bases, poured chalk into a line-making machine, and helped with lining up the infield, then sat down on the concrete bleachers. Aryan Brotherhood and Hell's Angels came in. Aryans went to the top of the bleachers and sat down; bikers took over the weight-lifting area. Two men smirked at him on their way to the steel bars and iron plates. The horn sounded across the yard. Les Plough moved a dozen inmates out onto the yard. Zeb, Harold, and Bunny were the last to enter. They sat down on the bleachers next to Patrick.

Since leaving the Akwesasne reservation Lone Bear had been careful not to exceed the speed limit. Skywalker drove one of Proud Hawk's refurbished sedans, staying close, never letting the van out of his sight. On the road since before dawn, they'd passed through Elmira and were now entering the Allegany Reserve. Lone Bear drove into the dark forest, meandering down narrow twisting dirt roads, then stopped. Skywalker pulled in behind him, got out and opened the van's passenger door and got in.

"Something wrong?"

"I was just thinking."

"About what?"

"It looks kinda suspicious, me in this thing and you following me."

"Yeah, but who would care?"

Think, Joey. Ranger Rick might see us. He may get it in his head we need assistance or something. Why would an ambulance be out here? He'd want to know why . . . don't you think?

"I suppose."

"Back there behind the barrels there's a tire iron. Get it. If I am stopped . . . well . . . you decide if you need to use it or not."

"Okay. Are we close?"

"Look at the map. This is Seneca Trail right here. See the mark Kaminski drew there? It's not too far."

The entrance to the base was just up ahead. Kaminski pulled onto the side of the road and partially unzipped the top of the cat carrier. Huey's head popped out. He meowed, looked out the window, then turned and looked up at Kaminski. The pilot gently rubbed the Siamese's head and behind his ear, then rubbed the silver bars on his left shoulder. Looking in the rearview mirror, he put his utility cap on, being careful to adjust it properly. The cat purred.

"Well . . . this is it."

He closed the carrier and drove up to the checkpoint. He was waved through, and he went to the parking lot adjacent to the helipads, where a half dozen army choppers and the Moreland General Air Evac were lined up neatly in a row. Air crew maintenance and flight technicians milled around as he briskly walked past them and climbed up into the new all-white H-model chopper. He placed the cat carrier on the aircraft commander's seat, then settled into the pilot's seat, where he found the key and began his preflight review. A small smile erupted on his face, then quickly disappeared. With great urgency he looked at Huey, who was anxiously sitting in his carrier looking through the screen mesh. They made eye contact.

"It's been a few years, buddy . . . what if . . ."

No time for that now.

He put his flight helmet on, then fired up the engine to start getting the big rotor to 380 rpms. He put his feet on the pedals, then placed his hand gently on the collective to the left of his seat. The pipe like rod he was holding looked and felt the same as it did on his old C-model aircraft. He paused from doing his routine mental startup to listen to the new, more powerful Lycoming 13 engine and wondered how it might affect pitch and lift. He looked down at the cat. He couldn't hear the cat but could see he was letting it be known in a loud way that he was uncomfortable with the engine sounds coming from above.

"Wish I had some noise suppression for you, pal."

He turned and looked at all the medical equipment packed into the aft compartment. *Damn it. Weight. This is no empty slick.*

He was going into base-brain auto mode, calculating added weight effects on lift takeoff angulation, when something outside suddenly caught his attention. He looked out his portside window and saw the colonel gesticulating at him. His headset exploded with FM chatter. He shut off the radio and also the identifiers so he could not be picked up by radar. He offered up a salute to his old CO, then pulled the cyclic all the way up to his armpit, causing the chopper to pitch up to a high hover. He dipped the nose of the chopper, moved forward, then dropped slightly. With all of his abilities and skill, he carefully throttled the collective, creating maximum power to the blades. They were up quickly, moving away from the aircraft parked below. The colonel just stood there, mouth wide open, staring into the sky as the chopper sped away.

By 10:00 a.m. they had reached the Pennsylvania state line and were heading south on Rote 14 with Vincent Wallace behind the wheel and Henry Crow Horse sitting alongside him on the F-250's bench seat. The old man sat quietly, studying the cab's surroundings.

"Automatic transmission, air-conditioning. Good truck," Henry Crow Horse declared.

"Belonged to my father. He drove it out to Nebraska to hunt pheasant."

"Ahhhhh . . . the ringnecks. I remember when I was young, my grandfather took me out many times to hunt those birds. Good meat. In the old days there were so many on Akwesasn lands. They're all gone now.

"Once he drove to the Pacific, then headed north on to the Alcan Highway. Made it all the way up to the rim of the arctic circle."

"This a seventy-one or seventy-two Ford?"

"It's a seventy-one. Three-quarter ton," replied Vincent.

"Rides a little stiff . . . like my jeep."

"Yeah. You can really feel it when you hit the bigger bumps. He requested more leaf springs in the back to accommodate the extra weight of the camper."

"Chevy's use oversized coil springs all around. Makes for a better ride, I think."

"Is that so? Huh. These big high-flotation tires make her ride a little harder." He would need them on the Alcan.

"It's like a turtle carrying its house around on its back. Much better than hauling a trailer around," said Henry.

"It's hunting season. If we stay on back roads as much as we can, with these guns here on the rack, we won't look out of place."

"Henry."

"Yes."

"Can you tell me a little more about these people that live at the bottom of the canyon . . . these Havasupai?"

"A couple of years ago we powwowed with some of them up in St. Regis. They're poor. Very poor. Probably the poorest tribe in the country. A few elders and some others came to see us and we spent time with them . . . they wanted to know more about our ways."

"Is that something you do often? I mean, invite other tribes from all over?"

"It's a common thing to do. We do this to better understand how some interact with the state and federal government leaders. Tribal elders are always willing to share strategy."

"Strategy?"

"Some are more successful than others in getting back what's been taken from us. Eight or nine years ago they got back over a hundred and eighty thousand acres at the bottom of that canyon."

"Havasupai. How does that translate into English?"

"People of the green-blue water. Been in that canyon for close to eight hundred years, they said."

"Always thought the Grand Canyon to be a huge hole in the ground with lot of reddish-looking rock all around it. Wonder how they got that name?"

"From what I could gather, there are some waterfalls in there that are very special. Give off color like no others."

"Well, you'll be seeing that soon enough."

Plough looked at his wristwatch, then blew a silver-plated whistle. Men gathered around the dirt area that served as home plate. The guard picked up two canvas bags containing equipment and handed one to Zeb. A short, slender man, Juan Rodrigues, stepped forward and took the other bag. Plough turned to Zeb.

"You got enough?"

Zeb looked at his players. "We're good," he said.

"How about you?"

The Cuban looked around, then pointed at each of his players. He started to count out loud ... *un, dos, tres* ... then continued, pointing in silence.

"*Sí.*"

"All right then. Too Tall ... you're up first."

Rodrigues looked up at Zeb, then smiled, exposing large upper and lower rows of white Chiclets-gum-like teeth; a solitary large gold upper front tooth shone brightly in the afternoon sunlight.

"May the best team win, *señor*," he said, then shook Zeb's hand. "*Bien mis amigos vamos a mostrarles como hacemos volver a casa*," he shouted; then he and his men walked slowly onto the weed-encrusted dirt field. Zeb walked over to the first row of concrete bleachers and stood in front of the men of South Block Level Two. Patrick Wallace got up from the bleachers and took his place behind the third baseline.

"Go get um Skeet," said Zeb.

Skeeter picked up a bat and stood at home plate. The game was underway. A giant of a man from the Aryan Brotherhood chosen by Payne stood behind him to call balls and strikes. A few biker weight lifters and Aryans started gathering in small groups, eyeing with interest the first softball game to be allowed in more than a year. Guards up on the walls peered down at the action beginning to unfold. Kowalski and a half dozen guards milled around the yard, trying their best to act professional and not be seen paying any attention to what was transpiring on the field in front of them. Kowalski looked up at the second floor of the administration building and noticed Warden Klump staring out the big plate-glass window of his office. He continued to slowly move around the perimeter of the yard. He walked past the tunnel entrance twice, then on his last pass entered the shadowy, dark passageway. A short while later he came back out into the sunlit yard, then walked slowly to the bleachers and stood in front of Francis Bunnyard.

"Warden wants to see you."

A muffled crack rang out as Skeeter made solid contact with a pitch and ran to first base, then headed for second. Some cheering erupted from the bleachers. Men stopped pumping iron and began paying attention. Harold picked up the bat and stood off to the side, near the third baseline.

"Did you hear me? Get up."

"What!" said Zeb.

"Shut up. Come on, Bunny boy, I don't got all day." Kowalski pulled his baton from his belt, then shoved the end of it into the black man's chest. "Get out of my way or I'll thump you for sure."

An expression of horror could now be clearly seen on Zebadiah's face. He looked over to the third baseline. Patrick locked eyes with the tall man, then in the foreground he could see Bunny being led away from the bleachers toward the tunnel entrance. Harold saw what was happening. He stepped out of the batter's box, stared at Kowalski, stared at Zeb, then looked down the third baseline at Patrick.

An impatient umpire with an oversized thyroid gland looked at Harold, then shouted, "BATTER UP!"

Before the men could think or act, Kowalski and Bunny were gone.

Les Plough now recognized what was happening.

Highway crouched alone in the corner of the dark pump house. There was an alcove running along one side of the tunnel and a set of large industrial electric motors and pipes at the far end. He waited behind one set of pipes. He got up. He paced back and forth like a maniac. This afternoon he would kill, but killing was not utmost in his mind. His short conversation with Philly a few hours ago carried him forward. His thirst for revenge permeated his every thought. His mania had turned into rage. The rage had an ending, a bloodstained climax, but the mania never let up. Madness engulfed every fiber of his nerves and muscles as he waited to pounce on his victim. He would tear into him like a panther, first paralyzing his prey by attacking the neck; then, after unconsciousness occurs, he would finish off the limp body as he saw fit.

Plough walked over to Patrick. Zeb did the same.

"Did you see that?" said Patrick.

The umpire shouted, "All right, let's go . . . PLAY BALL!"

Harold slowly, reluctantly stepped into the batter's box . . . the pitcher threw, Harold swung, and he missed.

"I am only allowed to take one inmate back at a time," said Plough. "Wallace, come with me. You . . . stay here."

"But . . ."

"Do as I say, Zebadiah."

The two men walked toward the tunnel entrance. Patrick glanced at the clock on the administration-building wall; it read half past three. He looked at the east wall and up at a clear blue sky, then entered the tunnel with Les Plough.

The cluster of pipes Highway was hiding behind traveled the length of the pump house then went straight up to the inmate's cells. He stopped pacing and peered out into the vague, uneven darkness of the tunnel. From his position he could make out the cavernous hall that connected the yard to the main prison compound. When he heard men's voices, he slowly took a step, then another. He pulled Bunny in. Kowalski vanished somewhere into the darkness. With one hand he grabbed hold of Bunny's forearm and twisted it backward and around his lower back, then he firmly clasped his captive's mouth with his free hand, rendering him silent. He stood near the tunnel, waiting for his prey to walk by. He watched as they passed side by side.

WALLACE! he shouted, then he retreated with his hostage back behind the pipes.

The two men stopped. Plough unhooked his baton from

his belt, then stepped into the pump house. Patrick was right behind him.

"Come on now. Come and get your boy."

With what little ambient light there was, Plough could make out two silhouettes behind the pipes. Out of the darkness a force pulled him backward. Kowalski stripped the black baton from his hand and slid it across his upper back through both his armpits, holding him firmly in place, upright and defenseless. Patrick scanned the area but could not see the guard. He took one step forward, then another one.

"All right . . . I am here . . . let Francis go."

"Sure. I'll let him go."

Highway slammed Bunny's head against one of the large asbestos-wrapped pipes, knocking him unconscious, then came out from behind the pipes.

"You got to hide in the dark, huh? Why don't you go after somebody that's your size for a change, you rat bastard. Come on, come on, you big pussy . . ."

Highway sprinted then lunged headfirst into Patrick's solar plexus, laying him flat out on the concrete floor. The back of his head bounced off the floor. He gasped for air. Highway jumped on top of him, staring into his eyes as he pinned him to the ground. On his back, dazed and with blurred vision, he could barely see Highway's hands coming toward his neck. He threw up a forearm, deflecting one oncoming hand, then reached for his ankle and pulled the switchblade out of his boot. Regaining control with both hands, Highway started choking off Patrick's airway causing him to lose clarity. With loss of dexterity, he fumbled with the knife and it fell out of his grasp. Highway smiled when he saw both of Patrick's eyes begin to quiver.

"This time you ain't getting out of this."

They heard a click. Highway arched his head upward, taking his eyes off his victim. Patrick plunged the long blade into his attacker's leg, just above the kneecap. Highway let out a moan and released his grip on Patrick's neck, then grabbed at his knee, pulling the knife out. He raised it over his head, preparing for a downward thrust into Patrick's heart, when suddenly a very large, fleshy hand appeared and clamped down on his wrist.

"We've had enough of you, Thorval," said the Terminator.

The Terminator broke Highway's grip on the knife; it flew out into the shadows, landing near the pipes a few yards away. Highway tried to push off from the ground, but the Terminator pounded the sides of his head with flaying fists, shattering both temporal bones and driving bone splinters into Highway's brain. His enormous body became still. The Terminator stood over the Hell's Angel. From somewhere out in the shadows, the Aryan leader appeared and walked up to the Terminator, then knelt down to inspect the body lying on the floor.

"He's still breathing," said Payne.

Kowalski slid the baton out from behind Plough's back, releasing his arms. Both guards moved out from the shadows and stood in front of the inmates. Payne stood up. The Terminator, Payne and Patrick stood side by side and faced the guards.

"That man needs medical attention," Plough quietly announced.

Bunny stirred, then woke and began crawling out from behind the pipes. He moved through the darkness across the floor by pulling himself along by his elbows; he saw Patrick's knife in front of him and picked it up, then continued moving in the direction of Plough's voice.

"That's right . . . I'll get some help," said Kowalski. He ran out of the pump house. The faint sound of an ambulance siren echoed through the tunnel.

"What's that sound?" asked the Terminator.

"It's got to be close to four o'clock," said Patrick.

Highway's eyes opened. He saw Patrick's back directly in

front of him. As he began to stand up, he pulled a knife out of his pants pocket, then suddenly he crumpled and dropped to the floor with a muted thud, a knife handle sticking out of his back.

"FRANCIS!" shouted Patrick, then grabbed him under his armpit. "Can you walk?"

"Yeah . . . I think so."

"Come on." Patrick pulled him along the tunnel.

"WALLACE, STOP!" shouted Plough as he walked toward them.

The Terminator followed them, slowly walking backward, all the while facing the guard and Payne. Payne stepped in front of Plough and faced him.

"It's all right," Payne said. "Wallace has an appointment to keep."

"What?"

They heard a loud whirring, fluttering sound, and a rush of wind and sand hit Patrick's face as he emerged from the tunnel. He pushed Bunny through the open doorway of the helicopter, then jumped in, falling on top of him. Both lay flat on their bellies as the Huey lifted off.

Zeb and Harold watched them move up and over the wall, then turned and looked at each other, shook their heads, and smiled.

He flew over the Susquehanna River just north of Lewisburg and took bearings, finding nav aids using the nap of the earth. He could see I-80 west, cutting its way through farmland, forests, and the Allegany Mountains. Looking at a relief map, he saw that Bald Eagle Lake was South of Lock Haven and a little more than five miles northwest of the interstate. He climbed higher to avoid transmission lines but was careful to maintain an altitude of no more than a thousand feet to avoid radar detection.

Don Kaminski turned around in his pilot's seat and looked at Patrick, and with a big grin on his face he gave him a thumbs-up, then banked to the north. The Lycoming engine roared. Bunny covered his ears with his hands. Patrick saw a pair of headsets hanging just aft of the commander's seat, grabbed them, and handed one set to Francis, while he put on the other.

Twenty minutes passed. "There it is . . . there's our lake," said Kaminski.

He made a quick pass, then circled, looking for Vincent. He saw the pickup camper at the very edge of the shoreline under some trees. Vincent Wallace and Henry Crow Horse were standing next to the hood of the truck.

"Hang on, boys, I am setting her down."

All three quickly exited the chopper and headed for the camper. For a brief moment they stood silently and looked at one another.

"This is Francis," said Patrick.

Vincent shook Bunny's hand. "Good to meet you . . . I really want to . . . um . . . get to know you but we got to get out of here," he said as he opened the truck door and slid behind the steering wheel. Don handed the cat carrier to Henry. Bunny walked behind the old retired sheriff to the rear of the truck and followed him up the steps and into the camper. Patrick and Don jumped into the cab. Don sat in between the two brothers.

"We're lucky . . . nobody's out here today," said Vincent as he started the engine.

"Let's keep that luck going . . . move out," said Don.

"Roger that, Captain."

Vincent drove the camper onto a narrow dirt road into the state park, slowly making his way through the thick forest that surrounded the lake. The forest began to darken as the late afternoon sun disappeared, obscured by thousands of acres of standing timber. Low-hanging hemlock branches scraped the top and sides of the camper as he negotiated the rough terrain.

Around six o'clock they emerged from the preserve onto one of many two-lane state roads they'd take on their way to West Virginia, Kentucky, then Missouri and Route 66. At half past ten o'clock Vincent saw an old, worn-out, rusty Sinclair filling-station sign and pulled in. A pale, skinny teenage boy walked up to the truck and looked at Vincent, Patrick, and Don, then eyed the rifles on the gun rack directly behind their heads.

"You're lucky," said the teenager.

"How's that?" asked Vincent.

"I was fixin' to shut her down for the night. You fellas huntin', huh?"

"Not today. We got a late start. We're just now coming into your fair state. You wouldn't happen to know of a place to camp—know of anywhere nearby, that is?" asked Vincent.

"Have to think on that for a spell . . . those are Henry lever actions you got there.

"Yep. You know your guns, all right."

"Looks like forty-four caliber. You goin' after the bears, huh?"

"Sure are."

"You want me to fill 'er up?"

"Yes, that would be great. Thank you."

The boy stood next to the driver's-side door and unscrewed a gas cap and began filling up the tank. "I don't reckon I know of any official-lookin' campsites around these parts, but there are some old abandoned coal mines just down that-a-ways."

"How far?"

"Not very. You'll see a beat-up old sign that says J. B. Greevy Company a few miles down this road. That's the closet one. I've known some who would camp around them areas. Yeah. That's what I'd do. That'll be nineteen even."

"Appreciate your suggestion . . . here you go," said Vincent.

He handed the boy a twenty plus another five and started the engine.

"Thanks, mister . . . thanks a lot. It's been a pleasure. Hell's bells, you just might get a bear comin' out of one of them mine caves. Good luck to ya all."

Henry pulled back a curtain covering the tiny side window of the overhead sleep compartment to see the boy sheepishly waving good-bye as they drove off into the dense darkness of a moonless, cool, crisp autumn night.

"There it is. Greevy Company," said Don.

"I see it." Vincent steered the truck onto a narrow, rutted track of dirt road. The rig rose up, then down, then swayed from side to side. Inside the painted aluminum-and-fiberglass paneled camper box, Henry and Francis bounced around wildly, hanging on to anything they could. The truck's headlights lit up the land ahead of them and they saw a tiny wooden shack with a partially collapsed roof and a boarded-up entrance to a mine. Vincent hit the brakes. The camper came to rest.

"This looks pretty good, Pat," said Vincent.

"This is a good place to camp, all right. That kid back at the gas station . . . he knew what we needed," Patrick replied.

"Yeah . . . he sure did. Come on, brother, let's see how our friends are doing in the back."

The brothers opened the cab doors and stepped out; Kaminski, who was sitting in the middle of the bench seat, followed them.

"Jesus. Can it be any darker out here?" said Don.

"There's a flashlight in the map box."

Kaminski grabbed the flashlight, walked around the hood to the driver's-side door, and played the light across the mine entrance. The mine had been abandoned for many years. The brothers and Kaminski walked around to the back of the truck. Don opened the camper door. Vincent stepped up and over the threshold and located a light switch just inside the doorjamb. He flipped it on and stepped back down. A low-watt lightbulb in a milk-glass fixture shaped like a miniature boat wheel began to flicker, then came on. Patrick peeked into the dimly lit cabin then asked, "How you two getting along in there? You all right, Francis?"

"Where you at, Henry? . . . I can't see you," said Vincent.

"Here we are Patrick . . . up here," shouts Bunny.

Don shined the flashlight up into the cab's overhead sleep compartment.

"Like two peas in a pod. See!"

"Well, come on down from there," said Patrick.

Bunny sat up, swung his legs over, and slid down into the galley, then helped Henry Crow Horse down. Henry slowly made his way to the back of the camper and down the steps. Bunny followed him outside.

"Patrick. How good it is to see you again."

"Henry."

Meowwwwwwwww. Meowwwwwwwww.

"Hold on, Huey, said Kaminski as he climbed up the steps. He grabbed the cat carrier, then turned around and rejoined the others.

"All right, let's get you out of there."

Vincent went inside and returned carrying a kerosene lantern, a plastic container of water, a bottle of bourbon, a pair of jeans, and a couple of wool plaid hunting shirts. He handed the water jug and whiskey to Don, and the clothes to his brother and Bunny.

"Here you go, Captain. I am going to start a fire and fix us some dinner. Come on, Francis . . . let's look for some wood."

Their camp was on the edge of a small, treeless Appalachian mountain surrounded by large piles of thick slabs of gray slate. They sat on army-surplus blankets in the moonless night and looked out at the desolate stillness and at one another. The fire's yellow flames, shooting up into the black sky, lit up their faces, exposing Bunny's whitish skin. His Scotch-Irish heritage, together with years of imprisonment, had bleached out all pigmentation, making him appear ghostlike as he sat next to the ruddy-skinned Mohawk Sheriff. Vincent cooked Rice-A-Roni and black beans, and they sat eating and looking up at the stars.

Patrick went into the camper and came out with some small bathroom-sized Dixie cups, walked over to where Don was sitting, and picked up the bottle of bourbon. "I can't remember the last time I had a drink, but I am going to remember this one," Patrick said as he poured whiskey into the cups. "Here Francis, pass these around. It's about time I said a couple of things that need saying. Francis Bunnyard here, or as he likes to be called, Bunny . . . show um your forearm."

Francis stopped chewing and rolled up his sleeve, exposing his Bugs Bunny tattoo, then put his plate down on the ground and took the cups, handed them out to the men, and sat back down.

"First . . . I want to let you know, this man I brought along has on more than one occasion been instrumental in keeping me alive. Without going into the particulars, let's just say I've got him permanently in my wheelhouse for the duration. Second . . . Thank-yous won't do it. There're no words that can begin to describe how I am feeling right now about all of you. I am thinking about Joey and Lone Bear and I know you are too. Tomorrow we've got to get Vin to that Hertz place in Charleston so he can get back and check on them."

"Those two are on the rez right now, sitting in Hooker's with Hawk, having beers and a smoke," said Don.

"That's right," shouted Vincent.

Patrick poured himself some whiskey, then stood up and raised his cup to the men who were sitting around the fire. They all got up and turned toward Patrick and raised their cups in the air.

"You did it. You've given me something I didn't think I'd ever have again. Here's to freedom."

"Freedom."

Henry put his hand on Patrick's shoulder. "If you'll permit me."

"Of course, Henry."

"Very soon you'll be in the canyon and there will be many there you can rely on to conceal your identity. I've seen to that. We must give thanks for the blessings already coming our way." He bowed his head, then looked upward into the night sky, and with hands raised high he pointed east, then north and south and finally westward, and began to chant in a rhythmic, repetitive cadence. When he finished his offering, he said good night and went into the camper to sleep.

"I guess its lights-out for me too. Thanks, Mr. Vincent, for that good supper we had," said Bunny.

"Good night, Bunny."

"Patrick."

"Yes."

"I don't know where we're headed but I got a feelin' it's goin' to be better each day that comes along. Too bad they all couldn't have jumped on. Hope Hal's okay."

"He's going to be all right."

"Good night, Patrick."

"Francis . . ."

"Yeah."

"I miss them too."

"See you in the morning." He took a few steps toward the camper, then suddenly stopped. "Mr. Vincent."

"Yes."

"You making breakfast?"

"Sure am."

Bunny stood still for a few seconds with a faint smile on his face, then looked back at Patrick."

"I'll work on it."

"Good night," Francis.

Vincent threw more wood on the fire and they stretched their blankets out and covered themselves; they stared into the embers and watched small yellow-and-blue flames grow larger.

"Damn."

"What's a matter?" said Don.

Patrick rubbed the back of his head. "It's nothing."

"Come on Pat. I detected some outright annoyance there."

"I took a hit right before you picked us up. It's just a little tender, that's all."

Don took off his jacket and rolled it up and handed it to Patrick. "Looks like you could use a pillow, ol' boy."

"Thanks."

"Kind of reminds me of all the nights we camped," said Vincent.

Huey appeared from out of nowhere and sauntered past Patrick, then settled down on the thick wool blanket alongside Kaminski.

"How long have you had him?" asked Vincent.

"Long time. Got him when I became a bachelor again in seventy-five."

Patrick watched the fire's flames grow.

"I can't imagine what might be going through your head right about now," said Vincent.

"Just thinking about a wannabe psychologist I met back there. One night we talked about the Holy Grail and how it appeared to a young boy in a fire just like this one."

"The Grail story, huh."

"That little book you gave me that day you visited—Plough saw it and that started a whole chain of events with him and me."

"When he visited you in that hospital, he seemed genuinely concerned about your well-being."

"Well-being. Hmmmm. Seems like all of you were concerned with my well-being. You all put your souls at risk for me."

"Remember what old Harper said back at St. James about the meaning of the Grail quest. He said it's about serving something greater than ourselves."

"I suppose he was right. Seeing old Henry offering up his incantations like that to his almighty spirit . . . how'd he say it . . . for the blessings already coming our way . . ."

"That's right . . . the blessings already on their way."

"Contrast that with, you know—Henry's blessings with what Harper offered up on another day . . . remember him reciting Aeschylus? Remember how it went . . ."

"I am afraid I don't. He talked a lot about what those ancient Greeks had to say. Not sure what you're getting at."

"I memorized it, Vin," he said. "'He who learns must suffer, and even in our sleep, pain which cannot forget falls drop by drop upon the heart until, in our own despair, against our will, comes wisdom through the awful grace of God.' Wisdom through the awful grace of God . . . that's an amazing line, isn't it . . . one that not only subverts an idea but also an emotion."

"It sounds to me like that old Aeschylus back then was trying to warn his readers about putting too much stock in what the heavens had to offer."

"You're right. I couldn't have said it any better. But is it a good thing to put down a mystery? Emotions are mysterious, aren't they? Sometimes emotions are all we have to go on . . . live for . . . you know what I mean?"

"Yeah. That's for sure. We couldn't live without them. Maybe that's why we were willing to put our souls at risk, like you said."

Patrick looked over at Don and his cat.

"Vin."

"Yeah?"

"Look over there. I put um both to sleep."

"Well, they have the right idea."

VIII

You wake up in the early-morning hours and while lying in bed you think about things. It's easy to begin to trick yourself. Keep telling yourself what you want to hear. You tell yourself that maybe you'll make it to a place where things are going to be all right. It's been a while since I could think things might come out all right for me. The friends that I left back there in that hellish place will never feel the way I feel right now. I am not sure what I will do or can do when I get to what will be my new home, so deep below the Arizona desert.

Me. Is that all I can think about? How can I think about me right now? Remember your Shakespeare, Patrick . . . "Freeze, freeze, thou bitter sky, that dost not bite so nigh as benefits forgot." Father taught us that ingratitude was the worst human quality of all. The long arm of the FBI will follow them for what they have done for me. You tell yourself that just maybe all of this will be over soon. But you know differently. You can wish all you want. The law never sleeps.

And what about the best qualities of man? Was Vincent right when he said we can't live without our emotions? Are our feelings as important as our ability to reason? Can there be a "feeling function"? What about love? Old man Harper said Sanskrit has ninety-six words for love. Persia has eighty. The Greeks had three. Americans have one. He said this "feeling" performs the same function as "thinking" but it does so without facts or reason. It is a sensation or urgency that one experiences in the body. Thinking is grounded in the left side of the brain where reason lives. "Feeling" is grounded in the right side of the brain . . . and is a bodily sensation of rightness and value. Through "feeling," one "knows" without knowing how he knows. Someone who is strong in this function feels the rightness of a choice, without facts, without logic. In fact, through the feeling function, the Unconscious Mind gives us guidance directly. To go to our facility of reason immediately stops the feeling function as well as intuition. Western culture has emasculated its feeling function. Not understanding what it is, it derides this gift of its own psyche, wrongly associating it with emotionality. My brother is very wise. So was Mr. Harper.

It rained in the night and the rain hissed in the fire and Huey crawled under Kaminski's blanket to keep dry, and in the morning it was cold and gray with the sun a long time coming. With everything soaking wet, Vincent decided a fire was not to be, went inside the camper, and came back out with a plastic water container, a jar of Tang and a bag of some kind of beef. They stood at the back of the camper and Vincent cut up strips of smoked jerky and they chewed it and drank the orange-flavored water.

They drove all morning through low rolling hills and hollows of Appalachia, past tar-paper-roofed shanties with porches filled with old washing machines and car parts and rusted-out swing sets in the front yards. Some roads were black top; others dirt and stone. Every five or ten miles two lanes merged into a one-lane dusty gravel road. The truck pitched and yawed as Vincent navigated steep narrow tracks that looked more like cattle trails then roadways. When he got to the main highway, he slowed, then pulled out onto the blacktop and drove west toward Charleston, and he kept to the speed limit every mile of the way. He stopped at an Esso station for gas and a newspaper. He handed the paper to Patrick, who unfolded it on his lap, and Kaminski stretched his neck to read along to see if there was any news about the prison break.

By noon they were in Charleston. Kaminski looked down at his clipboard and found the rental car address, then took his map out and directed Vincent to the west side of town and their first primary destination point. Vincent pulled up in front of a grocery store a block away from the Hertz parking lot and shut off the motor. The three men that could trace their friendship back to grammar school sat in the truck cab. They sat quietly.

After a while Vin said, "Don . . . it's all yours now."

"I guess I am the only one with a legit license."

"Henry must have one," said Patrick.

"Not sure you noticed . . . remember his note . . . he had some kind of a stroke after you were sent away," said Vincent.

"I did see him struggling this morning. He walks real slowly now. I guess we won't be asking him to drive the rest of the way."

"Yeah, that's for sure . . . his arm's all buggered up too. Let's hope his Supai friends can be trusted."

"I know hope is not an action plan but everything kind of rests on that now, doesn't it?" said Vincent.

"Sure looks that way."

"I've never been a big fan of hope. I hate good-byes. Don."

"Yeah, Vin."

"As soon as I sell your place, I'll get in contact with you through Henry's people in St. Regis. You have enough cash for now . . . right?"

"We'll be okay," replied Kaminski.

Vincent looked at Patrick and said, "Then this is it, brother. It may be a while before I can . . ."

"No worries, Vin."

Kaminski opened his door and got out and walked around to the driver's side of the truck and leaned against the front wheel well, then looked down at his map. He moved over and stood alongside the driver's-side door.

Vincent rolled down his window and looked at Kaminski. "I am going to check on the two of them first, then go in here and get some coffee for us and more food before we head out. That'll give you two a chance to sit and talk a bit."

"All right, Don," said Vincent.

Kaminski walked around to the back of the truck.

Vincent looked Patrick. "I believe he's about the best friend anyone could ever have."

"Yeah, I believe you're right. And what an amazing pilot, huh?"

"Yeah he is. I was told he was one of the best the army ever had. Be sure to check the tires at your next stop, okay? When he took this to Alaska he had more than one puncture."

"Remember when the old man first got this thing?"

"Do you think about them?" Vincent said.

"Our parents?"

"Yes. I do."

"Not too long ago I was in his study and found quite a few personal letters they had written to one another. You know you think about your family; you see them one way, then try to make some sense of everything that's happened."

"Are you all right?" Vincent said.

"I am all right."

"Hand me that water jug, will ya?" Vincent took a few swigs of water and watched Patrick. "I have to say you look different," he said.

"I am not the same as I was."

His brother nodded.

Patrick slid over to the passenger side of the truck. "Let me ask you something," he said.

"Okay."

"All of this that you and Don did—any regrets?"

The younger brother looked at him, gauging the question. "No," he said. "I'll tell you straight up how it was: we just couldn't allow it to go on any longer . . . you being locked up in there forever. We just got thoroughly pissed off at the whole thing—the trial, the government's new bullshit drug laws."

"But what about . . ."

"Hell, you know Don—once he gets that crazy mind of his going there isn't anything he thinks he can't do. Boy . . . that white chopper; that really did it, huh? They really thought there was some big emergency happening, didn't they?"

"Yeah, it sure was a good plan. Not a single shot fired. But what about when you get back home today?"

"Pat, you set your sights on what's ahead of you. Don't be thinking about me . . . you hear? Tomorrow I'll be back at the plant doing my marketing dog-and-pony show and then the Saturday night gig at the American Legion. A man's allowed to call in sick on a Monday once in a while."

"There's going to be a ton of questioning coming your way—you know that, don't you?"

"Will see. Continuity is the key. I'll just keep my head down, doing what I always do. *Keep on keeping on.* That's my plan."

"I'll miss the orchards and the jack when fall comes around."

"You and those trees—you loved all of it, didn't you?"

"It's the only thing that ever made complete sense to me. We are who we protect and who we stand up for, and when he put me in charge of them, well, it was as if . . ."

"Yeah, go on."

"It's kind of like what religion does for some. The role it can play in a man's life."

"Religion?"

"It plays an important part . . . not the religion itself but the feeling of something larger than ourselves, something that connects us to the spiritual realm. Being an orchard keeper taught me a lot about this. You have to understand that for you to live, life had to change. The apples that you've grown have made a pact, made a deal with you to keep them alive. Everything adapted to you."

"It's been a while since I've done this. I am going to take an oath. As long as I am alive, I promise you those apple trees will always be cared for."

"Well, that makes me very glad."

"There is one thing I need to ask you before I get going."

"What is it?"

"Just a second ago I mentioned family and trying to make some sense of it."

"Yeah."

"Well, when Angus King opened that will and read what was in it . . ."

"Oh that. I think I know what's coming," said Patrick.

"I mean by all rights, you being the oldest and all, Grey Stone was yours."

"How come just the cottage and the orchards?"

"I am not sure there's enough time to explain it. Hell, I am not sure I have any answers that make sense." Vincent looked at him. "When you came back from being in the city . . . you know, when you finished working on those towers, you seemed, I don't know . . . different. So removed from us."

"Yeah, I was. It was about that time I went to them and asked to remove me and put you in for sole ownership. It was only a few months later their plane went down . . . that kind of sealed my fate. I then just decided to permanently check out."

"That's when you hooked up with Ian."

"Yeah."

"But why, Pat? What on earth caused you to ..."

"Be a pot smuggler?"

"Yeah."

"Remember that wannabe psychologist I was telling you about ..."

"Yeah, Les Plough ... the guy that visited you."

"Maybe someday you can look him up. I think maybe he can explain it. Here comes Don. Vin."

"Yeah."

"I doubted everything I ever knew or thought I knew about myself. And when that happens, you just get lost and your decision-making gets real fuzzy and ... well ... you saw what happened."

"I think I understand."

"Thanks for taking care of the trees."

They crossed the Little Colorado River just north of Sedona, Arizona, and took Route 64 south. When Kaminski pulled into a filling station, the western sky was orange, red, and pale purple and the rock faces that surrounded a nearby ranch absorbed the colors that the setting sun had produced. He got change from the proprietor and made a telephone call and filled the tank and went back in and paid.

When they got to Williams it was nine o'clock. He sat with Patrick at the intersection in front of the Cameron Trading Post with the lights off and the motor running. Then he turned the lights on and pulled out onto Hermit's Rest Road headed east. He looked down at his clipboard at Henry's detailed instructions. He marked the mileage on the odometer and drove another two miles and slowed and turned off the road. He shut off the lights and left the motor running and got out and walked down and opened a gate and came back. He drove across the metal strips of a cow guard and got out and closed the gate again, then he got in the cab and drove down the dirt lane. He followed an ancient barbed-wire fence line, the truck wallowing over the bad terrain. The fence was just an old vestige, a couple of wires strung on weather-beaten, spindly wooden posts.

After a mile he came out on a barren red clay plain where a very old, partially spray painted, rusted-out Ford Econoline van was parked facing him. He slowly pulled alongside it and shut the engine off. Don and Patrick opened their doors and got out. A man got out on the driver's side of the van and greeted them. Patrick walked around to the back of the truck and opened the camper door. "We're here. Let's go," he said.

"Have you talked to him?"

"Not yet. Thought you'd make the introductions."

"All right then, let's get started," said Henry.

Henry stepped out of the camper. Bunny picked up the cat carrier and stepped down from the rear camper door, and together with Patrick they walked over to the van. Don stood by the front of the van.

"Look at all those stars up there," said Bunny.

"That's our desert sky," said the driver.

Another man, with long, flowing white hair, got out of the passenger's side of the van and stood beside the driver. "You must be Henry Crow Horse," said the man.

"Yes, and these are the men I wrote you about."

"I am Charley; my tribal name is White Feather. This is my brother George; he is Light Horse.

"This is Patrick Wallace, Don Kaminski, and Francis Bunnyard."

"I see you have an extra man."

"And I have my cat," said Don.

"Yes, will that be a problem?" said Henry.

"No, I don't think so—we have enough horses. I like cats."

"That is good."

"George will dispose of the camper truck. Not to worry, it will vanish as planned. The ride down is about eleven miles. With the horses it will take maybe five, six hours. There's a campsite waiting for us not too far from here. Tomorrow, after you've rested, we will get you down to the village."

Henry opened the passenger's-side door of the van and got in, while Light Horse drove the camper truck away. Patrick, Don, and Bunny climbed into the back of the van and sat cross-legged on a dirty mattress. Bunny opened the cat carrier and Huey came out and sat down next to Kaminski and rubbed the side of his head against the chopper pilot's knee and thigh. Charley White Feather got behind the wheel and headed toward the entrance to the west rim of the canyon. As he drove faster the tires kicked up red clay dust into the clear, starry night. He drove in a straight line except when he had to maneuver around giant tumbleweeds and armadillo. He stopped next to a firepit and shut off the motor, switched the dome light on, then turned and addressed the men.

"Our entrance to the canyon is not far; there will be no officials around here. Nobody will bother us."

"I don't see any camp gear in here," said Don.

"I brought some blankets, bread, and canteens of water, and there's some antelope jerky over there in that grocery bag."

"Where we will sleep?"

"Here inside," said Charley White Feather.

"All of us?"

"Henry and I will sleep on the roof."

"Why would you want to do that?" said Don.

"Well, you see, in the beginning when the earth and sky came together, I'itoi was born."

"I'itoi . . ."

"Yes, I'itoi . . . that's right, and he dislikes uninvited visitors. Everywhere, here, there, red shadows fall on Desolation. Tiny men live underground, the Yaqui hereabouts call them Surem."

"Surem . . . I see."

"And I'itoi directs them from his cave. The ancient ones said fallen angels were bound in chains and buried beneath a desert known as Desolation . . . that's what's all around us."

Charley let out a laugh. "But to get back to your question, much of the wildlife here is nocturnal, and it creeps through the nights and is poisonous and alien."

"Like what?" said Bunny.

"Well, there are quite a few, but here are the main ones we look out for: there's the sidewinder and the rattlesnake, scorpions, the giant centipede, the black widow, the tarantula, the brown recluse, the coral snake, the Gila monster . . ."

"Holy shit," shouted Bunny.

"And if that's not enough, nature has given us a further danger . . . "

"And what might that be?" said Don.

"Wild bees. And I've been told they are now Africanized. As if the desert felt it hadn't made its point, it added killer bees."

"Well, Mr. White Feather . . . sounds like this could indeed be Desolation."

"Inside it will be," said Patrick.

At midnight they heard three long howls to the north, then silence.

"Did you hear that?" said Don.

Huey opened his eyes, twitched an ear, and licked his paw but didn't budge from Kaminski's blanket.

"Yeah."

"It's a wolf, isn't it?"

"Yeah."

Patrick lay on his back in his blanket and looked out the two rear windows, where he could see a sliver of moon, and just below it he saw the Pleiades, which seemed to be cascading down and crossing the black sky, taking with it all the stars of the cosmos. His eyes were drawn to the outline of Orion and

Capella and the distinctive look of Cassiopeia; they were all rising up over the great canyon in one massive, orchestrated, speckled light show. He lay listening to the others' breathing in their sleep while he contemplated the past few days and wondered what would come next.

It was cold in the night, and in the dawn Charley White Feather was already up and had a fire going on the ground and was huddled over the flames. He stood up and walked over to the van to help Henry Crow Horse. He held steady a rickety old wooden ladder while Henry slowly climbed down from the roof. Once Henry was on the ground they crouched next to the fire to warm themselves. When the others got out of the van they were in plain view of the eastern rim and its multilayers of different-colored earth that the morning sun was just beginning to expose. They stood and stared at the baked terra-cotta terrain and the canyon's dimensions. Charley cooked bacon and beans and corn made from meal and water, and Henry made cowboy coffee, and they sat eating and drinking and spitting out bits of coffee grounds and looking out at the country. They watched the sun rise and saw a lone rider on horseback approaching on the plain about a mile away, leading horses toward them; dust blew from under the tread of the horses and twisted away behind them.

"How far down the road you think this'll get us?" Said Don.

"It's hard to say," replied Patrick.

"Francis looks a little nervous."

"He'll be all right once we get going."

"I think you're right. I got a feeling he's weathered tougher times."

"He sure has, more than you can imagine."

"You think there'll be a day when they give up looking for us?"

"Yeah. When hell freezes over."

"You have any idea when you think that'll be?"

"I don't have a clue, Don. The way I see it, the government won't like what we did. No, not one bit."

"Yeah, they don't like losing."

"What do you think, Henry?" asked Patrick.

Henry put a cigarette in the corner of his mouth and lit it and flipped away the match. "I don't know. Where we're going, not even the FBI will be able to sniff us out, so it won't matter one way or another."

Patrick stood watching the rider coming closer, his horses kicking up red dust and pollen into the clear morning air. They drank the last of the coffee and ate what was left of the beans. "Let's get ready to go," he said. "Francis."

"Yes, Patrick."

"You ever ride a horse before?"

"There were a few horses on the farm we worked. I never had a problem with um."

"That's excellent."

They were down into the canyon by midmorning. The man who brought them the horses had ridden toward the south, away from the canyon. They rode single file down a narrow, hard-packed caliche trail. They rode without speaking and took in the look of the landscape. A red-tailed hawk in the top of a crag dropped down and flew low along the canyon wall and rose again into a rock shelf a quarter mile away. When they had passed, it flew back again. By noon they were watering the horses next to a small crevasse where water gently flowed out of a rock formation and into a small hollowed-out stone pool. They filled their canteens and walked and drank. They rode on.

By eight o'clock the sun was already setting and the floor of the canyon had become cooler, and with daylight dwindling, an eerie grayness permeated the landscape. There were no cactus, no mesquite in sight, but plenty of candelilla and scrub catclaw. A storm front moved in quickly, towering over the edge of the western rim, and the wind was cool on their faces.

A long, rolling crack of thunder went pealing down the sky to the northwest. The ground shuddered. They sat their horses and looked up into the north sky. They rode on. There were spits of rain in the wind but no downpour. Distant heat lightning crackled. Still no rain. At the base of an enormous rock shelf about a mile away, Patrick saw wood smoke hovering over the roofs of a dozen or more small shanties. As they got closer, he could make out a few tiny patches of corn growing and goats grazing, then out of nowhere a thin, white-and-liver-colored long-haired sheepdog appeared and began walking alongside Bunny and his horse.

"Hey girl . . . where'd you come from?" said Bunny.

As they approached the village of the Havasupai, the night's darkness settled in and the warm yellow light of kerosene railroad lanterns dotted the landscape. Patrick eyed an open pavilion like shelter. In the middle of the dwelling was a fire-pit. The flames lit up the interior enough so that he could see pretty clearly the faces of young Supai children laughing at a tall, attractive Caucasian woman with puppets on her hands. They rode a little further, then Charley White Feather raised his hand into the air quietly and said, "Whoa," then dismounted in front of an adobe hut. The others sat their horses, then dismounted. The dog made a point of sniffing Bunny all over, then stood by his side. Patrick walked over to Henry to make sure he was doing okay after the long descent.

Kaminski looked uneasy. He turned to Charley White Feather. "Where is everybody? I see only kids over there."

"You hear that? . . . Sounds like chanting," said Patrick.

"I am not quite sure," replied Charley. "I am going to go around back. I think I know what's happening. Wait here—I won't be long."

Patrick walked a few steps away from the horses and leaned up against a cottonwood tree and watched the woman perform for the children. Bunny sat down on a wooden stool and petted the dog, while Don took the carrier down off his saddle and let Huey out. Henry stood alongside the hut, listening to the sounds being made a short distance away. A few minutes later Charley White Feather returned.

"It's as I suspected—Doc Berguson is in the middle of conducting a ceremony just behind us at base of that rock formation over there."

"You have your own doc here?" said Don.

"Right now he is the shaman to the tribe. That's his daughter over there with the kids. That's Barbra."

The chanting was getting louder. "What's he doing?" said Henry.

"He's offering up a Supai prayer for a tribal member's recovery. I've seen him do this many times. It'll be over in a few minutes. He gets his power from the thunder and it's necessary he conclude his ritual while the storm is still going on. He covers himself with the pollen of the tule plant that has just been struck by lightning . . . this appeals to the spirit of the lightning. It's harmless. A religious ceremony, not a medical one."

IX

An American-made rental car pulled up to the J. Edgar Hoover Building, then drove slowly forward, staying close to the curb.

"You can't miss that sucker, can you?"

"It's big, that's for sure. It goes on for blocks. Pennsylvania Avenue—it's been a while."

"They didn't waste any time."

"It'll be balls to the walls on this one, Tom. DEA and the US Marshals having a sit-down together—this should be good."

"There's the entrance."

They drove into the basement garage and were stopped by two guards, one on each side.

"Good morning, gentlemen."

"Good morning. Special Agents Tom Price and Randall Svensen."

The two DEA agents showed their IDs and were waved through. Ten minutes later they were in an anteroom outside of Robert A. Scully's office. Special Agent Gary Purcell from the Albany office was waiting to greet them.

"Tom, Randall . . . it's good to see you. How are you?"

"Busy as hell, Gary. Crack . . . it's everywhere."

A buzzer sounded on the desk of Scully's secretary. "They just arrived. Yes sir. You may go in gentlemen."

They entered a large conference room. Four deputy US Marshals and a half dozen FBI agents were standing at a dark mahogany credenza, pouring themselves coffee into white china teacups. Scully, second-in-command at the Federal Bureau of Prisons, was seated at the far end of a large table, engrossed in deep conversation with Special Agent Frank Coltvet.

"You were in Nam, right?" whispered Scully.

"Airborne."

"That's where they used to get us agents from. Now we get 'em from Carnegie Mellon, Ivy League. Accountants and computer whiz kids. Yuppies with guns."

"High-tech crimes require the best minds," said Coltvet.

"I suppose. Then we have this business in Pennsylvania. I guess this would be considered low-tech, huh? That's probably why they handed it to me. Gentlemen . . . can we get started?"

Scully proceeded with introductions.

"You all have been briefed and know why you're here. Special Agent Coltvet will highlight the specifics. Frank . . ."

Coltvet dealt eight-by-ten black-and-white photos like cards onto the table.

"Three days ago, two men, Patrick A. Wallace and Francis L. Bunnyard escaped from Lewisburg Penitentiary in Lewisburg, Pennsylvania. Let's start with some history about similar breakouts. On August 18th, 1971, in Santa Martha Acatitla, Mexico, a prisoner by the name of Joel David Caplan was extracted from a low-security prison with a 1960 whirlybird, then flown by single-engine fixed-wing aircraft to Arizona. There've been others . . . in Europe—France and Spain . . .

one in Germany. This is a first of its kind for us in the United Sates. We want to capture Wallace and Bunnyard as quickly as possible, for obvious reasons. As of this hour, here's what we have, Donald R. Kaminski, ex-army chopper pilot . . . has been a recluse since seventy-five, living for the past ten years atop a mountain in Moreland in Upstate New York. He flew two tours in Nam and is a childhood friend of Patrick Wallace and Wallace's brother. He's MIA. Vincent C. Wallace, Patrick Wallace's brother, lives in Moreland on a large estate that's been in his family for generations. The estate is adjacent to Kaminski's land. He's a VP at the Lunnis fabrications company there in Moreland. What we know for certain is our pilot here liberated a medivac from an army base and pulled his buddy out, then landed in a state forest some fifty-five miles away. It's our contention he didn't act alone. Let's fill in the particulars, shall we? I'll open it up now for your thoughts, questions, comments."

The meeting continued well past twelve and into late afternoon. Sandwiches and another large urn of coffee were brought in. They ate and drank more coffee. When it was over, each man had his assignment and together they agreed upon the mission, which was well established and ready to be executed.

Price and Svensen left the building and walked down into the underground garage and got in their car. The trip back to New York would take seven hours. Svensen drove out of the garage and headed north. Somewhere past Baltimore Price began to relive what went down the night he and State Trooper Scot engaged the smugglers on the reservation. Svensen listened attentively. He was already well versed in the intimate details of the story: the arrest and conviction of Wallace and how the bureau was confronted with one dead end after another with the Mohawk. They drove on.

They crossed over the Susquehanna River and drove to the center of Moreland. The clock on the dash read 1:00 a.m. The office was dark. They stayed in the car looking at the town. Streets empty. No one around, no movement of any kind. Both agents sat still, not saying anything to each other; then Price said, "It's about time we go home, don't you think?"

"Which one of us you think has it better?" said Svensen.

"I'll head for St. Regis after I get a little shut-eye, and you've got your work cut out for you with those bikers; I'd say we both have a pretty good uphill climb."

"You going to be okay with what you got to do?" said Svensen.

"A man is eternally in the debt of someone who saves his life."

Svensen didn't respond.

"To be honest, I am not sure how I feel right now. I'd be lying if I said I didn't think Wallace got screwed by the court. I just don't know, Randall . . . all these new laws . . . seems over the top . . . overkill."

"You're a good man, Tom—when the time comes, you'll do what you think is right."

The next morning Price left the house at seven thirty and took Route 14 north to Elmira, then I-70 to Massena. It was about a two-hundred mile run to St. Regis and he thought he could make it in under three hours.

He arrived at the reservation around eleven forty-five. He stopped at the Double T and sat in a booth and ate and sipped his coffee and watched the cars out on the highway. Something wrong. He sensed a feeling of uneasiness around him. He looked at his watch: 12:50 p.m.

He paid and walked out and got in the unmarked DEA car and sat there. Then he drove to the intersection and turned east and drove to the Bear Den Motel. He pulled into the motel parking lot and parked alongside a half dozen police cruisers. An officer was putting yellow police tape across a door on the second floor. Price got out and walked to one of the cruisers.

"Bad news seems to travel pretty quickly around here. I figured the DEA might show up sooner or later," the sheriff said.

"What's happened, Ed?" said Price.

"Could be more than one homicide. You know anything about this?"

"I don't know. You got any victims?"

"Two. Man and a woman. The ambulance left about a half hour ago with the woman. The man is dead. We have another man in custody—a witness or perp. Not sure yet. He's sitting over there."

"Do you know who they were?"

"Yes. Both Indians. The woman's name is Tushanna. The man is known as Lone Bear. The fella sitting over there . . . his name is Joseph Skywalker."

"What's he saying?"

"He told my deputy a biker started it. Says he dragged the woman out of her room and Lone Bear attempted to free her and the biker shot him. She was in pretty bad shape—looked like he wanted to get something from her and she wasn't about to give him what he wanted, so he roughed her up."

"You mean he beat her?"

"Yeah . . . may have even tortured her to get her to talk."

Price nodded. He looked over at Skywalker. He knew who he was from the trial. He remembered him sitting right behind Wallace. He looked down the row of motel doors. Some people were standing around talking.

Skywalker had asked for a cigarette and he lit it and sat smoking. He sat in the back of the deputy's cruiser looking agitated and worried.

"Can we go somewhere, Ed . . . to talk . . . can you get away for a minute?"

"I can. What's on your mind?"

"I just thought I might get you to ride over to Henry's with me."

"I've been trying to talk with him, Tom. Henry hasn't been seen around here for weeks. Just plain up and vanished."

"Well, Sheriff, Joseph over there may know something about that and maybe more."

"How about we get him to the office and you can fill me in on the way."

"All right."

The deputy secured Skywalker in the back of his cruiser and drove out of the parking lot with his roof lights on. Price got into the Sheriff's cruiser. It was a twenty-minute ride to the Massena County jail. During that time Price gave Ed Thomas a complete overview of the escape and his assignment. It was half past two when they arrived at the sheriff's office. At the front desk Thomas told his secretary to alert the state police that an interrogation would soon be underway. Price followed the sheriff down a hallway. Thomas stopped a few yards before the interrogation room and said,

"If what you suspect is true, then we've got to hurry up and move on this . . . you agree?"

"Time is a commodity in short supply when it comes to these kinds of things."

I've been sheriff here for a couple of years now, you know, since Henry retired, and I can tell ya the Mohawk here are fiercely loyal and close-lipped about . . . well, just about everything when it comes to dealing with outsiders."

"I think we can capitalize on that loyalty . . . Joseph and Wallace's relationship goes back a long way. There's a strong bond there."

"He was able to give us a pretty good description of the biker . . . we got to have something tangible to go on before the state police get here if your plan is going to work."

"If I am right, Joseph knows where that biker is headed, and he'll do his damnedest to get to Wallace ASAP."

They entered a small concrete-walled windowless room;

Skywalker was sitting at a steel table. Price sat opposite him while the sheriff stood off to the side.

"You want some coffee?"

"Yeah. I'll take some coffee," said Skywalker.

Thomas picked up a coffeepot that was off to the side of the room and poured some coffee into a Styrofoam cup and handed it, a plastic spoon, and a tiny container of cream to Skywalker.

"I am Special Agent Tom Price . . . I am with the DEA."

"I don't do drugs."

"That's not why I am here, Joseph. Can I call you Joseph?"

"That's my name."

"What I wanted to talk to you about, Joseph, was the man that you claim shot your friend. I wonder if there's anything that comes to mind about him. Anything more you might remember then him just being a biker, like you said."

"Like what?"

"Have you ever seen him before?"

Skywalker shook his head. "No," he said. He looked around the room.

Price watched him.

"How old a man would you say he was?"

"I don't know."

"You told the deputy he was in his thirties."

"Yeah. Something like that."

"How tall was he, would you say?"

"Not real tall. Sort of medium."

"Did he and Lone Bear fight? If so, did your friend hurt him?"

"I don't know. He was bleeding. Had a cut on his head. I couldn't say how bad he was hurt. After he shot him, he got on his bike and just took off."

Price stared at him.

"How badly was he bleeding?"

"I don't know."

"What did he say?"

"He didn't say anything."

"What did you say to him?"

"Nothing."

Price studied him. He got up and poured himself some coffee and sipped the coffee and set it down on the table.

"You're not going to help me, are you?"

"I told you all I know. I spoke to the deputy already. That's all I know to tell you."

"You have no idea why that man beat that poor woman almost to death?"

Price stood alongside him, watching him. Then he left the room. Thomas followed him out the door.

"We on the same page, Ed?"

"Yeah. When the Troopers get here, I'll let them do their thing, then cut Skywalker loose.

"There's just one more thing, Ed."

"What's that?"

"The deputy that arrived on the scene."

"Yeah."

"When he got there, was anything said? Any exchange?"

"I don't know. I haven't had a chance to fully debrief him."

"Could we talk to him now?"

"Sure."

The sheriff walked out of the office. Moments later he returned, his deputy walking close behind him.

"Deputy Andy Crow Horse, I'd like you to meet Agent Tom Price; he's with the DEA."

The men shook hands.

"Crow Horse. You wouldn't happen to be any relation to . . ."

"He's my uncle."

"I've talked with him on occasion. He's a good man."

"Yeah. Everyone in our tribe gives him respect."

"Look. I am a little pressed for time. I'll cut to the chase. Can you give me any info on what the two victims may have said when you came up on um? You were the first to arrive . . . right?"

"Yes."

The deputy took out a very small spiral notebook from his uniform-shirt breast pocket and looked at his notes, then suddenly his eyes began to tear up. "Do you mind if I sit down?" he said to the sheriff.

"You all right, Andy?" asked the sheriff.

The deputy sat down on one of the two armchairs that were on opposite sides of the small steel interrogation table. The sheriff put his hand on his shoulder.

"I've known Tushanna and Lone Bear forever. Went to school with um."

"Take your time," said the sheriff.

"When I got there, she was unconscious. Lone Bear was flat on his back a few feet away from her. When he saw me, he raised his hand. As I knelt down, I offered my hand and he grabbed it. He struggled to talk."

"And did he?" asked Agent Price.

"He whispered, 'Supai . . . Supai. He's with . . .' Then that was it." The deputy began to softly cry.

"Supay? What is Supay?" asked Price.

"It's pronounced Supai. I remember a few years back our tribe had this powwow, and tribes from the western states came here. The Supai representatives didn't have any money to travel here. But we've always known about um. They live somewhere deep in the Grand Canyon," replied the deputy.

"Thank you, Andy. Ed, I am going to contact my partner now."

Agent Price and Andy Crow Horse shook hands.

"You can use my office to make your call."

"Thanks, Ed."

They walked back down the hall toward the front desk.

"Sheriff," said the secretary.

"Yes, Darleen."

"The hospital called a moment ago. The woman didn't make it."

The deafening sounds coming from a chopper's straight exhaust pipes rattled Mom "the Butcher" Denton's kitchen window.

"That sounds like Razor."

"Sure does. Hand me the catch-up, will ya?" said Mom.

Martha walked over to the refrigerator and got the ketchup bottle out and plopped it down on the kitchen table.

"While you're up, how about some more of that sweet tea?"

"Jesus. Anything else?"

"Quit your hollering."

"I suppose I gotta make him something too."

"Keep it up."

Razor drove to the end of the driveway, got off his Harley, opened the garage door, and pushed his chopper in, then closed the door. Mom finished eating and walked out the back door of the kitchen and into the garage and saw him kneeling down, fitting a muffler onto his exhaust pipe.

"If you put that new muffler on, Martha won't know it's you coming."

Razor stood up.

"Shit, man, you're bleeding."

"It's okay."

"Better come in and have her patch you up."

"Soon as I finish this. I need to take some time off—I am thinking two weeks will do it. That okay with you?"

"Yeah. Sure. You've never asked for any time before. You heading out solo?"

"Going west. Just need to take care of some unfinished business."

"West, huh?"

"Yeah, Arizona."

"That's a couple of thousand miles, you know. What happened to your head?"

"I know it's a long haul."

"You don't owe me any explanations, Raze. Come in when you're done here and Martha will fix you up."

It was early evening; a good twelve hours after the bodies of Lone Bear and Tushanna had been discovered in the Bear Den Motel. Special Agent Tom Price of the DEA, Massena County Sheriff Ed Thomas and the New York State police had just finished their interrogation of Skywalker in the county jail.

Skywalker stood in the doorway of the interrogation room facing the hallway, then turned to the sheriff. "I need to make a call."

"Phone's down the hall to your right," said the sheriff. He handed Skywalker two quarters.

Skywalker took the coins and walked away. When he got to the pay phone, he took out his wallet and searched for a small slip of paper. He dialed.

"Dash."

"Yeah."

"It's Joey."

"Joey. Man . . . how the hell are you . . . it's been . . ."

"I know."

"Where you at?"

"Massena."

"What's up?"

"It's Lone Bear."

"Yeah . . . how's he . . ."

"He was shot. Dash."

"Yeah."

"He's been killed."

"What. What do you mean? He's dead? How can that be? . . . I just talked with him."

"Look, can you come get me? I am at the sheriff's office. I can tell you all about it when you get here. Can you come?"

"Yes. Of course I can."

"There's a little place across from the sheriff's office. I am looking at it right now—it's called Misty Anne's. I'll be sitting in there until they throw me out."

"It will take me at least an hour and a half to get there."

"If I am not in there I'll be sitting in the park that's next to the courthouse."

"Joey."

"Yeah."

"Who would want to shoot Lone Bear?"

When Special Agent Randall Svensen walked into his Massena DEA office, the phone

was ringing. He quickly made it to his desk and picked up the receiver. "Agent Svensen," he said.

"It's Tom."

"Tom. I just got in. You on the reservation?"

"Yeah."

"You must be thinking I am a slacker, Tom."

"Why's that?"

"I am just now showing up for work."

"Yeah, well . . . you're the married one. Marie probably wanted you to . . ."

"Okay, okay . . . how you making out up there in St. Regis?"

"Just a few hours ago I came upon a crime scene. A double homicide. Both Indians. Seems an Angel was the perpetrator."

"You think there might be a connection with our guy?"

"Don't know."

"I am getting ready to meet up with a possible informer across the border . . . wait a second, I see there's a message on my desk from Gary. Hold on. Let me see what he's learned," said Svensen.

Svensen looked down at the FBI teletype printout that showed the transcript of an interview with the warden in Lewisburg and another interview in Moreland. Price waited while Svensen read the results of the interviews.

"You still there?" Svensen asked.

"Yeah."

"All right, I am back. Well, it seems the agents in Penna have earned their pay for the month."

"What are they reporting?"

"Two things: first, they've discovered that a Hell's Angel by the name of Thorval Saxon, aka Highway, tried to kill Wallace . . . twice. Wallace was lucky to survive the first attack. In the second attempt the escapee Bunnyard killed Highway just before they flew over the wall. Seems Highway was blood brothers with one of the guys that got killed in that trailer you were in that night with Wallace. Second, one of Gary's men interviewed Wallace's brother and found zip so far but they're in the process of casting a bigger net on his whereabouts the week of the escape. That will take some legwork, some time."

"What are you thinking, Randall?"

"Well, we've got two Mohawks getting whacked by an Angel, then we have these attempted killings of our man by an Angel . . . mere coincidence, or is it something else? We saw how well Wallace was connected with the Mohawk up there."

"I am making some inquires here . . . nothing much to tell at this moment. I'll get back to you. That informer you mentioned . . ." said Price.

"Yeah."

Who is he?

His name is Billy Grimes. RCMP have him in Montreal on some trafficking charges. He was a member of Butcher's organization. They tell me he might be eager to talk to avoid some serious time in that hellhole in Causapscal. After I interview him, I'll find you and we can review our notes."

"All right. Good-bye, Randall."

Price stepped out of the sheriff's private office and walked toward the interrogation room; the sheriff was standing outside the room smoking a cigarette.

"Are the state police finally finished with him?"

"Yeah. Skywalker is outside. He's waiting for someone to pick him up. I have Deputy De'Grasse keeping an eye on him."

"Good, 'cause if he sees me tailing him, he'll go in a hole for sure on that reservation and that could make things difficult for me."

"You think this Skywalker has any idea what he's getting himself into?"

"I doubt it. I got a feeling there's some kind of strong connection there—deep roots. Some kind of Indian thing going on below the surface."

It was half past nine when they pulled into Hooker's parking lot. Dash drove around back and parked, then he and Skywalker got out and entered the garage through the back entrance and walked through the darkened bays and into the parts room, which doubled as an office. Dan Proud Hawk was sitting behind his desk and when he saw them he got up and walked around the desk and put his arms around Skywalker. Dash stood silently alongside them.

"Have you . . ."

"Yes, Joey. I just heard."

"It was that Razor asshole that did it. I need to call Mary."

"All right. But first sit down. Please. You too, Dash. Joey . . ."

"I got to call Mary—give me the phone."

"You're upset. Let's think this through . . . okay? Joey . . ."

"Yeah."

Proud Hawk looked over at Dash and then back at Skywalker. "Does he know about all we've done for Patrick? You know, the Pennsylvania thing?"

Skywalker looked at Dash then back at Proud Hawk. "Yeah, yeah, I told him everything on the way over here."

"Come on. Sit down here. Tell me what happened . . . what you saw . . . all I heard was there was a shooting . . . Lone Bear and Tushannah were shot."

Proud Hawk walked back behind the desk and opened up a drawer and took out a bottle of Wild Turkey. "Here. Have some of this . . ."

Skywalker took the bottle.

"Go on. Drink."

He sat down on an old bench seat from a fifty-seven Chevy sedan and took a swig of the whiskey, then handed the bottle over to Dash, who took a drink. Dash sat down. Proud Hawk pushed the telephone to the front of the desk.

"Before you call Mary you have to fill me in on what happened, all right?"

Skywalker grabbed the bottle and took another drink. "Both of um. Dead."

Proud Hawk slowly sat back in his chair and stared at Skywalker. "Let me have that . . ."

Skywalker handed him the bottle. He gulped down some whiskey and set the bottle down in front of him. "Do you think that biker knows where Patrick's at?"

"I am certain of it."

The telephone rang. Proud Hawk grabbed the receiver. "Hello. Yeah . . . Uh um . . . I just heard."

A few minutes went by. Proud Hawk hung up the receiver. "That was Chief Dan Tails. He just got off the phone with his man in the sheriff's office. He wants to see me. He's coming over. Did you know Tushanna was the chief's niece?"

"Uh . . . yeah, I think so. Yeah, that's right," said Skywalker.

Twenty minutes later Chief Dan Tails stood in front of the garage's entrance, then walked in. He went directly to Proud Hawk's office. He opened the door. Proud Hawk stood up and looked at him. He came around the desk and held out his hand; they shook hands. Skywalker and Dash stood up, then went over and stood along the wall; the chief acknowledged both of them, then he and Proud Hawk sat down on the old car seat.

"What is it you wanted to tell me?" asked Proud Hawk.

Dan Tails looked at Dash. "I remember you from Wallace's trial."

Skywalker turned to the chief and said, "His name's Dash. He's my friend. And so is . . . was Lone Bear. The three of us, we've worked with Patrick Wallace for some time. Patrick was a real close friend of my father," said Skywalker.

"Yes, I am starting to understand all of it now. The pieces are falling into place. That Hell's Angel, that Razor, he got what he wanted from Tushanna, all right. Lone Bear must've walked in on um as he was trying to get her to talk."

The chief looked at the bottle of whiskey. "Can I have some of that?"

Proud Hawk got up and handed him the bottle of bourbon. The chief raised the bottle to his mouth and took two swigs of the whiskey, then put the bottle on the desk and stared at Proud Hawk, then at Skywalker, then Dash.

"Things happen. I can't take um back," said the Chief.

"What do you mean?"

"I just got back from seeing Tushanna's husband Tommy— the kids were there. Those goddamn bikers. I never should have gone into business with them . . ." With tears in his eyes the chief lowered his head into the palms of his hands. "Ahhhh, Tushanna . . . ahhhh, Lone Bear," the chief groaned.

Proud Hawk gave Skywalker the keys to his blown 425-horsepower Hemi-powered Barracuda, the hottest car on the reservation. The chief gave Skywalker plenty of cash and two pistols and promised to look after Mary and his children if something were to go wrong. Skywalker and Dash left the reservation for the Grand Canyon just after sunset. Dash sat quietly staring out the passenger's-side window into the blackness of a moonless night.

Agent Price sat in his Chrysler K Car for a while, then picked up the receiver. "Randall . . . come in, this is Tom, your read me? Over."

"Yes Tom, I read you five by five."

"I lost them. One minute I was on them, then . . . just, well, they're gone. He's got one hell of a fast car."

"No worries. I'll call Gary—the bureau will have them targeted in no time. Give me that plate number."

"Let's hold off on that."

"Say that again?"

"Did you come up with anything in Montreal?"

"Yeah . . . I was just going to contact you."

"A good lead, huh?"

"Yeah. We may have something. This boy Billy Grimes, if he can be trusted . . . he may have just offered up something plausible."

"I'd like to keep this within the DEA circle for now."

"All right, but . . . I don't . . . okay, Tom it's your show. What do you want me to do?"

"Tell me everything this Billy Grimes had to say."

X

The sun was over the canyon, warming the cool air, ridding the ground of the ever-present morning desert-floor dampness. Bunny came out of his bedroom and walked out the front door past Kaminski, who was up on a ladder preparing to repair a section of the roof. Each man seemed to be settling into his new surroundings and using his talents to improve his living environment. Kaminski had a bucket containing red mud and was troweling the mixture into a crack that was allowing rainwater to leak directly below onto a large eight-by-four-foot piece of plywood that lay atop two rickety wooden sawhorses. The weathered, baked-dry, splintered sheet of plywood acted as a workbench and dining and poker table. In the middle of the night it had rained and water that hit the tabletop dripped down onto the dirt floor, creating a large patch of mud. Huey woke up on his ragged little piece of braided rug that lay in front of the fireplace, sat up, looked around the room and walked toward the open front door, then stopped and eyed the mud in front of him. He went around it and stood on the threshold and looked out at the communal well, where a woman was pumping water into a five-gallon plastic jug. At the back of their adobe dwelling, near the kitchen, Chopper—the name Bunny gave to the ever-present dog—aroused by the bark of a neighbor's dog, got up and walked through the mud, then at a quickened pace darted around and past the cat and out the door.

Bunny, returning from a trip to the outhouse, stood at the foot of the ladder. "Have you seen Patrick?"

Kaminski looked down. "Saw him over there behind Doc Berguson's a little while ago."

"Oh."

Bunny climbed halfway up the ladder and looked in the direction of the shaman's living quarters and saw Patrick standing alongside Doc Berguson's daughter Barbra.

"You're an easy man to talk to, Patrick."

"Is that right? What are the canyon walls saying today?"

"This morning they're silent. An unnerving silence except for the flies . . . those big horseflies, buzzing around the drying sage I hung from the rafters of my little shade arbor my father made for me. Every morning I play Lilly's little game. She only likes to be milked under that thing."

"She seems like a nice-enough goat. Maybe it's the smell of the sage."

"Yes, that could be, but my father thinks she's a trickster. Has that kind of spirit in her."

"I am still learning about your father's ways, Barbra . . . his . . . what did you call it . . . his insights into consciousness awareness . . . ahhhh . . . I am not sure exactly how to . . . you must think I am a . . ."

"I think you're wonderful. I was going to go to the falls . . . You want to come?

"Yes, I . . . I would enjoy that very much . . . maybe on the way we could talk about last night."

She gently took his hand and side by side they started down a caliche path past striated rock formations, moving ever so slowly and unhurried as if time had no meaning to them. After a few minutes they began walking single file upward on a narrow trail toward a rushing sound, slowly climbing higher and higher above the break, and then came back down into a mini canyon where blue-green water flowed from the upper rim straight down, more than two hundred feet into a grotto that was completely surrounded by lush vegetation. She walked up to the waterfall and said, "I am going to wash my hair."

She released from the back of her long, thin neck a small buckskin-like, turquoise-beaded collar that held her hair in place, then, looking up at the sky, she shook her head, releasing her long black hair, which cascaded down across and past the middle of her back. She opened a leather pouch that hung from her belt and took out a small plastic bottle of liquid soap, then bent forward near the edge of the spray, being careful not to extend too far into the main force of the flowing water. She knelt down where the water had pooled and washed her hair. Patrick stood off to the side and watched her. When she had finished, they sat down together where the sunlight shone down intensely so she could dry her hair.

"You were right about my father. He is a very remarkable man with some special gifts."

"How so?"

"The Supai say he has 'bear quality' . . . much nature power.

"How is it that the two of you happened to come to this place?"

"My father, you should know, was a very successful doctor in Philadelphia. A member of the Thomas Jefferson University medical faculty. He was a widower, and I was his only child. He was not an especially religious man, a sober Episcopalian.

One Sunday morning, five years ago ... he attended a Pentecostal meeting at the University of Pennsylvania ... and found himself speaking in tongues. He knelt down at the back of the room and began to talk fluently in a language that no one had ever heard before. This sort of thing happens frequently at Pentecostal meetings and began happening regularly to my father. It was not unusual to walk into our home and find my father sitting in his office utterly serene, happily speaking to the air in this strange, foreign tongue. I was, at that time, nineteen years old, having my first affair with a minority group leader. In my case, a Dakota Indian, a postgraduate fellow at Temple doing his doctorate in aboriginal languages of the Southwest. One day, I brought the boy home just as my father was sinking to his knees in the entrance foyer in one of his trances. The Indian wheeled in his tracks, and he said, 'Holy shit!' You see, my father was speaking a Supai dialect ... an obscure dialect, at that, spoken only by a ragtag band of unreformed Indians who had rejected the reservation and gone to live in isolation here in the bottom of this canyon. What do you think about that?"

"What am I supposed to say to that? I mean . . . really, Barbra."

"Yes, I can see your point. I need to explain it more ... no, better. It's not totally about my father's conversion, it's about mine. You see, I'd been hitting the hallucinative drugs pretty regularly at that time. I had some bad trips. Suicidal thoughts had entered my head, but nothing as crazy as fluency in an obscure Supai dialect. I mean, like, 'Far out, man!' Here was living miraculous communication of supernatural knowledge right before my eyes! In a few months, my father had closed his Main Line practice and set out to start a mission in the Arizona desert. I gave up my radical countercultural ideas and I followed him. It was a mistake, at least for me. My father had received the revelation, not I. He stood on a giant boulder, wide-eyed and gaunt, and preached the coming of the apocalypse to earnestly amused Indians. We lived in a cave, ate birds, and crushed piñon nuts. It was awful. Within a few months I was back in Philadelphia. An empty vessel, despondent, and dizzy with drug-induced flashbacks. I turned to conformity, cut my hair, and entered nursing school. I became worn-out, compelled . . . had shamelessly incestuous dreams about my father. I took up with some of the senior staff there. One of them, a chubby little psychiatrist, explained to me in no uncertain terms that I had a continuing unresolved lust fantasy for my father. I broke down. One day, they found me walking to work naked and screaming obscenities. There was talk of locking me up. So I packed a bag and came back here, to the bottom of this canyon. I've been here ever since. It's been three years now. My father is, of course, quite mad. I watch over him, and have been remarkably content. You see, Patrick, I believe in, well, in the whole enchilada . . . anything and everything."

"What was that all about?"

"I thought I was obvious. I'm trying to tell you, I have a thing about powerful, insightful men and I wanted to be honest with you about my past."

"I admire your candor."

"Patrick . . . last night, it was . . . you know when I first saw you I said to Mr. White Feather, 'Who's that hulking bear of a man?' The Supai are reverential about bears. Won't eat bear meat, never skin bears. Bears are thought of as both benign and evil, but very strong power. Men with bear power are highly respected and are said to be great healers. 'That man,' I said, 'gets his power from the bear.'"

"Barbra, I think last night may have complicated things . . . I am on the run and as sure as God made little green apples, there's going to come a time I'll have to pick up and leave abruptly, and where does that leave you?"

"In this part of the world, the Indian people followed the buffalo across the plains,—they learned to adapt. So can I, Patrick, so can I."

He held her in his arms. "Are you sure?"

"There are never any guarantees in this world, but I'll go where the bear goes."

"People think they know what they want, but most of the time they don't. Sometimes if they're lucky, a good thing will come their way. We complain about the bad things that happen to us that we think we don't deserve but we seldom talk about the good. Well I am saying it now . . . all that's good in the world has come my way these last few weeks, and you've been a huge part of . . . I can't find the right words to . . ."

"That's all right. Let's just sit here for a while and enjoy the falls . . . We can talk about all the good things out there or maybe just not talk at all. You know the Supai have a saying: *Nibi'dllziih Hasdidogaai.* It means good or bad, time has a way of sorting things out. We're just going to have to leave it there for a while . . . okay?"

Razor stood looking out across the desert. It had been a long drive from the Kansas border across Texas. He was ten miles out of El Paso when he stopped and parked the Harley on the berm and shut off the engine. After so many miles of unending road noise, wind, and sun, the quiet of the desert was all he wanted. He could hear a low hum as the wind blew across the telephone wires along the road. As far as his eyes could see there was sacahuiste and wire grass and high bloodweed along the sides of the road and miles of sand and mountains in the foreground.

He drove on into New Mexico. He rode all night, and in the first gray light he could make out a flat mountainous shape, which led him to believe he was close to his final destination. He drove on and saw signs for guided tours, souvenirs, and helicopter rides. He pulled over, dismounted, then lifted up the leather flap of his saddlebag and took out a box of ACP shells and put some of them in his pants pocket. He checked his .45 and made sure the magazine was loaded with all eight bullets, then put the weapon back into his belt and pulled his shirt over the butt end of the weapon and his stomach. He rode toward the national park east entrance, then turned off the main highway and traveled on a dusty road until he reached an old wooden barn with a sign on the roof that read Pistol Pete's Canyon Tours. The exhaust sounds from the chopper spooked a half dozen corralled horses; an Appaloosa reared up and took off and stood next to a shack with a small sign over the front door that read Office.

A gray-haired man with a scruffy beard came out and stood in the doorway and yelled, "Jesus H. Christ!"

Razor stopped in front of an ancient hitching post, dismounted, and walked up to the man. "Can you take me to the Havasu Canyon?"

The old man slowly took a step forward, backed up, and looked Razor up and down, then stared at the motorcycle. "Well, don't that beat all . . . a shiny silver steed parked where my horses like to set. The Havasu . . . what do you want to go there fur?"

"Heard it was a nice place."

"Nice place! Hell . . . if you like seein' them poor souls, it is. You some kind a water walker?"

"Yeah, right . . . bikers for Jesus . . . no, just want to see those waterfalls I've been reading about."

"You look like an hombre I might consider doin' business with."

"You Pete?"

"That's me."

"Where's your pistols?"

"This is 1984, pilgrim . . . hung um up a long time ago. Come on in, I'll go over my rates with ya. You like horses?"

Walking side by side, conversing with each other, Henry Crow Horse and Doc Berguson arrived at the adobe home where Don Kaminski and Bunny were standing looking up at the roof.

"It won't leak no more now."

"You have faith, Bunny."

"Ask for faith and faith will be given to you," Doc Berguson blurted out.

"I have faith in Captain Don."

"You see, Henry, I still have much more work to do here."

"Belief, faith, those can be good things. I am of the Mohawk tribe and can't speak for the Supai, but I think my Supai brothers and sisters are more interested in signs and wonders."

"Henry, I think science has done a pretty good job of stripping the world of its ancient mysteries. And the scientists have done a whole lot of housecleaning when it comes to belief. Makes you wonder: How will our imaginations be sustained, knowing the big bang has no divine purpose? Signs and wonders, Henry . . . I can live with that, but all people need to know there's more out there waiting for them."

Henry Crow Horse looked at the ex-army helicopter pilot. "We've been going around and around on this all morning—care to wade in on the supernatural way of seeing things?"

"I don't know Henry . . . not sure I want to get in the middle of that one, but I'll say this: I learned as a boy in matters dealing with the supernatural that if you just knock, a door will be opened for you. If you want to know anything about life, just knock."

"What do you mean, Captain Don . . . what door you talking about?" asked Bunny.

Kaminski looked at Bunny, then turned toward the two

old men: "Well, the way I see it, the whole of creation is perfect—there is nothing that goes wrong except what man does to it. We are part of that nature, that perfection—we are pure consciousness, pure awareness. But we have this duality, we get trapped into duality because we are human. This is because we are physical beings; duality is in us. We can liken it to a tree. A tree and its roots and its branches have sap running through them. Just as the sap feeds the tree, perfect knowledge is like the sap. We need to tap into that. Sit, then turn off your mind and float down the stream. That's what we have to do."

"I am not sure what all that's about, but I know in my life I've always tried to be kind," said Bunny.

"A long time ago, Francis, my grandmother said that to me—oh, and she also said to share. There, Henry, that's about all I know."

"I have to agree with you, there's truth in what you say . . . float peacefully down that stream, and while doing that, don't forget kindness and sharing along the way."

Don Kaminski looked at Doc Berguson, then looked back at Henry Crow Horse.

"He seems to be in a kind of trance."

"He's been doing that a lot lately."

Suddenly the doctor became lucid, eyes bright and focused. He faced the men and said, "As unnecessary as a well is to a village on the banks of a river, so unnecessary are all the scriptures to someone who has seen the truth . . ." Then he smiled and turned around and headed back down the hard sun-baked caliche path toward his red clay hovel. Bunny noticed Patrick and Barbra standing a few yards away. Barbra kissed Patrick on the cheek, then walked out of the yard onto the path and followed her father. Bunny walked over and stood next to Patrick and the two of them watched as the shaman's daughter caught up to him and put her hand on his upper back and tilted her head down onto the top of his shoulder, keeping it there as they continued walking back to the village.

"Boy, she's really pretty."

"That she is."

They stood there and watched them until they disappeared into the intense, glistening midmorning sunlight. Henry Crow Horse and Kaminski walked into the house.

"Patrick."

"Yeah." He studied Bunny's face. "What's wrong?"

"I was looking for you when I got up. Had another one. Guess I wanted to talk about it. Like you said it's good to talk about um with someone you know real good and trust."

"Was it the same as last time?"

"Kinda. Yeah. I think so. Yeah, but this one had the ending right."

"Come on. Let's sit down over there. You can tell me about it."

They walked over to a cottonwood tree and sat cross-legged under a thick bough that provided some shade from the intense rays of the sun.

"Patrick."

"Yes, Francis."

"Were you able to hear what Captain Don was saying?"

"I did. I heard what you said too."

"Before I tell ya about that dream, I got to ask you a question."

"Shoot."

"Captain Don's grandma and my nana had it right, huh?"

"Yeah, you bet they did."

"Did your grandma tell you some good life stuff too?"

"Well, I got to think about that for a moment. Yeah. I am sure she did. Let me . . . oh, yeah, I remember now . . . she said be good, do good."

"Grandmas know a lot."

"Indeed they do."

"My nana loved me. You love Barbra?"

"That question can't be answered so quickly."

"I had a girlfriend once."

"You did?"

"Yep. Her name was Lucinda."

Bunny got quiet and began to stare out in the direction of the distant canyon walls.

"You want to tell me about that dream, don't you?"

"It always starts out the same, you know, I am in the Quonset hut at eight a.m. cleaning out the trenches with that big shovel. Trucks filled with fresh-picked potatoes, tons of um are goin' to be dropped in soon, and old man Brighten tells me to get down in there in that deep dirt trench and make sure they're cleared of them rats. He lets out and shortly after, his son drives up in that souped-up old hot rod pickup of his with his drinking buddy, Pete Dye, who's slouched over inside the truck. Still both drunk from the night that just quit."

Bunny's hands began to shake.

"It's all right, Francis. You're safe here."

"You know, he comes over top of me demanding I drive Pete Dye home since he can't and I tell him his dad said that I am to clean the trenches and he . . . he picked me up out of that hole by my collar and slaps me hard across my face. I fall back down into the darkness of that hole in the ground. He's done it before, Patrick. This ain't the first time he done this to me; there's been others."

"Yes, I know he was a bully. He couldn't ever be fired."

"But this time it's different, Patrick. I put my hand to my mouth and there was a lot of blood and I can't see out of my one eye. He yells at me, 'Get up out of there, boy, so I can teach you some respect!'

"I come out all right but not from where he thought I would. I crawled through the dark and popped out from the other side of the floor and dropped him with that shovel. He never got up again. That's it . . . then I woke up. And for that they gave me twenty years. I am worried, Patrick."

"Tell me what you're worried about."

"If they catch me. What I did to Highway. They will kill me, I mean, execute me, won't they for the other one? I've killed two men."

"I think not knowing what's coming down the road . . . that's what's causing those dreams of yours . . . it's the unknown that haunts us while we sleep. It can't be helped, but we can try to understand it the best we can and maybe that will make the dreams stop coming."

"How?"

"I don't know for sure but I do know this: it's better to know than not know and it's better to be free than be a captive."

"A captive? You mean like a slave or prisoner?"

"What I am trying to get at is that we are captured and brought down by our own bad thoughts."

"How can I get free of the bad thoughts?"

"Well, there are many ways, but I think the primary cause of disorder in ourselves is the seeking of reality promised by another. We must think for ourselves, Francis. I'll work with you, but the goal will be to have you figure out for yourself what works best. Once that happens, the dreams should end."

"That sounds like a good plan, Patrick. But what if they find me and send me back?"

"I am not going to let that happen."

The deep roar of the Barracuda's Hemi engine drew the attention of the Navajos who were standing under a badly faded and tattered canvas canopy that they had just set up alongside their travel trailer. The tiny trailer looked very much like it could have been built back in the 1950s. They'd parked their little house on wheels just off the berm, parallel to a dusty red-clay road that led to an ancient native entrance to the canyon. The afternoon sun was beating down hard on the desert. Everywhere, in all directions, there was sand and reddish-copper baked clay that radiated the sun's heat back into the air, making it dense and oppressive. The canopy offered only the slightest bit of shade and some escape from the sun's rays. Two middle-aged women dressed in gingham blouses and ankle buckskin stood behind a flimsy wooden card table arranging bracelets and beaded pouches, while an older-looking man wearing faded blue jeans and a frayed white shirt and a black leather unbuttoned vest stood next to them emptying a box of small plastic sandwich-sized bags filled with strips of antelope jerky. The stocky, elegant-looking man wore alligator cowboy boots, and wrapped around his head was a narrow, embroidered turquoise-beaded headband that held in place his long, silver-colored flowing hair. Their skin was the color of dark tea and appeared exceedingly cracked and furrowed, like sunbaked dirt found at the bottom of a dried-out lakebed. After arranging the plastic bags on the table, the man sat down on a small aluminum beach chair and held a couple of bags up in the air. It was the strips of jerky that caught Joey's eye, since neither he nor Dash had had anything to eat since they left Santa Fe. Joey got out of the car and walked up and stood in front of them. The women didn't speak or make eye contact. The man sat stoically and didn't exhibit any affect but once he noticed Joey's features and realized he was Native American, he cracked a small close-lipped smile and said, "That a three eighty-three under the hood?"

"Four twenty-five Mopar."

"Ahhh. More ponies."

The women laughed.

"You look hungry."

"I'll take four bags of that jerky."

"That'll be eight dollars."

"What's the best way to get down into that canyon?"

"Any particular place you got in mind?"

"Last year I was invited to powwow with the Supai. Well, I am here now and need to get down into the canyon where they live."

"Walking takes some time and can be tough going. Horse-back is the best way to go."

"Do you know someone that can get us down there?"

"Yes. Me. Leo Fast Elk."

XI

*A*t first encounter the desert canyon appears two-dimensional, with clear nights exposing a rich black sky and a daylight uncovering stark, tawny earth tones. When one lives in the canyon environment for an extended period of time, one can begin to see nuances of beauty that in certain ways rival the Appalachian Mountains and forests where I grew up. Living with the Supai, I cannot help but be reminded of family. I miss my brother. I also miss laughter. Living among these impoverished people, I do not see laughter except in children's faces. Being as desperately poor as they are, they appear to have condemned themselves to live just to exist, not giving themselves the opportunity to experience the rewards and joy of opportunity. It makes sense to me now why Barbra and her father remain here. In the beginning it looked to me like a waste of time for them to try to expose a more positive way of life to this community. But now, after living among them like I have for these past months, I am convinced it is important to try— to try to bring a modern way of thinking to the people of *the canyon. If it is true that to live is to suffer and one must find meaning in the suffering in order to continue living, then I have to better understand how and why the Supai endure their harsh environment, and in doing so maybe I can learn a way to help them.*

One of the things you realize about living with an ancient people is that they're poor for a reason. Where there is suffering, there cannot be laughter, and without laughter the world looks bleak and feels cold all the time. They have some freedom but no opportunity. I got flown out of prison; why can't the same thing happen to them? But one must be pragmatic about such things. The good doctor, his daughter, and Don—their talents are being utilized to make things better here. What talents do I possess that can make this a better place? Time will tell. I am hoping I'll have time.

Patrick and Francis sat and talked under the cottonwood tree until the sun shone directly over them. The tree's branches and sun-drenched, wilted leaves provided just enough shade for the two men to enjoy some relief from the noon heat.

"My stomach's growling at me."

"So's mine," said Bunny.

"Why don't we head back and see what we can scrounge up in that kitchen of ours?"

They got up and walked down the red clay path that led them back to the front yard. They walked through an open door into their adobe house.

"Just in time," said Don.

Henry Crow Horse sat at the plywood table, where Don Kaminski stood ladling hot corn soup from an ancient dented tin pot into Henry's hand-carved wooden bowl. Patrick walked into the kitchen and came back out with two bowls and spoons. He took the ladle from Kaminski and filled a bowl and handed it to Bunny, then poured soup into the other bowl, and the two of them sat down next to Henry. Kaminski walked over to the fireplace and retrieved some tortillas and placed the flattened pancake-like bread on a large round plate in the center of the table. The hand-fired plate was large, with rich, brightly colored flowers and fruit painted into the glazed clay, and was the only thing of beauty that could be found inside the house. Don sat down and said, "Let's eat!"

Slowly, purposefully, they began to eat their soup. Henry reached for a tortilla and said, "I ran into Charley a little while ago. He's heading out tomorrow."

Kaminski frowned. "I'll miss him. He's a good man to have around. We've made some damn fine progress on fixing the plumbing around here."

"That new cistern and those shower stalls you built . . . they're working out real well," said Henry.

Patrick looked at Henry. "Did he say when he'd be back?"

"He said he may be gone for quite some time. Said he and his brother had some business to take care of in Phoenix. He's coming over tonight to say good-bye and to see if they're any messages we want him to deliver."

"We need to talk about getting a message out to Vin."

Don looked at Patrick. "Can we take that chance?"

There was a knock at the front door.

"Hello, the house." Charley White Feather was standing on the threshold.

Don got up to greet him. "Charley. We were just talking about you. Henry said you're leaving."

"Yup. Had a slight change in plans."

"You want to join us? There's plenty here."

"Thanks, but I got to be on my way. Just wanted to say my good-byes to you all. Don, can I talk to you for a moment?"

"Sure."

"Kaminski got up and the two of them walked outside and stood in the front yard."

"Don, I got a favor to ask."

"Okay. What's up?"

"There's this fella, lives about fifteen miles east of here. He's a hermitlike fella I've known for almost a year now. The doc's been treating him. He's a Nam vet like you. Name's Joel. I was hoping that while I was away you would from time to time look in on him for me."

"Be glad to, Charley. You going to do the introductions? How do I get to him?"

"Doc Berguson will be heading over there the end of the week . . . you can go with him if you like. I plan on leaving here soon, staying with Joel tonight and head out of the canyon first thing tomorrow morning. I'll tell him tonight you'll be visiting with him."

"Anything special I need to know about him?"

"He's been alone for a year now and that . . . well, just makes him kinda . . . makes him kinda prickly, if you know what I mean."

"I have a pretty good idea of what you're saying. Sure, Charley. I'd be glad to do that for you."

"I am much obliged to ya. You'll need a ride. Take Katie, that little Appaloosa mare of mine."

"You know . . . maybe . . . if it's all right with you, I could go with you right now."

"Sure, I don't see why not."

"I think having you there to introduce me would be better."

"You're probably right. Let me go in and say good-bye, then I'll head back and saddle up Katie for ya. Better take a bedroll. Sleeping accommodations are limited. Need to leave by one o'clock, if we are to get there by nightfall."

Kaminski looked at his Timex. All right then. Let's go back in. I just need to have a talk with Patrick, then I'll be along shortly."

Razor put his boot in the stirrup and mounted one of Pistol Pete's horses, then followed the old man down a trail that would lead them into the canyon's southern entrance. They rode for an hour, then began descending slowly on another trail that dipped down sharply below the rim of the canyon wall where Comanche once rode and the Kiowa passed, and suddenly Razor could see the Colorado River far below. Pete rode at a quick pace and navigated the trail with great agility. Razor made his horse quicken its step. It was windy when they had first set out for the canyon and the horses were agitated, but the wind abated as they rode farther down below the rim. Calmness ensued, and horse and rider began working carefully in tandem with each other to reach the canyon floor before darkness set in. Hours passed and the late afternoon sun was on the edge of the western sky, beginning to eclipse the rim of the canyon. The last of the day's light expanded slowly upon the canyon floor behind them, then disappeared again down the canyon walls in a grayish shadow, and a chill in the air came on and a few birds, nestled in the dark among brush and tumbleweeds, sang a few notes of good-bye to the day.

"In an hour it's goin' to be as dark as dark can be. We'll camp here tonight," said Pete.

"How much longer to the Havasupai Falls?"

"A few hours more. Don't worry, it'll still be there in the morning."

Don Kaminski made a couple of clicking sounds, then nudged his horse with the heels of his boots and rode up alongside of Charley White Feather.

"It's going to be dark soon. We getting close?" Kaminski asked.

"A little more than a mile."

With dusk quickly settling upon them they rode side by side at a quicker cadence.

"So Charley, how did you come to meet this Joel Lawrence? I thought it was just the Indians that could live down here."

"Joel's a special case."

"How's that?"

"Well, you see, he did something very special—so special that the great state of Arizona and, believe it or not, the federal government gave him permission to come here and live.

"What did he do?"

"You saw action in Vietnam, right?"

"Yeah."

"Well, in sixty-five he was in something called Operation Hump."

Kaminski paused, then said. "I see. You mean Joel Lawrence is . . ."

"Yep. Sure is. He won the Congressional Medal of Honor, all right. He's that Joel Lawrence."

"Well, I'll be damned. The first living black man to receive that medal since the Spanish America War, and he's just a short ride away. How'd you get hooked up with him? What in the hell is he doing here?"

"I grew up on a reservation in Arizona with a man, a son of a tribal elder named Joe Charles. That man's a congressman now, from a little town called Cave Creek . . . that's just outside of Phoenix." Charley White Feather laughed. "Little Cave Creek reservation out in the desert. Our rezzzzzz."

"What's so amusing?"

"A member of our own tribe made good. Real good. That's all."

"What do you mean?"

"Come on, Don. You've seen it all around you. It's no different out there, beyond this canyon, out in the plains all around the west or further east. Henry must have shared with you the Mohawk history."

"No, I don't know much. Not much at all. For too many years I've kept to myself, not wanting to be bothered by anyone or anything."

"Our people . . . our ways . . . we just can't seem to be able to assimilate with the white man. And because of that you see it everywhere. Struggling all the time. Scratching around for money. Just making it. Joe Charles. He's one in a million."

"Hell Charley, I am white. We've been kind of assimilating since we met, haven't we?

"Yeah . . . sure we have. Been doing good work back there; together we have . . . sure enough, we've tried to make a difference with the Supai."

"There's always hope, Charley. We can never give up on one another."

"Well that's uh . . . that's . . . I guess I can't deny what you're saying."

"We made a difference for sure, Charley."

"Gettin' back to your question—about Joel."

"Yeah, how'd they let him live down here?"

"Some years ago Joe got special permission to rent some land here for him to live on. It's not a permanent deal or anything like that. Joe asked me to get him settled in and ever since then I've kinda been the unofficial overseer. He does have his problems."

"He wanted to be left alone. Is that it?"

"Yeah, that's right, and since he did what he did over there people were sympathetic and set him up here where he could have his solitude. At least temporarily."

"Before I flew Patrick out over that wall, I lived alone in a mountain house. Just me and old motorcycles to work on, an over-the-road job flying eighteen-wheelers five days a week, and a cat to keep me company." Kaminski grabbed his pant leg and rubbed his leg brace through the khaki material with his hand. Sometimes I think I never left the Nam. Wanting to be left alone . . . yeah . . . I know something about that, all right. But people need people. I've started to relearn that these past months."

"Well, maybe you know better than most what it's like. Maybe you can help him. Yeah?"

"Maybe."

"Whoa." Charley pulled back on the reins. Kaminski did the same. Horses and riders became still.

"Looks like we got company up ahead."

"How can you tell, in this light?"

"You forget. I got them Navajo hawk eyes, my friend. Look. See um? Straight ahead to the right there."

They sat their horses and watched.

"What do you think?" Said Kaminski.

"I am not too keen on coming up on strangers, but they're the ones that decided to camp along this trail and I am not inclined to go out of my way just to avoid um."

"I like the way you think, Charley."

They rode a quarter mile and stopped within ten yards of Razor and his trail guide, Pete, who were sitting on their blankets on the ground with their horses staked a few yards away. The two of them just sitting in the dark with no fire. Pete sat holding a cigarette. Both men rose and stood and looked at the riders. After a while, Charley White Feather spoke up.

"Good evening."

Coyotes begin yapping on a bluff just to the south. Pete stared at Charley and tipped the ash from his cigarette and took a drag, then said, "Good evening back to you."

"Didn't mean to come up on you so sudden."

There was just enough gray light left to allow Razor to see Charley White Feather's hand on the stock of a lever-action .30-30 that was sticking out of its scabbard. Razor slowly stepped alongside his saddlebag, where he was able to quickly get to his .45 automatic, then he stood still and faced the men who were on horseback.

Charley kept his hand on the butt end of the stock. "You look kinda familiar ... aren't you ..."

Pete took another drag and exhaled. "Well, that all depends . . . you with the IRS?"

Charley smiled. "Well, if it isn't Pistol Pete. I've passed your face on that giant billboard a thousand times. Glad to meet ya in the flesh. I am Charley White Feather." Charley took his hand off the rifle, then took his cowboy hat off, exposing his long white hair, and pointed the front brim of his Stetson at Kaminski. "And this is Captain Kaminski."

The chopper pilot raised his hand but didn't say a word.

"Pleased to meet you. Just like two ships in the night, meetin' up like this," said Pete.

"Indeed," said Charley.

Both riders looked at Razor.

"This is Cletus Pendergrass," said Pete.

Razor stood silent and motionless by his saddle.

"He's from back east. Don't talk much."

Kaminski kept his eyes squarely fixed on the Hell's Angel.

"You fellas headin' out of the canyon tonight?" asked Pete.

"We've got a rendezvous to keep. Would like to stay and chew the fat with ya, but we gotta be movin' on." Charley ran his hand through his thick white hair and pushed it straight back, then put his hat back on and said, "Adios and happy trails to ya."

A coyote sang out a single solitary howl. Kaminski's horse bristled at the sound and it took him a few moments to get control of the young mare. Once he had her under his control, he looked back down the trail to get a final glimpse of the man from back east.

"She's a little spitfire isn't she . . . it's not much further, Don."

"Something strike you kind of strange about that guy Pendergrass?" said Don.

"He did seem out of place—not a typical-looking Grand Canyon tourist."

"That vest he was wearing."

"Yeah."

"Could you make out what it said on his back?"

"Maybe some motorcycle-gang patch of some kind—hard to tell in this light."

"That's what I thought . . . looked like gang colors to me."

"Could be."

Ten miles southwest of the Supai Village the three riders grouped in a clearing at the top of a rise and looked back. All the sky to the east of them was darkened and the terrain they had trodden over had turned a murky gray as far as they could see. They leaned forward, groggy-eyed in their saddles, and looked at one another.

"This is a good place as any," said the Indian Leo Fast Elk.

"I thought this day would never end . . . my ass is killing me," said Dash.

Joey laughed and shook his head. "Nothing like snowmobiling all day back home, is it?" he said.

Dash looked at Leo Fast Elk, their guide. "And I've got a saddle! Jesus . . . how'd they do this without a saddle back in the olden days?"

"Can't say for sure. I think maybe they were plenty thankful just to have a horse," he replied.

They made camp on a tiny escarpment high above a dried-out lakebed and spread their blankets in the red clay. Their Navajo guide took a rope and rode out. A short while later he came back dragging a dead tree, and they built a great bonfire against the cold. He then pulled out army-surplus tins of beef stew from his saddlebag and opened them with an old-style quarter-sized K-ration can opener and set them in the fire. He found collapsible aluminum cups and filled them with water from his canteen, then sprinkled powered tea into the cups. They ate the stew out of the cans with plastic spoons. After supper Leo Fast Elk picked up his blanket and stretched it out close to the fire, then lifted his saddle and set it next to the blanket. Both younger men watched him as he got himself ready to go to sleep, and after a while they got up and moved their bedrolls and saddles close to the fire.

As Leo was taking his boots off and getting under his blanket, he turned and looked toward them and said, "Hope the dinner was to your liking?"

"Didn't think food could last that long. My can had '1947' stamped on it," said Dash.

"It was good," said Joey.

"Last year the government gave us crates of the stuff and boxes of cheese and butter too. Before the war the army used to pay the down-on-their-luck cowboys to capture the mustangs that roamed these parts. When soldiers found out what was in those cans, the government put a stop to it."

Dash looked over to where the horses were standing. The fire was bright enough so he could see the horses' bloodshot eyes. "I don't know much about those animals but there's something about um."

"What's that?" Said Joey.

"They got those big eyes. Soulful eyes. That's what I see in um. Wild horses should stay free. They shouldn't've been hunted down like that."

"Son, I know how you feel, but I've lived long enough to know that in hard times people make allowances for such things. I am goin' to get some sleep. We've got another five or six hours of riding ahead of us."

It didn't take long for Leo Fast Elk to start snoring.

"Joey."

"Yeah."

"You awake?"

"Sort of. That snoring will keep the beasties away, that's for sure."

"You and Henry."

"Yeah."

"I've been thinking, Joey. Before what happened. I mean, before Tushanna and Lone Bear got killed at the motel. You met this Razor guy once before, didn't you?"

"Actually, I've never set eyes on him before. It was Henry who met him one night at Hawk's garage and told me about him," replied Joey.

"That's when he was asking about his brother."

"That's right. He wanted to know what happened to him. How he got killed on the reservation. What's got into you all of sudden? You should get some rest."

"I don't wanna sleep. All this seems so . . . this is some crazy shit."

"What do you mean?"

"You know . . . what you and Lone Bear did to those guys that night in that trailer."

"Yeah. So."

"And now look at all that's happening."

"I think I know what you're getting at. Razor going after Patrick like this. Instead of me. Is that it?"

"Yeah. That's it. Don't get me wrong. I'd be dead if it weren't for you and Lone Bear and what you did. But . . ."

"But what?"

"I don't know. Patrick's never seen this Razor guy."

"Yeah, but Henry has."

"What if he's already there? What if he's there now, I mean . . ."

"Look Dash, we'll be there tomorrow. We've got to stay positive . . . you know."

"Yeah . . . I know."

"Dash, it's like this . . . we start out doing something meaning no harm, something naturally in us to do. But somewhere along the line it gets changed around into something bad. A good man can kill. I did what I had to do that night . . . Lone bear too."

"I see what you're saying."

"What I did ... well, sometimes you have to take the bad with the good ... else you'll be running for the rest of your life."

They dismounted. Charley White Feather opened a gate and he and Don walked their horses through, then Charley closed the gate and they walked their horses around to the back of the cabin. As Charley was tying his horse's reins to the hitching post, Don's mare drew its head up and sniffed and snorted and backed away once, then again, and finally settled in next to Charley's horse. From the rear of the cabin they heard Joel Lawrence.

"That you, Charley?"

"Yep."

"Who's the desperado?"

"A friend."

"The back door opened."

"Come on in."

"This is Don ... Don Kaminski," Charley White Feather said.

The cabin had been built in the 1930s for people who came to do archeology digs. The single room they stood in contained a small, black cast-iron wood-burning stove that provided heat and a cook surface and two oil lamps that filled the room with a gentle light, revealing a water-pump handle and sink and a small, white enamel-top table with flowers hand carved into its wooden legs. There were bookcases made of oak with glass doors, filled with books and manuals, and on the walls were pictures cut out from *National Geographic* magazines depicting birds and animals from all over the west. Back in one corner of the room was a neatly made up metal cot, and on a nightstand next to the bed was a framed photograph of sixteen black Americans standing together around a very old woman who was sitting in a rocking chair.

"I've got a pot of hot water going ... would you like some tea?"

He stood six feet tall and was solidly built, and he wore heavy black-rimmed eyeglasses. His face exhibited a pleasant look of calmness, yet there was a secure sense of strength and assurance in his features and demeanor. They sat down at the small table and Lawrence served them Irish porridge he had just finished making, and they poured powdered milk over the steel-cut oats and ate and drank strong tea. As they talked, Kaminski kept looking at a battle flag from the army Ninth Division that was nailed up on the wall facing the foot of the bed.

Joel Lawrence took notice to how he was staring at it and said, "You're probably wondering why I have that hanging up over there."

"If my memory serves me right, there must have been over twenty thousand men in that division. They were the largest in country," Kaminski said.

"I had a feeling you spent some time in that part of the world."

"Do I still have the stare?"

"How about some more tea?"

"It's an honor to meet you."

"Thank you. So, how long have you known Charley here?"

"A few months."

"We've been making some progress with the Supai," said Charley.

"Yes, Doc Berguson mentioned that. Doc said you flew choppers—dust off?"

"No, gunships mostly."

"In sixty-five my MOS was first-aid man . . . they've changed it . . . they're known as medics now. Not sure why they did that."

"Well, you know the army," said Kaminski.

Joel Lawrence looked over at the flag, then turned back and looked at Kaminski and said, "I don't need to tell ya those dust-off boys meant a lot to us. When they just hovered up there above that triple canopy like that, taking constant fire;

man oh man . . . never seen such devotion. They were from the ol' reliable Ninth.

"They saved so many . . . and so did you."

Lawrence tilted his head slightly downward and turned away from Kaminski and looked at Charley White Feather. "So Charley, how you making out?"

"My days . . . Joel, are long and numbered."

"That sounds good to me, my friend. We have only so many summers left, don't we?"

"That's why I like to stretch out a day as long as I can. Joel, I have to head out of the canyon in the morning; not sure just when I'll be back."

"Is everything okay with you?"

"Just some tribal business I got to take care of. It may take me a couple of months to resolve some things back on the reservation. Joe will make arrangements to have your supplies delivered. Look, I know this is sudden, but I was wondering . . ."

"Yes, Charley."

"While I am away, if it's all right with you, is it okay for Don to stop by?"

Lawrence sat still and became quiet, then rose and walked over and stood next to the sink with his back toward his guests. "Well, Charley, you see, I don't uh, I just uh . . ."

"Look Joel, if it's going to be a problem, maybe I should . . ."

"Don, could you give us a few minutes?"

"You bet. I'll be out back checking on my mare. She may need me to sing her a lullaby before bedtime." Kaminski got up from the table and walked out the back door.

Lawrence turned around and faced the Indian.

"How long we've known each other, Joel? Almost a year now . . . right? And in that time I think we could both say we've gotten to understand certain things about each other—wouldn't you say that?"

"Yes, we have."

"The last few times I've been here, you told me that Doc Berguson and you were getting along real well and he was a good listener."

"That's right."

"Well. that's what a shaman does for a tribe. He listens. Back home our shaman made it a point to cup his hand next to his ear and hold it there to remind us how important it was that he listened carefully to our thoughts."

"Where you going with all this, Charley?"

"Don carries around in his head unhealthy thoughts. I'd say he has many demons attacking him. Joel, he's a good man but his mind is troubled. I was hoping that since the two of you had experienced great hardships during that war, it might be good to have you talk to one another—to listen to each other, and maybe some good could come of that."

"For both of us . . . that's what you were thinking, wasn't it?"

"Yes."

"You know, just 'cause he was in Nam doesn't make him my buddy. I've got my own issues I need to pay attention to; that's why I am here, you know."

"I hope I haven't stepped over a line here with you tonight. My people believe that what nature gives to us we must share with others. We take only what we need and leave the rest. When I see men in trouble, it is in my nature to step in and if it's possible . . . help um. That's what Navajo people think friendship is about. I am gonna go out back and take care of the horses. Will ya think about it?"

"I will, Charley. I'll think about what you said."

When he stepped out of the cabin he found only the horses, but then suddenly Kaminski appeared out of the dark, carrying a bucket of water.

"Careful, not too much—they'll bloat up."

They walked the horses into a small corral and set them under a half roof that extended out from the top of an old weather-beaten, splintered shed and unsaddled and unbridled them. Charley walked over to a large wooden crate, released a hasp, then lifted the crate's lid.

"Hand me your hat."

He scooped out some feed from a large burlap sack and poured the feed into Kaminski's cowboy hat.

"There you go. Just give her a little water when she's finished with that."

Charley filled his hat and fed and watered his horse.

From around back of the shed a gelding appeared and nudged its nose and forehead into Kaminski's back.

Charley laughed. "You might want to feed ol' brown eyes too."

After being fed and watered, Joel's horse backed out of the shed and went to the far side of the corral; the other horses walked over and stood next to the gelding, then both men came out and leaned over the top of the corral's split-rail fence and stood there silently for quite a while, studying the horses under the dim, grayish light of a gibbous moon.

"Looks like ol' brown eyes is enjoying the company he's having this evening."

"They're damn fine creatures," replied Kaminski.

"I always thought there was a kind of nobility to them," said Charley.

"I am curious, how'd it go in there?"

"He's thinking it over."

"I imagine being out here alone like this has given him plenty of time to think."

"You're no stranger to that, are you, Don?"

"It's been said we didn't lose that war—we just walked away. Sergeant Lawrence in there devoted himself to a cause and now it's my guess he's wondering what it was all about. Once that gets stuck in your head, it's tough to move on."

"I can't tell you what to do, Don, but I am going to bed down out here under that shed's lean-to. If anyone can reach him, it's you."

Kaminski walked over to the shed and retrieved his bedroll, then walked back to the fence. "I don't know."

"What do you mean?"

"He got the Medal of Honor for what he did. Who the hell am I to think I have the right to talk to him in any way, shape, or form?"

"Doc says he's having too many bad dreams; he can't sleep and he says it's effecting his health."

"How old is he?"

"My age."

"How old's that?"

"We were both born in 1928."

"Damn it. All right, I'll see you in the morning."

He climbed the three steps to the back porch and tapped lightly at the door with the back of his hand. He took off his hat and pressed his forehead with the palm of his hand, then ran his fingers through his hair and put his hat back on.

"Come in," a voice called.

He opened the door and stepped into the cool darkness.

"Charley? I am over here."

He walked through the tiny galley. Joel Lawrence was sitting at the table, staring into the flame of a candle. Don Kaminski stood in the doorway and took off his hat. Lawrence looked up at him. "Where's our friend?" he said. "I wasn't sure who it was."

"He's sleeping in the shed tonight."

"Oh. Huh. Well then it's you and me. Sit down. You want something to drink?"

Kaminski looked at the items on the table. Bottle of aspirin. An unopened bottle of Jack Daniels. Two glasses. A small yellow paper envelope with the word Kodachrome written on it in large red print. "Thank you, no," he said. "I appreciate it. Are you all right?"

"I am all right." Lawrence nodded.

Kaminski pulled out a chair and sat and he put his hat on a chair next to a transistor radio. "You get any decent reception on that thing?"

"On a clear night I can usually get a few stations."

"What kind of music do you like to listen to?"

"I am not too particular, most kinds I guess."

"I remember reading about you. Saw your picture with LBJ in *Life*."

"That would have been sixty-seven. I was a Spec Six then."

"I had just been assigned to the Ninth in sixty-seven. Our CO made sure to have a few copies of that magazine lying around in the operations room."

Lawrence got up and took the bottle of Jack Daniels over to the galley and put it in a cupboard, then came back and sat down in his chair. "I brought that out for Charley. He and the doc like the Jack."

"You didn't get into that habit over there?"

"No. Never did."

"In our squadron it was Jack, Jim, and Johnny."

"Yeah, I saw a lot of those empty bottles wherever I went."

"What year did you enlist?"

"Nineteen forty-six, at the ripe old age of eighteen; that was a couple of years before Truman signed Executive Order 9981. Before then we, uh, worked under different rules that delayed our entry into combat. We had to wait three years before we could begin combat training."

"You weren't always a medic . . . I mean, first-aid man?"

"Back then we had many jobs given to us. I saw action in Korea."

Kaminski looked at the picture on the nightstand and said, "Let me ask you something."

"All right."

"What are you most proud of?"

Lawrence looked at him, gauging the question. "You know

pride is one of the seven deadly sins."

"Saving someone's life on a battlefield, I can't think of anything . . ."

"More satisfying?"

"Yeah, you must be very proud of that."

"I don't know. When you go into battle, it don't matter if you're a grunt or first-aid man. It's a blood oath to look after the men with you. That picture there next to my bed . . . that's all of us next to our mother."

"All sixteen of ya."

"Yes, that's all of us. It took some time and planning to get everyone together for that photo."

"I don't have any siblings."

"About your question—it's an interesting one. Why do you ask?"

"I don't know. I heard about Operation Hump and what you did. Just curious, I guess."

"You know, being born into a large family like I was . . . I guess I'd have to say it starts with family. When I was eight years old, I had to go live with neighbors until I joined the army."

"That must have been rough."

"Yes, it was, but there just wasn't enough money to go around in the dirt fields of Winston-Salem, North Carolina. You're always called upon in a big family to lend a hand and make sacrifices. Doing for others, well, that's just what we did back home. Difference is, no one's shooting at ya."

"The army can be a big family, all right."

"Caring for others has always been a satisfying thing for me. I guess I am proud of that the most. What about you? What are you most proud of?"

"There's something about combat. Flying into a firefight and getting the mission completed. That would be high on my list."

"Combat does tend to bring out the best in men, doesn't it?"

"You know, Sergeant Lawrence, I've seen many things to make me lose faith in the human race, but our actions in that place is not one of them."

"Before sixty-eight, missions and rules of engagement were pretty clear. Good generals, good discipline. After Tet, you know . . . things back home got turned upside down. I have to admit, I saw things that would make what you just said . . . well, be called into question."

"That's war."

"Oh yes, the 'fog of war' . . . how that muddies the waters. Someone, I can't remember who it was said it best . . . 'we were all belligerents weren't we.'"

"That word describes the combatants all right, but I don't think it says anything about the politics that were in play. Look, uh . . . it's been a long day . . . I am little tired."

"I understand."

"Can I bunk over there in the corner? Is that all right?"

"Yes of course. I have some blankets you can have. Sorry I can't offer anything better."

"It'll be fine. Maybe we can continue this in the morning."

"I'd like that. It's been a long time since . . ."

"Yeah, I know. Me too."

It was dark when Barbra, railroad lantern in hand, knocked on the door. Patrick came out and hugged her and the two of them walked onto the path that would lead them out of the village past the blue-green Havasupai falls and on to a plateau that was adjacent to the northwest canyon wall. The sun would be up in a couple of hours and she wanted to be ready and fully prepared to help with an initiation the tribal grandmothers called *Kinaaldá*: a traditional maturity ceremony for Supai girls. They walked for a long time in the darkness through the rugged rocky terrain, getting off the path once, then finding their way back onto the path, and as they reached the base of the canyon wall, the sun was just appearing, providing enough light so they could see where the ceremony would take place. As they got closer, they saw a half dozen Supai women standing in front of a hogan, holding candles and looking in their direction, when suddenly, Maysun, the twelve-year-old girl Barbra was friendly with, ran past the two of them and stood in front of the women. Barbra gave the lantern to Patrick and raced off toward the hogan and stood next to Maysun's grandmother. The girl bowed to the grandmothers, then followed the women into the shelter, where they stood around the billowing flames of a fire. Patrick stood close by and observed their shadows. From around back of the hogan Doc Berguson appeared.

"Good morning," said Patrick.

"Good morning," replied Doc Berguson.

"I thought this was strictly a woman thing?" Said Patrick.

"This particular changing-woman ritual includes some songs to help Maysun enter womanhood; they asked me to sing one of them."

Changing woman?

"Didn't Barbra explain it to you?"

"She didn't use those words, she said it was something to do with assuring that the girl would grow up being strong and kind."

"Today's the last of the four-day ancient ritual. Each day the girl bathes, ties her hair back, and runs toward the east, and today, the final day, she bakes a corn cake in an earthen pit. The cutting of the cake at the end of the ceremony is significant."

"Who or what exactly is 'changing woman'?"

"A deity, one of the Supai holy people. Maysun will communicate with it today. Changing Woman helps the girl enter womanhood. When the ceremony is complete, the girl is introduced to many deities as a woman and is invited to take her place in the world. As medicine man, I perform the song that invites Changing Woman to come and do this for Maysun. When I am done and Maysun cuts the corn cake, they all sing, and the singing is the conversation they have with God. The songs they sing are saying the girl is coming out as a woman. They are surrounded by their deities in song."

"Where I lived, back in Moreland, New York, a Mohawk friend of mine had a picture that was painted before the Revolutionary War on the wall of his living room of a mom, dad, and their infant son in a snow-covered spring wilderness. The mom was sitting on the bank of a river, a campfire in front of her. The dad had just dipped his son into the icy waters and lifted him up in the air. The boy was crying, yelling in protest. The dad was laughing and the mom has a look of . . . here we go again, with the tough love thing. I asked my friend its meaning and he told me it showed how his people introduced male infants to all the elements of life; water, air, and fire."

"Ahhhh . . . the Mohawk baptism, huh? Nature has terrified and at the same time inspired these Supai people. And the beat goes on, Patrick, and on and on and on." Berguson smiled, then said, "You and Barbra . . . you look good together."

"Is that right?"

"Maybe there's your future . . . your own circle of life, so to speak. *And the beat goes on . . . and the beat goes on . . .*"

Razor was the first to rise, making so much noise in gathering his bedroll, tack, and saddlebags, it startled Pistol Pete out of a sound sleep.

"Pilgrim . . . you can't be doing that to an old man."

"I am in a hurry."

"I once heard a fella say he never looked back 'cause he was afraid something might be gaining on him. What's gaining on you, Pilgrim?"

Razor didn't answer.

"All right then. How about you gather some wood and I'll get us a fire started."

"Yeah. Okay."

After they drank coffee and had something to eat, Pete went over to Razor's horse and lifted a blanket off Razor's saddle and placed it on the horse's back and smoothed it and stood stroking the animal's neck and mane, then bent and picked up the saddle and lifted it with the cinches strapped up and the off stirrup hung over the horn. He placed it on the horse's back and rocked the saddle into place. He bent down and reached under and pulled up the strap and cinched it.

"There, you're all set to go. You'll be seeing them blue-green falls by noon."

Joel Lawrence was already up, getting a fire started in the wood stove. Kaminski woke to the smell of coffee. He got up and sat down at the table, and Lawrence handed him a cup of coffee and said, "How'd you sleep?"

"Had a couple of dreams."

"I had one I'd like to forget."

"Was it about Operation Hump? I mean, we don't have to talk about it . . . we can talk about something else."

"No, I dreamt about another time. Something that should've never happened but couldn't be helped."

"How's that?"

"You know a rifle platoon is used as bait."

"No, I wasn't aware of that."

"Charlie owned the night, with his booby traps and dug-in positions . . . the men were scared as always, but that night they were more angry then scared. That night was about something else."

"What was that?"

"Revenge. It was payback time for something that happened the day before. I am not going to paint a detailed picture for ya but I'll tell you this . . . they mutilated a rifleman that got separated from us and when it was daylight we found him tied to a tree with his manhood in his mouth."

"THAT'S IT!" shouted Kaminski.

"What?"

"Revenge! I've been wracking my brain over and over . . . on the trail yesterday. I remember now. The emblem on his vest."

"What are you talking about?"

"Someone I know back at the village . . . known him since we were kids. There's a man out there who wants to kill him and I've got to get back there. I can't explain it now, there's just not enough time . . . I've got to get back there right now."

"Could you use some help?"

"I could always use a good man like you."

"Count me in then."

Kaminski got up from the table and walked out the back door. He saw Charley White Feather standing by his bedroll, yawning and stretching his arms over his head. He quickly walked past him, grabbed his horse's bridle, then went into the corral. Charley watched as he tried to get the bit in the horse's mouth. Joel Lawrence walked by him and picked up a bridal and walked into the corral.

Charley followed them and said, "Am I missing something here?"

"It's Patrick."

"Patrick? What about him?"

"Help me with this, will ya?"

Charley took a sugar cube out of his jeans pocket and fed it to the horse, then slipped the bit into position. "Do you mind telling me what's going on?"

"Those two on the trail yesterday, that one with the vest; he's a Hell's Angel. The sergeant and I are riding back to the village."

"You think he's . . ."

"Yeah. The one I told you about."

They saddled the horses and they rode out of the corral, single file, into a morning that was fresh and cool and rode

north down a rutted track onto the dry scrublands of the canyon floor. Then suddenly they put their horses to a gallop up
a path onto a plateau, then onto a well-trodden trail that was
dotted with lechuguilla and side oats grama and basket grass.

They rode another two miles and had descended into an
arroyo when suddenly Charley White Feather pulled his horse
around and said, "Look over there."

They halted and watched some men on horses heading north.

"What do you see . . . is it the biker and that Pete fella?"
said Kaminski.

"No. There's three of um," said Charley White Feather

"What do you want to do?"

"Give um a minute, then we'll ride up that swale over there,
then into the road in front of um."

Charley put a cigarette in his mouth and took a wooden
match from his shirt pocket and popped it on the horn of
his saddle and lit the cigarette. He sat smoking and watched
the riders slowly heading north, then said, "Two of um aren't
very good riders. Come on. Let's go find out who they are."

They galloped over the swale, then down a bajada and set
their horses directly in front of Leo Fast Elk, Skywalker, and
Dash.

Don Kaminski looked past the Indian, then shouted, "Joseph
. . . what are you . . .?"

"Captain Don! We have to warn Patrick. He's here."

"The biker. I know. He's up ahead somewhere."

Razor guided his horse alongside Pistol Pete. "We need to talk."

"What's on your mind, pilgrim?"

"You remember what we talked about back at your ranch."

"We talked about some things, I recall. Can you refresh my
memory with some specifics?"

"When we get to the village. you said you had some people
you sometimes go see when you're down this way."

"That's right."

"I need you to go see them when we get there."

"You mean you want me to just leave you with the Supai?"

"Yeah. That's what I am saying."

"Well hell, pilgrim, you don't know nobody there . . . how you goin' to get along?"

"You let me worry about that."

They rode on. By noon they were just a few hundred yards away from the village; they sat their horses and Pistol Pete stared straight ahead. "There it is."

Razor could make out the shape of the village: unpainted, splintered, dried-out wooden windows in the old mud walls, the smoke standing straight up into the windless afternoon so still the village seemed to hang by charcoal threads. He dismounted and opened a saddlebag and took out a box of shells and put half in one pants pocket and the rest in the other and checked his .45 to make sure it was fully loaded, then put it into his belt and mounted the horse again and rode into the village. There was no one in sight. He tied the horse in front of the pavilion and walked down to the first adobe cabin and looked in. He started for the front door then walked around to the back and opened the door and walked in with the .45 in his hand. He crossed the room and looked out the front window, then he turned and walked back and sat down on a chair alongside the fireplace.

An hour later Henry Crow Horse arrived and opened the front door. He was startled to see him sitting there and he stood, hesitating. "Well, well, look who we have here. I remember you, Mr. Razor Blade," he said.

"Didn't think you'd seen the last of me now, did ya . . . Sheriff?"

The old man started to cross the room but Razor stopped him and made him take a seat in one of the wooden chairs next to the plywood table.

"What do you want?" The retired Mohawk sheriff's eyes darted toward the door.

The Hell's Angel stood up and pointed the automatic at him. He cocked the hammer. The click of the hammer falling into place was sharp and decisive. Henry Crow Horse remained still.

"I came to see the man that killed my brother."

"Your brother?"

"Axel was his name. Don't you recall me telling you about him that night at the garage in Massena?"

"I don't know what you're talking about."

"Wallace. Patrick Wallace. You better know where he's at. Get up."

"Things aren't going to turn out good for you."

"Who says they ever have? Turn around."

He turned around. Razor uncocked the weapon and stuck it inside the belt of his blue jeans, then ripped down a window shade pull from the window and tied the Indian's hands.

"You got a plan or you just going to improvise?"

"Never mind. You still think you're holding all the good cards, don't ya? Let's go." He grabbed Henry Crow Horse by the collar and pushed him forward. The back door was still open and they walked out and down a path and entered a small outbuilding behind the cabin.

Razor shoved the Indian's chest up against the back wall, turned him around, then stared into his eyes. "I am accustomed to getting what I want, old man. I am not new to the killing business, so if I were you I'd just stand there real still. Someone will be along soon enough."

"And then what?"

"It's been my experience that the best way to get someone to talk is to dangle a life in front of um. Any life will do . . . even yours."

"Is that so?"

"You may be old and crippled up and not afraid of dying, but someone else may have different ideas about seeing someone being placed in distress."

"That's your plan, huh? I thought you Hell's Angels were a little more creative than that."

"Shit. You think too highly of us, old man. We're at the bottom of the barrel when it comes to sophisticated thought." Razor laughed. We're just, well, plain, old simple angels from Hades. You know . . . it's time I shut you up."

Razor untied a bandanna from around his neck and pulled and stretched it out, then placed it over Henry's mouth and tied together the two ends of the cloth behind the back of the Indian's head. He walked him into a boxlike closet cluttered with rakes, hoes, and shovels. He pulled a knife out from under his denim vest and stuck the end of the long blade against his captive's neck and said, "You make a sound and the next pigeon that walks by, I'll cut um and gut um and throw him in there with ya. We clear?"

Then he shut the closet door and walked over and stood just inside the outbuilding's doorway so as not to be seen and stared at the back of the adobe brick cabin. A half hour passed, and when Francis Bunnyard stepped out of the back door of the adobe cabin, Razor had the hostage he needed.

It was a good hour before the riders appeared at the entrance to the Supai village, Kaminski, Lawrence, Charley White Feather, and Leo Fast Elk all leaning forward at a hard gallop, with Skywalker and Dash quite a ways back, doing their best to stay up with the more-seasoned, expert riders. Kaminski dismounted and entered the front door of his adobe cabin.

A few moments later he reappeared and stood on the threshold. "No one's here."

From around back, Grandpa Hobert Standing Buffalo slowly walked into the yard and stopped in front of the riders. Kaminski came out from the doorway and stood next to him.

"Gone. Both of them. Taken," said the Supai elder.

The women stood around a large mound of brownish red clay and straw. From under the earth-packed oven small amounts of smoke were slowly erupting and mixing together with the sweet smell of corn cake, which had been baking overnight. Doc Berguson stood next to the mound, then raised his hands into the air, chanted haltingly for a short time, then burst into song. When he was finished, he walked over and stood next to Patrick and Barbra, who were standing some distance away. They watched two women with shovels carefully dig out the terra-cotta pot and place it in front of Maysun. She waited for the container to cool, the women sang, then with a shovel she cracked open the clay container and took out the corn cake. With a knife she cut slices off and gave each grandmother a piece and thanked them for initiating her into adulthood.

A dry wind suddenly came up from the south and in the nearby eucalyptus trees the leaves crackled, shook, and sang, and Doc Berguson fell to his knees and prostrated himself in the direction of the north wall of the canyon, where ten thousand years ago ancient Supai living rooms were carved out of rock strata a hundred feet above the canyon floor. After melodically chanting a Navajo prayer, he stood up and gazed into Patrick's eyes, then turned and looked at his daughter. He reached down and took their right hands and joined them together, then put his hand on top of their coupled wrists and closed his eyes for a short while. He opened them again and smiled, then walked away. They watched him return to the hogan, and after a few words were exchanged, he followed the grandmothers and Maysun as they made their way, single file, onto the caliche dirt path that would lead them back to the village.

Barbra turned her tearstained face toward Patrick, and he continued to hold her hand as they walked in the direction of the canyon plateau. Maysun suddenly stopped, turned around, and stood and looked back in the direction of her friend and teacher, then smiled and continued on, joining the grandmothers on the mesa.

It had been an hour since they had come out of the village. They walked down into a narrow, flat arroyo then onto a low cap-rock mesa dotted with a few eucalyptus trees and yuccas that were just starting to flower.

Razor kept sticking the end of his .45 automatic in Henry Crow Horse's ribs prodding him forward as Francis Bunnyard led the way. "Hey old man, you see how this is working now, don't you . . . aren't you ashamed of yourself for doubting me?"

Henry Crow Horse kept silent as he struggled to keep up with Bunny.

"Your friendo here . . . he don't wanta see you get all shot to hell. It's good to have friends, isn't it?"

They walked through low hills covered with nopal and creosote bush until they came to a bajada in the plateau. A little off to the right was a stand of cottonwood, cactus, and a grouping of boulders.

"We got company!" shouted Bunny.

"What?"

Razor shoved Henry Crow Horse out of the way, then moved alongside Bunny. "Where. Show me."

He pointed to a ridge that ran diagonally to the mesa. "Over there, coming down from those rocks there."

"I see um. They all look like women."

"Yeah, that's them."

"That ceremony you were talking about . . . must be finished, huh? Right?"

"Maybe. I mean . . . yeah, it's over, today . . . today was the last day."

Razor took a firm hold of the front of Bunny's shirt and stood him up against a boulder, then pointed the barrel end of his automatic between his eyes and pressed it against his forehead.

"I don't see any men. Where's Wallace? If you've been lying to me, boy, I am goin'..."

"Razor ... he's telling you—"

"Shut up, old man. Both of you ... get over there. Move."

From Razor's position behind the boulders he watched the women and Doc Berguson walk down a narrow, rocky slope, then clamber up through traprock that led them onto a south-facing slope and along a windswept gravel ridge that would lead them to his position within a few minutes. There would be no place to go, no place to hide, once they came past him.

"I am going to find out where Wallace is right soon," he said.

He waited until the older women passed, then slid out from where he was standing and caught Maysun by the back of her shirt, stopping her dead in her tracks. She shouted. The women froze. Henry Crow Horse and Bunny started to move toward Razor, then quickly stopped when he shoved the barrel into the girl's back. She slowly twisted her head around eyeing him nervously.

"See, Sheriff ... leverage. I got it. It never fails in these types of situations."

He held the gun up at shoulder level and with his free hand grabbed Maysun's upper arm and turned her toward the women. "All right, *ladies*, no one's going to get hurt if you tell me right now where Patrick Wallace is."

Maysun stood on the caliche trail, trembling, staring at her grandmother. He held the automatic on her and repeated his demand. Then they all waited, when suddenly her grandmother walked forward and stood before him.

"Well?" he said.

The grandmother nodded and stepped back and put her

hand on Maysun's shoulder.

He pointed the gun toward the sky and fired, then shoved Maysun down to the ground.

"Get up."

She knelt in front of her grandmother. He looked down at her, then stared at the older woman. "What's it going to be?"

A unified cry erupted from the women and she looked at him and said, "I'll take you there, you . . . you . . . hombre.

Maysun was still kneeling.

"Stand up."

"Now wait just a minute here . . . what's this all about?" Doc Berguson said.

"It's pretty simple, *friendo*. Granny here is going to lead me to the man . . . we have some unfinished business to settle and I am taking Miss Skinny Britches here along for insurance. As long as I get what I want, you'll see them again. Simple, huh?"

XII

I was taught that to whom much is given, much is expected. Watching the grandmothers conduct the Kinaaldá made me remember when my mother said that to me; I was seven years old. I also remember a day in prison when an old inmate recited a poem to me. He half sang, half spoke these words: "One fine day the wind called to my soul the odor of jasmine, and the wind said, 'In return for the odor of my jasmine I will take all your rose petals.'" "I have no roses, the man said, "all the flowers in my garden are dead." The wind said, "Then I'll take the dried petals and yellow leaves," and left. The man sat on a rock and wept and said, "What have I done with the garden that was entrusted to me?"

Years wasted on the way to this moment. The generations of Wallaces that came before me; how much of a disappointment I have been to them. Was Barbra's father envisioning something I cannot or don't want to see? Les Plough, Parzifal, and the Grail King—serve the other, and truth and beauty will come your way. Plough was right about the Holy Grail. But that has eluded me.

Why? I feel something icy and unfeeling entering me like another being—it's smiling malignantly at me now and will never leave me as long as I live. My life has led me to this moment and yet it has led me nowhere at all. Remember Macbeth . . . "Out, out brief candle . . ." I am just a walking shadow.

As I stood next to Barbra looking up at the ancient rock-face homes of the Havasupai I couldn't get it out of my head what her father was thinking. Why he would want his daughter to get mixed up with someone like me? I thought, Yeah, I am a young man with a whole lot of living left to do; maybe I can make it work with her. But my present situation and future is dire and no one can dispute that, so why? What was he thinking when he joined our hands together like that? Was it just another one of his visions or was it time and aging acting on his thoughts? Both can be great motivators. A father wants to see his kids get a fair chance at happiness. I always thought if I lived my life in the strictest way I could somehow keep it together. After Skywalker fell to his death, I said to myself I was young and I was entitled to one mistake, especially if I could learn from it and start becoming the sort of man I had in my head that I wanted to be. I was wrong. It doesn't work that way. What could her father see in me that I can't? Could it be that he wants me to take her away from here? Has he finally come to his senses when it comes to her well-being? I've managed to mess things up pretty good up to now. What did he say? We look good together. Yeah, maybe that's good enough. Maybe that's a good start to a life—a life of looking after another and maybe making all that has happened to me somehow seem worthwhile.

Razor pointed his .45 in the direction of the caliche trail that led to the rocky slope and the ridge the grandmothers, Maysun, their shaman Doc Berguson, and Bunny had just come down hours ago. The three of them set off back up the trail with Maysun's grandmother leading the way. As Razor walked forward, he turned and looked back to see those he left behind standing together, staring at him. At the edge of the ridgeline, where the ground flattened out, a flock of pigeons burst, flapping, out of a rounded-out cavity made of baked red clay. They walked onto an arroyo that bore north and they followed it for a good distance until it began to narrow and grew rocky, stepping cautiously, looking toward the slopes above them. He prodded them on and they clambered up through basalt rock, then onto the south-facing slope and along a barren plateau, and as they came around to the far side of a butte, they heard a tremendous roar and stopped. There they stood staring at the Havasu green-blue waterfall, the cascading water plunging down two hundred feet into a pool directly in front of them. The falls mist covered the entire area and spilled into dozens of pools and secondary falls that cascaded over small natural travertine dams.

Masun and her grandmother lay on their bellies on the red rock cliffs where the day's heat was still rising and sucked at the cool water and laved water over their faces and the backs of their necks. Razor stood. He held onto the gun. He looked at the grandmother. She was sitting a few feet away on the ground, bent over slightly sideways with her hands stretched out in front of her. When Razor looked down at her he shook his head.

"*Loco hombre*," she said.

"Yeah, yeah, I know."

He looked up at the falls and surveyed the lush green amphitheater that was in front of him and said, "Pistol Pete was right, it's a paradise, all right. Let's hope the two of you get the chance to see it again. How much further?"

They stood, holding each other's hands, gazing at the multilevel village that had been built into the canyon wall long before Christopher Columbus had ever set foot in North America. Barbra walked up to a rickety old wooden ladder and climbed to the top rung, then stepped onto the narrow ledge of the first level, which contained a half dozen compartments. Patrick followed her and the two of them stood on the ledge then turned around and faced the vast wide-open terrain and the high rock bluffs on the far side of the canyon, dotted with small patches of thin cottonwood trees clinging to the escarpment. The sound of the waterfalls faded. Then it returned. A cool wind blowing up from the canyon valley flowed gently over them, the afternoon sun shining down brightly on them, with clear blue skies overhead.

"Let's sit down for a minute," she said.

They sat on the rock ledge and swung their legs over the edge.

"It's so beautiful here. No wonder the Supai have never wanted to move away. I was always a city girl. What was it like where you grew up?"

"Where I . . . it was wonderful. Plenty of farmland for my father's thoroughbred horses. He raised a few winners in his time."

"That sounds exciting."

"For him. For me it was my apple orchards. My brother and I worked very hard there. Our father would not have it any other way."

"He was pretty strict?"

"You could say that. He demanded respect and we gave it to him. We feared him most of the time though. But I have fond memories of those orchards."

"Tell me one of those memories . . . please, Patrick. I want to know everything about you."

"All right. Let me . . . okay . . . when I was a kid I camped in the fall on a cold, bitter night out in the middle of my apple orchard and I lay listening to a flock of some migratory birds overhead. I remember first hearing their partially muffled sounds then suddenly, I could see them as they traversed the early evening sky in chevron flight going farther and farther until they were gone. I wished them God speed till they were gone. I never heard them again."

"I think you have a wonderful way with words. Have you ever written any poetry?"

"Me?"

"Yes, you."

"Some. In college. They were mostly about nature I encountered growing up around the Appalachian Mountains and the forests and lakes around Moreland. Guess I was enamored with Thoreau."

"Will you recite one for me?"

"No, I can't remember any of mine."

"Please."

"Well, I remember a few lines of another. A part of one, that is. By Baudelaire. The poem *L'invitation au Voyage* is about as beautiful and exotic as they get. *Aimer à loisir / Aimer et mourir / Au pays qui te ressemble!* My French is pretty rusty."

"Please, in English."

"One can translate this poetically or literally . . . or pick something in between. So, here are two treatments: In loving at ease, / Until life has gone, / In that land in the image of you.

"To love easily / to love and die / in the land that you resemble.

"If you read the entire poem, you will see that this is just the tip of the iceberg, as it is the entire culture which is meant by the land that you resemble; we don't really have an English word for *pays*. It includes everything about an area and its culture: soil, smells, even sense of time. Most people don't get that or care about such things. It's invisible to them. They care about curb appeal—you know, what the neighbors will think."

"I spent my whole life in Philadelphia. City culture is, well, surely very different than what you experienced. I love living here. I am able to breathe and investigate and see things that

I never thought I could or would want to."

"The desert is mysterious. You do love it so, don't you?"

"Patrick."

"Yes."

"I've been thinking about what happened a little while ago when my father joined our hands together."

"I have to admit . . . what he did made an impression on me."

"'To love easily . . . to love and die.' I want that with you, Patrick. You know, when I was a little girl, my father once lit all these candles on the dining-room table and said to me, 'Barbra . . . thousands of candles can be lighted from a single candle, and the life of the candle will not be shortened. Happiness never decreases by being shared.'

"Barbra, I promise I'll do my best to share what I can, what's in me to share."

They hugged each other and sat on the rocky ledge for quite some time, telling stories and joking with each other, enjoying each other's honest thoughts and feelings as the sunshine and the cool breezes coming up from the valley fell on their faces and they smiled and laughed.

Barbra then fixed her eyes on something moving below them on the canyon floor and said, "Huh."

"Something wrong?"

"Thought I saw some people moving down there."

"Where?"

She pointed to an area 150 yards away, where the flat canyon floor rose and met a half dozen or more small sand hills that butted up against brown-red boulders of various sizes and shapes, some the size of a two-story house.

"Over there," she said. "They came out that little gully over there, then went behind those rocks."

He could see them. "It's Maysun . . . and her grandmother . . . someone's with them. He doesn't look familiar, he said."

Barbra stood up and waved. He stood and looked down the

caliche trail the three of them were on, the trail that would lead them to where he and Barbra were now standing. He looked at her, smiling and waving. The three of them were now fifty yards away.

"Ever see that fella around the reservation before?"

"I don't know. No. Don't think I have. We'll climb down," she said. "Come on."

The three of them walked out from behind the group of boulders, then stopped.

"*There!*" Maysun's grandmother said as she pointed upward, toward the ancient cave village where Patrick and Barbra were standing. "NOW YOU LET US GO," she said loudly.

They continued on. They stopped in front of the multitiered rock dwelling. Razor told her to call Wallace down and she called to him twice. He knew he would not leave the canyon without settling the score; the man he thought killed his brother was standing a few yards away, staring at him.

Patrick stood in front of Barbra, holding her arm so she would remain still. He looked at the man.

"You have me at a disadvantage sir," he said. "Who are you and what do you want?"

"I want you to follow me," Razor said.

"Now why would I want to do that?"

He pulled the .45 out from his belt and managed a sardonic smile. Patrick nodded. He'd already figured out that there was some kind of bad blood between the two of them.

"I know what you're thinking. But if you think I won't use this, you better think some more. You understand? You got to answer for what you did."

Barbra moved to his side. He tried to stop her but she got lose from the hold he had on her. "For what he did? Who the hell are you?" she said.

"Your boyfriend there killed my brother Axel—broke his neck—and now it's time he gets what's coming to him.

Patrick looked at Barbra and touched her cheek with the tips of his fingers, then turned and stared down at Razor.

"You'll get no second chance with me, Wallace. Get down here. Do it."

"He's unarmed," Barbra shouted.

"I am coming down."

"Wait ... don't ..."

"It'll be okay. I am going to talk to him."

Patrick climbed down. Razor followed him with his eyes. The women didn't move. He circled the ground and stood between Razor and Maysun. Razor smiled.

Patrick looked at the Hell's Angel and said, "I didn't kill your brother."

"Bullshit. Do you think you can bluff your way out of this?"

"You let Grandma here and the girl go back down that trail; they don't need to see any of this."

"See what?"

"Well, you're holding the gun."

"It's funny."

"What's funny?"

"You don't look scared."

"Come on ... let um go," said Patrick.

"You think I am going to kill you, don't you? You mustn't love life very much."

"PATRICK!" shouted Barbra.

"Tell her to come down. Do it!"

A few miles below the canyon's north rim, Charley White Feather pulled on his horse's reins. "Whoa, whoa," he said quietly, and the Appaloosa responded. Horses and riders stopped a few hundred yards from the ceremonial hogan. Kaminski and Skywalker set their horses alongside Charley, who was staring at the hogan and the surrounding terrain. Joel Lawrence and Leo Fast Elk rode up, followed by Dash. All of them were now lined up in a row looking forward toward where the elder patriarch of the Supai told them to go—where he believed Wallace and Doc Berguson's daughter were headed before dawn.

Kaminski spoke first. "If he's in there and we want to surprise him, then we better move up there on foot."

"I agree," replied Joel Lawrence.

Skywalker slowly moved his horse forward then turned and faced Kaminski. "He killed them."

What are you saying? What do you mean, Joey?" Kaminski asked.

"Lone Bear and . . ." Skywalker's head dropped down, his chin almost touching his chest, then slowly he looked up and stared into Kaminski's eyes. ". . . and Tushanna. Killed um both. He made Tushanna tell him where Patrick was headed."

Dash moved forward and set his horse next to Skywalker. Together the two of them faced the others. Skywalker continued quietly addressing the men.

"Look. I killed his brother and I have to do what I know to be right. I owe Patrick. If this biker needs to be taken out, I am going in and I am doing it. I can't speak for my young partner here; he'll have to do that for himself."

Dash glanced at Skywalker, then looked back at the men and began to speak.

"Lone Bear. He was like a brother. I have to do something, or I just won't ever be right again inside. You know what I mean? I have to—"

Charley interrupted. "They're coming out."

All eyes were on the hogan now. The women, Doc Berguson, Bunny, and Henry Crow Horse first stood in front of the adobe house then came toward them. Don Kaminski sat straight up in his saddle, then leaned forward, trying hard to clearly see the small group of people a few hundred yards away, and said, "Do you see the biker?"

"No, he's not with them," replied Charley.

"Let's go!" Kaminski took off. At a full gallop it took only a few minutes for them to reach the hogan. Kaminski pulled on the reins and stopped just in front of Henry Crow Horse.

The Mohawk sheriff grabbed the horse's bridle, then looked up at the chopper pilot and said, "I am glad to see you. He looked at the other riders. Joey . . . what are you . . ."

Kaminski dismounted, then Skywalker. They embraced Henry Crow Horse.

"It's Patrick," said Skywalker. "That crazy biker is . . ."

"Yes, yes . . . I know," replied Crow Horse. He turned to Kaminski. "He's up there about a quarter mile, at that old rock dwelling; you know, those rooms made into the cliffs. He has this man's daughter and a young girl and the girl's grandmother."

Bunny and Doc Berguson came forward. The tribal women remained in the background except for Maysun's aunt Maddie, who ran off in the direction of the Supai village.

Henry Crow Horse looked at Kaminski, then at Skywalker. "It seems this Razor fella has it in his mind Patrick killed his brother. I am afraid he plans on taking his revenge out on our friend."

"We'll stop him, right, Captain Don?" shouted Bunny.

"We sure will, Francis."

Charley White Feather and Joel Lawrence got off their horses. Dash and Leo Fast Elk dismounted. Together they stood with the group. Charley White Feather quickly surveyed the land, then addressed the men.

"Look. We need a plan. And we need it fast, if we're to have a chance of getting your friend out of this mess. This man here. This is Joel Lawrence. He has experience in combat missions."

"That's right. He was part of a *lerp* team," Kaminski said.

Skywalker turned to Kaminski. "What's that?"

"Long range reconnaissance patrol. Joel . . . how would you . . ."

Doc Berguson moved quickly forward and stood in front of White Feather. "Now just hold on a minute. What about my daughter? What about Maysun and the old one?"

Kaminski put his hand on the shaman's shoulder. "Paul, there are many of us and he's alone. We can't just sit back and let him take over like this. The element of surprise is with us."

"But, what if . . ."

Charley White feather moved closer to Doc Berguson and picked up a stick that was lying close by on the ground, then he squatted down and drew a rectangle in the dirt. The men crouched down and watched and listened to White Feather. "I've been there many times. So have you, Doc. We know the place—he doesn't."

"Well, I am going with you."

"Of course. We'll all go, but we first have to plan and execute the plan as best we can."

White Feather continued carefully drawing on the ground the lay of the land and the multilevel rock homes.

Kaminski turned to Lawrence. "Joel, up ahead, what do you think we should do?"

From the moment Maysun's aunt Maddie had backed away from the hogan and started down a narrow caliche trail, she tried to run, then walked at a quick pace and finally settled on a fast jog-like shuffle. All of her sixty-plus years were tugging at her lungs, her breathing labored, a constant stinging pain hurting both her knees. She steadily pressed on, keeping in her mind the image of her niece being pushed down onto the hard, red caked ground then forced against her will to take the hombre to the ancient cliffs. She quickened her pace down into a wide, flat arroyo, her legs throbbing terribly. The arroyo went west in the direction of the late afternoon sun and she followed it for a good distance until it began to narrow and grow upward into some basalt rock. She had to slow down and walk, then climbed up through shards of red canyon rock, which had fallen from the rim, onto a west facing slope and along a barren dirt ridge where she could see the village about a quarter mile below where she was standing, trying to catch her breath.

Having the village in view, she hurried down the steep slope, trying not to fall. Within a short time she came out onto the wide dirt road that dissected the village, and as she turned a corner, she saw three unfamiliar-looking men standing next to Grandpa Hobert Standing-Buffalo. She ran up to the Supai leader, then collapsed at his feet.

DEA Agent Thomas Edward Price, Pistol Pete and his brother-in-law Clarence first stared, then knelt down and administered first-aid and tried to comfort her as best they could. After a few minutes the three men carried Aunt Maddie's limp body into Standing Buffalo's cabin and laid her on a small cot and covered her torso with a serape. She lay unconscious. Standing Buffalo sat next to her while the three men walked outside.

Clarence said to Price, "What kind of a jackpot do we have going on here? Pete, you have any idea what the hell's going on?"

"All I know is, this Pendergrass paid me to take him here to see the falls and get him to the village. Then on the trail he tells me that when we get to the village, get lost—that he would hook up with me later. I rode over to old Mac Comstock's place to wait. After visiting with Mac for a while I came back here. This guy Pendergrass never did. His horse is tied up over there. That's all I know."

Clarence stared at Price, then looked back at his brother-in-law, then back at Price. "When I agreed to take this fella down here I didn't want no trouble. What do you got to say for yourself, Mr. Price?"

The special agent took out his wallet and showed Clarence his badge.

"Shit. I knew it. I just . . ."

Standing Buffalo appeared in the doorway. "She's awake now. What she's saying may be of interest to you."

The agent went into the cabin and knelt down next to the cot, while the others followed and stood behind him.

"*Loco hombre*, he is. Maysun, Maysun."

"Where is he?"

"He's after *Shashtsoh* man."

"Who is that?"

"That's Mr. Patrick's Supai name, Bear Man," said Standing Buffalo.

"Up on the rock house, they are. He's going to . . ." Aunt Maddie's eyes closed. The Suapi leader moved in and bent down and took hold of her wrist, then put his ear close to her mouth and nose. He raised his head then pulled the serape up and over her face.

"*Nilch'I* has taken her away."

The men stepped back and stood by the door and watched as Standing Buffalo began to chant loudly, moving his arms upward, repeating the motion over and over again. His chanting then became slower and diminished in sound to a soft-spoken prayer as he circled the body.

Price motioned to the men and they walked out and stood in the front yard. The agent looked at them and said, "Either of you know where this rock house is?"

"Yeah. I do," said Pete . . . but it's not just one. There're many houses kind of like stacked together on top of one another, dug into of the cliffs of the canyon wall."

"So Agent Price. What's this all about? You seem to have a big interest in all of this. Why did I bring you down here?"

"Can you take me there?"

XIII

Patrick's eyes were fixed on Razor. Barbra Berguson stood still. Razor advanced a bullet into the .45's chamber. The sound of the sliding action and the round falling into place were sharp and clear. He put the end of the barrel next to Maysun's temple and held it there. Grandma put her hands up to her forehead and closed her eyes. The Hell's Angel looked at Barbra, standing by the ladder on the bottom tier of the multilevel rock homes that stretched laterally for more than fifty yards, two hundred feet below the great plateau that made up a portion of the canyon's north rim.

"What's it gonna to be?" he said.

Razor looked at the grandmother. She still had her hands on her forehead but she had looked at him.

"Come over here," he said.

She did what he ordered her to do.

"All right. You've made your point," Patrick said.

"You know, I changed my mind. You stay up there." Razor

pointed the gun at Patrick and pushed him backward. He gestured at the women with his chin.

"Get up there," he said.

Maysun held the ladder while her grandmother slowly climbed onto the first tier, then she looked over at Patrick. He looked at her and smiled and said, "Don't worry, sunshine, it's going to be okay."

Then she looked up at Barbra and her grandmother and climbed to the top. Razor pulled the ladder away and it fell to the ground.

"Let's go." Razor shoved the .45 into Patrick's back, prodding him to get moving. Patrick looked up at Barbra and saw how frightened she was—how helpless she appeared, unable to do anything but stand there and stare back at him.

"Move."

"How did you find me?"

"What difference does it make?"

"It makes a difference to me. What's your name?"

"That's not important."

"What do you aim to do? You aiming to get to the truth or just kill me straight out?"

"Truth! I know all there is to know about the truth. I didn't drive a couple of thousand miles to discuss it with you, your bullshit truth, Wallace. You broke his neck. You proud of what you did?"

"Belief and seeing are two different things . . . and often wrong. You see what you want to believe."

"Keep talking, Wallace. Ain't gonna do you no good." He pushed Patrick ahead of him at gunpoint. "Let's take a little walk up that-a-way."

He pushed him again and they started up a trail at the northeast corner of the plateau. The trail narrowed and as they walked farther up, they went straight through a crevasse that was created by boulders the size of two-story houses. Patrick could hear the waterfalls as they came out on the other side. High above his head a vulture screeched, and he turned, and a man stepped onto the trail behind them and stood in silhouette within a light gray shadow the late-afternoon sunlight and boulders had created. The man stood, then moved back into darkness. No one spoke.

"Hell's Angel," Skywalker called out.

No one answered. Razor watched the sunlit ground beyond the boulders. He could see the shadow of another man where he stood to the side of some rock formations just beyond the boulders. Then the shadow withdrew. He listened. He pushed Patrick Wallace toward the edge of the waterfall.

"Hell's Angel," Joel Lawrence yelled.

The riders had staked their horses on the open plateau just above Razor and his captive and Razor counted not two, but six of them.

"You must have many friends, Wallace," Razor said.

"I am starting to think so."

The continuous roar of the falling water echoed loudly across the canyon floor. Below the falls, a hundred yards away, Agent Price lay on his belly, resting the barrel of his Mauser-action rifle on a smooth rock, and pushed off the safety with his thumb and sighted through the scope. He placed his finger in the curve of the trigger. Suddenly he saw a figure step up and come into view. Razor raised and pointed the .45 at Patrick Wallace's head.

Skywalker climbed up over a small rocky ledge and was now no more than twenty feet behind the biker. He stood in plain view of both men and said, "You got the wrong man there."

"They won't shoot you," said Patrick.

"You want me, not him," Skywalker quietly said.

"Joey!"

He never heard the crack of the rifle. His upper body twisted in the air as the bullet entered his upper arm and he gave out a groan and fell to one knee. The .45 was gone. Men came forward from behind a sheer rock gorge.

Don Kaminski walked up to Joel Lawrence. "Good work, Sarge."

"Good teamwork, Lieutenant. That DEA man wasn't bull-shitting us. He's a Cracker Jack shot, all right."

"A good man to have around. Like you."

Skywalker moved forward and stood in front of the biker and Dash walked up and stood alongside his friend. "You all right, Patrick?"

"Yeah. Damn, Joey. I thought I was a going over those falls. Good to see you. And you, Dash. Both of you."

Skywalker grabbed the collar of Razor's vest. "Get up. Dan Tails made the whole thing up. All this time. It was me you wanted."

"You?"

"You have to answer for what you did back at St. Regis. Do you understand me?"

"Joey don't," pleaded Patrick.

"Patrick!" Bunny shouted as he walked up from the trail. Barbra, Maysun, and her grandmother were a few paces be-hind him. Razor looked at the women, then looked at Patrick and said, "You were telling the truth back there, weren't you?"

"I was."

Razor looked over at Henry Crow Horse.

"What I tell ya, *Sheriff* . . . we Hell's Angels . . . we weren't ever much to begin with."

Razor brought his uninjured arm up quickly then thrust it downward, breaking Skywalker's hold, then threw himself over the edge and into the falls.

Barbra ran up to Patrick and put her arms around him. Doc Berguson went over and stood next to Charley White-feather and watched his daughter and Patrick holding each other, then smiled and said, "They look good together . . . don't they, Charley?"

Bunny walked over and stood next to Don Kaminski and

Henry Crow Horse and the three of them watched the couple embrace. Suddenly, they saw the Supai villagers, both young and old, standing in a semicircle just above them on the upper plateau. Grandpa Hobert Standing Buffalo was in the center and he looked at the three of them, then nodded and gave them a slight close-lipped smile. The women came down and put their arms around Maysun and her grandmother, while the Supai men allowed Agent Price to make his way through to the edge of the falls.

"What now?" asked Kaminski.

"Hmmm. Well, I saw a man fall to his death. Suicide, I'd say. That's going to be my report when I get back."

"Yeah. And . . ."

"They'll come and investigate all of it."

"But what exactly are you going to say when you get back?"

"It'll be up to others to decide who that person was. But for now let's just say I couldn't make a positive ID, given the limited facts in front of me.

XIV

I'll suddenly sit straight up in bed and Barbra will wake up and she will softly say my name.

"Do you need anything?" she'll ask. "No, I am good," I'll say.

Some days I'll go into the kitchen and get her some apple juice and OTC crackers and crush them with my hands, and she will eat them and drink the juice. It seems to eventually settle her morning sickness. We will often just lie there and not say a word for quite a while. Sometimes she'll fall back asleep and when she does I'll lie there thinking about the Wallace clan and my home back in Moreland. My great-great grandfather built that place from the stones he had dug up in the surrounding fields. I remember sitting on the grass as a kid in the backyard of that gray-looking manor house, inspecting the walls and how all those stones were aligned and perfectly level and anchored so well together. I didn't know how long the place had been there. A hundred years. Two hundred.

This morning I concentrated my thoughts on the man that built his homestead up from nothing and what he had to endure to carve

*out a life like he did. That area around Mohawk country had not
had a time of peace for many generations. Fighting for this and
that was a normal part of life back then. But this man, my ancestor,
had placed down stone upon stone, timber tied together with other
timber with a hammer and nail; with the strength in his back he
created a house to last for a very long time. Why was that? What
did he believe in to do all that? I don't know. I'd have to say that
the only thing I can think of is that there was some sort of vow
he made to himself, and he kept that vow deep within his soul.*

*About the time I finished my morning musing I turned my eyes
toward Barbra. She was sleeping ever so peacefully, I thought;
having only good dreams. I am not laying up a stone house—have
no intention of doing that. But I am going to try to make that
same kind of vow and stick it in my soul if I can. Maybe that will
be enough to help me keep the promise I made to Barbra. To love
easily . . . to love and die in the land that you resemble.*

Francis Bunnyard was downstairs, getting ready for the workday. He lived above an old Esso gas station and was up before
dawn, arranging tools that he thought they would need to
finish a job by the end of the day. It was a cold, gray, damp
Alaska morning when Patrick walked into the gas station. He
and Barbra lived just out back in a cottage. Barbra was up and
was outside feeding the chickens, then starting to tend the
garden. He looked at the truck and its detached snowplow
in the bay. He looked at the broken plow and wondered how
he'd fix it. He walked to the rear of the building and stood in
the doorway and watched her. He looked behind the cottage
at the dozen apple trees he had just planted a month ago.
A feeling came over him. He couldn't name the feeling. It
was happiness, he thought, but it was also something else.
And the something else was what had him standing there
instead of starting to work on the plow. He'd felt like this
before, but not in a very long time, and when he thought that,

then he believed he knew what it was. It was in that small ancient-looking book bound in tattered, faded red cloth. *Le Morte d'Arthur* and the noble tale of the Sangreal. It was the meaning of the Grail legend—more beautiful and meaningful than any idea he'd ever known or could conceive. Serve the other and truth and beauty will come your way. *You have to believe in that*, he thought.

Then he and Bunny went to work on the snowplow.

Acknowledgments

Helga Schier, PhD., for her remarkable editing skills and continuous encouragement I am deeply grateful.

Lama Ole Nydahl, an old soul who helped me see things more clearly.

Monsignor McGough, the strongest and most dedicated man I've ever met who continues to remain a constant guiding light to all who are seeking peace, love and the brotherhood of man.

And finally, the gentleman that helped me to see the wonders of taking the path of the artist in everyday life – To the memory of Arthur Vincent Campbell IV. A Renaissance man par excellence. Artist, financier, engineer whose great intelligence and talents were exceeded only by his lust for life and love of adventure.

About the Author

Robert Slothus, pronounced SLow—Thus (1952 to present) began his Health Sciences career in 1971 as an Airman in the United States Air Force and began his teaching career in 1979 as an instructor at The Pennsylvania College of Technology, where he taught Medical Imaging for thirty-six and a half years.

For more information and updates from the author, vist www. robertslothus.com